ELLSIE ANNE

Life Without You

The Lola Series - Book 1

To anyone living with a mental health condition,
as well as those who love and support them.
You are not alone. It's my hope that Lola's story will give you
a voice when everything else tries to silence you.

Contents

Acknowledgement

Thank you, God, for entrusting me with this amazing story. You have pushed me well past my own personal comfort zone, to bring to life Lola's story- a story that has so far been a voice for many people in my personal life. Thank you for loving me and being the foundation of my life.

To my amazing husband, thank you for supporting me in this tireless endeavor. I am so thankful for your endless love and listening ear for all of my crazy ideas. Thank you for believing in me, even when it was hard for me to believe in myself. I thank God every day that He brought you into my life and that with His help, you have healed a very broken spirit. I couldn't have done this without you.

I would like to say a special thank you to a few of my best and dearest friends. Britt, Dawn, Liz, Samantha, and Naja thank you all so much for helping me bring *Life Without You*, and the entirety of *The Lola Series*, to life. Your never-ending love and support have helped me persevere even through the moments of self-doubt and writer's block.

Liz, you helped me rediscover my love for writing through a fun visual storytelling platform.

Samantha, my precious friend from work, I am so thankful for all of the hours and nights of searching for just the right songs. I am also thankful you ended up introducing me to Britt, who just so happened to be on the same visual storytelling platform as Liz.

Britt, words cannot express just how thankful I am for your love and support- not just with writing, but with everyday life. You love my characters as much as I do, and I am grateful that you truly do see Logan as your son. There's no one else I'd entrust him to.

Dawn, you aren't just my bestie for the restie, you are literally my kindred spirit and soul sister- the Lizzie to my Lola- and to have you as a part of this journey means the world to me.

Naja, I am so thankful our friendship has grown and blossomed from the visual storytelling platform and that we can share ideas and just life in general together.

I would like to thank my amazing supporters on Instagram, specifically Jade, Daisy, Beckii, Kelly, Luka, Jenn, Ashley, and Aggelina, you are the real MVPs for sticking with me through this journey. I am so thankful for each and every one of your friendship. I truly couldn't write this book without your love and support.

Thank you, Jordyn and my other beta readers for taking the time to help me grow as an author.

Lastly, thank you dear reader for taking a chance on this story written by an indie author.

Author's Note:

Please read carefully!

I just wanted to start by thanking you for taking the time to read Life Without You. This is the first in a three-book series. This story is Lola's and will intertwine between both past and present spanning from the years 1980-2016. This story is written with the utmost sensitivity to those who suffer from mental illness as well as those who live with and love someone suffering from a mental illness. I hope that you will take the time to truly appreciate and engage in Lola's story.

Life Without You will discuss uncomfortable topics such as, but not limited to: self-harm, eating disorders, bullying, age-gap relationships, the realistic and negative impacts from a toxic relationship, and other triggering topics. The characters speak in a very real and raw way; their thoughts and actions do not mirror my own.

~Ellsie

1

Prologue

August 29, 2014

In the middle of a rustic-modern bedroom, with beige wallpaper strategically torn away to reveal exposed brickwork, Logan Asher Warren paced back and forth with a pen and notebook in one hand while holding his cellphone to his ear with the other; annoyance ingrained upon his face. The same tireless conversation of the past two years occurred once more, with a well-meaning loved one.

"Look, Shaw, I know you mean well, but I promise you I'm fine."

"It's been two and a half years since we went on hiatus, don't you think it's time to move forward with your life … move forward from …"

"For fuck's sake, Shaw! How many damn times do I have to say, she's not up for discussion. And just to get you guys off my damn back, I've come up with a new album title and am working on some songs."

"Logan, I'm not tryin' to overstep but it's hard watching you be a shell of who you were. I get that she was dealing with some shit but ya nearly let her destroy you and that shit ain't right!"

"Drop it right now or this fucking conversation is over!"

Inhaling deeply, Shaw knew this was a losing battle, for when Logan made up his mind, it was easier to will a glacier to melt. "So, what's the idea for the album name?"

"If y'all are okay with it, I'd like to call it **Momentary**."

"I like the title, but let me mention it to Pablo and Pierre. Or, you could just come to L.A. yourself. I know the Morettis' would be happy to see you, too."

Rolling his eyes as he was about to respond, the beep of an incoming call stole Logan's attention, "Hey man, I got another call comin' in."

Looking at the unknown number, Logan internally debated answering, however, curiosity being the fickle maiden she is got the best of him. "Hello?"

Being met with silence, again he queried, "Hello?"

"Umm … is this Logan?"

Feeling his heart catch in his throat, Logan couldn't believe his ears. Weakly, he responded, "Lola? Is it really you?"

"H-hey. Y-yeah … it's me. Umm … how are you?"

"You're shitting me, right? This is actually you calling?"

Nervous laughter filled the other end of the line as Lola tried to gather her composure, "It's really me. Uh … anyhow, I was wanting to know if you are free next Friday night at around seven o'clock?"

Anxiety gripped his heart as he feared this was humanity's cruel joke. Gathering his thoughts, Logan responded, "I am free at that time, but even if I wasn't, I'd drop everything for you in a heartbeat! I love you more than anything, you know that right?"

Guilt filled Lola's heart as she responded, nails in her palms, "I know. I remember you telling me and that's what we need to discuss. Let's meet at Cate's Cafè."

"Lola, are you sure? We can meet somewhere else if it's easier for you."

With a twinge of annoyance in her voice, Lola retorted, "It's fine," before catching her breath in a calming manner, "besides, I'd like to see her and your dad."

"If you're sure, then it's a date. I love you, Lola."

With a heavy sigh, Lola flatly replied, "See you then, Logan," before cutting the call.

2

Return

September 5, 2014

The rush of wind from the open window blew through Lola's vibrant, curly red hair. She clicked on the radio of the 1967 cherry red **Ford Mustang** that had been her dad's prized possession and was now in her care. "Good morning lovers! DJ Samantha here, and it's another beautiful day, as I come to you live from Parkway, Oregon. Up next, we have a classic and a personal favorite of mine, 'Until the end.'"

As the words of the song on the radio faded into the back of Lola's mind, she thought to herself. *I honestly never thought I would return to this place. Especially after all that **he** has done. Yet, here I am. Well, Averie and I, making this journey back. It's the least I owe to Logan after the **incident** and things turned out the way they did. In the end, what's done is done. Dr. Indigo says that if I want to move forward I can't keep letting the past hold me back.*

Lola inhaled deeply and thought to herself as she pulled her car into an empty parking space in the parking lot for **Cate's Café**, *Well, here goes nothing and everything all at once.*

~

Meanwhile, inside of **Cate's**, Logan sat anxiously in self-reflection as he waited for Lola to enter; with solicitous thoughts at the forefront of his mind. No contact with Lola was not due to lack of trying on Logan's part; having tried to reach out for close to a year, Lola simply wasn't ready to talk. Logan was beyond ecstatic the moment he received Lola's phone call the week prior. Just the thought of seeing his best friend, and the woman he loved more than life itself, rekindled all of his old feelings.

As Logan patiently waited at the table, the noise of the radio filled the café. "Good evening, Oregon! DJ Samantha here with you once again. This next song, 'The Scientist,' goes out to all you lovers out there who are missing the one who holds your heart."

The music faded into the background, as Logan was once again left with his thoughts, while he subconsciously drummed out the song's tune against the table; a nervous habit he had developed when faced with uncomfortable situations that couldn't readily be fixed. While he had originally agreed to meet Lola at 7 p.m., he arrived three hours earlier under the guise of helping Cate and his father, with the hopes of unwinding the ball of nerves that had made residence within the pit of his stomach. *Shit, this is like I'm meeting Lola for the first time all over again.*

Logan's thoughts were interrupted by the chiming of the café's door; looking up, he saw her. Even though it had been a year and a half since they had last faced one another, Lola still caught his eye instantly when she walked into the room; she was breathtaking. With her delicate five foot nothing stature; petal-soft fair skin; rose-red hair.

Lola's hair reminded Logan of a burnt orange sunset with ruby hues; it was beautiful and her warm curls tumbled over her shoulders like rusty water. And her eyes, Logan's most favorite thing about her. For him to describe her eyes as green would be too plain. Lola's eyes were the color of evergreen; they were the green that brings the earth back to life after an unforgiving cold.

~

As Lola stood outside the café door, she thought to herself, *Coming back here to this town, to this place has taken so much strength. Hell, it even took me three months just to muster up the courage to call Logan, my best friend, up. Some best friend I am. I know he loves me beyond words, but I am so afraid to let him in, or even let him love me. Everyone I have ever loved has left my life in one way or another and the demons inside are terrifying. Dr. Indigo keeps telling me that I have to let people in if I ever want to live again.*

As soon as Lola crossed the threshold, Cate, along with her fiancée- who happened to be Logan's dad- Cade, ran over to hug her. The sudden embrace caused Lola's body to stiffen for a moment before she reminded herself that these people were safe. They were the friends who loved her dearly and would never hurt her … unlike **him**.

Cate, with her beautiful raven-colored hair, which flowed down her shoulders in loose waves; perfectly tanned skin; and delicate, aqua blue eyes were still as kind-hearted and compassionate as Lola had remembered. Although they were only six years apart in age, **Cate's** warm, maternal embrace was something that Lola had longed for the last two years, especially after the **incident**. Cade, with his chestnut brown cropped hair, light complexion, and ocean blue eyes, stood beside Cate and gently wrapped Lola in a loving hug; both of these people felt like bittersweet memories of home.

As Cate embraced Lola, she spoke, "Luxie! Oh my gosh, girl! It's been so long. You look amazing. Please tell me you are coming back to work for me. I need my best girl here. You know, it's just not the same without you. The customers miss you so much!"

Lola thought to herself and laughed, *I forgot how fast Cate can talk when she gets super excited*; before nervously looking up at her friend. "Hey, Cate! Thanks for the compliment. I love you guys and have missed you dearly. But … sorry, it's still hard."

"Take your time, *sweetie*," Cade reassured as best as he could.

Regaining control of her voice, Lola continued, "This place will always hold a special place in my heart, but with trying to get back into the swing of things with my own company, and the damage **he** did, I just can't."

Looking away with shame and sorrow, Cate tried to hide her tears. "I know, Luxie. I know almost better than anyone the damage **he** has caused."

Seeing the heartbreak upon his lover's face, Cade held Cate close, in hopes that he could absorb some of the self-hatred she felt after the truth of everything came to light. Leaning into Cade's loving hug, Cate's chipper tone quickly returned. "Please just know you're always welcome here, even if it's just as a customer."

Turning from Cate, Cade finally embraced Lola. "Luxie! How's my second-best girl? Are you here to see my boy?"

Lola laughed and retorted with playful sarcasm, "Cade, you know me so well! Yeah, Logan and I need to talk and catch up. I don't know how long everything will take, but my therapist, Dr. Indigo, seems convinced that telling Logan **everything** will be the key to my healing. After all, he's the one I hurt the most."

"Well, *sweetie*," Cate teased with a playful wink, "Logan has a key so he can lock up tonight. He still lives in my old apartment up above the Café, so if you feel tired, I **know** you can crash at his place."

"Thanks, guys. Really. I love you both more than you will ever know."

As Cate and Cade exited the café embracing each other, Lola again became lost in her thoughts as she searched for Logan. She laughed to herself when she found him seated in the back booth.

Just looking at him sends butterflies into my stomach. His light golden skin; rose-red hair, like my own, with his bangs haphazardly in his eyes like always; and amazing ocean blue eyes. I could get lost in the sea of his eyes. Damn! He's even wearing my favorite outfit of his. I love seeing him in his tight, ripped black jeans, blue open buttoned-down flannel, and his grey sleeveless undershirt.

After momentarily chastising herself, Lola gingerly made her way through the crowd as Logan stood to greet her. Once she reached him, Logan couldn't help but wrap Lola in the warmest hug ever; the kind of hug you secretly craved though never really knew you needed it. However, once you had it, you never wanted to lose it.

~

As Lola made her way to Logan's table, he took in every single detail of her because he was afraid that this moment was a dream; one that would disappear when he awoke. Lola was stunning in her black dress that was covered in red roses and perfectly hugged her tiny curves. She had elegantly paired it with a gorgeous maroon-colored moto jacket and black combat-style booties with a four-inch heel. In her ears were beautiful red, long dangling star earrings. One might think it was a color scheme far too dark for someone as fair-complected as Lola, but this color scheme only amplified everything Logan loved about Lola. Logan stood there, lost in awe before finally speaking.

"Lola! You look amazing!"

Lola looked at Logan as she playfully stuck out her tongue and winked, "Ditto, Amigo!"

The red-haired duo burst into jovial laughter and for one single instant, all seemed right in the world once again.

"Lola, why don't you have a seat and fill me in on what you wanted to talk about?"

"Straight to the point as always," Lola giggled.

Logan stated with a flirtatious wink, "You know me, babe!"

After taking several minutes to catch her breath and calm her anxiety, Lola finally began. "Well, I know how you feel about me and have felt about me all this time. I truly care about you, but I *need* you to be patient with me. I must tell you my story and see how you feel at the end of everything.

"I have so many demons inside and everyone leaves. If you are going to be serious, I need you to know everything."

Logan tried to listen but elation got the better of him, as he quickly blurted out, "Lola, I already kinda know what happened with Shane and Ronan and that changes nothing. I love you all the same."

Lola looked at Logan as anger flashed in her eyes. "Logan, please! If you can't hear everything I am gone. Dr. Indigo says I have to do this and I can't keep running."

Shocked and on the brink of tears, Logan panicked. "I'm so fucking sorry for my impatience, Lola. I've just missed you so much. I promise, no matter how long it takes, that I will listen to everything."

3

Where it all begins

September 5, 2014

Lola took in Logan's appearance as he sat across from her with desperation in his eyes; knowing the fear he felt at the possibility of losing her again was very present. Lola took a deep breath as she thanked Logan. "Thank you, Logan. This seriously means the world to me."

Hearing Lola's words caused a wave of panic to flood Logan's soul. *As I hugged her, she still smelled of fresh berries on a warm summer's day. I just wanted to hold onto her forever and never have her live in fear again. That's why I jumped the gun so quickly while she was talking. I can't help myself. I'm such a fucking **idiot**! When Lola said she would leave and never return, I knew she meant it. Fear overtook me and I nearly lost it.*

After thirty minutes of silence, Lola looked at Logan with tear-filled eyes. "To understand how everything came about two years ago, you must first learn about my past and the time that was before me: the time of Jackson and Anne-Marie."

Logan looked at Lola and smiled, "Lola, you could spend a thousand years telling me your tale, and I would listen intently no matter what."

~

It was the summer of 1980 when at the age of 16, Anne-Marie Flowers lost both of her parents in a car crash. She had no family to care for her, only a former nanny, Patricia Sommers. Anne-Marie did her best to fit everything she could into a singular suitcase, before making the long drive from Seattle, Washington to Parkway, Oregon. Anne-Marie adored Patricia and her husband Luke, as they had always been like second parents to her.

While Patricia and Luke had been married for 20 years, they had yet to conceive a child. Even though this was a sad circumstance, Patricia and Luke were overjoyed to care for Anne-Marie. Settling in as best as she could that summer, Anne-Marie readied herself for her Junior Year of high school.

As the first day of school rolled around, Anne-Marie thought to herself, *This is it. New school, new me. Oh lord please don't let me make a fool of myself!* Quickly throwing on her uniform, she made the short drive to Parkway High. Upon pulling up to the high school, Anne-Marie sat in her car for a couple of minutes and sadly thought of her parents, whom she missed more than anything. And while Luke and Patricia had been more than accommodating, it simply wasn't the same as having her parents there.

Anne-Marie's first day of school was a smashing success … until her last class of the day, which just happened to be her worst subject: *Chemistry.* Much to Anne-Marie's chagrin, her classroom was located at the complete opposite end of the school from her other classes. Hurrying as quickly as she could, Anne-Marie sprinted down the corridors, barely missing her fellow students. She barreled into the classroom, out of breath, barely beating the final bell. In her haste, Anne-Marie nearly knocked down the teacher, Professor Williams, to the ground.

Professor Williams quickly adjusted her glasses and spoke with surprise in her voice, "Uh … hello?"

Mortified by her actions, Anne-Marie quickly apologized before she hurriedly sat down. Taking a deep breath to ease her embarrassment, Anne-Marie spoke to herself, a little louder than she meant to. *"Come on girl! This is it, the last class you can make it through, and then it's home free."*

A vibrant blush settled into Anne-Marie's golden cheeks when the voice beside her spoke up and said, *"I'm glad to see I'm not the only one who pumps myself up for this class!"*

Startled, Anne-Marie turned her head and blushed even deeper, for the most handsome boy she had ever seen was her lab partner for the year. Gazing intently, she couldn't help but take in his every feature: his amazing rose-red hair, deep forest green eyes, fair skin, and glorious height. *"Cat got your tongue, beautiful?"*

Mortified by how creepy her obvious staring must have been, Anne-Marie apologized for the second time that class period, before nervously introducing herself. "Sorry! I'm new here and kind of awkwardly shy. Oh my gosh! I cannot believe I just said that. Anyhow, all embarrassment aside, I'm Anne-Marie Flowers, and you are?"

"I'm Jackson Swan, and don't worry, *beautiful*, I'm pretty awkward too."

The remainder of the class felt rather mundane for Anne-Marie, although she was glad to end her day on an easy note. When the last bell of the day signaled sweet freedom, Anne-Marie began gathering her things, when she felt a gentle tug on her bag. Glancing over her shoulder, she found herself staring into Jackson's smiling face.

"Hey, *beautiful*. I'd like to give you my number so we can study together sometime. I've heard that Professor Williams is pretty tough, so we might as well get ahead of the class."

"Thanks, Jackson. I appreciate it; here's mine. I look forward to seeing you tomorrow." Anne-Marie turned to leave before she suddenly stopped to ask, "Wanna walk me to my car?"

Jackson looked at Anne-Marie and happily agreed. "Sure thing, *beautiful*! Besides, I want you to meet my best girl and favorite redhead, Averie."

Upon hearing the mention of this Averie, Anne-Marie's heart sank. *Am I being played? How can I even compete with someone named Averie?* Anne-Marie sat in the classroom lost in her melancholy thoughts when Jackson's voice brought her thoughts again to the present.

"Come on, *beautiful*! We don't want to keep Averie waiting all afternoon."

Crestfallen, Anne-Marie silently obliged. Making their way through the campus grounds, Anne-Marie thought to herself, *Well, let's get this humiliation over with.* Jackson called from over his shoulder, "Don't dilly dally, Averie's just around the corner. Move that cute behind!"

As soon as they made their way to the parking lot, Anne-Marie doubled over with hysterical laughter. Jackson looked at Anne-Marie a bit bewildered as he awkwardly rubbed the back of his neck.

"Uh … is everything okay, Anne-Marie?"

Wiping the tears from her laughing eyes, Anne-Marie said, "Oh … yes, sorry! I am so ridiculous."

Jackson was a bit shocked and asked, "What do you mean, *beautiful*?"

Anne-Marie, now feeling a bit sheepish and foolish exclaimed, "I honestly thought I was being played. I thought Averie was another girl."

Jackson chuckled and said, "I can assure you, *beautiful*, that there's no other girl, aside from Averie here, in my life."

As Anne-Marie looked at Jackson, her heart filled with joy once again. "Averie sure is beautiful. Thank you so much for showing her to me."

Jackson looked deeply into Anne-Marie's chocolate brown eyes and flirtatiously said, "Averie is the second most beautiful girl right now."

Anne-Marie sighed happily and said, "Well, I had best be heading home. Thanks for walking me out and make sure you call me." Jackson looked at Anne-Marie one last time and stated, "Trust me, *beautiful*, the pleasure has been all mine."

As Jackson walked Anne-Marie to her car that day, he knew instantly that this girl was the one for him. As Anne-Marie drove off, Jackson said to himself, *"Anne-Marie, I can't imagine Life Without You."*

~

When Anne-Marie arrived home, she was the happiest she had been since before her parents' deaths. Dreamily walking toward her room, Anne-Marie paused in the kitchen for a brief moment. Patricia looked up from the dinner preparations to ask, "Hi, *sweetie!* How was your first day of school?"

Anne-Marie looked at Patricia and sighed, "Hi Patricia. It was **amazing!**"

Patricia giggled at this lovestruck girl and said, "Oh, *sweetie!* I am so happy to hear that. Why don't you go change for dinner?"

Anne-Marie agreed and said she would be back down soon. Upstairs in her room, Anne-Marie laid across her bed and reflected upon her day. She had been so nervous in the beginning, but meeting Jackson just had to be fate. Some people come into your life that you just know are destined to be there, and for Anne-Marie, Jackson was one of those people.

Patricia called upstairs, "Luke and I will be at the table waiting for you. Please come join us when you are ready." Anne-Marie quickly snapped out of her reflection and changed before heading down to dinner.

The conversation was lively as this little family sat at the table. Luke turned to Anne-Marie and asked, "How was your first day, *sweetheart*? Did you make any friends?"

Anne-Marie sighed blissfully once again, and said, "Oh, Luke! It was simply the best day ever. I did manage to make one friend. He was this handsome redheaded boy in my chemistry class."

Anne-Marie blushed as she made this statement, which in turn, caused both Luke and Patricia to chuckle heartily. Luke asked, "What's his name? Maybe we know his family."

Anne-Marie sighed and said, "His name is Jackson Swan."

Patricia giggled while saying, "Ah, young love!"

Luke was very excited, for they were longtime friends of the Swan family. "Anne-Marie, this is wonderful news!"

Anne-Marie was a bit startled and exclaimed, "How so?"

Luke chuckled and stated, "Well, we know the Swans personally! They are dear friends of ours and I work for Jackson's father, Jack, at **Swan Industries**, and more specifically **Swan Hotels**."

"What is **Swan Industries?**"

Patricia smiled warmly as she answered Anne-Marie's query, "**Swan Industries** is the parent corporation for several hotels and other small businesses."

Anne-Marie was very impressed and pleased to learn that she would now have far more opportunities to visit with Jackson. Laughter filled the dining room table as everyone continued to talk about their day.

Once Anne-Marie had finally readied herself for bed and lay down that evening, she drifted off with happy thoughts of seeing Jackson once again.

4

The light I leave behind

September 5, 2014

Lola continued, "Anne-Marie and Jackson dated their entire junior and senior years of school, and were the happiest couple alive. Patricia and Luke were so happy that the daughter of their hearts was able to overcome so much grief with Jackson by her side. To Anne-Marie, Jackson was her everything. 'Jackson, if I ever lose you, I know I would die. There is no way I can have a **life without you.'** Jackson in turn would always reassure her by saying, 'You've got nothing to worry about, *beautiful.* I'm never leaving you because you're my entire world.'"

~

1981-1982

With luck, Anne-Marie and Jackson were able to keep some of their classes together, but even if they hadn't, it wouldn't stop them from meeting during class time during a 'bathroom break' for a steamy make-out session. Each time they managed to sneak out, Jackson would lead Anne-Marie to a secret alcove, lined with bright, blue lockers; then proceed to lift her and gently press her narrow frame into the lockers, as he smashed his lips to hers and kissed her passionately. In turn, Anne-Marie would giggle excitedly, before returning his kisses just as passionately.

~

The morning of the senior prom, Anne-Marie awoke with a butterfly-filled stomach. This was yet another milestone she was crossing without her parents by her side. Although she missed them dearly, each day seemed to hurt a little less, knowing she had everyone, especially Jackson, by her side.

Patricia entered Anne-Marie's room and was all abuzz with excitement. How she had longed for this moment, to have a daughter to help get ready for prom. In her hand, Patricia had a small gift box which, she neatly laid beside Anne-Marie's gorgeous dress.

A few weeks before prom, Jackson and Anne-Marie agreed upon blue and white as the colors they would wear for that magical evening. Anne-Marie spent countless hours searching for just the perfect shade of blue; one that would compliment her golden skin and chocolate eyes. In the end, she chose a vintage-style dress with a stunning white lace bodice, one that had the most amazing light blue satin buttons along the back. The body of the dress was the same light blue satin with a light blue tulle overlay. For her dainty feet, Anne-Marie found strappy heels in a similar blue with delicate ruffles on them; she couldn't wait to feel like a princess.

As Anne-Marie looked at the garments laid out across her bed, she noticed the dainty gift box Patricia had placed there moments earlier. Upon opening the box, her eyes filled with tears, for Patricia had gifted Anne-Marie her most prized possession, a stunning diamond heart necklace. Anne-Marie ran to Patricia and thanked her through her tears.

~

Across town, while Jackson readied himself, he couldn't help but smile, because, with any luck, tonight would bring forth a new stage in his relationship with Anne-Marie after asking her the question that burned brightly in the forefront of his mind.

When Anne-Marie suggested they wear blue and white as their color scheme, Jackson felt over the moon. Before meeting Anne-Marie, Jackson never had a favorite color; however, once he saw her wearing a navy blue dress when he introduced her to his parents, blue instantly became his favorite color. For, blue only magnified Anne-Marie's rich golden skin, honey blonde hair, and stunning chocolate brown eyes. These were the very eyes he could stare at in wonder for the rest of his days.

Instead of a traditional tuxedo for prom, Jackson opted for his tailor-made navy blue blazer, slim white slacks, and black dress shoes. Now that Jackson was becoming a man and would be taking over **Swan Industries** in the future, Jack felt it was finally time to pass on the family heirloom which had gone to every male Swan heir since 1930 when the company was founded. While Jackson readied in his room, Jack knocked on the door.

"Come in." Jackson greeted his father merrily when Jack entered the room. "What's up, dad?"

Jack took a deep breath and replied, "Well son, as you know, you will be taking over the company once you graduate both high school and college. You are growing to be such an amazing and compassionate man and I want to pass this gift on to you. Normally, it would occur at the time of the changing of leadership, however, I feel you deserve it now."

Jackson couldn't believe his ears! He had longed for this day to come since he was a small boy. This was nothing less than an honor and the sign of a *true*, Swan heir. Being a man of few words, Jack handed his son the gift box, shook his hand, and left the room for Jackson to continue his preparations. Jackson opened the box once his clothes were on and his eyes lit up. Inside was his very own silver-banded **Rolex** with a sapphire face. If all went well at prom, this would simply be one of the best days of Jackson's life.

When Jackson arrived promptly at six o'clock in the evening to pick up Anne-Marie, he was awestruck by the pure beauty standing before him. Surely, only God himself could create such a masterpiece. Placing his hand to his chest, Jackson took a deep breath and said, "Are you ready, *beautiful*? Averie is waiting." Anne-Marie simply replied with a head nod and a giggle.

~

The moment Anne-Marie saw Jackson make his way up the walk toward the front door, she was taken aback. This man couldn't possibly be more handsome. His tailored suit was made just for his lanky, 6'2" body. The navy blazer he chose magnified his rose-red hair and evergreen eyes. Normally, one wouldn't typically call a man gorgeous, but to Anne-Marie at this moment, he was simply that … *gorgeous*. Anne-Marie descended from the house stairs to the living room and smiled even brighter when she saw Jackson in front of her. When he said, "Are you ready, *beautiful*? Averie is waiting," Anne-Marie couldn't help but giggle, as she recalled her silliness of thinking Averie was another girl.

~

The gymnasium was exquisitely decorated when Jackson and Anne-Marie arrived. While most couples sought out their friends at events such as this, Jackson and Anne-Marie only had each other. Once Anne-Marie met Jackson, he was all she ever needed, so she never attempted to form friendships with anyone else.

"Waiting for a Girl Like You" by Foreigner came on and Jackson knew, that now was his moment. He flirtatiously asked his alluring beloved to dance with him and of course, Anne-Marie happily obliged. While on the dance floor, Jackson stared into the chocolate diamonds of Anne-Marie's eyes and said, "My beautiful love, you are my everything."

Anne-Marie giggled and said, "Jackson, if I ever lose you, I know I would die. There is no way I can have a **life without you**."

Hearing these words made Jackson smile and he replied, *"Beautiful, I'm never leaving you. You are my entire world."* Jackson took a deep breath and then asked, "Anne-Marie Flowers, would you do me the honor of moving in with me after graduation? I don't want to spend a single moment apart from you!"

Anne-Marie was so overjoyed that tears streamed down her face. Her only reply was a passionate kiss placed upon Jackson's lips. Anne-Marie and Jackson simultaneously thought to themselves, *This truly is one of the best days ever.*

~

May of 1982 brought both high school graduation and apartment searching. Jackson wanted something close to the university in Portland, so he and Anne-Marie found the cutest studio apartment just three blocks from campus. One would think that at only 17 (Jackson would turn 18 on August 24 and Anne-Marie would turn 18 on September 24), these two would have a hard time adjusting to adult life, but nothing could be further from the truth. Jackson and Anne-Marie settled into adult life beautifully. Jackson began taking on more responsibility at **Swan Industries** headquarters in conjunction with his full-time college load, while Anne-Marie joined Lorriene on the **Swan Industries Charitable Board**.

Even though Jackson had yet to propose, Lorriene knew her son well and knew that Anne-Marie was the only one Jackson would love for a lifetime. With this knowledge, Lorriene lovingly took the time to prepare Anne-Marie for her future role of "Mrs. Swan," and the main function of every Swan woman was to ensure that the company gave back to the very community which had helped to turn the business into what it now was. The big event that Lorriene was laying upon Anne-Marie's shoulders was the annual New Year's Eve charity gala.

Anne-Marie thought to herself nervously, *Who knew that being with a Swan came with such responsibilities? I'm already taking on such a big task when Jackson hasn't even proposed to me yet. We've already been together for two years at this point, so Lorriene feels that it could happen at any time. I hope she's right.*

~

Jackson and Anne-Marie enjoyed hosting both Thanksgiving and Christmas for their families in their tiny studio apartment. The warmth of everyone together magnified the space instead of restricting it. Anne-Marie thought of her parents for just one brief moment before pushing those sad thoughts aside to be present with the ones who were surrounding her.

Those events passed quickly in the blink of an eye and before they knew it, December 31, 1982- the night of the gala had arrived. Anne-Marie was a nervous wreck as she called everyone on the list for what truly felt like the millionth time.

Jackson looked at her and chuckled, as he drew her into his warm embrace. He gently began placing tender kisses on her cheeks and slowly trailed them down her neck. Each kiss only made Anne-Marie giggle lovingly. Breathlessly Anne-Marie spoke, "Are you trying to seduce me, Mr. Swan?"

With a hungry gaze, Jackson lustfully looked into Anne-Marie's eyes and exclaimed, "Always, Ms. Flowers. Always."

Anne-Marie wrapped her legs around Jackson's waist as he carried her to their bed, passionately kissing her neck. Staring deeply into the beautiful chocolate brown eyes that held his heart, Jackson couldn't help but love this woman with every fiber of his being. He thanked God daily for the love she showed to him in return. In a teasing manner, Jackson began nibbling on Anne-Marie's shoulder and said, "You seem so tense, *beautiful*! Why don't you let me calm you down before tonight's event?" Passion took over as their love for each other set the world on fire.

~

A few hours later, it was time to start dressing before heading to the venue. Anne-Marie chose a stunning champagne tulle dress with a gorgeous black lace bodice and black lace floral details in the skirt. She decided to pair this stunning dress with simple, classic black strappy heels. Since this was an unusually warm winter evening in Portland, and the winter snow had yet to make a major appearance, Anne-Marie felt these shoes fitting. Jackson opted for a classic tailored white dress shirt and slim black slacks, which he paired with a burgundy blazer and patent black leather dress shoes.

Jackson admired Anne-Maire's delicate body as she dressed for the evening. He was looking forward to the end of the night when he would have the chance to remove Anne-Marie's dress and once again be enchanted and captivated by her presence as he made love to his divine beloved. Anne-Marie could feel the passion burning in Jackson's eyes as he intently watched her dress. So, she took this moment to tease him just a little by slowly dressing and making sure each movement was done in the most sensual of manners. Anne-Marie thought to herself, *I cannot wait until we are home and Jackson can remove this dress and again ravish my body.*

~

The gala was a huge success and no one could believe that this was Anne-Marie's first time organizing such an intensive event. Many board members were greatly pleased by Jackson's choice in a girlfriend and agreed that Anne-Marie had all the makings of the perfect future, Mrs. Swan. Jackson smiled as the board members and charity donors showered Anne-Marie with praise and compliments; although, their opinions were null and void in his mind.

Before heading home, Jackson asked Anne-Marie if he could take her to see the garden set up underneath the stars and fairy lights. Anne-Marie happily agreed because, for her, all of this attention was rather intense and not something she was particularly used to. *Oh well, if this is what comes with being with Jackson, then I will gladly be cast into the spotlight even if it does make me uncomfortable.*

Jackson gently grabbed Anne-Marie's hand and lead her to a giant Sycamore tree which had been beautifully decorated in tiny fairy lights. This spot felt simply magical and altogether, otherworldly. Anne-Marie sighed in delight and exclaimed, "This is truly a magical end to this amazing night."

From behind her, Jackson stated, "I can only think of one thing that would make this night even more magical, *beautiful.*"

Anne-Marie giggled lovingly and said, as she turned to face Jackson, "What's that, my love?"

When Anne-Marie turned around, she faced Jackson, who had gotten down on one knee. Tears of joy filled her eyes as Jackson began to speak. "Anne-Marie, I love you more than life itself. I can't imagine living a **life without you**. Will you marry me, *beautiful?*"

As Anne-Marie gazed down at Jackson, this moment- this one single moment in time was everything to her. Lovingly she replied, "Yes Jackson! With everything that I am and everything that I have, **yes**!" There are defining moments that we all have in our lives, and for both Jackson and Anne-Marie, this was one of them.

~

1983

Time moved forward from that magical moment and reality began to set in, in the form of daily life. Yet, Anne-Marie and Jackson's love and desire never once faltered. A year of engagement came and went so quickly and along with it came a slight decline in Jackson's health. Jack thought maybe he was pushing his son too hard, so he decided to lessen Jackson's load at **Swan Industries**, just until Jackson would be ready to graduate college. Anne-Marie fretted but Jackson reassured her that everything was fine and he simply needed to make sure he was resting. Hearing these words of reassurance quickly calmed her anxious heart.

~

February 14, 1984

Valentine's Day quickly arrived, and with it brought a new change to the lives of Jackson and Anne-Marie. As she prepared dinner, Anne-Marie thought to herself, *I can't wait to give Jackson his gift. I know it will cheer him up, especially since he has been pretty sick lately.*

While lost in her thoughts, Jackson came home from work and greeted his bride-to-be. Gingerly, he placed Anne-Marie on the countertop and kissed her passionately. Breathlessly breaking their kiss, Anne-Marie spoke, "Happy Valentine's Day, *baby*! I love you so much."

Before he could reply, a coughing fit overtook Jackson. Concern etched deeply upon Anne-Marie's furrowed brow. As soon as he was able to catch his breath, Jackson simply placed a kiss upon her forehead and stated, "I love you too, *beautiful*. Happy Valentine's Day to you as well."

Though she was still worried, Anne-Marie did her best to not ruin the evening, as she switched emotional gears quickly and exclaimed, "Let's go ahead and eat dinner. I can't wait to give you your gift afterward."

When they were seated at the table, Jackson sheepishly said, "Hopefully, Dr. Fischer's office will call soon, so we can find out why I haven't been feeling well lately."

Anne-Marie reassuringly placed her hand on Jackson's leg. "I hope that his office calls tomorrow because I would like for us to enjoy our evening together."

After dinner, Anne-Marie asked Jackson to wait on the couch as she tidied up a bit, before bringing in his gift. When Anne-Marie entered the room, she asked Jackson to stand up as he opened the gift. "Happy Valentine's Day, *baby!*"

Nervously, Jackson took the small package wrapped in blue paper from Anne-Marie. Taking a deep breath, Jackson carefully opened the box and what was laid before him took him by complete surprise! Jackson went through an array of emotions in just a few seconds! At first, he was completely in shock. Then, he chuckled and asked, "Are you serious? We are going to be parents?!?"

Jackson cried tears of joy as Anne-Marie exclaimed, "Yes, *my love*! I am twelve weeks pregnant and our precious baby is due after both of our birthdays."

Jackson happily exclaimed, "This truly is the best day ever!"

Anne-Marie giggled as Jackson walked closer to her and began to kiss her passionately. Jackson broke their kiss and told Anne-Marie that she should go over to the Sommers' residence to tell Patricia and Luke. Anne-Marie agreed but requested they go tell Jack and Lorriene tomorrow during brunch. Exhausted, Jackson replied, "If that's what you want, *beautiful,* we'll do just that. But for now, I'm going to lie down for a bit. Please make sure to wake me when you return so I can show you **just** how happy I am."

"Are you trying to seduce me, Mr. Swan?"

"Always, Ms. Flowers. Always."

The moment Anne-Marie backed out of her parking space, Jackson's heart fell. Guilt ate away at him, as he knew Dr. Fischer's office wouldn't be calling. He knew because he already had the answer. How could he destroy this precious girl he loved so much? Jackson prayed a silent prayer. *Hopefully, our baby will keep her alive. Please, God, let this baby remind her every day of me. If it's a girl, I'll tell Anne-Marie her name has to be Luxe.* With that, Jackson undressed down to his underwear and slipped into bed.

~

As Anne-Marie made the 15-minute drive to Luke and Patricia's, her heart swelled with a mixture of joy and sorrow. This was one of the few times, in recent memory, where she truly felt that she missed her parents. Knowing there wasn't any point in dwelling on what she was missing, Anne-Marie chose to focus on what she had. Patricia and Luke had been so wonderful to her and she was so excited to give them the gift of being grandparents.

When Anne-Marie walked through the front door and into the living room, she was shocked to see both Luke and Patricia laughing, crying, and altogether, full of hysterics. Cautiously, she remarked asked what was going on. Patricia quickly dried her eyes with a tissue and exclaimed, "Hi, *sweetheart*! What are you doing here? We were going to call you in the morning because we have the best news!"

Anne-Marie chuckled at Patricia's enthusiasm and stated, "Really?! I have great news for you guys, too. Why don't you go first?"

Luke started crying once again as his bride of more than twenty years delivered the heartfelt news to Anne-Marie. "We are pregnant!"

With this announcement, it was as if time stopped. To say Anne-Marie was flabbergasted would be putting it mildly. Happy tears streamed down Anne-Marie's face as she remarked, "Oh my gosh! Are you serious?"

Patricia just chuckled joyously in reply. "Yes, *sweetheart*, I am 16 weeks along. I truly thought this day would never come."

Anne-Marie just stood there in a mixture of shock, joy, and disbelief. Could this be happening? If anyone deserved a child, it was this wonderful couple. After a few minutes, Anne-Marie giddily stated, "This **truly** is the best day ever!"

Luke, finally able to compose himself asked, "What's your news, *sweetheart?*"

A bit sheepishly, Anne-Marie replied, "I came over here to tell you guys that I am 12 weeks pregnant! Our babies are going to be the best of friends."

Luke exclaimed, "A dad and a grandpa all at the same time. God is truly smiling down on me."

Luke and Patricia were overjoyed for this moment with the darling daughter of their hearts. And while she may not have been theirs by birth or blood, she was theirs nonetheless. Anne-Marie celebrated the double announcement with Patricia and Luke for an hour, then bid them goodbye to head back home.

~

When Anne-Marie arrived home, she looked upon Jackson and then down at her belly. The little baby created in love, and growing inside of her, was an amazing blessing. Anne-Marie climbed into bed and began playfully kissing Jackson as she spoke, "Jackson, I'm back. Jackson, wake up!"

Jackson awoke with a yawn and then gave Anne-Marie a flirtatious wink. "Hi, *beautiful!* How was your visit with Patricia and Luke?"

"They are pregnant too! Patricia is 16 weeks along."

Jackson remarked, "That's amazing!"

Anne-Marie replied, "It truly is! Patricia said that the doctor is monitoring her since she is 44. Apparently, she is what they call 'advanced maternal age.'" Anne-Marie rolled her eyes at the words "advanced maternal age."

Jackson looked at his love and smiled as he gently stroked her hair and thought now would be the perfect time to tell her the name he had picked for their baby. "I have a name for our baby girl."

Anne-Marie looked at Jackson and giggled. "*Honey,* I'm only 12 weeks along. How do you know this little one is a girl?"

Placing his hands on his hips, Jackson responded, "I honestly can't say. It's more of a feeling, really. I guess I just know."

Anne-Marie just laughed at this silly man of hers. "Okay, well *if* this little one is a boy, he will be named Jackson Archer Swan III. I want him named after you and your dad." Pausing briefly, Anne-Marie then asked, "What was the girl's name that you had in mind?"

Jackson was so excited and honored! "I love that if we have a boy, you want him to be named after dad and me. However, if we have a girl, which I know we will, her name will be Luxe."

Anne-Marie was a bit shocked and confused. "Luxe? It's definitely beautiful and unique but, why Luxe?"

Jackson amorously responded, "I have my reasons and will tell you tomorrow when we announce to my parents, but right now, I want to show you just how much I love you."

With that being said, Jackson climbed on top of his beloved and began placing kisses on her neck. Passion overtook Anne-Marie as Jackson's kisses moved lower and lower down her body. Jackson only stopped long enough to teasingly nibble here and there before slowly making his way back to her enticing, cherry red lips.

~

The next morning, Jackson and Anne-Marie awoke and readied themselves for the weekly brunch with Jackson's parents. Jackson opted for a neutral gray sweater vest over a white dress shirt and red skinny jeans. He paired these with his **Rolex** and favorite black dress shoes. Anne-Marie decided upon a delicate red lace dress which she paired with matching strappy heels and her necklace from Patricia. As Anne-Marie dressed, she couldn't help but feel hesitant. *Hopefully, Jackson's parents will be excited about our baby.*

Jackson waited in the living room for Anne-Marie to finish up. As Anne-Marie entered the room, Jackson noticed the downtrodden look upon her face. Nervously he asked, "What's wrong, *beautiful?*"

Holding back tears, Anne-Marie replied, "I'm so nervous. Do you think that your parents will be angry? We are pretty young and we aren't even married yet."

Jackson chuckled a bit at his sweet girl and her silly, nervous thoughts. Lovingly, he placed a kiss on her cheek and responded "*Baby*, I can promise you this is going to bring them so much joy!"

~

The 30-minute drive to Swan Manor was quiet and peaceful; Jackson and Anne-Marie both sat thinking quietly about the news they would soon deliver. As Jackson pulled into the drive and parked the car, a single tear rolled down his cheek. Taking a moment to catch his breath, Jackson said, "Come on, *beautiful*! I am starved."

Anne-Marie smiled and said, "Me too, *my love*! This little one has left me famished."

Upon entering the manor, Jackson called out, "Mom! Dad! We're here," to which Lorriene replied from another room, "Hi, *honey*! We're just finishing in the kitchen, so why don't you two wait for us in the sunroom?"

Out of all the rooms in Swan Manor, the sunroom was quite possibly Anne-Marie's most favorite place. The linen-colored walls paired perfectly with the snowy, white pillars, and furniture Lorriene had chosen. The vast windows let in the sun's warmth and allowed her to feel entranced by the natural beauty which surrounded the property. This truly was the perfect location to announce their baby.

After the delicious brunch, the little family sat in the sunroom, simply enjoying this beautiful winter day in Oregon, when Jackson looked around and cleared his throat before speaking. "Mom. Dad. We have some news for you guys?"

Jack looked at his son and asked, "What is it, son? Have you guys finally set a date for the wedding?"

Anne-Marie and Jackson looked at each other and just smiled before Anne-Marie simply stated, "Well, Grandpa …"

Upon hearing the word *"Grandpa,"* both Jack and Lorriene stood in shock! After a couple of minutes the shock wore off and both just smiled at each other lovingly. Jack spoke excitedly, "Grandpa?"

Jackson responded with great enthusiasm which matched his dad's. "Yes! Anne-Marie is 12 weeks pregnant."

Anne-Marie chimed in, "If the baby is a boy, he will be Jackson Archer Swan III." Hearing this name announcement made Jack and Lorriene both beam with pride.

Jackson cut in and said, "However, if this little one is a girl, her name will be Luxe Swan."

Lorriene was confused for a moment; this was not a family name nor one she had heard of before. So Lorriene asked, "Why the name Luxe? Don't get me wrong, it truly is a beautiful and unique name, but why Luxe?"

Curiosity finally crept its way back into Anne-Marie's mind and she responded with a shrug, "Ya know, I asked Jackson that same question last night when he told me the name."

Again, a single tear ran down Jackson's cheek and he knew that he could no longer keep his secret. So, he spoke, with his voice wavering, "Her name will be Luxe because … because it means light. And- and our daughter will be the light in this world that I leave behind."

Jackson could no longer hold the flood of bitter tears welling up inside of his very being. Anne-Marie, Jack, and Lorriene were all in complete and utter shock! What on earth could Jackson have meant by *"The light I leave behind?"*

5

Don't get too close

September 5, 2014

Lola paused from the start of her tale to look around; she was exhausted and already dreading the drive back to Lizzie's house. Once again turning her gaze to Logan, she remarked, "Look, Logan, it's getting late and I am exhausted. I still have an hour's drive back to Lizzie's house. I can always come back tomorrow and start where we left off."

Sadness overcame Logan. Lola had just come back and would now be leaving again. So, he said the first thing that came to both his heart and his mind, with absolute resolve, "Lola, please just stay upstairs at my place. You look exhausted and I honestly don't think it's safe for you to drive."

Knowing he was right, Lola playfully replied with an eye roll, "Yes, *mom*," and burst out laughing.

Logan looked at Lola and laughed while saying, "Alright, *Miss Sarcastic*, move your sweet ass upstairs! You know, I didn't miss this part of you."

Lola exclaimed, "Ouch! Take it out!"

Logan rolled his eyes in reply, "Take what out?"

Lola playfully slammed her hand against the table and exclaimed, "The knife you just used to cut me down. You know my sass is a **gift**!"

Logan laughed to himself and playfully sighed, "Fine, woman! Just please move it so your sass can get some sleep. I will be up in a bit, just let me finish cleaning up. Why don't you make yourself at home."

Lola looked uneasy but caught her breath for a moment and said, "Uh … Okay. If you're absolutely sure, then I guess I have no other choice."

As Logan watched Lola leave, he clicked on the radio before beginning the late-night cleaning. The soothing voice of the Radio DJ flooded the empty café. "Good evening, Oregon! DJ Samantha here with one last late-night jam before I call it a night. This song goes out to all those dealing with internal demons and struggles. 'Demons' by the amazing band, Imagine Dragons, is up next after a word from our sponsors."

The music faded into the back of Logan's mind as the thoughts of his heart made their way front and center. *There she is- My Lola … hell, my heart … a glimmer of her still remains. I hope I can get her back. Life without her has been pure agony for me, but I know I can't be selfish right now. She has to come back, but only if she's ready."*

An hour later, as he walked into his tiny studio apartment, Logan saw Lola already fast asleep on his bed. Her rose-red hair was beautifully displayed around her soft heart-shaped face. She was simply enchanting. Logan bent down and gently kissed Lola's forehead. It was then that he noticed her tear-stained face and the wet pillowcase. Logan's heart shattered as he saw the sight of this beautifully broken girl.

How can anyone so beautiful and full of light also be filled with so much sorrow? I know she'll tell me everything in her time, I just wish that

bastard *would've never brought her to her breaking point. I almost lost her for good. Thank you, God- she's back, even if only for a little while.*

As Logan crawled into bed beside Lola, she shifted toward him and snuggled in. There it was again, her intoxicating smell of berries on a warm, summer's day. Logan whispered into Lola's ear, "You seriously have no idea just how much I love you. I'll do what I can to protect you and keep you from harm … even if it means saving you from yourself."

~

September 6, 2014

Morning approached and Lola began to awaken. She realized this was the first time in what felt like forever that she wasn't plagued by nightmares. A comforting warmth surrounded her as she began to open her eyes. She realized that Logan held her close, so close in fact, that it was almost as if his life depended upon it. Lola smiled quietly to herself but then, guilt began to flood her mind. Inside, her mind began to taunt her *You don't deserve happiness. Look at how damaged you are! You are selfish to think you can give the love he deserves!*

"**Stop it!**" Lola screamed and ran out of the room.

Logan began to stir but, thankfully, he slept through Lola's outburst; she couldn't handle it if he had awoken to her internal struggle. Lola said to herself as her stomach growled, *I know it's early, but I need to call Dr. Indigo. First things first though, it smells like Cate has made some delicious goodies. I'll get food and then call Dr. Indigo.*

Although he had been asleep, Logan had felt Lola awaken and start to stir; he knew her struggle had begun. Her self-directed outburst confirmed Logan's thoughts enough to rouse him, yet he made sure to keep his eyes shut because he knew Lola would be mortified if she found out about his awareness of her internalized struggle.

Lola went to Logan's closet to look for something presentable in public.

After searching through the limited wardrobe she had, Lola decided on some denim jeggings, a cute grey camisole which she layered with a red, long sleeve flannel that she chose to button a tiny bit and then tie at her waist. She chose to pair this simple outfit with red ballet flats and a crescent moon necklace, then added a cute tribal headscarf to tie up her long curly hair.

As Lola looked upon herself in the mirror, she chuckled and remarked, "Well, this is about as good as it gets. I guess I decided to embrace my inner Oregon girl with this outfit."

Once slightly satisfied with her appearance, Lola returned to the bedroom and left a note for Logan stating, *"If I'm not here when you find this, I'm downstairs at **Cate's**. XXX"*

Lola made her way downstairs and straight toward Cate and Cade. Cate looked up as soon as Lola entered the room. "Hi, sweet Luxie! Glad to see you didn't make the drive back to Lizzie's. How did you sleep?"

Lola responded, "Actually, pretty decent for the first time that I can ever remember."

Cate asked, "Did you let Lizzie know you weren't coming back?"

Lola sighed and stated, "No, it was so late that I didn't want to disturb her."

A look of concern quickly came across Cate's face as she remarked, "Well dear, please call her soon. You know how much Lizzie worries."

"I will. I need to call Dr. Indigo too."

Just then, Cade walked through the door carrying some muffins. He sat them on the display, while simultaneously handing one to Lola, before giving her a fatherly kiss on the head. Cade said, "For our favorite girl."

Lola giggled and said, "Thanks a million, you guys. You really know how to make a girl feel loved."

After Lola finished her muffin and coffee, she stepped outside behind the café and made her phone calls. First up was Lizzie.

"Hello!" the sweet voice on the other end of the line answered.

Lola stated, "Hey, sister. Sorry I didn't message you last night. I stayed here in Parkway at Logan's apartment above the café."

Lizzie breathed a sigh of relief and said, "Hey, sister. Yeah- thanks for calling me. I was gonna blow your phone up if I hadn't heard from you by the time I awoke."

Laughing, Lola stated, "Sorry, *Momma Bear!*"

The noise of a young girl in the background took Lizzie's attention. "Momma, is that *Auntie Bear*," the voice quipped.

Lizzie replied, "Yes, *my love* it certainly is."

The little girl remarked, "Hi, *Auntie Bear*. I wanna see you soon, Okay? I love you and miss you," and then happily exited the room.

Lizzie returned to her phone conversation and said, "Alright, *Baby Bear*, I've got to get off of here pretty soon, so please just let me know when you're coming back."

Lola replied, "Will do, *Momma Bear*! Kiss Raelee for me."

Pausing for a moment, Lola remarked with a bit of melancholy in her voice, "I can't believe Baby Rae is now 10."

Lizzie chuckled at the thought, "I can't either!"

Lola quickly added, "Oh, before I forget, I think I'm going to try staying here in Parkway with Logan for a little while. As you know, Dr. Indigo is making me go through **all** of my story with Logan as a part of this complete healing bullshit. So, I'm not sure how long it will take."

Trying her best to remain calm, Lizzie breathed a sigh of frustration and remarked, "Luxie, don't start this crap again. You and I both know that she's right. *Sweetie*, I get it, I do. However, you're gonna have to trust the process. At your last meeting, Dr. Indigo said it would be hard as hell. I love you, *Baby Bear*. Call me every day and don't roll your eyes at me!"

Lola rolled her eyes right as Lizzie told her not to, and laughed. "Aye Aye, *Momma Bear*. I love you too."

Lizzie replied with a smirk, "I will talk to you soon, okay? Right now, I need to get Raelee to her ballet lessons."

Lola hung up the phone and thought to herself, *I am so grateful to have a lifelong best friend in Lizzie. I know I shut her out for a while, but she never once gave up on me, like a true Momma Bear.*

~

In a beautifully teal painted kitchen, Lizzie stood at the edge of her breaking point. Normally, Lizzie was the epitome of composure, but not today. Today, two years of sadness flooded her heart. The pent-up tears she had yet to shed, came streaming down Lizzie's face all at once.

A gentle, masculine voice called out, "Hey, *babe*. I'm about to head into town. Do we need anything while I'm there?"

Hearing no reply, Mark made his way into the kitchen and sorrow overtook him. There were very few times Mark had ever witnessed his wife break down and this sight tore his heart in two. Quickly walking over to Lizzie, Mark asked, "What's the matter, *babe*? Why has your sweet smile disappeared?"

At the sound of her husband's soothing voice, Lizzie did her best to regain composure. Taking a deep breath and pausing for a moment, Lizzie finally replied, "It's Luxie. I am just so worried about her. I don't know if my heart can take another **incident** like before."

Upon hearing these solemn words, Mark shut his eyes to fight back the tears. The **incident** had been so heartbreaking for everyone. Although she had not let it get to her and tried to be the firm rock for everyone during that time, Mark knew his wife. He knew that it had all been too much for her to bear.

Pausing briefly to gather himself together, Mark finally spoke, "All that we can do is pray for her and support her. She has to take the steps to move forward on her own."

Breathing deeply, Mark embraced his lovely wife. Lizzie's beautiful chestnut-colored hair had started to fall into her face so, Mark gently moved it aside to place a kiss on her forehead. Looking into her husband's sea glass-colored eyes, Lizzie softly stated, "Thank you for always being my rock, *my love*."

Kissing her forehead once again, Mark replied, "Any time, my beautiful *hurricane*."

~

As Lola hung up the phone with Lizzie, she began to pace back and forth anxiously. Now came the call Lola dreaded, the call to Dr. Indigo. It's not that Dr. Indigo wasn't amazing to talk to, she was. Lola just hated having to feel like she was "reporting in" *every.single.damn.day*. Lola sighed to herself, *"Let's do this."*

The phone rang for a good thirty seconds and just as Lola was about to hang up, a voice came across the line. "Good morning, Ms. Harper."

Lola balled her empty fist in anger and said with a haughty voice, "Good morning, *warden*. What have I said about calling me 'Ms. Harper?'"

Dr. Indigo laughed to herself and responded, "My, my! It would seem like someone woke up on the extra sassy side of the bed this morning. Is calling me 'Warden' necessary?"

Filled with sass and rage, Lola remarked "Why yes, I did wake up on the extra sassy side. How many times do I have to tell you that my sass is as big as my..."

Dr. Indigo quickly interjected, "Ahem, Ms. Harper, let's keep it PG, especially when you are in a setting outside of my office."

Lola rolled her eyes, "Yes, Warden!"

Dr. Indigo sighed, "Alright dear, enough with the 'Warden.'"

Lola stated, "Fine! I only do it when you call me Ms. Harper. You know that's not me anymore. It's Swan again. Lola Swan. Lola fucking Swan! We have been talking for two years now and shouldn't need such formalities."

Dr. Indigo replied, "Very well, Ms. Har … I mean, Lola. Let's move on. How was your first night back in Parkway?"

Lola dreaded these questions. "Well, I'm not gonna lie, it was so hard coming back. All the memories washed over me and I felt like I was going to suffocate by the emotion. I wanted to open the old scars and let the emotion flow free, but I didn't. I know now that it only hurts the people who care about me."

"Lola, that is amazing! It sounds like you're making real progress. Now, will you please tell me how you slept and what you felt this morning?"

Thinking for a moment, Lola answered truthfully. "Well, last night, I arrived here kinda late and began telling Logan a little bit of my story, the part with Anne-Marie and Jackson and their beginning. Then, Logan made me go upstairs and sleep at his place because he was being all mom-like and wouldn't let me drive back to Lizzie's."

Dr. Indigo laughed and replied, "I think that's very wise and I am again, proud of how much progress you have made by being able to focus on genuine help and not letting the emotion cut into you."

Lola paused for a few minutes before she continued. "Well, like I said Dr. Indigo, it was so draining on me that I really had to fight the urge to let the old scars open up and the emotion flow free, so instead, I cried myself to sleep. At some point, Logan came in and slept beside me. When I woke up this morning, he was holding me so firmly yet lovingly and protectively."

Dr. Indigo remarked, "How did you feel when you woke up to Logan's embrace?"

Lola thought for a moment before replying, "Honestly, at first, I felt happy and safe, but then it passed and guilt flooded my mind."

Inquisitively, Dr. Indigo asked while making her notes, "Tell me about this guilt. If you need a few moments to gather your thoughts, it's fine. I would rather this conversation take a while and have you be open and honest."

Lola breathed deeply and waited for around three minutes before she continued nonchalantly. "You know the same old same old. My mind plaguing me with thoughts of how selfish I am and that I am too damaged to ever deserve love and happiness."

Dr. Indigo inquired, "How did you handle these thoughts and emotions?" Lola responded, "Well, I was angry at myself because I didn't let the scars open last night to flood the emotion out but then, I was angry at myself for thinking that way. What would they say if they found me like that? So, I yelled '**stop it**' to myself and got dressed for today."

Dr. Indigo stated, "Okay Lola, just a few more questions. Who do you mean by *they*? Logan specifically? Also, did you eat this morning?"

Unsure of how to respond, Lola said, "Kind of Logan specifically, because … well, you know. But also Cate, Cade, and Lizzie. I just can't let them all down again. I did eat today. I had one of Cate's muffins and yes, before you ask, I ate all of it and kept it all down."

Pleased with the outcome of the call, Dr. Indigo exclaimed, "Well Lola, I can honestly say that I am beyond thrilled with your progress as of now. You have made great strides on this journey so far. Please remember, that I am only a quick phone call away no matter the time if you ever feel that you have to let the emotion flow out. It's healthier to talk and lose a little sleep than to keep it hidden, only to let it out through the old scars. Have a good day, Lola."

Relieved that this conversation was finally ending, Lola replied,

"Thanks, Dr. Indigo. You too."

After the phone conversation, Lola felt immensely drained and in desperate need of a nap. Before wearily making her way back to Logan's apartment, Lola turned on the **MusicLove** radio app, in hopes that some music would distract her thoughts.

"Hello, Oregon lovers! DJ Samantha here with an early morning love song. This next jam goes out to all those giving their everything to the one they love. And those afraid to move forward with their hearts. 'Bleeding Out' by **Imagine Dragons** will play after a quick message from our sponsors."

Once Lola made her way back, she undressed and climbed back into bed. For a brief moment, as she stared intently at Logan, Lola was overcome with the desire to gently kiss his forehead. However, reality quickly set in- anxious thoughts constantly an unpleasant reminder of her countless failures. *I know Dr. Indigo is right, but I'm scared shitless. I just don't want to get too close.* As Lola snuggled in next to Logan, she let his warmth overtake her. Logan's scent reminded Lola of the Oregon coastline, a unique mixture of evergreen trees and the ocean breeze. This scent was comforting and could feel like home if only Lola could allow herself to be loved.

Logan lovingly embraced Lola, kissing her forehead to welcome her back, "I'm glad you're back. This bed was getting awfully cold."

A sleepy chuckle escaped Lola's lips while she bemused, "Shouldn't you be getting up for work anyhow?"

"Nah! My shift at **Cate's** doesn't start until noon, so we can rest for a few more hours."

"Why are you workin' at **Cate's** anyway? I thought you had a couple of other jobs?"

"I help here periodically. Now, shh! No more talkie, unless you want me to kiss your sweet lips."

Lola playfully slapped Logan's bare, tattooed chest before allowing the rhythmic sound of Logan's heartbeat to lull her back into a peaceful slumber.

~

Around 11:00 a.m., Logan's alarm went off and both he and Lola woke for the day. Logan asked, "What's your plan for today? I have an 8-hour shift at *Cate's* and we need to continue our talk."

Lola pondered, before replying, "Well, before I left to come here, Dr. Indigo said in my last session that I needed to start writing letters to the people in my life. Not necessarily to be read but to help with this healing path B.S."

Logan replied thoughtfully, "I know you aren't happy, but honestly, I think this is a good thing."

With that, Logan kissed Lola's head and then went to dress before beginning his shift. Looking at his wardrobe, Logan decided that instead of his usual flannel, he would wear an old faded black band t-shirt, which he paired with his favorite ripped black jeans and all-black Converse.

As he finished dressing, he chuckled to himself. *If mom could see me, I know she would bitch about my jeans, but why mess with a good thing.*

Logan left Lola to herself and entered the café, where he found business was fairly steady and Cate and Cade were both hard at work restocking all of the bakery items.

Once Logan entered, Cate said, "Hi, *sweetie!* How's Luxie?"

Cade simply greeted, "Hi, son!"

Logan thought for a moment and then breathed deeply before replying. "Hey, guys! Lola is okay. Honestly, I am not pushing anything with her."

Cate looked at Logan lovingly and stated, "That's probably for the best."

Looking down at her long list of things to do, Cate turned to Cade and Logan and said, "Alright my loves, I am off to run errands." Turning to Cade, Cate said in a sultry voice with a flirty wink, "I'll see you later tonight, *Daddy*."

Cade blew Cate a kiss and blushed with infatuation, desire, and lust. While Logan, on the other hand, was mortified and feigned vomiting.

As Cate exited the room, Cade couldn't help but chuckle. "You're 30 years old son and you still can't handle the fact that your old man is a sexual beast."

Logan slammed his hand against his face and sighed, "For fuck's sake dad, please **do not ever** refer to yourself as a sexual beast again!"

Cade laughed merrily at the torment of his son and jested, "Don't hate the player son, hate the game!"

An idea quickly came to Logan's mind. It was the perfect way to get back at his dad. "Okay dad, so, I am going to call Pop and ask if he and Grammy are still gettin' it on."

Cade instantly regretted his decisions and laughed, "Alright son, checkmate in your favor!"

Both father and son laughed heartily for a few minutes before Cade decided it was time to turn the conversation at hand to one of a more serious nature. "So son, how are you really doing? And don't give me this blanket cop-out shit. I know you and I want to know the truth."

Logan knew his dad was coming from a place of love and concern. Breathing deeply and pausing for a few minutes, Logan sadly looked down at the ground and replied, "Honestly dad, I'm scared shitless. I want to be there for Lola to catch her but at the same time, I'm worried I'll push her away. I also don't know if my heart can take her breaking in two again. I feel like I'm on a fucking slippery slope with nowhere to go."

Cade looked at his son with sorrow. There was nothing he could do in this situation but be there. Seeing how much the ***incident*** hurt Logan in the process scared the hell out of Cade. After all, what parent wouldn't be concerned after the truth came out about everything that went down. Looking at his son, Cade said the only thing he could think of, which still managed to feel empty and hollow. "All I can say son is to remain diligent and patient."

Trying to steer the conversation in a different direction, Cade remarked, "On another note, have you called your mother lately?"

Logan rolled his eyes at Cade and exclaimed with a haughty attitude, "Dad, I'm a grown-ass man. I don't need to call my '**mommy**' every day."

As soon as those words left Logan's mouth his phone began to ring, as if by instinct. Logan looked at the caller ID and an expression that was a mixture of horror and surprise flooded his face. "Oh, shit!" was the only thing Logan could mutter.

Cade just laughed and laughed as Logan regained his composure and answered, "Hh-hey, momma! How's it going?" Logan headed to the back to take the call and Cade carried on with his work, all while praying a silent prayer for his son.

~

The day passed mundanely for Lola as she procrastinated with her letter-writing and decided to read a book instead. Her current favorite was The Raven's Song by E.R. Blackwell. As Lola cracked open her book, she thought to herself, *I wish I could meet E.R. Blackwell someday; her books inspire me. The love that Raven and Willow have for each other, is something I would love to have again one day. Sadly, I'm far too damaged to be loved.*

Lola quickly lost track of time and before she knew it, Logan's shift was over and he was back upstairs. When he walked in, he found Lola passed out with her book haphazardly strewn to the side. Logan looked at Lola lovingly before gently waking her. "Lola. Hey,

Lola- I'm back?"

Lola stretched and rubbed her eyes before sitting up and stating, "Wow! Has the day passed so quickly?"

Logan playfully shook his head and chuckled, "Come on, get dressed. We are going for dinner."

Lola shrugged in reply. "I'm not hungry."

Logan angrily crossed his arms and remarked, "Lola, what have you eaten today?"

Lola thought for a moment before giving her reply, "Umm … a muffin and some coffee, but I'm totally fine."

Her stomach grumbled as she lied about being fine. Logan placed his hand on his face in frustration. "Damn it, Lola! You need to fucking eat. No ifs, ands, or buts about it. The only butt should be yours moving out of this bed to get dressed for dinner."

Lola laughed and replied, "Ugh! Fine, Warren!"

She quickly dressed in the outfit she wore that morning and the couple headed downstairs, in the direction of **Marty's Diner** for some take-out.

As they walked down the street to the tiny diner, Lola let her hand gently graze Logan's. A tiny flutter of something started in her heart but, she quickly dismissed it, not wanting the demons inside to ruin this peaceful walk. Once Logan and Lola entered the parking lot, Logan said, "Come on, we're just doing a pickup."

Lola rolled her eyes but quickly followed Logan into the diner. Once they entered, anxiety began to fill Lola's mind. Lola stated with a tinge of annoyance and exhaustion, "Let's just get this over with."

Logan remarked cheerily, "This'll be fun, you'll see!"

Marty's Diner was a small, classic American-style diner. It had beautiful red brick walls which were elegantly accented with black equipment and decor. Along the ceiling hung strands of beautiful lights that carefully cascaded to create an atmosphere of hominess and refinement. **Marty's** was owned by Marty Franklin and his adoring wife, Betty, and had been a Parkway staple for more than 40 years.

Behind the counter, Betty moved like a busy little bee, preparing orders for the eager guests. As they walked toward the counter, Logan exclaimed, "Hi, Betty."

Betty returned Logan's greeting and then looked upon Lola with sheer delight. Tears of joy welled up in Betty's beautiful violet eyes. "Well, as I live and breathe! If it isn't little Luxie!" was the only remark Betty could muster.

Lola giggled and exclaimed, "Hi, Betty! It's nice to see you."

Betty laughed lightly and said, "Sweet baby child, I am so happy to see you. You know, every time I look at you, it seems like you look more and more like your father."

Quickly Betty turned away from Logan and Lola and called out, "Marty!"

When no reply came, Betty called again. "Marty! You'll never believe who is here?"

From the kitchen, Marty could hear the gusto in his lovely wife's voice and quickly turned to see what all the commotion was about. As Marty entered the dining area, he was in complete shock. "Well, if it isn't little Luxie! How have you been sweetie?"

Marty embraced Lola in a sweet hug and Lola replied, "Hi, Marty! It's great to see you."

In the background, "Order up!" and the dinging sound of a bell brought Marty back to his senses. "Well Luxie, I must get back. Now don't be a stranger, ya hear!"

As Marty hurried back into the kitchen, Betty quickly cashed Logan out and the couple enjoyed the nice summer night breeze on the way back to Logan's apartment.

Upon entering the apartment, Lola quietly excused herself to the bathroom. Logan took this time to set his coffee table up. Logan thought to himself and laughed, *Even if we are just here at home, I want Lola to know she deserves nothing but the best. After all, momma didn't raise no punk ass bitch!*

When Lola returned, her eyes lit up at the beautiful sight before her. She wanted to feel joyful because of this sweet gesture. However, her mind wouldn't have any of that. *Don't even think about getting any bright ideas. You know you are nothing but a worthless shell of a person.*

Taking a few deep breaths, and trying not to cry, Lola simply stated, "Thank you, Logan. Let's sit and eat."

Logan couldn't help but look away in disappointment at Lola's flattened tone. *Does this mean nothing? She says thank you, but does she mean it?*

Quickly chastising himself for even thinking such thoughts, Logan kissed Lola's head and said, "After you, *my heart.*"

They ate their meal in silence which, if Lola was going to talk again, is what she preferred. Once the meal was completed, Lola cleared her throat and began. "Where were we ..."

6

Joy turns to sorrow

February 15, 1984

When Jackson and Anne-Maric shared the news with his parents about the pregnancy, his revelation for choosing the name Luxe gripped everyone with fear and disbelief. Lorriene, whose face paled from shock, finally broke the silence and spoke. "Son, what exactly do you mean by the light you will leave behind in this world? If this is some kind of sick joke, take it back!"

With tear-filled eyes, Jackson replied, "Why would I joke about something like this, Mom? I talked with Dr. Fischer yesterday morning. I have cancer. They don't know how long I have but right now, it still seems pretty early on."

Silence. Nothing but deafening silence; the heavyweight of it filled the room like a dark cloud bringing a vicious tornado. Jack reached out his arm to steady Lorriene then asked, "Son, did they say what kind of cancer you have?"

With a heavy heart, Jackson sorrowfully stated, "Leukemia. Specifically, *Chronic Myeloid Leukemia.* Dr. Fischer does seem hopeful that with Chemotherapy treatments, I should be fine. However, he said we must look at all avenues of possibility."

What was supposed to be a day filled with love and happiness quickly turned mournful. Everything became instantly overwhelming, causing Anne-Marie to break down and run out of the room. Jack looked at his son and said, "You need to go after her now!"

Sorrowfully, Jackson went after Anne-Marie. Searching frantically throughout the manor, Jackson finally found her outside in the snowy garden. Wrapping his arms lovingly around Anne-Marie, Jackson stared into the chocolate brown orbs which captivated his very soul.

Holding onto her gaze as the powdery snow gently fell around them, Jackson quietly stated, "Hey- look at me, *beautiful*. Please?"

Frustration filled Anne-Marie and for the very first time, she found herself angry with Jackson. He was the man who had become entwined into her very being had kept something so life-altering from her. Balling her fists in rage, Anne-Marie released a gut-wrenching scream. "What the hell do you expect from me, Jackson? We are supposed to be a team! We are supposed to grow old together! We are supposed to raise this baby together!"

Jackson pulled Anne-Marie into his chest as she released her angry tears. Thirty minutes in the cold Oregon snow passed as Jackson held onto his beloved, letting her weep in desperation. Jackson inhaled deeply, finally finding the courage to speak."Look at me beautiful. I planned to tell you last night but you were so happy. Our baby is a blessing and will be the very best of both of us. Even if I pass on, can't you see that I will always be with you through our precious child?"

With no tears left to cry, Anne-Marie bitterly remarked, "Please take me home."

~

The weeks quickly passed by and Jackson began his chemotherapy treatments. Anne-Marie was in complete shock the first time she saw Jackson after his initial treatment, and each time after never did get any easier. Patiently taking her in his arms, Jackson would lovingly kiss Anne-Marie and say, "Look at me, *beautiful*."

Looking into his evergreen eyes, Anne-Marie would smile, which in turn, always caused Jackson to laugh a bit. "Dr. Fischer says that this is all par for the course. He's the best at what he does and I trust him. So please, *beautiful*, just trust in me. Okay?"

Each time, Anne-Marie would gently kiss his lips and reply, "I trust you more than anything, *baby*. You are my very reason for living."

~

April 1984

April 15 started off no differently than any other day, however, this would be the day when the sordid side effects of the chemo would finally make themselves known. The instant Anne-Marie's usual reply escaped her lips, she could no longer hold herself back. Passionately she kissed the love of her life because she needed to feel Jackson close to her.

Graciously, Jackson returned the kiss. Slowly, he moved his kisses down the side of her neck, as Anne-Marie ran her fingers through Jackson's firey, red curls. Jackson paused for a moment and looked upon Anne-Marie's body in awe as her precious baby bump had begun to show.

Lovingly, Jackson kissed Anne-Marie's belly before he slowly and seductively made his way down her thighs and to her quivering center. Anne-Marie, lost in the midst of pleasure, continued to run her hands through Jackson's hair. Reaching the point of climax, Anne-Marie looked up from her moment of ecstasy to notice her hands held clumps of the red curls she adored.

"Oh my god, Jackson!" Anne-Marie screamed in horror as she quickly recoiled to the upper corner of their bed and sobbed.

Jackson just held her because what more was there to say.

~

Once Anne-Marie fell asleep, Jackson retreated to the bathroom. Gazing upon his ghastly reflection, Jackson couldn't help but feel angry. Angry at the world. Angry with God. And worst of all, angry with himself. He was a good and honest person. He honored his parents and loved Anne-Marie and their baby with his entire being. So why was this to be his fate?

"Why, God? Why the hell is this happening to me? How can you just sit there and let that beautiful girl suffer?" Angry, bitter tears left Jackson's eyes as he plugged in his electric shaver, removing the remainder of his curls before the chemo could steal any more from him.

Satisfied with his buzzcut, Jackson showered then returned to bed. Jackson's joyful heart turned sorrowful; however, he refused to let that sorrow bring any more burdening thoughts to Anne-Marie. Kissing her forehead sweetly, Jackson drifted off to sleep.

Anne-Marie awoke the next morning to a slight prickling feeling upon her face; looking down, she saw the outcome of Jackson's actions. Silently weeping to herself, she prayed, *God, please don't leave me here alone. My parents are already gone. Please don't take the man I love and the father of my baby. I am not strong enough to live without Jackson.*

~

June 1984

The revelation of Jackson's illness took a toll upon Jack and Lorriene. Jackson was their only child and had been a miracle to conceive. Lorriene wanted to be hopeful but her mother's heart told her that no hope remained, her son would be gone before the end of the year. Jack did his very best to remove the workload from Jackson so that he could rest yet, Jackson would not hear of it.

"Dad, if you would allow me to speak bluntly, cutting my workload is complete and utter bullshit."

Jack looked at his son and said with sorrow in his voice, "Son, I just want to make sure you are resting and enjoying this time with Anne-Marie before the baby arrives."

Rolling his eyes in anger, Jackson said, "For fuck's sake, dad! I'm not dead yet."

Although Jackson knew his dad meant well, he was tired of everyone acting weird around him. In a bitter rage, Jackson exploded, "Don't you think I already know I am dying? Dammit! I don't need your fucking pity old man. Just back the hell off!"

Grabbing the whiskey from the boardroom table, Jackson poured a small amount for himself and downed it before smashing the glass against the wall behind his father.

Exiting the room, Jackson exclaimed, "You want to lighten my load. Fine. I fucking quit!"

It was at that very moment, Jackson decided that he would take his own life back into his hands. Knowing his time was short, he chose to stop his chemotherapy treatments; something he did not discuss with Anne-Marie. *She has finally come to terms with the sickness, I am not going to let her know I have added the final nail to my coffin.*

Stepping into his office, Jackson grabbed a pen and paper, then wrote out a letter for his unborn baby, which his heart told him would be a beautiful daughter.

Upon finishing his letter, Jackson headed down to his car and drove to his parent's house. Once inside, Jackson gave the letter to his mom and asked, "Mom, please give this letter to my baby girl on her tenth birthday."

Lorriene looked at Jackson and sighed. "Son, what if your baby is a boy. What then?"

Already frustrated by the events of the morning, Jackson replied a bit hastily, "Mom, don't start. Please. In my heart, I **know** this baby is a girl. I know she will look just like me but have her mother's cute little nose."

Trying not to cry, Lorriene remarked thoughtfully, "Maybe God is giving you peace in this scary time."

God was the last thing Jackson wanted to hear about but knew arguing with his mother would be a moot point. So, in turn, he simply replied, "Yeah … maybe."

Trying to change the conversation to a brighter point, Lorriene asked, "How is Anne-Marie? I miss having her here for weekly brunch. Honestly, son, I miss you both."

Jackson sheepishly stated, "She's as fine as can be expected. Her pregnancy is going okay. As you know, the news of my cancer diagnosis hit her hard. Just as she was coming to terms with my illness, my hair started falling out. Her doctor has told her to rest a lot and try to avoid stressful situations."

Lorriene asked, "Is this why Anne-Marie has chosen to step down from the Charity Board?"

Annoyed, Jackson responded, "What do you expect from her mom?" Taking a moment to steady his emotions and prevent himself from snapping at his loving mother, Jackson made his mother promise one last time that she would give his letter to his daughter when she turned ten.

With tears on the verge of breaking the dam that was the last of Lorriene's composure, she kissed her son's head in the same loving manner she had always done, but somehow, this time it seemed to feel final. "I will. I love you, son. Forever in my heart." Standing at the window, Lorriene couldn't help but clutch her heart as she watched her only child drive down the road.

~

Anne-Marie's pregnancy was going exceedingly well, despite the immense stress she felt from Jackson's diagnosis. Both the doctors' visits and fetal scans showed a strong and healthy baby. While Jackson and Anne-Marie longed to know the gender of their baby, her doctor refused to look, in case there was a chance of an incorrect result. During this time, Anne-Marie felt completely and utterly alone; this was the one time she regretted having closed herself off to other friendships after meeting Jackson.

~

August 2, 1984

Just after midnight, being only 36 weeks along, Anne-Marie went into labor. Frantically she woke Jackson from his slumber, letting him know it was time to head to the hospital. Jackson dressed as quickly as he could, despite the weakness permanently housed in his limbs.

When the young couple arrived at the hospital, Anne-Marie was admitted to the pregnancy ward, as she was already at five centimeters dilated. Kissing his darling upon her cheek, Jackson excused himself to find a payphone to contact his parents as well as Patricia and Luke, who had just had their baby two weeks ago; a beautiful chocolate brown-haired baby girl that they named Elizabeth Renee, but planned to call Lizzie. After Jackson made the calls, he turned to head back to his beloved. Darkness closed in around him as he suddenly passed out.

~

Anne-Marie patiently awaited Jackson's return when her contractions intensified and she called for the nurse. She sat in agony for nearly 30 minutes before someone finally came in to check on her. The nurse hurried in and spoke, "Sorry you had to wait so long, *sweetie!* My name's Abby, and I'll be taking care of you. We had to carry a man downstairs to the Emergency Department because he had passed out. Let's see where you're at."

Anne-Marie fearfully quipped, "Who passed out? Was it my fiancée? Did the man have rose-red hair?" Although she knew the answer, Anne-Marie cried out in rage and distress, "Please tell me, I'm begging you! I need him here with me for this. I'm not strong enough on my own."

Abby, trying to remain professional and positive, simply stated, "Oh, *honey-* I'm sorry to say that it was him, but I'm sure he'll be fine. Now, your body is already fully dilated, and I need you to do your best to not stress. You don't want the baby to be affected. Even though it may not seem like it, you are stronger than you think."

After pushing for four long, lonely hours, Anne-Marie's baby was born at 6:00 a.m. Nurse Abby placed the baby on her chest and said, "Congratulations, momma! You have a beautiful baby girl. She has the fairest skin and the most amazing red hair, that I've ever seen. I've never seen hair the color of roses before."

Looking down at her daughter, Anne-Marie let the painful tears fall, as she entertained the darkness, bitterness, and sadness encroaching upon her heart. She cried because Jackson was right; their daughter was beautiful and looked just like him. She cried because Jackson was elsewhere in the hospital and had missed this moment he longed for.

Oblivious to her patient's pain, Nurse Abby joyfully asked, "Have you and Dad come up with a name for this gorgeous girl?"

Anne-Marie thought for a moment as she turned her head from her daughter. *I'm sorry Jackson. I have to call her Lola for at this moment, my joy has turned to sorrow. I will still honor your wish by giving her the middle name Luxe.* Finally, she answered, "Yes. Her name is Lola. Lola Luxe Swan."

Nurse Abby stated, "What a uniquely gorgeous name for a uniquely gorgeous girl. Now, if you'll excuse me for a moment, I'm going to see what I can find out regarding your fiancée." Upon her return, nurse Abby let Anne-Marie know that Jackson was finally stabilizing, and would be able to see both Anne-Marie and their baby in two hours.

Anne-Marie spoke wearily, "Thank you, Nurse Abby. Do you mind taking her to the nursery so I can rest?" Just as she was about to settle in for a nap, wishing to sleep away all of the uncertainty of the last few hours, there was a knock on the door. "Come in!"

As the door opened, Jack, Lorriene, and Luke all entered. Luke was the first to respond, "How's my girl? What did you have?"

Anne-Marie smiled the best she could and said, "Hey, guys. Umm … We had a baby girl. I named her Lola Luxe Swan, but please don't tell Jackson about the name yet. When he comes back down, I will tell him."

Finally realizing that her son was not present in the room, Lorriene worriedly quipped, "*Sweetie*, where is Jackson?"

No longer able to contain her tears, Anne-Marie exclaimed, "He's in the ER. My nurse, Abby, said he is stable and they would wheel him down in two hours."

Fear and anger caused the otherwise level-headed Lorriene to snap. "Why is my son in the ER?!"

Through her tears, Anne-Marie stated, "Abby said he passed out in the hall after making the phone calls. Which I don't understand. I thought the chemo was helping."

Lorriene exhaled deeply and remarked with pity in her voice, "Oh, *honey* … he didn't tell you?"

By this time, frustration filled Anne-Marie as she felt she was the only one out of the loop. "Tell me what?"

Normally a stoic man, Jack said with tears in his eyes, "*Baby girl,* he stopped taking chemo back in June, because he said it wasn't helping."

Anne-Marie broke down and the darkness began to engulf her

heart even more.

Two hours passed and Jackson was finally wheeled down to Anne-Marie's room. His bed was placed beside Anne-Marie's and she climbed into his and kissed him passionately. Even though he kept the lack of treatment from her, her heart longed for him. At this moment, Anne-Marie knew. She knew he was leaving this world and her to raise their baby alone, and her heart shattered even more at the thought.

Jackson greeted his love with a weary smile and kiss before asking, "Where's our baby? Was I right?"

Anne-Marie chuckled, "She is on her way back in. You were right, *my love*. She's so beautiful, and looks just like you with my nose."

Nurse Abby brought the baby in and handed her to Jackson. "Congratulations, Papa! You have a tiny but healthy baby girl that weighs 5 pounds 12 ounces and is 17 inches long."

Jackson and Anne-Marie sat together looking upon their daughter and all seemed to be a happy family. Unfortunately, appearances are often deceiving. Jackson held baby Luxe for an hour, before he handed her over to Lorriene, and turned to Anne-Marie. "I love you more than life itself. Please take care of our daughter. She is our love and light. I'm sorry to leave you so soon." With those final words, Jackson Archer Swan II kissed his beloved, Anne-Marie, one last time before closing his eyes, as he welcomed death's hauntingly, sweet embrace.

Deep in her heart, Lorriene knew that this was an answer to her silent prayers over the past months. Every day she prayed, *God, if you must take my son, please let him live long enough to hold his baby at least once.*

Jackson's funeral was held exactly one week after the birth of their daughter and in a sense, Anne-Marie was buried that very day alongside Jackson. The preacher spoke the standard funeral jargon, but those words were hollow and empty, for nothing could change the fact that Anne-Marie was now completely dead inside. Not even listening to the words being said, Anne-Marie looked down at the daughter in her arms and felt completely alone in this world. How could she move forward when her very soul was in that coffin?

One by one, friends and colleagues left and all that remained were Jack, Lorriene, Anne-Marie, and baby Luxe. Lorriene couldn't help but look at Anne-Marie with such heartache. "Sweet Anne-Marie, do you want me to take little Luxie for you, so you can pay your final goodbye?"

Handing the baby to Lorriene, Anne-Marie kissed the casket one last time and said, "Instead of wedding vows, I am saying goodbye. You promised you would never leave me and now I am lost. I don't know how to live this life without you Jackson. My heart will **always** love you. So that I'll never forget you, I am leaving this red poppy here. A red poppy from our daughter and I. Forever in my heart, always."

7

Tender Moments

September 6, 2014

After telling Logan about Jackson's death, Lola decided it was time to call it a night. Grasping his hand gently in hers, Lola asked, "Are you fine if we head to bed and pick this up in a few days? I really need time to decompress after all that has been said."

Logan sighed heavily- the weight of Lola's beginning hit him hard. While his own life began in a rather unconventional manner, he could not imagine what Lola must have felt growing up. Bringing Lola's hand to his lips, Logan placed a gentle kiss upon it before replying, "Anything you want, Lola. I have waited two years for you and will continue to wait for as long as it takes for you to be ready."

Once both Logan and Lola were in his bed, Logan pulled Lola into him. He needed her to feel his heart. His heart could only beat for her because she was his heart. Lola gazed upon Logan's chest and finally saw all of Logan's tattoos. Timidly, Lola placed her tiny hand upon Logan's chest and said, "Tell me the story of your tattoos."

Logan laughed and said, "What makes you think I have a story to tell about my tattoos?"

Lola playfully rolled her eyes and retorted, "Warren, I've known you for years. Hell, we've even become best friends in that time. And while I may not know much, the one thing I do know for certain is that you never do anything without a purpose."

Logan couldn't help but laugh at how well Lola pegged his thought process. "Well, you're not wrong there." Gazing longingly into Lola's forest-green eyes, Logan brushed away a stray curl that haphazardly fell into her face. While he longed to kiss her again, he knew this was something that could not be rushed. Instead, he settled for a gentle kiss on her forehead.

"Well," Logan began, "All of my tattoos were done by my friend from high school, Luka Daniels. He started apprenticing at age 16 with his dad, Lucian. He now has full ownership of the shop. I would never dream of letting anyone else ink this magnificent body, which you see before you."

Lola laughed so hard she snorted! "Oh my gosh, Warren. You're too much!"

Putting his hands up, in self-defense, Logan said, "Just stating the truth. Anyhow, I decided to get my first tattoo when I was 16. My three best friends and I thought we were so cool and angsty and decided to get our first tattoos together. My grandfather had been the sheriff in Vienna for a long time, so, yeah … I could pretty much do what I wanted. Plus, at the time, I wanted to piss my mom off."

Lola chuckled, for she could definitely imagine Logan as a little punk-ass teenager. Logan continued, "We all chose to get the same standard look with a 'cool' nickname. You can never go wrong with skull and crossbones keys on your left forearm, so that's what we did. I used my initials **LAW** because I was so original."

Lola laughed her heart out at the image of 16-year-old Logan. The heaviness of her heart needed this. *I have been so worn, battered, bruised, and broken for so long. Isn't it time that I had even the tiniest amount of joy?*

Logan continued. "On my 18th birthday, I wanted to do something that would be meaningful for my mom and dad. I was still pretty pissed at my mom and her boyfriend, but with my sister Eloise on the way, I wanted something to take my focus off the anger. So, I had this huge side piece that's on my right side done. It's a victrola with lyrics from both my mom and dad's favorite songs; two roses for them; and of course a 'W' for Warren."

Hearing how Logan spoke about his parents touched Lola's heart. Although she tried not to be, she couldn't help feeling jealous of those who had a completed family. Yes, Logan's mom and Cade were divorced, but Logan still had them both. A tear fell from Lola's eyes, which she tried to wipe away without Logan noticing. Of course, Logan noticed; he noticed everything about her. "Shit- I'm sorry, Lola! I should've been more aware, especially after learning about your dad."

Lola placed her finger on Logan's lips and said, "Shh! It's okay. I'm ridiculous, really. I mean, how can I miss someone that I've never known; someone who's always been a ghost haunting me."

Lola tried not to cry and tried not to listen to **his** voice that plagued her mind. *What did I tell you long ago my little vixen? Perfect people can't handle messy and you, my sweetheart, are as messy and fucked up as they get! We are the same.*

Logan tried calling Lola's name, as he noticed her jaw tighten and her fists ball. Her mind kept taunting her, *We are the same. You can't escape your darkness. You can't escape me. No amount of therapy will help. I own your soul my little vixen, and from that, there is no escape.*

By this time, Lola's palms were bleeding from the digging in of her fingernails, as she tried to not let **his** voice overtake her again. Logan quickly headed to the bathroom, before returning with a dampened cloth. *"My heart,* look at me."

Hearing Logan's words and gentle touch, Lola felt herself resurface from the depths of her mind. Questioningly, Lola looked at Logan. "Did you just say, *'My heart'*? I thought you said it yesterday, but then figured I was probably imagining things."

Logan chuckled and replied, "Yes, I did. Now, if you'll let me finish, I'll explain why."

After the blood was off of Lola's hands, Logan gently kissed them, then held them in his own strong ones. Lola had not felt a touch this gentle since Shane and it scared the living shit out of her. Once he was certain that Lola's breathing and heart rate were now regulated, Logan continued.

"So, for my 25th birthday, I decided it was finally time for some new ink. I love camping and the night sky and my favorite animal is a stag. So, I figured why not combine the two things I love into one unique and badass tattoo."

Lola had to agree- for it truly was like nothing she had ever seen before. The neck of the stag stopped just above Logan's right wrist and the entire head fit perfectly upon his forearm. The rack of antlers was truly a masterpiece in itself, as they wrapped perfectly up the top part of the arm; stopping approximately halfway through Logan's bicep. The space between the antlers felt empty and caused Lola to quip, "Why is there so much empty space between the antlers?"

Logan chuckled, as this was not the first time he had heard this question. "My hope is to one day have an add-on for something special." Lola smiled at the response; Logan was always so well thought out with every decision. Continuing, Logan asked, "Do want to you know why the stag is my favorite animal?"

Lola eagerly stated, "Of course!"

Brushing his thumbs over Lola's, Logan explained. "My grandma on my mom's side would always tell me this story that she claimed was a great Swedish tale. Honestly, I have no idea if it was or not, but it was something that stuck with me throughout my childhood. My grandmother, Dianne, said that Swedish tale told of the stag, or *Alces alces*, being the protector and king of the forest. It was his duty to ensure that all life was kept in check. If anything were unbalanced, he would use his mighty rack of antlers to bring life back into it."

Logan smiled as Lola listened to his childhood tale in awe, as he spoke again, "I have always had a great desire to protect the ones I love from those who would do ill will towards them."

Logan inhaled deeply as he paused for a moment. "This same story is what inspired my last tattoo, which is over my heart. I got this tattoo, shortly after the **incident**. You were gone and refused to see anyone, and after what happened, I needed to have something of you close to my heart. That day, I was so fucking scared, Lola! So fucking scared."

Logan's heart broke as he relived the painful memory of what happened two years ago. Guilt flooded Lola's heart and mind; a painful, permanent reminder of the **incident**.

Logan spoke on. "I went to Luka and begged him to do this tattoo for me. He almost refused because he felt that I wasn't in my right frame of mind. This was the only time I'd ever threatened to go to another artist. I had him draw up the lone, yearling stag looking into the northern lights, surrounded by forest. In the light, he sees the most beautiful maiden in all the land. Her sorrowed face telling many a tale and her stunning red hair flowing down, until she became one with his world and home."

Lola placed her hand on the tattoo- enamored by the most majestic-looking tattoo she had seen in her entire life. Curiosity got the better of her, and she just had to know, "Why is this on your heart, Logan?"

Logan closed his eyes and said, "Lola, **you** are the very reason my heart beats. I have loved you for so fucking long that it's all I know.

Even when I was with Naja, my heart only ever belonged to you. I tried to not let it happen, but it did. When the **incident** occurred, and I thought I was going to lose you, it literally felt like my heart was being ripped from my chest."

Logan paused to catch his breath. "Lola, don't you see, you are my very heart. You are my beautiful maiden who has become one with my world and home."

Lola wanted to believe every pretty word that Logan said and smile through these tender moments they shared. How could she though, when she couldn't even trust her own thoughts. This was by far the most precious and romantic gesture she'd ever heard of yet, she couldn't help but doubt the sincerity … even if Logan's face appeared truthful, and as far as she knew, he had yet to lie to her. She would have to talk to Dr. Indigo about all of this because she didn't know how to process these emotions.

Politely, Lola replied. "Thank you, Logan. I know it may not seem like I am grateful, but I am. Right now, I am just speechless. You are too good for someone like me." With those words, Lola drifted off to sleep, her hand on Logan's heart. Logan prayed, *God, please continue to help her. Help me also to be patient and compassionate.*

8

What is a mother?

September 7, 2014

When Lola woke that morning, she quickly dressed for an early run. After a year of regular sessions, Dr. Indigo suggested Lola try running; and soon enough it became her primary alternative to relieving stress and tension. Seeing a note taped to the bathroom mirror, Logan reminded her that he had business to take care of in Portland.

Just as she was drifting off to sleep the night before, Logan told Lola that to help occupy his anxious heart during the past two years while she had been gone, he had not only come back to Parkway to help Cate whenever she needed it; but also maintained both his freelance photography and digital media marketing businesses. Though Lola should have been happy to have this day to herself, it meant being left alone with her thoughts- something she hated more than anything. After a quick shower and dressing for the day, Lola called Dr. Indigo.

"Good morning, Lola. How are you today," Dr. Indigo warmly greeted.

Lola inhaled deeply for a moment before replying, "I'm alright. I just finished a five-mile run not that long ago."

The scribbling of a pen to paper filled the phone line, followed by Dr. Indigo's standard inquiry. "How was your night last night and how did you sleep?"

Lola blankly replied, "My night was decent, and, to my surprise, I slept really well again."

Dr. Indigo made another notation, then asked, "Wonderful to hear, Lola! Will you please tell me what all you have discussed with Logan so far?"

"I told Logan about Jackson's death. I asked him if we could postpone anything more for a little while. I felt we both needed time to process." Pausing for a moment for a sip of coffee, Lola then stated, as she made a small revelation. "As we were going to bed, I asked him to tell me about his tattoos. Oh! Something I just realized-"

"Alright Lola, I will say that I think it was incredibly wise not to pile so much upon yourself all at once. And what was your realization?"

"Well, this is the second night I have slept with Logan by my side, and I thought it would be awkward, but ... well ... I guess it was comforting. It kinda reminds me of the time before ..."

"What were you able to learn during your discussion about Logan's tattoos," Dr. Indigo proceeded to inquire, taking additional notes while listening earnestly.

"Well, I learned that every tattoo seems to be well thought out with purpose and meaning. Which, I think is cool, but also makes me feel kinda sad because I realize how shitty of a friend I was for not taking interest in anything really personal to him unless it could benefit me." Lola couldn't help but tear up at the thought of the insensitive nature of her past self.

"One thing to remember, Lola, is that people with your condition often have difficulty sympathizing with the emotional well-being of others. The fact that you can recognize these actions from your past self, shows how much progress you have made already."

"Thank you, Dr. Indigo. I know I may not always come across as grateful, but I really am." Lola admitted, before nervously continuing with her original thought process. "While I love all of the stories and meanings behind Logan's tattoos, and how everything he does is purpose-driven, I can't help but be confused by his last tattoo."

Intrigued, Dr. Indigo led on, "What specifically about this last tattoo leaves you in a state of confusion?"

Thinking for a moment and allowing the scene to replay in her mind, Lola timidly spoke. "Well, he told me this tale about a stag protecting the forest. This young stag is looking up into the northern lights, and there he finds the most beautiful maiden. Her hair flows down until she becomes one with him and his world."

"Was there anything else about this tale that seemed to resonate with you?"

By this point, Lola felt as if her nerves were on fire. She desperately wanted Logan's affirmations to be sincere, however, she couldn't help but have doubts. Finally speaking, Lola exclaimed, "Well, Dr. Indigo, Logan said that the tattoo was of me, and he got it tattooed over his heart immediately after the *incident*. He said I was the very reason his heart beats. Even when he was dating his last girlfriend, Naja, his heart only beats for me."

Both ends of the call were silent for a moment as Dr. Indigo made more notations. After a minute or so, Dr. Indigo continued with her questions. "Lola, please tell me, what went through your mind when Logan delivered this revelation to you?"

Exhaling once more, Lola said, "Honestly, I was scared shitless. Hell, I still am. I can't even begin to process what he is saying. I'm messy, broken, and damaged. And while a huge part of me wants to believe in every word he says, the voices always make me question if he's lying or not."

Dr. Indigo paused for a moment, then continued, "Lola, I understand your hesitation and weariness. I will ask, has Logan ever been one to lie to you in the past? What have his actions said when you see him with those around you? Please do not respond right away. I want you to take some time and truly reflect upon these questions. Please write down these thoughts in a journal so that we can reflect together. Do you have any questions before we end our session today?"

Lola frowned, as this was not the answer she wanted. She wanted Dr. Indigo to tell her what to do, not more reflection bullshit. Hastily, Lola quipped, "When can I finally go back to *my* company? You do know that it doesn't look good for a CEO to be out as long as I have."

Dr. Indigo shook her head and chuckled for a moment. "Lola, we have discussed this. At the moment, you are not fit to return full time. After the last time, you know the stipulations your Uncle Gregory has set out for you. Besides, you said you trusted Jade and Daisy in your absence. How about this as a compromise? You may begin weekly phone calls with them or your assistant, Marina. No more than once a week, though."

Lola knew this offer was as good as she was going to get, so she thanked Dr. Indigo and ended the call.

~

September 13, 2014

One week had passed since Lola told Logan of Jackson's death; as well as staining her palms crimson with her fingernails. When Lola spoke to Dr. Indigo, she probably should have mentioned the reflexive moment of weakness, but felt it was easier just to hide it away for now. *It's just one time. I'm fine. I know I will be fine.* Lola tried to reassure herself with these thoughts.

Since her in-depth conversation with Dr. Indigo regarding what Logan had said, Lola still wasn't sure what to make of the matter. Dr. Indigo reminded her that this was par for the course with her official diagnosis. For so many years, she had been handling emotions in such a harmful manner, that she wasn't quite sure how to process them healthily.

Lola was tired of trying to think about this and dreaded the conversation she knew would have to come with Logan later on in the evening. *It's so draining having to go back through **all** of this. I've already told Dr. Indigo, so what difference is it going to make if I tell Logan every damn iota of information? He's just going to realize how fucked up I am, and then he'll just end up leaving me too.*

Slamming her fist on her desk in front of her, Lola tried her best to silence the voice in her head. Needing to shift her focus to something else, Lola dialed the number to her office in hopes of reaching Marina.

Marina Isobel Vasquez was an eager 24-year-old woman, who had joined **Swan Industries** two years ago, immediately upon her graduation from college. Jade and Daisy had both raved upon her hard-working performance in their written reports, that Lola was ready to get back into the office to officially meet this young woman.

"Good morning and thank you for calling the office of Ms. Lola Harper. This is Marina speaking. How may I direct your call?"

Lola exhaled excitedly. "Hello Ms. Vasquez, this is Lola."

Marina was excited to hear Lola's melodious voice on the other line. "Good morning Lola, I mean, Ms. Harper."

Lola laughed heartily, "Lola is perfectly fine, as long as you allow me to call you Marina."

Marina breathed a sigh of relief, "Of course. How may I help you today, Lola?"

Lola made a mental note to finally change her surname back to

Swan, as she chuckled once again, before getting down to business. "I am calling today to see if Jade or Daisy has made any headway on procuring a deal with **Carson Tech?**"

Nervously Marina replied, "I'm sorry, Lola. We all thought since you had prior knowledge of Mr. Andre, he would easily agree to the terms."

Lola shook her head, "It's not their fault, Marina, Andre is just a total hardass."

Marina had a burning question and was uncertain if now would be a good time to ask. "Umm …"

"Tell me what's on your mind, Marina."

Marina let out a nervous laugh before replying. "Well, I was wondering if there was any way I could advance in my career. I have been a faithful assistant for two years now and am needing more of a challenge to put my degree to use. I love this company so much and don't want to leave, but don't know what else to do."

Lola admired Marina's bravery. It took a hell of a lot of guts to ask a boss she had barely even met for a raise. An idea formed in Lola's mind. "Marina, I admire your gusto and have heard nothing but praises from Jade and Daisy. You said you need a challenge, correct?"

Marina couldn't believe what she was hearing; she had been so certain that Lola would fire her for asking for an advancement. "Yes!"

Lola remarked, "Well, if you can do what Jade and Daisy have been unable to, and are able to procure the agreement with **Carson Tech** and Mr. Andre, then you will be promoted to head of the division which will handle all work with **Carson Tech**. If you are unable to acquire the deal, I am happy to keep you on as my assistant. However, if you choose to go elsewhere, I will gladly give you a glowing recommendation."

Still flabbergasted, and doing her best not to puke from her elevated nerves, Marina simply said, "Thank you for this opportunity, Lola. I will do my best to not let you down."

~

September 20, 2014

It had now been two weeks since Lola had returned to Parkway and started telling Logan about her sorrowful start to life. Logan had let Lola have her room to breathe and process; though the space was difficult for him, he did his best to be considerate of Lola's needs. Aside from occupying his mind with various jobs, he also made sure to connect with his friends; if for nothing more than his own benefit, Logan chose, for the time being, not to mention Lola's return. Everyone had thought he was bat shit crazy for having a tattoo of someone who brought him so much anguish two years ago.

And while he could keep most everyone in the dark regarding Lola's return, his mother, Britt, was not so easily fooled. Britt adored her son more than life itself and it pissed her off that some girl nearly destroyed her baby boy so selfishly. Watching Lola nervously pace around the room, Logan couldn't help but recall the phone conversation with his mother, the day after Lola's arrival.

~

September 6, 2014

"Hi, *baby mine*. How's it going?" Britt asked as Logan answered.

Logan rolled his eyes and laughed. "You do know that I am a grown-ass man, mom. You don't need to keep referring to me as 'baby'."

Britt laughed, "Watch your tone, boy! You know momma knows best. Besides, who brought you into this world?"

Logan groaned in annoyance, "You did."

Britt laughed again, "That's what I thought. Just remember that because I can take you out of it too!"

Annoyance filling his mood, Logan snapped a bit, "For fuck's sake mom!"

Britt was taken aback, "Oh hell no! Boy, check this attitude right now."

Logan knew he had overstepped his bounds, he hadn't meant to, he was just stressed and nervous with Lola finally being back. "Sorry, momma. I'm just nervous and stressed."

Concern filled Britt instantly, "*Baby mine*, what's going on? You know you can tell me anything."

Logan sighed and rolled his eyes. His mother was **literally** the last person he wanted to talk to about this, however, he knew she wouldn't relent. Sheepishly, he began, "Well … what I have prayed for, for the last two years has finally happened."

Britt was shocked for a moment before anger, and a bit of her justice-seeking personality began to manifest "*Mi stai prendendo in giro?* (Are you shitting me?)"

Logan was shocked. It was extremely rare for his mother to use such language. Treading lightly, Logan remarked, "I see *Zio* has been teaching you the bad words in Italian again. Do I need to tell *Zia* to monitor his calls again?"

Britt was fuming! "Don't you dare change the subject, young man! Did you forget the torment that *cagna egoista* (selfish bitch) put you through?"

Logan was angry, and rightfully so. Of course, he didn't forget, how could he; that moment tormented him constantly. "Look, mom, I love you, I really do, but I am **not** going to do this with you right now. You don't know a damn thing about anything regarding this. Hell, I don't even know half of it.

"If you wanna be petty then so be it, but don't call me until **you** change **your** fucking tune. Tell Elle-belle and Rosebud I love them and say 'hi' to Dean for me. I guess I'll talk to you later."

Not even waiting for his mother to object or even try to speak, Logan quickly hung up and placed her number on **Do Not Disturb**, for he didn't have the energy to deal with her.

~

September 20, 2014

Shaking that moment from his mind, Logan walked over to Lola and lovingly wrapped his arms around her; an action that caught Lola off guard and caused a small amount of panic to form in her. Logan sensed the tension and kissed the back of Lola's head before speaking. "I am so sorry, *my heart*! I didn't mean to frighten you. I was only hoping to calm you down before you wear a hole in my floor."

Lola released a sigh, as she momentarily allowed herself to rest the back of her head into Logan's chest; his warm scent filling every part of her being. Logan's scent was so fresh and pure, it was like an ointment for Lola's wounded soul. Lola allowed herself to stay in Logan's arms for a few minutes before she gestured for him to follow her to the couch. It was now time for Lola to continue with her story.

~

1989

After the funeral, Anne-Marie was a complete wreck. While she had wanted to be able to love the last remnant of Jackson enough for the both of them, poor Anne-Marie never recovered from Jackson's death; therefore she couldn't see her daughter as anything other than a constant reminder of her sorrow.

Little Lola spent the first part of her life primarily cared for by her grandparents. Aside from her grandparents and Lizzie, the only person of any remembrance to Lola from her early years, was a nanny, by the name of either Kay or Kayla, not that she could ever seem to correctly recall.

As fate would have it, when Lola turned five and was due to start Kindergarten, Jack and Lorriene were finally able to take Anne-Marie to court and were awarded full custody of their precious granddaughter. Jack and Lorriene, ever gracious to their dear friends, the Sommers', worked out an arrangement so that Lola and Lizzie would not have to be too far from each other very often.

Judge Callum Garrison looked sorrowfully at Anne-Marie, before speaking with a heavy heart. "Now, Ms. Flowers, do you understand why we are all here in this courthouse today?"

The judge's query fell upon deaf ears as anger burned inside of Anne-Marie's once loving heart.

"Ms. Flowers, unless you are willing to cooperate, you leave me no other choice but to grant full guardianship to Mr. and Mrs. Swan."

Again, Anne-Marie chose to remain steadfast in her anger; she had failed Jackson and now there was nothing she could do.

Being a man of great compassion, Judge Garrison delivered his verdict. "The court hereby grants full custody of the child in question, Lola Luxe Swan, to the paternal grandparents, Mr. and Mrs. Swan. However, the court would also like to add, that if Ms. Anne-Marie Flowers attends parenting classes in addition to the recommended counseling hours, we will reconvene in six months to once again address the custody of the child."

When the judge made his decision, Anne-Marie quickly gathered her belongings before exiting the courtroom. Never once did she turn around, for if she did, she might have lost all strength she had. Some people might call her actions selfish, but for Anne-Marie, she was just trying to survive.

~

With each passing birthday, Lola's heart desired nothing more than to call the woman who had long since abandoned her,

"Momma!", and to feel her embrace. Every year that Lola blew out the candles, her wish failed to come true, thus causing sweet, little Lola to stop believing in wishes at the tender age of nine.

~

August 2, 1994

By the time Lola's tenth birthday rolled around, she requested no candles nor statements of "Make a wish".

"Oh my sweet girl, please do not be disheartened," Lorriene lovingly soothed.

"What's the point of wishes when they are nothing but giant **lies**," Lola bitterly spat out.

As Lola stomped up the stairs, toward her room, Lorriene called out, "My dear, Luxie, I promise you, this birthday will be the best one yet."

Stopping dead in her tracks, Lola turned to face her grandmother as she rolled her eyes, before vehemently screaming, "Yeah! What's so special about this stupid day anyway! I wish I was never even born because then maybe, just maybe my Daddy would still be alive and my mother would be happy. Instead, she just hates me!"

Lola quickly ran to her room, where she flung herself upon her bed and sobbed. Lorriene held the small girl in her gentle embrace for an hour, until Jack made his way upstairs to inform his beloved that the guests had arrived.

Lorriene looked at her husband with anguish in her eyes. "Jack, honey, please tell everyone to help themselves to the food. Then, go into my desk and get the very **special** envelope that has been put away just for this day; our Luxie's tenth birthday!"

Jack hurried back as quickly as he could; making sure to bring with him the envelope and the annual birthday tiara. Lola looked at him with teary eyes and meekly laughed as she said, "Grandpa! You know, I'm 10 now. I'm almost too old for the birthday tiara!"

Jack looked at Lola, bewildered, and exclaimed, "Nonsense my darling! You're our light and life. Why, if it was up to me, you would wear this every day so everyone would see that you are our princess."

Jack placed a gentle kiss upon Lola's head, which earned him the faintest of smiles, while Lorriene took the letter and handed it to Lola. "Darling Luxie, this envelope contains a letter from your father that he wrote shortly before your birth and his passing. We've never opened it because he made me promise to save this until your tenth birthday. Would you please read it out loud?"

Lola looked nervously at her grandmother before replying, "Yes, Grandma …"

*My darling daughter. My Luxe Swan. I am so sorry to know that I will never be a part of your growing up. I will never be a part of all of your firsts. I pray you will look like me to gently remind your precious mother just how much she is loved. I chose your name because it means light. I am leaving this world soon and I know that you are the light I am leaving behind. Shine bright through all of your days my love. No matter what sorrow and heartache may come before you, please **never** stop shining. I hope you know that I will love you forever and always. It kills me to know that you will have a life without me but I promise you will do amazing things, baby girl. Daddy loves you, forever and always!*

As Lola finished the letter, she huddled closely together with her grandparents; tears loudly echoed the torment of three wounded hearts. While Lola was happy to finally have something that her father cared enough to leave for her, it crushed her to know the real reason why her mother could never truly look at her.

The burden she now carried within her tender heart was more than any 10-year-old child should have had to bear.

9

Broken

September 20, 2014

Lola looked up at Logan and paused for a moment, with tears welling in her eyes. The letter from Jackson was both her most treasured and despised possession. Lola loved it because it was one thing, along with Averie, that was left for her by her father. At the same time, Lola hated the letter, because it was a ghost haunting her of endless what-ifs.

Lola and Logan sat in silence for about thirty minutes before she continued, "Time quickly passed, and before I knew it, I was preparing for my 14th birthday, as well as the start of my Freshman year of high school. This was also the time when Anne-Marie decided to come back into my life. No one knew where she had been, but she looked happy and healthy. It was easy to see that she hated how much of my life she had missed out on, but at that point, I didn't even care. She was a stranger standing in my house."

~

July 31, 1998
Ding! Dong! Ding! Dong!
The sound of the doorbell startled Lola from her required summer

reading. Busy in the kitchen, Lorriene called out, "Luxie, *sweetie*, would you please get that?" Being the ever obedient girl, Lola happily did as requested. Had Lola known what would await her on the other side of the door, she would have never agreed.

The moment Lola opened the door, her jaw dropped. While she didn't have many memories of her mother, there was no denying the honey blond-haired woman who stood before her was her birth giver, Anne-Marie Flowers. Lola clenched her fists and jaw in anger, as she looked Anne-Marie up and down, before asking in a tone laced with venom and annoyance

"What the hell are you doing here, Anne-Marie?"

Sheepishly, Anne-Marie looked as she responded, "Can't I come to see my daughter since she's about to turn 14?"

Maniacal hysteria overtook Lola as she spat out, "Daughter! Daughter! That's **rich** coming from the likes of you."

No longer able to control the years of hurt, sadness, and anger all simultaneously surfacing within her, Lola slapped the shit out of Anne-Marie *three* times before screaming, "Don't you ever call yourself a mother! You are **nothing** to me but some egg donor. *I fucking hate you*!"

Hearing the commotion at the front door, Lorriene quickly made her way from the kitchen. Just as she had arrived, Lola ran quickly up the stairs to her bedroom, where she sobbed into her pillow.

Lorriene looked upon Anne-Marie with complete and utter shock, before composing herself as the lady she always was. "Hello, dear. Do come in. I'll make us some tea and you can explain why you are here." When the tea finished, Lorriene had Anne-Marie sit at the table with her.

"Now dear, while our door has always been open for you, I'm going to need you to please explain why it has taken you nearly ten years to show your face."

Looking down in shame, Anne-Marie timidly exclaimed, "I am so sorry. I didn't mean to cause Lola, or you, any heartache or trouble."

Lorriene replied, "Just so you know, everyone calls her Luxe or Luxie like Jackson wanted. Ever since she learned that her first name means sadness and sorrow, she has hated it with every fiber of her being."

Already feeling the judgment of the world upon her shoulders, Anne-Marie retorted, "With all due respect, Lorriene, **Lola** is <u>my</u> daughter and I will call her the name I gave her."

Not one to lose the upper hand, especially when it came to her precious granddaughter, whom she would lay her very life down for, Lorriene snapped. "With all due respect, Anne-Marie, pushing a baby out doesn't make you a mother. So, you can either tell me why you're here, or I will call the police and have you arrested for trespassing!"

Anne-Marie took a deep breath- things were not going as well as she'd hoped. Taking a few more deep breaths to calm herself, she pleaded, "I feel this has quickly derailed. I came back here because I want to try to have a real relationship with my daughter and with you all. I am so very sorry for all of the hurt I caused.

"I've been going to therapy as well as group counseling. I had severe postpartum depression which turned into a deep depression and anxiety. Guilt ate me alive for all of the hurt I caused. Honestly, I just want a fresh start."

Because she loved this woman as if she were her very own flesh and blood, Lorriene set aside her personal feelings as she looked deeply into Anne-Marie's weary eyes; the burden of Jackson's death, along with her painful life choices, had caused their once shimmering, chocolate hue to fade into a murky brown. "Now darling, while that is all well and good, you need to understand how much this is to take in, especially for Luxe. I'll need to talk with Jack and see what he thinks before we move forward with any type of decision."

Trying to remain hopeful and not feel too defeated, Anne-Marie simply stated, "I understand. I also want to let you know that I met an amazing man, named Everett Silver, who has been a huge help to me. If Jack says 'yes,' please call me. I would like to set up a dinner for all of us to talk."

Lorriene gracefully patted Anne-Marie on the hand as she said, "Alright, Anne-Marie. I'll be in touch within the week. Thank you for coming to call."

Once Anne-Marie left Swan Manor, Lorriene made her way upstairs to comfort Lola. At the sound of her bedroom door opening, Lola looked up and gazed into the sweet, honey-colored eyes of her grandmother. This woman, the woman who raised her, was her *real* mother. Lorriene sat on Lola's bed and whispered sweetly, as she brushed Lola's beautiful curls from her face, "Oh, my precious girl. Please don't carry the weight of the world on your shoulders. I know you are hurting, but I think you should try to give your mother a chance."

Filled with sorrow and anguish, Lola bitterly replied, "Why should I, when she hates me!"

Knowing that she couldn't take Lola's hurt and heartache away, panged Lorriene greatly. "My darling girl, this is the farthest thing from the truth. Her love was too much that she just couldn't handle it all. Grief hits everyone differently and guilt generally follows soon after."

Stubbornness was both a blessing and a curse when it came to Lola, and at this moment, she was done. "I don't want to talk about this anymore today, Grandma. I am tired and going to sleep."

Lorriene lovingly kissed her granddaughter upon the head, before exiting and calling out, "Okay, Luxie. Have sweet dreams, my love."

~

September 20, 2014

Talking about Anne-Marie's return always left Lola feeling emotionally drained. "Logan, do you mind if we continue this conversation in a few days? I am exhausted."

Noticing Lola's heavy eyes, Logan said, "Of course, *my heart*! You need to rest."

Logan and Lola readied themselves for bed and both lay there just staring at the ceiling. Sometimes, silence speaks more than what we are capable of. Yet, at the same time, silence leaves so many questions unanswered. Logan reflected upon all that he had learned so far. How could a mother not want her own child? How could at only 10, Lola (his Lola) have already wished she were dead. It broke his heart. Logan reached across and pulled Lola into a warm embrace because he needed her to know that he was there. **Always**.

Surrounded by Logan's strong arms, Lola's mind was once again riddled with selfish guilt. *I am so grateful to have Logan in my life. I feel safe here, in the silence, with him. But no matter how much I try, I just don't see how I can be with him the way he wants. I know Dr. Indigo said that this journey was supposed to be one of healing, but how can I heal when I have to feel every single ounce of pain over and over and over again.*

Logan leaned over and gently placed a kiss on Lola's head, as he whispered, "I love you." While the only thing Lola could muster in return was, "Good night." Hearing her whisper of acknowledgment, Logan laid back upon his pillow, allowing his thoughts to fester in the forefront of his mind. *I need her to feel safe. I need her to feel love because without her, I am broken inside. Lola is my everything. When she was gone, I felt like I was dying. This. This right here is what I have needed to end my day- surrounded by her curly red hair brings me so much peace. I love her so much that if I don't tell her, it feels like my heart will explode.*

Trying to settle in, Lola allowed her restless thoughts to continue their acts of chastisement. *I know Logan loves me, but somehow all I can manage to say is "Good night." How can he possibly love a person like me? I am not alright. I am deeply broken inside. Everyone leaves. Everyone dies. When and if I can ever return his affections, I fear that he will be gone too. Is it selfish to have Logan hang on like this? Maybe, but at least he is here and living. I know* **he** *is gone now, but I live with fear every single day that* **he** *will come back for me. I barely survived the last two times and I fear the third will be my end.*

Just as Logan was about to shut his eyes, his phone rang. Annoyed, he reached over to the nightstand, ready to hit decline, when the name **Antonio Moretti** flashed across the screen. Logan considered declining the call but knew his *Zio* was a man of persistence and not one to easily be ignored.

Sighing in defeat, Logan looked at Lola and said, "Sorry, I have to take this, it's a family call." Lola nodded. Logan answered, somewhat begrudgingly, as he headed out of the room, "Hey, *Zio*! What's with the late call?"

Lola tossed and turned. As much as she hated to admit it, she was comforted by Logan's warmth that enveloped her as she slept. The silence became deafening so Lola decided to find some music to calm her nerves, at least until Logan returned. Switching on her *Music Love* Radio App, Lola soon heard the soothing voice of DJ Samantha filling the airwaves.

"Good evening lovers! DJ Samantha here with a late-night, soul-filled jam. This little lady has a set of vocals that will bring even the strongest man to his knees. 'Born to Die,' by the lovely **Lana del Rey** is up next after a word from our sponsors."

The music faded into the back of Lola's subconscious as she drifted off to sleep. With so much hurt and loss residing in her heart, painful memories of losing Shane soon tormented her dreams.

~

September 21, 2014

Logan awoke around 4 a.m. to the sound of Lola crying and screaming. He tried to awaken her but had no luck. Finally, after 15 minutes, he was able to wake her. Lola, barely awake, cried out "Shane! Please don't leave me. Please take me with you! I'm sorry, Shane!"

Logan's heart broke because he knew that no matter how hard he tried, he just couldn't take the pain from Lola. Unsure of what else to do, he quickly exited the room, only to return moments later with a cup of water. As Lola drank the water, Logan surrounded Lola in a deep, warm hug.

Taking his large, slender hand Logan gently cupped Lola's cheek. "Lola. Hey, it's okay, it was only a dream. You're okay. I am here."

Lola cried out bitterly, "That's the fucking problem! It was only just a dream. He's gone and I am here alone."

Lola quickly stood up and stormed out of the room. Fear and panic overtook Logan. Memories of the **incident** quickly erupted in his mind, as he followed Lola into the walk-in closet, grasping onto her hand as if it were his own lifeline while crying out, "Lola, please wait!"

Annoyed, but also happy that Logan cared enough to follow her, Lola snatched her hand away as she curtly remarked, "Look, Logan! I can't deal with this shit right now. Please just let me be. I just need to go for a run to clear my head. I promise I will be back." Logan begrudgingly let Lola leave without further questions because he knew there was no use trying to stop her.

~

Nervously, Logan paced back and forth around his room. *Who should I call? I am freaking the fuck out right now and am on the verge of absolutely losing my shit!* **Fuck***! I haven't felt so damn helpless since* *the **incident**.*

Finally, it dawned on Logan that he should call Lizzie; after all, she was the only person who knew Lola the best. Logan quickly dialed Lizzie's number and prayed she would answer. He almost gave up hope, when finally a sleepy voice answered, "Hello?"

Distraught, Logan responded, "Hey, Lizzie! It's Logan. Sorry to call in the middle of the night."

Shaking the sleep from her mind, Lizzie responded, "No. It's fine. Is everything okay with Luxie?"

Having already broken down during his phone call earlier, Logan did his best to maintain a sense of composure. "Honestly, I don't know. She was asleep and then started crying and screaming out for Shane. Then, when she awoke, she snapped at me and stormed off for a run."

A hitch in Lizzie's voice was all that Logan heard through the other end of the line. Lizzie paused for a couple of moments before sweetly stating, "Oh dear- I'm so sorry, *hun*. Just let her calm her emotions with this run. Dr. Indigo told Luxie that running is a healthier alternative to processing her hurt instead of opening her old wounds again. Just please make sure you keep an eye on my sister and don't hesitate to call Dr. Indigo if anything seems out of the ordinary."

Breathing a sigh of relief, Logan expressed his gratitude. "Okay, Lizzie, I will. Thanks for answering."

After a big yawn, Lizzie replied, "Anytime, Logan. I know Luxie and knowing her means that I know she does love you, just in her own way. Just try to be patient with her. Goodnight."

Once he ended the conversation with Lizzie, Logan anxiously awaited Lola's return; so to calm his mind, he tried to read a book. *I may as well give Lola's favorite book, **The Raven's Song** by E.R. Blackwell a read.*

~

As Lola ran, the guilt of her reactions began to consume her. *I feel so guilty for leaving Logan after yelling at him. I know he was only trying to help, but it hurts too much. I miss Shane and Ronan both so much; they are gone in different ways and can never come back. It's all my fault really. The pain is unbearable and I know that I have to run to feel something or else I will revert to my old habits of pain release. I **need** to feel something and, according to Dr. Indigo, tired muscles are apparently the "healthy alternative."*

Lola ran until her legs were weak and then pushed herself to keep going until she finally made it back to Logan's apartment. It was already 7 a.m. by the time she returned, and while she had no idea the distance she'd covered, time was what mattered the most. Three hours of feet on the pavement. Three hours of trying to process and keep from opening her scars. Three hours, which meant it was nearly time for Lola's morning call with Dr. Indigo. As she entered, Lola noticed that Logan had fallen asleep at his desk, with her book, awaiting her return. Lola thought it best to let him sleep since it was his day off.

Lola thought to herself, *I wish I could just skip this call. I am exhausted and just want to sleep. I want to crawl into a hole and die. I want to leave this place.* As the inner demons started to fill her head, Lola's phone rang. Dr. Indigo was calling, as if by a sixth sense that Lola was not okay.

Stepping back into the living room, Lola took the call, rolling her eyes as she haughtily answered, "Good morning, Warden! You know, you're early."

Dr. Indigo chuckled as she started, "Good morning to you too, Lola. I see we have set back a few weeks. Will you please tell me how your day went yesterday and how you slept?"

Being deprived of both sleep and food caused Lola to snap. "Well, you know, life sucks and I slept like shit!"

Dr. Indigo made notations before continuing her query. "Can you tell me what caused you to not sleep well?"

Lola was beyond pissed. "Seriously?!?! As if you don't know! This healing process **bullshit** you have me on is killing me! I can't do this. I want to stop. It hurts too much. I would rather be dead inside than feel this hurt." Lola choked out the last few words as tears overtook her.

Dr. Indigo patiently waited as Lola cried for five minutes, before bringing composure back to herself. Once Dr. Indigo heard Lola's breathing start to regulate, she stated, "Lola, I know that this journey has not been, and will not be, easy for you. However, you **have** to feel. In one of our first sessions, you told me how you didn't want to be an empty shell of a person, like Anne-Marie. And this is why we agreed on this healing journey."

Lola sighed heavily, "You are right, Dr. Indigo. I don't want to be like Anne-Marie. It just hurts so much."

Warmly, Dr. Indigo responded, "I know it does, Lola. Why don't you recount the events for me? Remember, this is a safe call, no different than my office." Lola took a deep breath and recounted her events.

"The past couple of weeks have been going well. Logan gave me space and I was able to contact Marina about some things at work. Everything was going smoothly, but I knew I couldn't keep putting the conversation off for long. So, I told him about my tenth birthday, as well as when Anne-Marie came back into my life."

Dr. Indigo interjected, "How far did you get into Anne-Marie's return?"

Lola continued, "Just shortly after I slapped her a few times and stormed off crying."

After making more notations, Dr. Indigo continued, "I see. I remember how hard this conversation was when we were first meeting. Can you tell me what happened afterward?"

Pausing for just a moment, Lola stated, "Logan and I got ready for bed and then he kissed my head and again told me he loves me. As we were lying down, Logan received a family phone call and stepped outside of the apartment to answer it. The silence was deafening me, so I turned on some music. Unfortunately for me, *'Born to Die'* was playing as I drifted off to sleep."

Dr. Indigo queried, "How does Logan's confessions of love and affection for you make you feel?"

Without an ounce of hesitation, Lola states, "Honestly?! It makes me feel scared. Actually, terrified is the right word."

Engaging further, Dr. Indigo asked, "Why does this make you feel terrified?"

With a heavy heart, Lola replied, "Because, in the end, everyone I have ever truly loved with all of my heart is either dead or has abandoned me. And then, when I thought I finally found it this last time, it was all a painful lie."

Dr. Indigo reminded Lola, "Lola, please remember, you still have Lizzie, along with her family. You also have Cate, Cade, and Logan. These are all tangible, healthy examples of love."

With nothing else to say, Lola blankly remarked, "I guess …"

Dr. Indigo began her next series of questions. "Since you had a heavy evening, can you please tell me how you slept?"

Lola pondered a moment before responding, "I only slept, if you can even call it sleep, for maybe two or three hours. I awoke at 4 a.m. to Logan shaking me because I was crying and screaming for Shane. The pain of causing my own betrayal is utterly unbearable."

Dr. Indigo quipped, "Can you please elaborate more about your dream of Shane? Also, how long has it been since you have dreamed of him?"

Lola replied, "It's been about two months since I last dreamt of Shane. It's always the same dream over and over again. I relive the horror of that night. Then, I see Shane waiting for me. I am running for him because I need to feel him and hear him. I need to just be in his presence. Sadly, no matter how hard or how fast I run, I can never get to him. I am alone."

Dr. Indigo made notations. *Lola not having a dream of Shane in two months is tremendous progress.*

Continuing, Dr. Indigo asked, "After you awoke, how did you process the heaviness of these emotions?"

Guilt flooded Lola's mind as she recounted her actions. "Well, first off I screamed at Logan. Then, I just ran and ran until I felt weak and then I continued to run some more."

Dr. Indigo asked, "How long was your run for?"

Lola responded, "Three hours. I had literally just returned when you called."

Dr. Indigo asked, "How do you feel after this run? Is your desire to open your scars at bay or is it still lingering?"

Lola was silent for a while. She wanted to lie and say that she was fine and that the cutting wasn't haunting her every waking moment. She wanted to say that she didn't miss the sweet release it gave her to feel a different form of pain. A pain that was pleasurable compared to eternal heartache. Lola couldn't lie when directly asked, however she still had yet to inform Dr. Indigo about her nails digging into her palms.

After ten minutes of silence, Dr. Indigo questioned, "Lola, are you still there?"

Shaking herself from her thoughts, Lola stated, "Umm … yes, sorry. I was just thinking. I could lie to you, but I won't. After the run, the desire and urge aren't nearly as strong. This is why I ran for three hours. I was so scared that if I stopped, I would cave.

Something is wrong with me. I am not alright. I am broken inside."

After making more notations, Dr. Indigo spoke warmly into the phone. "Lola, I can promise you, that you've come such a long way. I am so proud of your progress and your honesty. You are broken, but please trust me that this healing process will patch the brokenness. You will have scars but that means you are a survivor and a warrior."

Feeling slightly encouraged and relieved, Lola said, "Thank you, Dr. Indigo. Have a good day."

Dr. Indigo replied, "You too, Lola. Please do not hesitate to call me, even at 4 a.m."

After her conversation with Dr. Indigo, Lola showered, then woke Logan up. Stretching, Logan remarked, "*My heart*, I'm so happy you're back. How was your run?"

Still feeling guilty for her outburst, Lola replied with chagrin. "Hey … it was okay. I'm so sorry for screaming at you and storming off."

Logan sat up and patted the bed for Lola to come in beside him. Lola happily obliged, as she was exhausted. Engulfing her in his arms, Logan lovingly whispered, "Lola, *my heart*, it's okay. I know you have a lot to process and I am not going anywhere. You're not alone in this. I'll continue to fight against hell and back, just for us to be together."

Lola yawned and laid her head down upon the pillow. Logan placed a kiss upon her head before standing. "Have you heard of the awesome band, **Beyond Oregon**?"

Lola thought for a moment, then replied, "I have, but only their early stuff from like 2002-2006. It was pretty awesome."

Logan smirked and puffed out his chest a bit as he allowed Lola's compliment to go to his head. Laughing, Logan asked, "So, do you know who any of the band members are?"

Pondering for a moment, Lola stated, "I don't, I'm sorry."

Logan's eyes lit up as he thought to himself, *Just another reason why I love her. She doesn't even realize we are talking about **my** band.* "Well, you're in for a treat, *my heart*. It just so happens that I do some work for the band occasionally. Even though they're on hiatus right now, rumor has it that they may get back together in the future."

Lola was shocked! She knew Logan had his businesses, but she'd never imagined that he would work with celebrities. In complete awe, Lola exclaimed, "Wow, Logan- that's pretty cool!"

Warmth and love overflowed within Logan's heart. "So, *my heart*, would you like to hear a preview of the last song they recorded before going on hiatus? It was never released to the public." Lola nodded her head in excitement as she closed her eyes.

Logan pulled out his phone, searched through his bands' music, before he finally came to the song he was looking for, and pressed play. Music filled the air, as Logan rejoined Lola in bed. Lovingly brushing her hair, Logan said, "You know, the lead singer told me he wrote this song, 'Alone' after he nearly lost the most precious thing in the world to him."

Gentle breathing filled the air, which signaled Lola was finally asleep. Logan placed a kiss upon Lola's forehead, before murmuring, "I wrote this for you. You are the most precious thing in this entire world to me."

As Lola slept, a peaceful smile spread across her face. This simple sight caused Logan's heart to swell. His beautiful girl was broken and there was nothing he could do but wait patiently, like Lizzie said, as Lola went on this journey. Only Lola could choose to heal from the past. Healing takes time and it hurts like hell, but in the end, we are all stronger because of it. His beautiful girl was a beacon of light even if she couldn't see it herself just now. His beautiful girl was a survivor and he would be damned if anyone stood in her way.

10

It comes crashing down

October 5, 2014

Lola had now been back in Parkway for a full month- far longer than she had originally intended- and two weeks had passed since Lola's traumatizing dream of Shane, which lead to her freak out and three-hour running session. After the nightmare, Lola couldn't help but feel resentment towards herself for instinctively becoming emotionally distant once again. And whenever Dr. Indigo asked how the letter writing was coming along, Lola felt frustrated, because every time she sat at Logan's desk to start, it felt as if the blank pages were mocking her.

In those two weeks, Logan did his best to make sure Lola had space, but at the same time, making sure she knew he was available. He chose to occupy his mind with shifts at **Cate's**, as well as time with his sisters and friends. After his phone call with Antonio, Logan decided it was best to suck up his pride and call his mother. The two had agreed to come to some sort of truce regarding the *Lola* situation. Britt's heart ached at the thought of Lola possibly wrecking her son once more; however, she decided to trust that her son truly was, *"A grown-ass man"* and that he could handle this with a level head.

Logan was elated having Lola so close to him for the past month; life had not been easy since her return, but he wouldn't trade it for a second. Having sensed Lola's restlessness and apprehension, Logan decided that a change of scenery would do her a world of good. Ensuring that his schedule was free for the next month, Logan decided it was time to surprise Lola with a drive to his family's cabin. The drive along the PNW (Pacific Northwest) coast was one of Logan's favorites.

Logan walked into the bedroom and happily announced, "Get ready, *my heart*. Make sure to pack a bag for a little road trip."

Lola looked at Logan in utter confusion. "Road trip … I thought we were just staying here."

Logan laughed in reply. "Well, we were, but I have decided a change of scenery would do both of us some good. Besides, I've never taken you to my dad's cabin."

Lola nervously chuckled, "Oh fine," as she began to pack her wardrobe back into her very large weekender bag.

As soon as everything was packed, Logan and Lola headed down to **Cate's** to say their goodbyes, before stopping at the market to pick up some food for their little getaway. Once in the car, Logan looked at Lola with a big smile. It wasn't just any smile though, it was a smile that made her feel butterflies and grow weak in the knees. Lola thought to herself, *I am glad I am sitting down.* Out loud she said, "Eyes on the road, Warren! Eyes on the road." Logan laughed and turned his attention to the road for the drive ahead.

An hour into their drive, Logan and Lola tried to break the silence at the same time, and after a great deal of going back and forth as to who would speak first, Logan finally said, "You need to call Dr. Indigo and Lizzie and let them know you will be in an area without cell service or WiFi. You don't want to cause them any worry or panic."

With sarcasm dripping in her voice, Lola retorted, "Oh god no! That would be horrendous!" Pausing for a moment, Lola chuckled as she stated, "Lizzie would freak the fuck out for sure."

"What was on your mind, *my heart*?" Logan asked once Lola ended her final phone call.

"Well … umm … I was just wondering who those girls were that flocked around you in the market. They all acted like they knew you, but you seemed uncomfortable."

Logan sighed as he hoped Lola would have simply ignored the people surrounding him, but his luck in avoiding the truth could only carry him so far. Answering as honestly as he could, he simply stated that they were fans.

"Huh? I never knew photographers had crazy amounts of fans. The way those girls were acting, some unsuspecting person would think you were some kind of rock star."

Lola's analogy left Logan feeling like a deer trapped in the headlights of the semi carrying his deceit that was ready to hit him head-on. Regaining control over his senses, Logan told a few playful jokes before, both passengers sat back and enjoyed the silence and serenity of the view around them. Finally, three hours after having left Parkway, Logan and Lola arrived in Pinecrest, where Cade's cabin was located.

When the car was unpacked and Lola made lunch, Logan suggested they go for a walk through the woods and head down to the coastline. The smell of forest and sea filled Lola's lungs and brought a sense of much-needed peace to her; especially after she dreamed about Shane constantly plaguing her mind. The pair walked in silence for 30 minutes before finally arriving at their destination, where Logan found a nice bench and gestured for Lola to sit beside him.

Lola took a deep breath and sat. She knew this conversation had to continue so she took several more breaths to steady and prepare herself. Logan took her hand closest to him and held it tenderly, "Just take your time. You've got this!" Lola looked into Logan's eyes, took another deep breath and said:

"Okay so, where did we leave off?"

"Your mother had just returned." Logan graciously reminded her.

"Oh yes, Anne-Marie had returned and I did not take it well at all. Grandma and Grandpa talked about meeting over dinner with Anne-Marie and the guy she was seeing, Everett. Grandpa said we had to have this dinner because my father would want us to hear Anne-Marie out. Love runs deep, or some shit like that.

"Anyhow, dinner was scheduled for a Friday night and I was to come straight home from school. I dreaded this night but I would be lying if I said that I wasn't at least somewhat intrigued by actually spending time with my mother. Even though she had abandoned me, a teeny, tiny piece of my heart still longed for this woman who brought me to life."

~

August 1998

The night of the dinner with Anne-Marie and her suitor, Everett Silver, had arrived. At first, the situation felt very awkward and uncomfortable for all who surrounded the dining table. However, as the night progressed everyone began to feel at ease and had an enjoyable time. Curious about their dinner guest, Jack and Lorriene began their inquiry of Everett and his life. Even though Anne-Marie had left for quite some time, in the minds of the Swans', she would always be their daughter. All the while, Lola quietly surveyed her surroundings.

Lorriene began, "So, Everett, will you please tell us a bit about yourself."

Slightly wide-eyed, like a deer in the headlights, Everett breathed deeply and chuckled to himself, as Anne-Marie gripped his hand. "Well, Mrs. Swan, I am originally from a small town in North Carolina called Clarington and am the second eldest of six children. I work as an architect. My firm, Silver Structural, is one I built from the ground up."

Everett paused for a moment before laughing. "Sorry guys! Architect pun." The group found themselves equally bemused with Everett's sense of humor. Continuing, Everett stated, "I design buildings all across the globe and travel quite regularly."

Jack felt it his "fatherly" duty to ask the question weighing on everyone's minds. "How did you and Anne-Marie meet?"

Recalling the tale in his mind, Everett's eyes lit up. "Well, as I said, I travel quite regularly all across the globe, so being Stateside is quite a rare treat. My family was having an annual beach trip to Wilmington and for the first time in years, I was able to attend. I'm the only one of my siblings who isn't married or has children, so I never made it a priority to attend. Anyhow, on the third night, I saw the most beautiful woman sitting on the dunes, gazing into the night sky."

Lola felt herself tear up a bit as her thoughts tried to turn bitter. *While I awaited my mother to love me, she traveled and went to the beach? What a load of horse shit!* Noticing how her granddaughter's countenance began to falter, Lorriene quickly grabbed Lola's hand, letting her know that everything would be okay.

Oblivious to the impact his words were having on Lola, Everett proceeded with his tale. "I needed a break from all of the kids, so I asked if I could join her for just a moment."

Anne-Marie blushed deeply, as she too recalled their initial meeting- then exuberantly chimed in. "I was slightly startled but readily agreed. I had been alone in my sorrow for so long that just another presence being there somehow felt … I don't know … welcoming. We sat in silence, listening to the sound of the waves crashing against the shore. As the sun began to rise, we looked at one another and couldn't help but laugh. I mean, who sits with a stranger for hours, while saying nothing?"

Everett laughed as he said, "Seeing her face in the sunrise made my heart stop. Her brown eyes looked like they had lost the world and it broke my heart. I asked her for her name and we exchanged information. I decided to stay in North Carolina for a little while and Anne-Marie and I instantly hit it off. She was very honest about your son, Jackson, and how much she regretted leaving her daughter behind. It was hard to hear, but I felt in my heart that God had brought us together that night."

Anne-Marie squeezed Everett's hand as she spoke, "With Everett's help, I was able to start therapy and get the help I needed. It also meant being able to finally come home and face my fears. Guilt has a funny way of holding you hostage."

The group settled into lively chatter as Lorriene brought out dessert, a delicious-looking black forest cake, and coffee to the table. As Everett bit into the cake, he was overwhelmed by the decadent chocolate flavors. "Mrs. Swan, I must say, this is the best black forest cake I have ever tasted."

Lorriene laughed as she said, "No need for such formalities, Everett. Please, call us Jack and Lorriene. Also, our sweet Luxie is the one who made the cake, so all the thanks go in her direction."

Lola blushed as her grandmother put her on the spot. "Thank you, Mr. Silver. Grandma has made this every year for my birthday and said it was my father's favorite, so I wanted to give it a try."

Once dessert was finished, Lorriene looked at Jack and said, "Jack, darling, please take Everett to your study. You should show him the new concept you are considering for your next hotel."

As Jack stood, he kissed Lorriene's head before replying, "Of course, *my love*. Perfect meal as always."

Once Jack and Everett headed off to the study, Lorriene looked at Anne-Marie and asked how she was feeling after this dinner. Anne-Marie, in turn, looked directly at her daughter and smiled. "Honestly, it felt really good. It felt like I was coming home."

Lorriene exclaimed, "Just so you know you always had a home here. Jack and I would never have abandoned you or kicked you and our Luxie out just because Jackson died."

Hanging her head in defeat, Anne-Marie stated, "I know I can't take back the years of being gone and the hurt and disappointment I caused. All I can say is thank you so much for a fresh start. I would like to ask if Lola would be okay to start staying at our house on weekends."

Thoughtfully Lorriene stated, "Luxe is 14 now and I feel she can make that decision for herself. What do you think darling?"

Lola sat there for several moments in complete and utter astonishment. This was the very moment she had wished for all of her life. Finally, she exclaimed with childlike joy, "I think I would like that a lot. And, it will be nice to learn more about you and Everett."

~

December 1998

A few months had passed and Lola was having the time of her life with Anne-Marie and Everett; she finally felt as if she had **actual** parents. Even though her grandparents were the absolute best people in the entire world, **nothing** compared to the feeling of finally having her mother so close.

Christmas time was approaching and this year Lola wanted to spend it with Anne-Marie and Everett. Normally the week before Christmas, Jack and Lorriene would take Lola to visit the Sommers family, along with their other family friends, the Carsons, and

Bennetts. After spending time with family and friends, Jack and Lorriene would take Lola on an adventure to anywhere in the world her heart desired.

This year Jack and Lorriene planned a Christmas trip to France, however, Lola begged to stay home as this would be her very first Christmas with her mother. Jack and Lorriene were a little sad to not have their annual tradition with Lola, but wouldn't trade Anne-Marie finally being a mother to their precious granddaughter for anything.

Christmas Eve and Christmas Day with Anne-Marie and Everett were everything Lola had hoped, wished, and prayed for. The thing Lola was most excited about was the normal traditions of baking cookies, singing songs, watching holiday movies- all things most people typically took for granted.

~

December 31, 1998

New Year's Eve arrived and with it, was to bring the return of Jack and Lorriene from their trip to France. Lola was eagerly awaiting her grandparents and the familiarity and comfort of her own home and bed. Hours passed without a sign of Jack or Lorriene, which caused Lola to nervously pace back and forth. Finally gathering the courage to speak up, Lola asked, "Anne … I mean, Mom, would you and Everett please take me home? Maybe Grandpa and Grandma are unpacking first before they come here? Do you think we could meet them halfway or something?"

Anne-Marie lovingly kissed her daughter's head as she replied, "Of course, *little one*. Go gather your things and then we'll head out."

The hour drive from central Portland to Parkway dragged on for what felt like eons to Lola. To ease her nerves, Lola brought out her **Discman** and **U2** CD her friends, Shane and Andy had given her for Christmas. Skipping forward to "*With or Without You,*" Lola closed her eyes as she strummed her fingers and allowed the music to calm her nerves.

The sound of sirens began to overpower Lola's music. Realizing they were just a few streets from Swan Manor, panic balled up inside of Lola's stomach. **"Stop the car now**,*"* Lola yelled to Everett; barely waiting for the gear shift to be placed into the park, she bolted from the car.

Tears fell from Lola's eyes as she saw her grandparents' car completely totaled. Trying to run through the crime scene tape, an officer stopped Lola. Anger and hurt filled the 14-year-old girl as she punched the officer's chest and screamed. **"Let me through you son of a bitch!***"*

With pity-filled eyes, the officer sadly exclaimed, "Easy there, *little one*. We can't let anyone through."

Lola begged and pleaded for the officer to tell her what had happened. Stating he needed to talk to his commander, the officer walked away as Anne-Marie and Everett came up to embrace Lola. After an hour, the officer returned to Lola. With sorrow in his voice, the officer stated as professionally as he could, "The driver, Mr. Swan had a heart attack, thus crashing the car. The passenger, Mrs. Swan was killed upon impact."

Lola stood there in disbelief. *The officer has to be mistaken. This is someone else, it just has to be. Grandpa and Grandma can't be gone. How can my family just be gone? Don't they know I need them?* Breaking free from her thoughts, Lola ran through the crime scene, straight to the lifeless bodies laid upon the stretchers. No one stopped her, for who would be so cruel as to rob this young girl of her grieving. Not a single word was said as Lola cried until she passed out.

~

January 1999

After the funeral, Lola was sent to live with Everett and Anne-

Marie, as Anne-Marie was technically her legal guardian at that point. Now that Lola would be living with them, Anne-Marie encouraged Everett to purchase a home in Parkway, thus ensuring some kind of normalcy remained in Lola's life. Swan Manor was now officially Lola's property, but at this point in her life, the thought of returning there was painfully haunting.

Lola requested the judge place Swan Manor, in her trust, along with **Swan Industries** and the 10 million dollar fund Jack and Lorriene had left for her, all in the hands of her grandfather's best friend, and **Swan Industries'** current CEO, Gregory Miller. The conditions of her trust were very strict:

1. *No money was to be touched, aside from basic school needs and living expenses. Full access to the trust is only given through marriage, or age 25, whichever scenario comes first.*
2. *The recipient may return to Swan Manor whenever ready; in the meantime, a full staff will care for the grounds and daily maintenance.*
3. *The recipient must, upon legal working age, remain gainfully employed while maintaining acceptable grades.*
4. *The recipient must attend college, in the business management program, as the recipient is the legal heir to Swan Industries.*
5. *Upon graduation from college, the recipient will receive the custom watch, designating the recipient as the sole heir and proprietor of Swan Industries.*
6. *If any of these stipulations cannot be met, the entirety of this trust is therefore null and void.*

Lola readily agreed to the conditions, knowing since she was little, **Swan Industries** was her inheritance; and was a cross she would happily bear if it meant being a Swan. The money or lack of access to it meant nothing to her because what good or use was money when the people Lola loved most in this world, were ripped away from her?

~

August 17, 1999

Time marches on, as it always does and in Lola's life, this was no different. Life with Anne-Marie and Everett wasn't bad, but it also wasn't the same. The couple did the best they could to make Lola feel loved. Not having any children of his own, Everett came to love Lola as his daughter. So much so, that he asked for Lola's permission to propose to Anne-Marie. Lola readily agreed, as her mother was truly happy. Shortly after Lola turned 15, Everett and Anne-Marie wed.

After the wedding, Everett's workload began to increase; thus causing him to travel through Russia, Canada, and most of the U.S. more and more. Anne-Marie was sad, but she knew that he was a highly sought-after architect and his job was demanding. Whenever Everett was home, he did everything to ensure it was as if he had never left. Slowly the little house became a home and its inhabitants a family.

~

February 14, 2000

"*Little one*, would you please come here when you have a moment?" Anne-Marie called out from her bedroom.

"Yes, ma'am. I can as soon as I finish this math problem. If that is alright?" Once she had finished a bit of her school work, Lola entered the room her mother shared with Everett. Happily, she called out, "What's up, mom?"

Nervously, Anne-Marie asked, "Have you ever wanted siblings? I know you have Lizzie, but have you ever wanted others?"

Lola thought for a moment before exuberantly responding, "Of course!"

Breathing out a sigh of relief, Anne-Marie stated, "Well, *little one*, you're going to have two new siblings in October. I am pregnant with twins!" Lola couldn't believe her ears. Tears of joy filled her eyes as she lovingly embraced her mother.

"Mom, when did you find out and do you know when you are due?"

"I found out today when I went to the doctor for my yearly exam. My doctor said I am ten weeks along. You know, that's just two weeks shy of when I learned I was pregnant with you." Anne-Marie smiled at the bittersweet memory of Jackson's excitement 15 years ago.

When Everett entered the door, Anne-Marie told him the good news. Tears of joy fell down his face, for he never thought he would have children of his own. Everett loved Lola dearly, but to a man, there was just something extra special about having your own flesh and blood.

~

April 24, 2000

The time for Anne-Marie's 20-week scan and gender reveal of the twins had finally arrived. So far, everything with the pregnancy had gone well and the little family was hopeful today's appointment would be no different. Anne-Marie and Everett couldn't wait to start buying items for the babies and set up their nursery. Lola couldn't wait to learn if she would be having brothers, sisters, or one of each.

As the nurse scanned the doppler wand across Anne-Marie's belly, a look of concern came across her face. "Excuse me for just a moment, please. I need to go and fetch your doctor."

Silence filled the room as the nurse quickly exited. Nervousness filled Anne-Marie's heart as she silently prayed, *God, you have taken so much from me. Please let my little babies be alright.*

The nurse returned to the room, with the doctor in tow. As she scanned again, the doctor grew very concerned. He asked for Everett and Lola to step out of the room and called in several nurses to double-check the scan. The pair paced up and down the waiting area for fifteen minutes, which felt like an eternity. The doctor finally called them back in and asked them to please sit. With a somber expression upon his face, he said, "Mr. and Mrs. Silver, Miss Swan- I have some rather regrettable news. As we were doing the scan, we were unable to detect any heartbeats. I am sorry to say that your twins have passed on."

~

August 17, 2000

The loss of the twin boys took its heavy toll on both Anne-Marie and Everett in different ways. To heal her shattered heart, Anne-Marie began drinking heavily; while Everett drowned his sorrows by turning to his work and travels, anything to escape the empty room which haunted the once happy home. Whenever Everett was home, Anne-Marie screamed and hit him. He tried to comfort her, but the loss of her babies was too much for her broken heart. Lola's home became a broken, dismal place that she dreaded. Both school and Lizzie's house had become a reprieve, but in the end, she always had to return home to Anne-Marie's drunkenness.

Once Lola's sixteenth birthday passed, she set out with determination to find a job. The stipulations of her trust were always in the back of her mind. Lola set out in what had once been her dad's car, Averie, into town to find a job. That warm day in August, it was as if fate knew Lola needed an escape, as a new business had opened a few months prior in Parkway.

Pulling into the parking lot just off of Main Street, Lola saw a "Help Wanted" sign in the window of the cutest little café. As she entered the establishment, a cheerful young woman, who looked no older than 22, called out, "Hi! Welcome to ***Cate's Café***. I'm Cate. How can I help you?"

Lola smiled brightly at the kind woman standing in front of her. Cate had a naturally tanned complexion; raven-colored hair, which was beautifully feathered; and powder blue eyes straight out of a faerie tale. Extending her hand, Lola greeted Cate with a firm handshake. "Hi, my name is Luxe, and I'm here to apply for the job."

A week later, Cate called Lola in for an interview and she was hired on the spot. Lola was ecstatic to finally have a job and couldn't wait to tell Anne-Marie and call Everett and Lizzie. *Hopefully, this good news will bring a smile to my mom's face,* Lola thought to herself. When Lola told Anne-Marie her good news, Anne-Marie had been drinking and was anything but excited.

Enraged, Anne-Marie stomped over to Lola, screamed, and slapped her hard across the face, as she seethed. "You think I would forget about you slapping me, you ungrateful piece of shit! You should be dead and not your father! Not my babies! I hate you! Do you hear me? **I fucking hate you!**"

Lola was in complete and utter dismay as both her face and heart stung. Never in her life had she felt so foolish. *Of course, my mother could never really love me.* No longer able to remain in that house of torment any longer, Lola ran out the front door, just as a heavy summer rain started to fall. It was as if the sky cried with Lola. Lola ran until she reached the park. Once there she collapsed upon a bench and sobbed in the rain. In the distance, a young, masculine voice called out to Lola, but it would fall upon deaf ears as it was drowned out by both the sound of the rain and Lola's cries.

11

Is this love?

August 17, 2000

As Lola sat on the bench crying in the rain, she was unaware of her surroundings, and a voice calling out to her.

"Excuse me, Miss. Are you okay?"

The sound of the voice drawing closer finally reached Lola's ears enough to stop her tears. As she looked up, the owner of the voice spoke, "Luxie? Is that you? It's me, Shane Carson!"

Feeling rather sheepish for not having recognized Shane's voice, Lola blushed as she replied wearily, "Yes, it's me. Sorry, Shane. I didn't recognize your voice and I'm so sorry you have to see me in this state."

"It's okay, Luxe. I'm not sure what is going on, but if you want, I don't mind sitting here with you," Shane tenderly stated while moving a curl that covered Lola's eyes.

Lola thought for a few moments as she gazed at Shane before replying, "Honestly, I'd like that a lot. You've changed a lot over the summer. Did you have a good time in the Netherlands visiting your grandparents?"

While Shane spoke with excitement about his time with his mother's family, Lola couldn't help but be mesmerized by Shane's new look. He had grown so much over the summer while he was away and had filled out quite handsomely. Shane had also let his platinum blonde hair grow out just enough to be put into a top knot, while he kept the undersides shaved close. His light skin had tanned nicely, thus making his blue-green eyes stand out even more. Although the piercings he now donned- the bridge of his nose and double ear gauges- certainly helped to enhance his new look.

After Shane spoke of his trip, he gently held Lola's hand in his; the pain etched across her face made him heartbroken for his friend. The pair sat on the bench in the rain for an hour with nothing said, which was a comfort to Lola. Once the rain stopped, Shane asked, "Would you like me to drive you home?"

Not quite ready to face Anne-Marie just yet, Lola asked Shane to drive her to Lizzie's house instead. The two friends joyfully spoke of their excitement regarding the start of their junior year. The pair were ecstatic to learn they had three classes, as well as lunch period together. Lola laughed as she thought to herself, *At least I won't feel like a third wheel with Lizzie and Mark this year.*

"Hey, Shay, do you know what lunch period Andy has? He won't be alone will he?"

"Shay, huh?"

"Yeah, if you don't mind, I think your new look deserves a new nickname."

Shane laughed as he told Lola that he did not mind the nickname at all, but only she would be allowed to call him Shay.

"Andy will have our lunch period. Ever since what happened in seventh grade, my parents have made sure that Andy and I have our schedules exactly the same."

Lola breathed a sigh of relief, "I remember that day, and I am so glad."

After a twenty-minute drive, Shane's car finally arrived in front of Lizzie's house. Once Lola had exited, she turned to thank Shane again for the company and ride, she noticed that he pulled out a small, green notebook from the side panel of his car door and began to write something down.

"What are you jotting down, Carson?"

"Oh! Sorry. I just like to write down important memories. Have a good night, Luxe. I'll see you soon."

As soon as Shane was out of the driveway, Lola gave a quick "hello" to Luke and Patricia, before making her way to Lizzie's room to quickly change from her drenched clothes. Immediately upon changing, Lola lay across Lizzie's bed with the biggest smile plastered across her face. Lizzie couldn't help but pick up on Lola's infectious smile.

"Hey, *baby bear*! What's got you so smiley?"

"Oh, *Momma Bear*! My day started great, turned to complete shit, and still somehow managed to end on the best note ever!"

"Don't keep me in the dark! Tell me what's going on, sister."

"Well, remember when I applied for the job at that new café, called **Cate's**?"

"Yeah! Did you hear back?"

"I did. I went for an interview and ended up getting the job!"

The two girls embraced each other and squealed for joy as Lizzie called out, "That's amazing, *sweetie*!" Once their celebratory ruckus died down, Lizzie needed to know what had caused Lola's day to go horribly wrong.

"If something so wonderful happened, what caused your day to go wrong?"

Taking a moment to catch her breath, Lola paused before telling Lizzie just what happened. "Well ... I was so excited that I wanted to tell my mom because I figured some good news would make her smile. After all, the loss of the twins is still pretty hard on her."

"Okay … where is this going, Luxie?"

"When I got home … well … she was drunk."

Instantly at the mention of the word "drunk," Lizzie frantically grabbed Lola's shoulder and began scanning her. Almost as soon as Lizzie started her observation, her eyes landed upon the bruise which had darkened upon Lola's cheek. The overflow of emotions that Lizzie had raging inside spewed out like a tsunami.

"What the hell did that **bitch** do to you?"

"Calm down, *Momma Bear*. It's just a small bruise, besides, it will be gone before I have to start work or back to school."

"Lola Luxe Swan! You do not tell me to calm down! How the hell can you just sit there and act like this shit is okay? She fucking hit you **again!** I know she did."

Lola knew Lizzie was serious, so she had no choice but to tell Lizzie everything that had happened with Anne-Marie.

"Lizzie, I know it's not alright, but she's my mom. One parent and two grandparents are already dead. What do you want me to do? I'm sure this will pass soon."

"I should at least tell mom and dad."

"No! Lizzie, please promise me you won't say anything," Lola pleaded, as she grabbed her friend's hand in desperation.

"Why should I do that Luxie? Isn't that the same thing as saying what she is doing is okay?"

"Lizzie, I'm begging you! If you ever loved me as a sister, please don't tell your parents. Let's just forget this whole stupid thing even happened. I have good news to tell you, so why sully it?"

Lizzie hung her head in defeat as she swore, on their sister code, that she would again keep the abuse Lola was experiencing at the hands of Anne-Marie, secret. "So, what's this good news?" Lizzie asked, plastering a faux smile upon her worried face.

"Well, after I left home, I ran into the rain until I found a bench to sit on. While I was crying a voice called out to me. You'll never believe who it was?"

"Who? Don't leave me hangin', sister!"

"It was Shane! He's back from the Netherlands."

"Shane, as in Shane Michael Carson, who you've had a crush on for the last two years?"

Just the thought of her silly crush made Lola giggle, "One and the same, sis." Sighing in awe at the memory from earlier that evening, Lola laid back on the bed as she continued. "Lizzie, he really is the sweetest. After we talked, he sat in the rain with me and held my hand until it stopped raining, then offered to give me a ride."

Lizzie couldn't help but smile at her friend's elation. Lola didn't have many happy moments in the last couple of years, so to see her smiling like this, made Lizzie's heart swell. "You know Luxie, according to Mark, Shane has been in love with you for, like, ever."

"As if!"

"For real!"

"Well, if that's true, then why has he never said anything or even tried to make a move?"

"The same thing could be said for you, *baby bear*. Anyhow, Mark said Shane's scared you'll reject him. Plus with everything going on with Andy, he wasn't even sure you would want to date him."

"Are you kidding me? I adore Andy, he is the best. Besides, we have all been friends for so long, you'd think Shane would understand that by now."

"Well then, it's settled! You leave everything to *Momma Bear* and she will work her magic."

~

September 4, 2000

One month had passed since Lola's sixteenth birthday, and in that month so much had changed. Lola was excelling at her new job and managed to balance it with the first few weeks of school. Shane had also asked Lola out for their first date, thus officially making them a couple. Things at home, however, had gone from bad to worse. This led to Lola staying away from home as much as she possibly could; be it staying after school to study, work an extra shift, spend time with Shane, or even just hang out with Cate or her friends. Anything was better to Lola than being in her own personal version of hell.

For Lola and Shane's first date, Shane decided to take her for coffee at **Cate's**. Living in a small town like Parkway meant date night options were limited. Each date brought the teens closer together and meant more important memories for Shane to keep a note of. Although Mark and Lizzie would often have Andy hang out with them, Lola would make sure he felt included with her and Shane as well.

~

September 9, 2000

The Way of the Gun had just been released in theaters and Andy was dying to see it, so Mark and Lizzie decided to treat him to the movie, thus giving Shane and Lola the chance to drive over to Proxy Falls, in Willamette National Forest, where they would hike for the day and enjoy a nice picnic in the beauty of nature. After hiking for an hour, Lola and Shane found a beautiful grove near the base of the waterfall where they could set up their picnic.

"What do you think about setting up our picnic here, Luxie?"

"Oh my gosh, Shay! This spot is so pretty."

After the teens had eaten the contents from the basket, they took some time to truly take in the scenery surrounding them. As Lola lay back upon the blanket to gaze at the clouds, Shane made more notations in his notebook.

"Shay, can I ask you something?"

"Shoot."

"Are you going to be an author one day?"

"Ya know, I haven't given much thought to it. Why do you ask?"

"Well, you're always making notes, so I was kinda curious."

Sighing heavily, Shane responded, "I'll probably just end up taking over my father's business, being his only heir and all."

"Lay back with me and look at the clouds!"

Shane willingly complied with Lola's request, making sure to grasp her hand in his as he did.

"Tell me, Shay, is taking over his business what you want to do?"

"Honestly, I don't know. I'm 16 and feel like I should have options. Instead, my whole life was planned for me the day I was born."

Lola laughed, a little bitterly, for she knew those feelings all too well. The weight of Shane's statement was a burden, she too, had to carry.

"So, if you had options like you want, and could do anything in the world, what would that job be?"

Shane thought for quite a while as he gazed upon the clouds. No one ever took the time to ask what he would want to do if options were set before him; they always just assumed he would be the next leader of **Carson Tech**.

"I love what my dad's company does, but that's just it, it's **his** company. If I could do anything I wanted, I would do missions work by helping build schools, orphanages, and maybe even preach and help spread the gospel. My family is loaded, and it wouldn't hurt anything to help people. What about you, Luxie?"

"Shay, I think that is amazing. I don't know what I believe because if there is a God, he has never been kind to me. Maybe one day though, I could go with you and work in an orphanage. I would just want to love on the kids because I know what it's like to be alone."

As Lola spoke, Shane squeezed her hand. Even though she hadn't told him about every hardship in her life, he did know quite a bit. Lola nervously looked over at Shane because this was the first time she had ever told anyone about her beliefs. *There has to be something out there, but how can I know what to believe when I only have heartache and despair.*

"Shay, can I ask you one more thing?"

"Sure Luxie, what's up?"

"Are you mad at me that I don't know what to believe?"

"No, I'm not mad. I think it's normal to question what's going on and why things happen the way they happen. I think you have to come to your beliefs on your own because if someone forces you, it will just push you away."

Lola took a few deep breaths as she closed her eyes for a moment. *I should tell him the truth, I mean, after all, it's the least I could do. But, what if he hates me because I put up with it? Here goes nothing and everything at the same time.*

"Anne-Marie … my mom … she beats me and abuses me every day. I hate it there."

"Why don't you move back to your grandparents' house? It's been nearly two years since they passed away."

"I know, but … I'm not ready. Besides, I don't want to live alone in such a big house."

"Have you told Lizzie?"

Laughing, Lola replied, "Do you really think much gets past that **hurricane**?"

Shane laughed in reply for he knew this was an honest truth like no other. Thinking for a moment, he paused before asking, "Do her parents know? I know that your mom is special to them."

"**No**, and they never will! They finally have her back in their lives and I am not going to be selfish enough to have them lose her again. This is my burden to carry. Besides, even if I wanted to, I doubt they would believe me. I know they love me, but… I don't know."

After Lola's confession, Shane and Lola continued to lie in the beauty surrounding them, and before they knew it, the sun started setting. Once everything was packed, the pair made their way back to Shane's car to begin the drive back home. The ride was silent, with Shane holding onto Lola's hand and Lola held captive by the unease of returning home.

When they finally arrived in Lola's driveway, Shane looked over to Lola and smiled brightly. Lola was overcome with the urge to kiss him, but she was also afraid. *We have barely been dating a month and this will be my first kiss. What if it's awful? What if this makes things super awkward and we can't even be friends anymore?*

Sensing Lola's nerves were at an all-time high, Shane inched closer to her, then whispered into her ear, "May I kiss you, Luxie?"

Lola felt like she could die from the amount of pure joy bursting within her, which caused her to shout out "Yes!," a little too eagerly. Shane laughed before pulling Lola into a warm, loving kiss; the kind of kiss written in the stars.

Nervousness soon overtook Lola, causing her to pull back and look at the floor. *I have wanted this moment for so long, but I don't want to be just a fling to him.*

When Lola pulled back, Shane instantly grabbed her and worriedly asked, "What's wrong? Was the kiss bad? Was it too soon? Did I mess it all up? Oh, God! I did. I went and messed everything up."

Lola, a bit teary-eyed at the fact her uneasiness had caused Shane to think he messed up, shook her head as she replied, "No, it was amazing. It's just … this was my first kiss and … I'm nervous. I don't want you to break up with me now that you got it."

Lovingly, Shane placed his hand upon Lola's cheek as he gazed into her eyes. "Luxie, *Mijn Bloem*, you are more special to me than words can describe. You are my first girlfriend and my first kiss. I'm not going to screw this up by acting like some tool. Besides, I don't let just anyone call me Shay."

Lola laughed at Shane's last statement before asking, "What does *Mijn Bloem* mean?"

"That, my dear girlfriend, means *my flower* in Dutch."

"Shay, I absolutely love that."

"Well, I shall call you *Mijn Bloem* from now on."

The couple, both glad to be over their nerves, took a moment to kiss one another again. "Hey, *Mijn Bloem*, before you leave, can I ask you something?"

"Always, Carson. Always."

"Well, there is this concert in Portland, at *The Mad King*, the second week of October. It was going to originally be a guys' trip with just Andy, Mark, and I, but you know that Mark and Lizzie can't be apart from each other that long."

Lola burst out laughing as she remarked, "It's so true! You know, with as much as they fuck, I'm really surprised that Lizzie isn't pregnant yet." This statement caused the young couple to double over in a fit of laughter. Once Shane wiped the tears from his eyes, he asked, "Will you come with me?"

"Who's playing, and how long will we be gone?"

"Well, the guys and I were thinking since school is out that week, we'd just go to Portland for the whole week. The concert is on a Thursday night, so we'd be gone Sunday through Saturday. As for who's playing, some new local band from Vienna, called *Beyond Oregon*, is opening. *Brand New* and *Taking Back Sunday* are the two main headliners. My dad's company is providing all of the tech and sound equipment."

Lola was ecstatic! "Are you shitting me right now, Carson? I fucking love **Brand New** and **Taking Back Sunday**! We're going and I've got rooms covered. Perks of being an heiress to the biggest hotel chain in the PNW."

Shane kissed Lola once more before walking her to the front door. "Goede nacht, **Mijn Bloem.** Good night, My Flower."

"Good Night, Shay!"

When Lola entered the house, she praised whatever being in the universe would listen, because Anne-Marie was asleep; unfortunately, the house reeked of booze. Lola quietly made her way to her bedroom, where she giddily fell back upon her bed with thoughts of the day running through her head.

How the hell did I get so lucky? Shane was so nervous too and didn't judge me for my lack of believing like he does. He brings my heart so much joy, that when I'm with him, I don't even think about all of the hurt. I just feel ... happy. Whoever's listening, is this love? Because I think I am in love with Shane Michael Carson.

12

Silence screams the loudest

October 5, 2014

Lola broke from her tale as she needed time to regain her composure. Looking out over the bluff and into the Pacific Ocean as the sun began to set, brought a calming peace to Lola. The grey hues that magically fused into the pinkish-orange sunset truly were a sight to behold. Lola closed her eyes for a brief moment to take in her surroundings one last time before she asked, "Can we please walk back to the cabin now? I'm tired and hungry."

"If you're ready, then yes, *my heart*, we'll head back."

Silence filled the path as the pair made their way back, each lost to their own thoughts. Logan wanted, no, **needed** to know more but at the same time, he didn't want to be overly pushy or insensitive. Lola looked over at Logan and studied his face. When it came to reading people and being in tune with the emotional well-being of others, she was severely lacking, however, even she could clearly see the queries reeling inside Logan's head.

"You know, Warren, if you have a question, you should just ask it," Lola quipped in her matter-of-fact manner.

Nervously rubbing his neck, Logan playfully quipped, "How'd ya know I had a question?"

"I'm pretty oblivious when it comes to reading people, but you, you're pretty blatant in your curiosity. You make this weird scrunched-up face." Lola jested as she mocked the face Logan was, in fact, making at that very moment.

Rolling his eyes, Logan exclaimed, "So, when are you going to fill me in on Andy. You speak of him so fondly but also bittersweetly."

Sighing heavily, Lola remarked, "I guess now is as good as any time to tell you about Andy Bennett."

~

August 7, 1989

The first day of Kindergarten was a day of great excitement for Lola, as it meant a full day with her sister, Lizzie. While for Jack and Lorriene, the first day meant a big milestone had passed for their sweet Luxie, both nervously prayed the child would make more friends, aside from Lizzie.

As the girls entered the classroom, they eagerly searched for their seats. The teacher, Ms. Edwards, after much discussion with both the Sommers' and the Swans' felt it best to place Lizzie and Lola at separate tables, thus encouraging better socialization in both girls. Lizzie found herself seated beside a small boy with glasses framing his sea-green eyes, and fawn-colored hair. Lizzie, always a child with a bold personality remarked rather abruptly, "Hi, cute boy! My name is Lizzie and you **will** be my boyfriend."

The little boy beside her started crying out for the teacher, "Ms. Edwards! Ms. Edwards!"

Ms. Edwards quickly rushed over to check on the boy as she gently called out, "What's wrong, Mark?"

As Mark told the teacher what had happened, Ms. Edwards couldn't help but laugh. "Oh, Mark, don't fret. Okay? Lizzie here just wants to be your friend." Turning to Lizzie, Ms. Edwards said,

"Elizabeth, we must **ask** people to be our friends, not demand. Please apologize."

On the other side of the room, at a table in the back, little Lola found herself seated between two boys. The boy to her left had platinum blonde hair and blue-green eyes, while the boy to her right had honey-blonde hair and clover green eyes. Trying ever so hard to be brave, Lola turned to the boy on her right and introduced herself. "Hi, I'm Luxie! What's your name?"

Silence was the only response given, thus causing little Lola to feel very self-conscious.

"His name's Andy."

Turning to her left, Lola looked at the boy sitting beside her. "What?"

"That's Andy and him don't talk much."

"Oh … okay. What's your name?"

"My name's Shane. Andy's my best friend but him don't talk much."

Even though Andy said nothing at all, which Shane more than made up for, Lola was very excited to have made two new friends that day.

~

1993

Time moved forward for Lola and her friends, and during their elementary school days, Lola quickly learned Andy was very fond of plants, flowers specifically. Lola also learned that Andy's father, Andre Bennett, worked with Shane's father, Jordan Carson, and this was how the boys became such good friends.

Andy's mother, Taralynn, was pleased to learn that her son was making friends, however, she was concerned about his lack of interest in anything other than horticulture. She would often vent to Shane's mother, Mona, "I swear, this boy isn't right! He shows no ambition toward anything unless it's in my garden. He doesn't even participate on the playground."

Mona, who adored Andy as her own son, would remind her friend, "Taralynn, my dear, he's still just a child. Athletics and other activities will come. Why worry about these things now?"

"It's not **normal**," Taralynn would bitterly reply.

"Darling, what is normal anyway?"

Andy's most treasured possession was a pocket-sized book gifted to him by Lizzie and Lola for his eighth birthday, called **The Language of Flowers**, as they thought Andy's interest in flowers was truly amazing.

~

1995

One day, during the lunch period in fifth grade, Lola finally decided to ask Andy what his book said about the meaning of Red Poppies.

"Andy, what does a red poppy mean? We always leave them on my daddy's grave, so I wanna know what's so special about them."

Pulling out his book, Andy turned to the section labeled **P**. "Poppy; *Papaver rhoeas*. Symbolic for remembering, bloodshed, and death."

Teary-eyed, Lola thanked Andy for sharing the meaning. Poppies were the beautiful flowers that always decorated her father's grave and helped her to hold him in her memory, even though she never knew him; thus making them her favorite flower.

Now, not being a stereotypical boy, Andy often was bullied by boys who could not fathom how one of their own would rather spend his time doing "prissy things." When no teachers, or friends, were present, Andy was often the victim of bullying.

"Faggot!"

"Go smell the flowers, you stupid gay boy!"

"If you say anything to your boyfriend, Shane, we'll destroy your precious book."

Andy would try to fight back, but his gentle nature often left him uncertain as to how to handle the situation. "I'm not gay! Shane's just my friend. Even if I was gay, I would still be a better person than you cowards!"

Shane nearly caught on to what was happening on the day he found Andy crying at his locker. "Andy, what happened?"

"Nothing! Just leave me alone!"

That same school year, Taralynn had finally had enough of her 10-year-old son not acting "normal," so she took him to a therapist for testing. After several weeks of testing, Andy was diagnosed on the Autism Spectrum with Asperger's Syndrome. The therapist told Andre and Taralynn that Andy could and would still lead a very functional life, however, he would face challenges along the way. To overcome these challenges, family support was crucial.

The diagnosis of their son was devastating for Andre and Taralynn, as their hopes of a "normal" child were thrown out the window. Neither could look at their son and sadly began to treat him as more of a burden than a blessing. Mona's heart broke for the lack of love Andy received from his parents, for she loved that boy as if he were her own son.

After a serious conversation with her husband Jordan, Mona decided that it was time the Bennetts let Andy live with the Carsons, given that the Bennetts would continue to provide financial support for their son. Once Shane learned of Andy's diagnosis, he became overly protective of Andy; Andy was the brother of his heart and Shane would do anything to protect his brother.

~

1997

Andy tried his best to adjust to life in the Carson house; it was comforting for him to be surrounded by people he had known his entire life, sadly though, these people were not his parents. Unable to understand why his parents suddenly disappeared from his life, Andy began acting out. Mona, being a woman of great virtue and patience, worked hand-in-hand with Andy's therapists to find ways of calming Andy and helping him have as stable of a life as they could.

After two years of different therapists for Andy, Mona felt hopeless. *God, please provide me with something to help this dear boy.* Finally, on recommendation from a nutritional therapist named Kaleb Johnson, who worked at the **Lorriene Swan Center**, Mona was finally referred to a new therapist, recently graduated from college, who specialized in Autism Spectrum Disorder (ASD) and family counseling.

Andy's new therapist, Dr. Derek Winters, recommended starting a very specific routine every day, along with Andy naming his five favorite flowers when times were stressful for him. Dr. Winters spoke with Mona in earnest as he exclaimed, "Mrs. Carson, are you aware of the importance of routine for people on the Spectrum, specifically with Asperger's?"

In her lovely Dutch accent, Mona replied, "No sir, I am not. I am willing to learn anything to help my Andy."

"Routines are **vital** for a proper functioning life. You need to have two routines in place, one for school days and one for non-school days. A calendar and clock will be very helpful tools for Andy as well."

"Thank you, Dr. Winters. What about the calming technique?"

"Andy, please tell me what your five favorite flowers are? As I recall from a previous session, you said flowers are your favorite."

"Lilies, orchids, roses, tulips, and daisies are my favorite."

"Well, Andy, when things feel overwhelming for you, I want you to try to name off those five flowers. Doing this will help give you something to focus on and calm both your nerves and your mind."

For the first time in two years, Mona finally felt as if she had answers. "Dr. Winters, is there anything else that you recommend to help?"

"If Andy is okay with headphones, I recommend him wearing them and listening to music when navigating through any congested areas in school."

~

Over the course of six months, Andy's daily school routine (wake up, shower, dress, eat, walk to and from school with Shane) worked very well, and all was right once again in the Carson home. During the beginning, there were a couple of setbacks but nothing that would cause alarm or concern; whenever Andy would feel overwhelmed he would recite his five favorite flowers or turn on his music.

All was well and good, until the day both Shane and Andy's worlds changed...

The fateful day when the boys' worlds changed started off just like any other day of their seventh grade school year but ended in a way no one expected. On this day, Shane had to stay after class to finish up a group project with Mark; absentmindedly forgetting to tell Andy ahead of time.

"Shane, are you ready to walk home?"

"Crap! I forgot to tell you," Shane expressed remorsefully.

"Tell me what?"

"I have to stay after school and finish a project with Mark."

"What?! No! We have to go home! That's how it is every day!"

"You can wait here for a couple of hours while Mark and I finish this project, or, you can walk home on your own."

"**No, Shane**! We can't change the routine! Every day has to be the same! You can't just change things like this on me!"

With a heavy heart, Shane replied, "Look, brother, I'm sorry! I know change is hard for you but it's just for today. Why don't you work on your calming exercise and listen to your music while you walk home? I promise I won't be any longer than I have to. Besides, this will give you time to collect more flowers for your science project."

"Whatever, I'm going home now! I don't need you anyway," Andy angrily spat.

Shane sighed once more as he headed into the library with Mark.

Little did Shane know, the bullies had been lying in wait for a moment such as this; they were finally going to deal with this *gay weirdo*, as they ignorantly referred to Andy, once and for all.

Nervously, Andy walked home with headphones in place, blissfully listening to 'How's It Gonna Be,' by **Third Eye Blind**, as he recited "Lily, Orchid, Rose, Tulip, Daisy." All the while, the bullies were behind him taunting.

"Wait up little florist!"

"We want to know about your gay flowers!"

"You're such a fucking burden! No wonder your parents dumped your stupid ass."

"Oh look, the gay freak thinks he can ignore us with headphones!"

Soon the bullies surrounded Andy, taunting him even more, as they ripped his headphones and backpack away from his body. A couple shredded the contents inside the bag, while others spit in his face and punched him. Andy tried to calm himself down, but the pain overtook him as he blacked out.

~

Shane was relieved when he and Mark's project was finished and he could finally head home. He had found it hard to focus on anything because he felt guilty that Andy had to walk home alone. As Shane walked down the road he saw a familiar set of headphones,

Walkman, backpack, and notebook. Fear gripped Shane's heart and he knew something was wrong with Andy.

Shane desperately followed the paper trail to a back alley where he found Andy, unconscious and beaten to a bloody pulp. Shane's heart broke that day. *This is all my fault! I should have made him stay. I'm sorry that I have failed you brother.*

Swiftly rushing to a nearby story, Shane called 911 and Andy was rushed to the hospital.

Externally, Andy recovered just fine. Internally, however, he died a little bit. After that day, Andy refused to speak to anyone outside of his friend group or Jordan and Mona Carson; his refusal to speak caused people to start treating him like an invalid. Shane's guilt caused him to become exceedingly overprotective. As for Lola and Lizzie, they saw a sad and broken boy. Both girls, however, refused to treat Andy any differently than they had before.

~

October 5, 2014

Lola looked at Logan before they entered the front door of the cabin, as she paused for a brief moment. "Andy and I became super close our 7th-grade year, neither of us had our *real* parents in our lives; something that the others just couldn't understand."

Logan had no words to say, as the murderous rage built up inside of him. Bullies were something he never could stand. "It pisses me off to no end how people think they can just treat others like shit!"

Lola squeezed Logan's hand; a tiny action that helped to mildly soothe the justice-seeking beast within him. "After everything I have been through, I still don't understand why people think they should have control over someone else in such a destructive manner."

Logan quickly embraced Lola. He needed to feel her warmth so that he could fully calm down. Trying not to freak out, Lola patted Logan on the cheek as she playfully remarked, "Easy there, *tiger*," before giving him a friendly peck upon his cheek.

Logan made Lola a delicious and authentic Italian lasagna for dinner. As the wonderful smells permeated the room, Lola couldn't help but sigh in pleasure. "Oh my gosh, Warren! This smells fucking amazing!"

"Thank you, *my heart!*"

"I hope it tastes as good as it smells."

"It better, or my *Zio's* mother, my *nonna* would haunt me. Plus, my mom would kick my ass," Logan remarked with a chuckle.

"Who? Zio? Nonna?" Lola asked in utter confusion

"Sorry, Lola. My *Zio* is my mom's kind of adopted brother, Antonio. *Zio* is Italian for uncle; their parents were best friends. *Nonna* is Italian for grandmother. Antonio's mother, Carmella, taught this recipe to my grandmother, Dianne, and my mother, Britt; both of whom taught it to me."

After some playful conversation, Logan and Lola sat at the table, eating their meal in silence. So much information had been given, yet there were still so many holes to fill. The silence that filled the room was screaming to be spoken … to be heard … to be healed. Sadly though, silence was what it stayed.

When their dinner ended, the pair readied themselves for bed. Once in bed, Lola sadly smiled as she gazed upon Logan's face. Logan looked up through the skylight, staring into the stars. *There is so much more I want and need to know. I need to know how that bastard broke her.*

Instead of speaking, Logan gently wrapped Lola into his embrace as he kissed her head, smiling at the memory of her kissing his cheek earlier that evening. Heaviness and confusion flooded Lola's mind as she cried silent tears upon Logan's chest while drifting off to sleep.

13

Mijn Bloem

October 7, 2014

A couple of days had passed quickly, with Logan and Lola just enjoying time on the coastline and hiking through the forest behind the cabin. Having some time to clear her head, Lola felt ready to continue once more. As Lola made her way towards Logan, she took a couple of deep breaths and prayed a silent prayer for some kind of peace; talking about her first meeting with **him** never failed to make her a nervous wreck.

"Hh-hey, Logan-" Lola called with a shaky voice.

"Hey, *my heart*, what's up?"

Exhaling sharply, Lola remarked, "I am ready to continue if you want to grab a seat."

~

September 11, 2000

Lola was eagerly counting down the days leading up to the Portland trip. Since she couldn't wait to spend a whole week with her boyfriend and best friends, Lola decided to ask Cate for as many extra shifts as possible at the café; she wanted her own money and didn't want Shane feeling like he had to pay for everything for her.

After school, Lola entered the café where Cate greeted her with the biggest hug.

"Luxie, I am so glad you are here! I have the best news ever to tell you."

Laughing at her friend's overly exuberant enthusiasm, Lola replied, "Hey, Cate! What's going on?"

"Well, you know how Cade and I have been seeing each other right?"

"Yeah. How is that going by the way, with the 10-year age difference and all?"

"It's going really well, which is why I am so ecstatic," pausing for a moment, Cate continued her statement. "Ya know, I am really glad that you are supportive of my relationship with Cade, even though I'm 22 and he is 32. My father nearly lost his shit when I told him. I swear that man needs to let me be a damn adult!"

"Cate, the way I see it is this- if he treats you well and treats you right, and you are happy, then what does it hurt," Lola replied with a shrug. Bringing her hand to her chin, Lola remarked, "Anyhow, what is your exciting news?"

"Ah yes! Well, since things with Cade have been going well, he is taking me to his hometown- Vienna, Oregon- to meet his family … and most importantly … his son."

Lola was completely flabbergasted! "Cade has a son?!?"

With a nervous laugh, Cate replied, "Yeah- he's actually your age, 16."

"What the actual fuck?"

"Well, Cade got his ex pregnant when they were both 15 and their son was born right after they turned 16."

"Oh, man! That had to be really hard."

"I can't even imagine, honestly. Cade said he and his ex were married for 13 years; their parents made them choose marriage or give their baby up for adoption."

With tears in her eyes, Lola was in awe of Cade's selfless heart. Most guys would have left the girl to figure it out on her own, but he did the right thing. "What's his son's name?"

"His name is Logan Asher Warren."

"So, when are you going?"

"I actually leave in a couple of weeks."

"Umm … will you be back in time for my concert trip I told you about?"

"Of course, *sweetie*, but I will have to close the café while I am gone. You can't run this thing on your own and your schooling is the top priority."

At the mention of closing the shop, Lola was crestfallen. *Shit! What am I going to do now?*

Noticing the look of sadness upon her friend's face, Cate exclaimed, "What's wrong, *sweetie*? I thought you might enjoy some extra time off."

"I really need the money Cate … and … it's just nice to not be at home. Isn't there anything you can do?"

Thinking for a moment, an idea came to Cate. "It's a long shot, but I might be able to see if my twin brother can cover me for the time I am gone and then you won't have to miss out on any money."

Wide-eyed, Lola exclaimed, "Twin! You have a twin? I thought you were an only child this whole time."

Cate laughed heartily at Lola's remark before preening in response, "Well, dear Luxie, you know I have to keep the mystery alive."

Lola laughed in response as the two girls set off to work, in preparation for the evening customers.

~

September 12, 2000
Cate paced back and forth nervously as she awaited Lola's arrival

after school. *I wish Luxie would fill me in on what's really going on with her and her home life. I want to help her but there's nothing I really can do. Maybe this news will cheer her up, although my brother can be a major hardass.*

"Hey, Cate! How was the morning shift after I left?"

"Finallyyyyyyy," Cate jested with a flair of drama.

Lola couldn't help but shake her head and laugh. "Ya know, I always thought Lizzie was dramatic, but man, she's definitely got nothing on you."

Cate blew Lola a kiss as she replied, "What can I say, babe, it's all a part of my charm."

After a few minutes of laughter and jokes passed between the friends, Cate clapped her hands together as she exclaimed, "So, I was able to convince my brother to come down and run the shop while I am gone for two weeks. He also wants to check the books and make sure that I'm actually making a profit. Our dad is such a hardass and has said countless times, he will close this shop if I'm not making money."

"How can he do that if it's your business?"

"Oh sweetie, that's Maximillian Gallagher for you. He's the world's biggest pain in the ass, followed quite closely by my lovely twin brother."

"Yikes!"

"Eh, it is what it is. Besides, my brother wasn't always such a hardass. Dad really pushed him to graduate uni early and then there was the whole debacle with *Bunni.*"

"*Bunni?*"

"That's a tale for neither here nor there. Anyhow, let's get to work, my friend."

Cate exhaled in relief as Lola eagerly agreed to start her shift. *Oh, man! I almost royally fucked up. I can't believe I mentioned Bunni.*

~

September 26, 2000

Things had gone very well for Lola in the past two weeks, as she had been able to pick up several extra shifts. 15 minutes to close the chime on the door alerted Lola to the arrival of a new customer. As she was putting things away, Lola replied, "Welcome to **Cate's**. I'll be with you in one moment."

The customer waited a couple of minutes before making his way towards the counter where Lola was busy stocking items. Clearing his throat, he quickly caught Lola's attention. When Lola turned around to look upon the person behind her, her jaw literally dropped. The man before her was 6 feet in height; had a gorgeous natural tan complexion; jet black hair styled into a Mohawk that swooped on the side in a beautiful curl pattern. The man was adorned in various tattoos; a tight-fitted white v-neck tee underneath a denim studded vest; tight ripped black jeans; and black combat boots. He was every punk girl's dream come true.

However, the thing that captivated Lola the most was his eyes. Never in her life had she seen a pair of eyes so blue they were white. Lola knew propriety said it was rude to stare, yet she couldn't break away from the entrancing hold these eyes had upon her. Knowing she wasn't paying attention, the man called, "Excuse me?"

Stepping closer to the counter, he chuckled and stated, "Tsk tsk! Excuse me. Eyes up here, *sweetheart*."

Lola blushed as she shook her head from the trance. Sweetly she called out, "Oh! Sorry, sir. Hi and welcome to **Cate's**! How may I help you? We close up in about 10 minutes, but I'm more than happy to help."

The man spoke, in his deep, husky voice, "Black coffee. What's your name, *sweetheart*?"

Lola looked up with her bright smile and gave a chipper reply.

"Sure thing, it's coming right up." As she poured the coffee into a to-go mug and placed the lid on, Lola replied, "My name is Luxe, but most of the people around here just call me Luxie."

Thinking to himself, the man inquired with a devilish smirk, as he took the cup from her hand, his fingers grazed her delicate skin. "Tell me, *sweetheart* …"

A look of concern, mixed with slight arousal, came across her face as his fingers grazed her hand. Quickly she snatched her hand away and picked up the towel to finish cleaning. "Tell you what, sir?", she interjected.

Looking down upon her, he said, "Tell me a name that hardly anyone calls you."

At the sound of this statement, Lola's discomfort grew and she began to stutter, "Umm … well … Luxe is my middle name. I hate my first name!" The firm finality at the end of her statement caused the man to chuckle once again. He decided to step a bit closer to the side of the counter she had now moved to as she cleaned.

The man positioned himself upon the stool and slowly drank his black coffee as he watched her clean. *Black like my soul*, he thought to himself. "Tsk tsk. Tell me, *sweetheart*. It can't be that bad."

Lola breathed in and out deeply for a moment or so before finally whispering something inaudible and more to herself than anyone else.

"I'm sorry, *sweetheart*, you need to repeat that and this time where I can hear you," the man before her remarked with authority in his voice as he crossed his arms; icy orbs boring into her very soul.

Closing her eyes and breathing deeply, she replied in disgust, "Lola. My name is Lola."

Feelings of desire began to build up, on the tip of his tongue as he pulled her arm closer to him, with only the counter to separate their bodies. *Fuck! I want to take her right now. Good things come to those who wait though*, he said to himself. Whispering into Lola's ear, the man purred, "Lola. An exotic name for a goddess." The shiver that went through her tiny body did not go unnoticed.

Trying to pull away and regain control of her situation, Lola sheepishly replied, "Umm… thank you, sir. What is your name?"

Pulling Lola back closer to him, the icy-eyed man breathed into her ear once again and replied, "Jacob. Jacob Gallagher."

He chuckled as a look of horror came upon Lola's face once she realized just who he was. Pushing herself away, Lola stammered, "Jacob Gallagher?!? Are you related to Cate?"

Jacob chuckled and responded, bemused, "Yes, *sweetheart*. I'm her twin."

Just as Jacob was about to pull Lola to him once again, the voice of a young man called from the back, "Are you ready, *Mijn Bloem?*"

Lola's eyes lit up at the sight of him. Quickly, she tossed her towel on the counter and ran to the owner of the voice. "Shane!", Lola squealed with glee. "Hey, *baby*! Yes, I am. I missed you so much," Lola continued and planted a huge kiss on Shane's cheek.

Looking lustfully at his girlfriend, Shane replied, "Let's go *Mijn Bloem*. I can't wait to show you how much I missed you."

Lola giggled at this flirty banter and exclaimed, "Alright, Shay! Just let me tell Cate that I'm leaving and that her brother, Jacob, is here."

Shane responded, "Alright, *Mijn Bloem*."

As Lola made her way down the hall, Shane looked at Jacob as one would an enemy on the battlefield. With smug certainty, Shane stated matter of factly, "My girl sure is something isn't she. I can't imagine life without her."

Once Lola had informed Cate of Jacob's arrival, she and Shane exited the building, getting into their vehicles, they quickly headed back to his house to work on homework as well as have dinner with his parents; Jordan and Mona, who had just returned from an extended business trip.

~

Jordan Carson was a New York native and business mogul. Before starting **Carson Tech**, he worked worldwide rebuilding failing businesses and showing them how to maximize profits. Mona DeVries-Carson was a gorgeous lady from the Netherlands who came to the U.S. on a student visa. Mona and Jordan met in college at **NYU** and instantly fell for one another.

Although Mona spoke English, she preferred Dutch to be spoken in their home. So, to make a good impression, Lola requested that Shane begin teaching her to speak Dutch. After all, who doesn't want to impress their boyfriend's mother?

To make the language lessons interesting, Shane and Lola decided to take the rules from strip poker and apply them: If Lola pronounced a word incorrectly, she had to remove one item of clothing. Yet, if she pronounced the words correctly, Shane had to remove one item of clothing. They both agreed that neither would go past losing their undergarments, as they were not at a point in their relationship where they were quite ready to have sex; both teens valued their virginity but knew they wanted their first experience to be with each other.

When the young couple entered the Carson residence, Mona lovingly called out, *"Hoi, zoon! Hoe was je dag?* (Hi, son! How was your day?)"

"Hallo, mama! Mijn dag was geweldig! Mijn Bloem is hier voor het avondeten! (Hi, mom! My day was great! My Flower is here for dinner tonight!)"

"Oh! Je vader en ik leren eindelijk je mooie meid kennen! (Oh! Your father and I finally get to meet your beautiful girl!)"

Nervously Lola spoke up, *"Hallo, Mona! Mijn naam is Luxe. Ik ben zo blij om eindelijk jou en Jordan te ontmoeten. Ik hoop dat mijn uitspraak in orde is.* (Hello, Mona! My name is Luxe. I am so happy to meet you and Jordan. I hope my pronunciation is correct.)"

Mona looked at Shane with the biggest smile on her face and said, '*Shane! Je hebt Luxe geleerd om Nederlands te spreken?* (Shane! You have been teaching Luxe to speak Dutch?)"

Chuckling despite his nerves, Shane replied, "*Eigenlijk moeder, het was het idee van mijn bloem. Mijn bloem wilde het voor je leren, omdat ze wist hoeveel dit voor jou zou betekenen.* (Actually, mother, it was the idea of my flower. My flower wanted to learn for you, because she knew how much this would mean to you.)"

Mona was awestruck by this gesture of kindness, for not too many girls would have been willing to learn her native tongue. Quickly smoothing out her navy blue pencil skirt, Mona hurried everyone into the kitchen before heading up the stairs to retrieve Andy from his room.

Mona decided to serve a traditional Dutch meal called Stamppot followed by Poffertjes for dessert. The conversation was lively and Lola tried to follow along as best as she could. When she needed help, Shane happily translated back and forth. After the meal, Shane went to talk with his dad while Lola offered to help Mona clean up the dishes.

Mona turned to Lola and spoke in English, "Sweet Luxe, you're the first girl my Shane has ever brought home. Thank you so much for learning Dutch. Not many would try."

Blushing deeply, Lola said, "Thank you so much for welcoming me into your home, Mona. Please call me Luxie. I am honored to learn Dutch. Shay is so special to me and I would do anything to make him happy."

"Darling, do you love my son?"

Lola nervously rubbed the back of her neck, as she murmured,

"Well, we haven't been together very long …"

Mona laughed as she cut Lola off. "Oh, *schat* (darling)! I know those eyes and that look. It's the same look when I met Jordan. You do love him and I can't think of a better girl to become my future *dochter* (daughter)!"

Lola blushed in deep admiration, "I do love Shay very much, but I am afraid to say it because he may think it too soon and get scared away."

"I know my son. He loves you and will tell you soon in his way and time."

Once Lola and Mona had finished cleaning everything, Lola and Shane retired to Shane's room where they studied for a little bit and kissed quite a lot. Before they knew it, it was time for Lola to head home. As the pair stood in Shane's driveway, Lola's heart fell. *Oh, how I wish Lizzie was home. I hate walking into hell.*

Noticing the look upon Lola's face, Shane asked, "What's wrong, *Mijn Bloem?*"

Releasing an exacerbated sigh, Lola stated, "Honestly, I'm scared to go home. I'm scared that Anne-Marie will be drunk."

Shane closed his eyes as he silently prayed for God to protect his precious flower.

"I swear, it's like she has some kind of fucking radar telling her that I had a good day. That way she can make my life as shitty as hers!"

Lola broke down as the emotional weight overtook her. Shane lovingly embraced Lola as he said, "Listen, *Mijn Bloem*! Breath!"

Noticing Lola had taken several deep breaths, Shane lovingly kissed her forehead. "I will protect you. You are mine. We will get you out of there soon. Have you given any more thought to moving back to Swan Manor?"

Through frustrated tears, Lola replied, "I need to, but with the trust in place, there isn't much I can do. I'm scared one day Anne-Marie's rage will bring her to the point of killing me. I am so scared to live there."

Shane kissed Lola's forehead once more as he dried her tears. When Lola was safely in her car, Shane stated with an affirming tone, "Don't worry, *Mijn Bloem*. I will figure something out. I promise."

~

On the drive home, Lola's mind was plagued with heavy thoughts. *Is mom awake? Hell, is she even sober? Or is she going to be drunk and violent? My God! I can't take this life of uncertainty...the weight of it all is simply too much to bear.*

Pulling in the drive, Lola killed the engine and made her way to the front door. *No sense in delaying the inevitable.*

Once Lola opened the door, she was greeted by the overwhelming smell of vomit, trash, and booze. A loud crash in the background told Lola she had a night of **hell** awaiting her.

"About time you come home, you fucking slut," Anne-Marie spat the venomous words out as a king cobra would, rendering its prey paralyzed.

Inhaling to maintain what little composure she had, Lola greeted, "Hey, mom-" before defending herself to the best of her ability. "First off, please stop calling me a slut. I'm still a damn virgin for crying out loud! Secondly, I **told you** that Shane and I would be working on our project at his house and having dinner there so I could finally meet his parents."

"Don't you fucking tell me what you are, you ungrateful bitch!"

Years of rage and hatred expelled from Anne-Marie's mouth like an exercised demon, as she hurled her empty beer bottle; which careened directly with the side of Lola's head.

Grasping her head in pain, Lola refused to let her mother have the satisfaction of seeing her cry. Lola swiftly moved to her bathroom, where she proceeded to survey the damage caused by the impact of the glass bottle. *Oh god! She broke the skin and it's fucking swollen. How the hell am I supposed to cover this shit up?* **Fuck!** *Why can't I catch a damn break?*

Angrily, Lola turned on her radio, where DJ Samantha's calming voice flooded the bathroom as Lola started her shower.

"Hey there, Oregon lovers! DJ Samantha here with a little throwback to 1995 with *Don't Speak!*, by **No Doubt** after a quick word from our sponsors."

With the music drowning out the sound of her tears, Lola tried to let the hurt leave her body. As the hot water soothed some of her stress, Lola did her best to remain calm as she started shaving her legs. The sound of several glasses smashing against a wall in the kitchen overpowered Lola's music, startling her. The swift jerk of her hand caused Lola to cut her thigh; the pain mixed feelings within her.

As Lola watched the blood drip down her leg, she breathed a sigh of relief. *Finally...just a little ounce of freedom. Wait! What kind of messed up shit am I thinking? I know I shouldn't find comfort, but it sure as hell makes this easier than carrying all the pain inside.* Lola battled the inner voice, shaking the detrimental thoughts from her head before ending her shower and trying to find solace in sleep.

14

Sweet Release

October 9, 2014

After telling Logan about cutting her leg in the shower, Lola felt it was best to wait a couple of days before continuing on. Two days later, she still found herself lamenting over the dismally, slow pace this tale was taking.

"Logan, I know it's probably pretty annoying waiting forever on a fuck up like me. I'm sorry that I'm so damaged. I mean, what do you even see in me that is worth sticking around?"

Drawing Lola close to him, before placing his arms around her neck and gazing into her forest green eyes, Logan smiled as he exclaimed, "Lola- *my heart*- like I told you a month ago, I would wait forever for you to tell me everything. Sure, I **had** a life before you, but hell, I wasn't even living. After knowing you and loving you, *baby* … you set my world on fire."

With a blush warming her fair, rose skin, Lola quickly closed her eyes and gasped as she felt a gentle kiss upon the top of her head. "*My heart*, why don't you relax on the bed while I bring us some apple cider and start the fireplace. If you want to continue on, I am ready to listen; if not, I will continue doing some work. Sound like a plan?" Logan thoughtfully asked.

"You know, I'd like that a lot."

Fifteen minutes later, Logan joined Lola on the bed in the master suite of his cabin, with fresh, hot apple cider in hand. Lola took the mug and slowly inhaled the comforting cinnamon aroma. "I really appreciate your patience, and if you're sure you're fine with listening, I am okay to go on ahead."

~

September 27, 2000

After her shower, Lola did her best to doctor up her leg before falling asleep. However, sleep would avoid her completely. Shaking the restlessness from her brain, Lola decided that it was best to just go ahead and awaken for the day. Glancing at her alarm clock, she read the mocking numbers **4:00 a.m.** and threw off her blankets. Quickly pressing her feet to the floor, Lola groaned in agony as a sharp pain went through her leg. The memories of what occurred after she came home quickly slapped her in the face; Lola shuddered at the thought of the small amount of relief she felt as the blood dripped down her leg.

While doctoring both her head and her leg, Lola did her best to focus on the one single joy she had at the moment ... her upcoming trip to Portland for the concert. *I am so thankful Cate is giving me so many extra hours. I just really hope she told Jacob that I would be coming in to help him.*

Once her leg was re-bandaged, Lola quickly slapped on some concealer, as she tried to hide the bruising near her hairline from her mother's assault the night before. With the remainder of her make-up in place, Lola searched in her closet for something that would not only cover the bandaging but also keep unnecessary pressure from being applied. As she surveyed her options, Lola was very thankful that she rarely wore jeans. Ten minutes of searching later,

Lola decided that the best she could do was a pair of hole-filled black tights (thankfully they were designer, with strategic holes which just so happened to not have any on the upper thigh area of the left leg), which she paired with a belted blue and white mini skater dress; to complete the look, Lola opted for a pair of gunmetal grey high heeled combat boots which had small silver studs adorning them, a dark blue moto jacket, purple leather bracelet, and three-star choker.

~

When Lola arrived at the café, she saw some of the lights were already on and figured that Jacob had decided to go ahead and try to open up on his own. Lola yawned as she shook the sleep from her weary head and unlocked the door; stepping inside she called out, "Good morning Jacob, it's Luxie", before heading to the bathroom to double-check the side of her head. Although her reflection showed that the bruising was covered to the unsuspecting eye, Lola felt as if it were a scarlet letter announcing her wretched life to the world.

Back in the dining area, Lola started brewing three pots of coffee and set up the plates in the display case. When the first pot of coffee had finished, Lola poured a cup for herself and Jacob before heading into the kitchen. Upon entering the kitchen, Lola couldn't help but laugh at the sight of the tall, muscular, tattooed man before her who appeared to be stumped by Cate's muffin recipe. Hearing the sweet, silky laughter behind him, Jacob turned around and remarked with a flirtatious wink, "Hey, *sweetheart*! I didn't expect you in until after school."

The sultry sound of Jacob's voice, in conjunction with his enigmatic gaze, caused a warm blush to rise in Lola's fair rose-colored face. "H-hey. Uh … yeah. I guess Cate forgot to tell you that I have been coming in before school to get extra hours."

"Mind telling me why you need extra hours?"

"Not at all," Lola said with excitement in her voice, "My boyfriend, some friends, and I are all going to this big rock concert up in Portland, at **The Mad King**, in a few weeks. We will be staying a full week and I will need extra money for shopping and stuff. Ya know?"

With a devilish smirk and the need to get a rise out of the little vixen before him, Jacob retorted, "I figured a sweet young thing like you would just ask mommy and daddy for the money. I mean if you are anything like Catarina, it's the typical go-to move."

This statement caused a fire to burn in Lola's deep green eyes, thus causing arousal within Jacob. The brevity in her statement made his dick rise in ecstasy. He loved the fire in her and knew he had to use this to his advantage. Lola snapped. "I don't know who the fuck you think you are, but you don't know my life!"

As soon as the words left Lola's mouth, she instantly regretted them. The events from the night before had taken their toll on her. This normally sweet-natured girl had reached a small breaking point. Tears filled her eyes as she realized her stupidity for yelling at her boss. "Jacob, I am so sorry. I shouldn't have snapped at you. I am so sorry, sir! Please don't fire me. I really need this job. I had a bad night and didn't sleep well," Lola pleaded.

Watching the tears stream down Lola's face, Jacob thought to himself, *Way to be a fuck up. Although, this can work to my advantage.* Looking into Lola's sorry eyes, Jacob replied, "'Look at me, *sweetheart*! I'm sorry. I shouldn't have assumed anything."

Lola quickly wiped her eyes and breathed a sigh of relief, as she exclaimed, "It's fine. I'm fine … I'm fine. Thanks for apologizing though."

Not wanting the conversation to end, Jacob felt the need to press a bit further. "So, *sweetheart*, did that boyfriend of yours make your night shitty?"

At the mention of this question, Lola started laughing. "Are you talking about Shane? Heaven's no! Shane is amazing and perfect." After settling herself, Lola quickly stated, "I just don't want to talk about it."

Moving a step closer, Jacob breathily replied, "Okay, Lola."

At the mention of her name, Lola began to feel flustered, a mixture that was both sexual and annoyance in nature. Thus causing her to state, in an almost begging tone, "Ugh…please don't call me that name. Call me Luxie, please!"

The sound of her begging voice nearly sent Jacob over the edge. *Fuck, fuck, fuck. I need to bend her tight little ass over this counter now.* Shaking his head from his thoughts for the second time, Jacob devilishly smirked, and noticed that this smirk seemed to have an effect on the vixen before him. "Well, you see, *sweetheart*, that's the thing I **will** call you Lola. I am the boss after all and you owe me."

In annoyance, Lola rolled her eyes and stated, "**Fine**!"

Moving to where he was now directly in front of Lola, Jacob said, "I'm sorry sweetheart, but fine what?"

Lola nervously spoke, "Fine, **boss**! You can call me Lola."

The sound of Lola's words were magical and melodious to Jacob's ears. This was the girl he had been waiting for. *So beautiful. So sweet. So innocent. I can't wait to feel you break, my little vixen.* Jacob placed a hand under Lola's chin, so as to bring her forest green eyes into his icy gaze. "That's a good girl, *sweetheart*."

Placing a kiss on Lola's forehead, Jacob told Lola to start on the muffins. As Jacob left the kitchen, he made sure to snap a picture of Lola bent over to grab a bowl, ass straight up in the air. *This will come in handy later tonight.*

~

At 6:45 a.m., the door chimed and Lola's eyes lit up with joy. "Shane! Good morning, *baby*," Lola called out.

Anger seethed through Jacob as he saw this blonde boy touching

his vixen. *That stupid son of a bitch will regret ever touching her.* As Lola and Shane began to leave for school, Lola quickly turned back. "Bye, Jacob. I'll see you after school. I'll show you how to do all of the closing stuff, too."

Giving Lola a wink, Jacob replied, "Sure thing, *sweetheart*. I'll be waiting."

~

When Shane and Lola parked their cars in the lot reserved for juniors, Shane quickly embraced Lola in a deep hug. His gut told him something was bothering Lola, whether she would admit it or not, was the question. Mark and Lizzie had arrived shortly after, to which Shane asked Andy if he would walk in with them so that he could talk with Lola before the morning bell rang.

"*Mijn Bloem*, are you okay today? Also, how long is that creep going to be here?"

Sighing heavily, Lola responded, "I'm fine Shay. I just didn't sleep well last night. Mom was … well … mom. Don't tell Lizzie though, I really don't need her up in my shit today. I know she cares, and I fucking love her for it, but I'm too tired to deal with *momma bear.*"

With a deep yawn and rub of her eyes, Lola continued, "And Jacob is only going to be here until Cate comes back from Vienna. Besides, he seems harmless. Everything'll be fine, you'll see."

"*Ik heb hem naar je kont zien staren!* (I saw him staring at your ass!)"

"*Shay, Schat, je hoeft je nergens zorgen over te maken. Ik hou van je met heel mijn ziel.* (Shay, honey, you have nothing to worry about. I care for you with all of my soul.)"

"*Ik vertrouw je mijn bloem. Hij ben het die ik niet vertrouw. Als u echter zegt dat alles in orde is, zal ik uw woord op prijs stellen.* (I trust you, my flower. It is him that I do not trust. However, if you say that everything is fine then, I will take your word.)"

Kissing Lola passionately upon her lips, Shane wrapped his arm around her shoulders as they made their way into the school building.

~

The school day dragged on for Lola, who was barely able to keep her eyes open. *Ugh...I wish I would have brought another coffee with me.* Allowing her head to rest on her left hand which was propped up on her desk, Lola finally succumbed to the sleep she so desperately needed.

"Miss Swan."

"Miss Swan! If you do not wake up right this instant, you will need to leave my class."

Lola jolted awake at the sound of her name being called and laughter surrounding her. "Sorry, Mr. Mayweather. What was the question?"

"Miss Swan, this is AP American History, not a nap center. If you can't handle the course work then you need to leave."

"My apologies, Mr. Mayweather. It won't happen again, I promise."

Lola hung her head in embarrassment, as this was the first time she had ever fallen asleep in class. *What the hell was I thinking? Taking seven AP classes while working. Well, it would also help if I had a mother who gave a damn about me. Instead, she's a cold-hearted bitch. Life just keeps shitting on me.*

Feeling a slight throbbing in the side of her head, Lola instantly recalled the altercation with her mother the night before. Anger seethed throughout Lola's body as she dug her fingernails into her palms hard enough to draw blood. The sensation of her skin breaking was painful, but the warm liquid upon her nails caused Lola to exhale in relief. *That wasn't so bad ... in fact, it was such a sweet release. I feel better. This is fine ... I'm fine ... I. AM. FINE.*

~

The school day dragged on for Lola until the last bell finally sounded, allowing her to head to work; the place that had quickly become her safe haven.

Finally, at 4:00 p.m., the bubbly redhead entered the shop and lovingly greeted every guest. Preoccupied at the register, Lola playfully greeted Jacob with a wink, "Hey, **boss**!"

As Lola greeted him, Jacob's thoughts instantly turned sexual as he stared at Lola's sweet, luscious pink lips. *Fuck me now! The things I would do with that mouth. She should definitely do as the tattoo says, and give Daddy a kiss.* Jacob returned the greeting with a sexy, lust-filled wink, "Glad you're back, *sweetheart.*"

The shift ran smoothly and closing time quickly arrived. Lola cheerfully walked Jacob through each task, then headed to do her own work in the lobby. Once Lola had completed her tasks, she walked back to the office to let Jacob know she was leaving for the night. As she approached, Lola saw Jacob standing in the office shirtless and only in his boxers, ready to change into basketball shorts for the night. Having yet to see a fully grown man nearly naked (she had seen Shane in his boxers from their language lessons, but this ... this was something more), Lola's heart began to flutter and she was truly speechless.

Sensing Lola's arrival and sudden arousal at the sight of his body, Jacob chuckled and stated with a wink, "Come on in, *sweetheart*. I only bite when you ask me to."

Hesitantly and a bit nervously, Lola slowly made her way into the office. Jacob walked over to Lola and grabbed her tiny hand; thus leading her directly in front of the desk. Placing one strong hand on Lola's waist and the other on her cheek, Jacob looked into Lola's eyes. The gaze was so intense, Lola tried to look away but the icy orbs enchanted her.

With Lola entranced, Jacob took this moment to lean in close enough to Lola's face; his lips mere millimeters from her, "Tell me, *sweetheart*, what brings you in my office?"

At this moment, Lola couldn't breathe or speak. Everything felt so wrong, so right, and like her nether regions were ablaze. With no words coming from Lola's mouth, Jacob brought his lips close enough to gently graze against hers; while pressing her back further onto the desk. Again Jacob asked, "Now, now little *Vixen*, what brings you in my office?"

Lola was completely at a loss as to what she should do. She knew she should answer, but answering with Jacob's lips so dangerously close would lead her to kiss him. The thought of kissing him both pained and intrigued her heart. She loved Shane so much, but also knew that she could not deny the fact that Jacob's mere presence caused a stirring in her body, that was made known to Lola by the fact that her panties were now damp and clinging to her heated core. Unable to stand the icy gaze any longer, Lola closed her eyes and exhaled gently.

The gentle breath reverberated against Jacob's lips and sent a pulse through his body, straight to his already aroused member. *Fuck! Why doesn't she just surrender to me now? I've never had to work so fucking hard in my entire life for a damn kiss. I blame that blonde bastard she's with. I'm glad I have that picture from earlier because my balls are fucking blue.* Unable to restrain his lust and hunger any longer, Jacob forcefully smashed his lips to Lola's, devouring them like a lynx on a fox. Lola was so caught off guard that she did not hesitate for even an instant to return Jacob's kiss.

Swiftly, Jacob moved his experienced lips down Lola's neck and collar bone, while laying Lola completely flat on top of the desk. As a moan escaped Lola's lips, her cellphone ringing in the background, became her saving grace. The ringing caused Lola to quickly come to her senses and realize the grievous mistake she was making. The longer the phone rang, the angrier Jacob became. *This fucking close. Damn it to hell!* Jacob's annoyance overtook him as he snapped at Lola. "Are you fucking stupid? Answer your damn phone right now."

Completely dumbfounded by Jacob's sudden change in tone, Lola made her way to her phone. Uneasily she answered, "Hello?"

The masculine voice on the other end responded in relief. "Oh thank God, *Mijn Bloem*! I was getting worried. Are you okay?"

Blushing deeply, Lola responded, "I'm sorry, Shane. Jacob and I were finishing up some cleaning and I misplaced my phone. I'll be home soon. Okay?"

As Jacob listened to the conversation, his jaw clenched. *Of course, that son of a bitch calls.* Guilt filled Lola's face when she responded to the inaudible voice on Jacob's end, "I know, *baby*. I know. It's just for a week or two, I promise. Then, it'll be us, well us and our friends in Portland." A blush filled Lola's face as she giggled, "You know I'll make it up to you, Shay. Let me get off here and I'll call you when I get home. I love you."

Not even turning to look at Jacob or tell him goodbye, Lola hastily made her way out of the main door and into the parking lot. Opening the door to her 1967 Cherry Red **Ford Mustang**, Lola swiftly entered, turned the key, and drove off down the road.

As Jacob watched Lola leave, he returned once more to his thoughts. *Oh, my sweet little vixen. I shall enjoy hunting you. Just you wait, little one, we are in this for the long haul.* Jacob turned heel to the bathroom, where he pulled out the picture he had snapped of Lola; to this, he pleasured himself at the mere thought of taking her, ass up in the air whilst begging him for more, as he imagined himself pounding into her unmercilessly.

~

Arriving home, Lola was relieved to find Anne-Marie's car gone.

She quickly headed up to her room where she changed into some lounge shorts and a camisole then checked her leg. Seated on her bed, Lola decided to give Shane a call before starting her homework; pushing the wave of guilt to the back of her mind.

15

A Glimmer of Joy

October 10, 2014

To say Logan was astounded, was an understatement; in fact, he was seething and felt a rage burning within him that he hadn't felt since his last altercation with Dean 14 years ago. Placing his hand upon his chest, Logan closed his eyes and breathed deeply for several moments, with the hopes of soothing his rage.

Looking upon Logan's face, Lola instantly felt plagued with guilt. Closing her eyes, Lola presses her nails into her palms, once again feeling the comfort in pain. "I'm sorry … I know how much you hate Jacob…I can stop now and just not tell you anymore if that would be easier?"

Watching the tears slowly fall down Lola's lightly flushed cheeks, Logan gingerly lifted her chin, before placing a delicate kiss upon her forehead. "*My heart* … yes, I hate that sick bastard with a burning passion, but I promised you, that no matter what, I would listen. Although, at this point, I think it would be a good idea for both of us to take a break for a day or so. Yeah?"

Giggling to herself, Lola playfully teased, "It's like you can read my mind, Warren."

"Of course, I can, *babe*. It's one of my superpowers."

Yawning deeply, Lola excused herself from the room to get ready for bed. Once she was settled in, Logan pulled Lola close, ensuring she was engulfed in the safety of his being.

As soon as Lola had entered a deep sleep, Logan quickly threw on some clothes, grabbed his camera, and left a note for Lola.

My precious heart,
I've gone for a quick drive to get a few nature
photos. Don't worry though, I should be back before
you wake up. I love you always and forever. -Logan

~

Sunrise had always been Logan's favorite time of day to capture nature shots; there was such a deep serenity being the only one to witness the dawning of a new day. Although he was beyond exhausted, Logan knew for his sake, as well as Lola's, he had to clear his head. If he allowed his anger to come out, any progress he and Lola had made would fizzle away. Thankfully, the next town over was only a thirty-minute drive and he would be able to have some cell service. *I guess I should give Zio a call, even though I am sure he's tired of hearing me bitch and moan. No one really understands and pretty much everyone thinks I am stupid for **Loving Lola**, but God, I swear I would stop if I could. Yet, somehow I can't.*

~

Immediately upon parking his car, Logan bolted out the door, needing to feel the fresh early morning autumn air around him. With his nerves on high alert, he wished for once in his life he were a smoker. *Just something to calm me down. Hopefully, Zio answers and doesn't give me shit. Oh lord, I hope he doesn't tell mom I am calling about the bane of her existence...Lola.*

"Come on … come on … pick up. Fuck!"

Just as Logan was losing hope, a very groggy and gruff voice answered the line.

"*Nipote*? Is everything alright?"

Rolling his eyes, Logan playfully remarked, "Of course it is. Can't I just call you to chat?"

A hearty laugh answered Logan as Antonio made his way out of his bedroom. "Logan, you forget how well I know you. You and I only call each other at 2:30 A.M. when something is bothering us."

Sighing in defeat Logan stated, "I'm that transparent, huh?"

"I wouldn't say that. I've just known you since you were born, it's my job as the best and favorite *Zio* to know when you need to get something off your chest."

With his voice breaking, in both hurt and anger, Logan decided to go ahead and let vulnerability manifest itself as it should. "So, I know I told you about Lola being back … and please, for the love of God, do **not** tell mom I am talking to you about her."

Pausing for a minute and taking Antonio's silence as confirmation this call was solely between them, Logan continued. "Well … she told me something new tonight and I am seriously on the verge of losing my shit and ripping a mother fucker to shreds! I am beyond pissed, *Zio* … like the level of pissed I was when I cleaned Dean's clock."

"Breathe for a moment, Logan. Have you taken some time to process this information by yourself?"

"That's why I am calling you; 'cause if I'm left alone with this anger that is building, I'm going to fucking lose it and then everything will have gone to hell with where Lola and I are right now."

"I'm glad you called me, and I hope you don't ever fear waking me. Do not let this anger consume you. Trust me, I know how hard it is. Is there anything that she told you that is particularly bothering you?"

"She told me that bastard, Jacob, started harassing her when she was 16! The shit he put her through and how he tormented not only her mind and body. I mean, in just four years, Eloise will be the same age as what Lola was when that son of a bitch took advantage of her. I know, they didn't have sex at that point, but my god! I swear, *Zio*, I want to hunt this mother fucker down and cut his balls off before putting a bullet in his brain. And don't even get me started on her mother …"

Antonio had to take a deep breath before replying. The rage his nephew was feeling was so strong, and he was having a hard time keeping the anger down himself. He hated men that took advantage of adolescent girls. "Now that, *mio nipote*, is a true monster. Just remind yourself that he's gone, that she's safe, and she's with you. While I'd love to make your wish come true, you and I both know your mother would kill the both of us," He did his best to add a sliver of humor in an attempt to help Logan ease his mind. "Do you have your guitar or camera with you?"

"You know, I could say that it would be worth it for mom to murder me, but … then Lola would be left alone … so … Fuck! Sometimes being noble sucks balls. Anyhow, when I see the deep scars on her sides where that asshole bit her repeatedly over the years, I just … I don't know. I want her to know she is beautiful, but how do I handle this shit, when it makes me so fucking angry?"

Pausing once again to regain his composure, Logan stated, "Yeah … I have my camera. Lola doesn't know I am musically gifted."

Sighing, Antonio did his best to think of something to say, but he was at a loss. "You know I'm a blunt man, *sí*? Can I be blunt with you?"

"Always. You wouldn't be my *Zio* if you sugar-coated things."

Antonio chuckled before responding. "Lola is still very much healing. I think you've mentioned before that she is telling you her story, and by the sounds of it she is nowhere near being done. I know that you want her to know how beautiful she is … but when someone is still healing like that, it takes time for their walls to come down. When the time is right, you can show her by loving every inch of her, and being tender with the scars where she was once brought pain. It is going to take you a lot of patience, but you can do it. Meanwhile, use your camera to take pictures of things that Lola finds beautiful."

"Thank you, *Zio*, I mean it. You have bailed me out more times than I can even begin to comprehend. I really would be lost without you."

"You never have to thank me. I'll always be here for you. I love you," Antonio shrugged and then rolled his eyes realizing that Logan couldn't see him.

"I love you too, *Zio*. Now go get back to bed for *Zia* has both our heads!"

Belting out his throaty laugh once more, Antonio bid his nephew goodnight and hung up the phone.

~

Just after hanging up the phone, Logan let the last of his angry tears fall. *Now is not the time to lose your shit, Zio is right.* Once he had regained composure, Logan walked down a small path a few yards from his car, to look for the perfect sunrise images. For his hope was to have enough time to develop the film before Lola awoke.

Satisfied with the images he had been able to capture, Logan returned his camera to his car before going to make a few purchases from the shops in the little town. Convinced he had purchased everything to surprise Lola with a nice breakfast, Logan entered his car once again and made the short journey back to the cabin.

Much to his relief, Lola was still sleeping soundly as he quietly placed his purchases upon the counter before taking both his coffee and camera to the darkroom; when Logan showed an interest in photography as a teenager, Cade built a small addition onto the cabin, which housed all of Logan's photography supplies. In the city, Logan used a digital camera, but when he had the chance to focus on the natural beauty Oregon had to offer, nothing replaced the dynamic of film.

Although he had taken several shots, two, in particular, stuck out to him as ones that would give the love of his heart a glimmer of joy. Being awake for over twenty-four hours was beginning to take its toll on Logan, but he pushed on preparing the breakfast for Lola and him to enjoy. *Sleep can wait, the light glowing in her eyes, even for a moment, cannot.* With everything placed on the tray, Logan made his way into the bedroom.

~

Sensing the warm sunshine upon her face, Lola awoke only to feel slightly chilled and was quite surprised to find that Logan was nowhere in sight. Looking around the room in a bit of panic, Lola found the note and exhaled notably in relief. Taking a moment to relieve herself in the adjoining bathroom, Lola walked back to the bed, where she made note of her sleep in the journal Dr. Indigo had requested she keep since she would be outside of cellular service.

While Lola made her notes, Logan walked into the room and was surprised to find her awake.

"I must say, God has blessed me with the most beautiful view, not once but twice this morning," Logan beamed flirtatiously.

Lola couldn't help but chuckle, "I saw your note. So tell me, how did the photo session go?"

"Why tell you, when I can show you?"

Walking over to Lola, Logan held the photographs behind his back, "Close your eyes, *my heart!*"

Adhering to Logan's request, Lola playfully retorted, "Fine Warren, but your sweet, ginger ass better be feeding me before I starve to death."

"Don't get your panties in a twist, woman! You'll get food after the surprise; then, I need to sleep and would like it if you could rest beside me…maybe even read me a little bit of **_The Raven's Song_**."

Beaming behind closed eyes, Lola's heart savored a small bit of joy that Logan would want to take an interest in the only book that had helped her through her struggles in the last two years. "Sounds like a plan, Warren, now hurry before I say 'fuck you' and just go straight for the food."

Trying not to let his hormones put a foot in his mouth, Logan walked over to the bed, where he placed the pictures on Lola's lap. "Okay, _babe_! Open your eyes."

As Lola opened her eyes, the sight before her left her in complete awe. "Logan," Lola breathed out, "these are the most stunning images I have seen in my entire life. The way you captured the fog in the mountains melding with the tree line. Are those fir trees? Also, the way everything reflects into the water? I swear it looks like a painting in a way. And, where did you manage to find poppies?"

Yawning as he brought the food over to the bed, Logan told Lola about his early morning excursion, ensuring he left out the conversation with Antonio. Once their meal was finished, Logan stripped down to his boxers before snuggling into the one who gave his very soul a reason for being; letting her comforting scent encompass him and finally bring the peace he needed.

Picking up her copy of **_The Raven's Song_**, Lola began, "_Through a misty haze, in an eclipsed and overshadowed land, lay the realm of Corvus Corax; home to the Dark Elves. All was calm and peaceful in Corvus Corax until a deafening and vehement scream rang through the entirety of the land._"

Listening to Lola's delicate voice, Logan blissfully drifted off to sleep.

16

The Quiet Things

October 11, 2014

After a somewhat restful night, Lola awoke from her slumber; readied herself for the day, and went out to prepare breakfast. Turning to exit, Lola looked over at Logan, and thought to herself, as a warm feeling began to fill her chest. *Why does he have to love me so? Why can't he just leave like everyone else? I'm okay with being alone because loneliness means I won't get or cause hurt.* With a melancholy expression now etched upon her face, Lola left the room.

~

Logan awoke, as his stomach grumbled, to the smell of French toast. Quickly dressing, Logan left the room and headed to the cabin's kitchen; he stopped short when he saw his love finishing breakfast preparation. Lola was stunning no matter what she wore; but this, the slightly messy hair pulled up haphazardly and casual clothes with no makeup on, was when she was the most gorgeous thing he had ever seen.

Logan walked over to Lola, placed his hands on her hips, as he gently kissed the back of her head and neck. Lola laughed as Logan's lips tickled her neck. In a laughter-filled voice, Lola said, "Well good morning to you too, Mr. Warren! Are you hungry?"

Logan looked at Lola lustfully and said, "I am hungry for something, alright, but I guess French toast shall suffice."

Lola looked away as she felt her face grow hot with blushing and her body shudder. Gathering her composure once more, Lola said, "Let's sit at the table and eat. Afterward, I will tell you what happened the day Cate and your dad came back, as well as what happened at the concert."

Chuckling, Logan remarked, "If it's the concert I'm thinking of, my friends and I were there."

"Huh?! No way! What are the odds?"

Logan brought Lola's hand to his lips and delicately kissed each small finger. Biting her lip to help her remain calm, Lola cleared her throat before continuing once more.

~

October 3, 2000

Lola awoke with a sudden start; a mixture of dread and elation flooded her soul. "One last day with Jacob … you can make it. Thankfully, by the time I'm out of school, Cate'll be back," Lola encouraged herself as she searched through her closet for anything to cover her legs. Between the double-whammy of her mother and Jacob, Lola's palms and thighs bore the brunt of her anxiety. Finally settling upon a pair of deep blue high-waisted skinny jeans that were embellished with black splatters; a white mock neck three-quarter sleeve shirt, which cropped at the waist; a chain bracelet with light blue studs; and a pair black wedged espadrilles with satin ribbons. After a quick once over to tame her curls and some light makeup to bring life back into her face, Lola drove to the café for her morning cup of torment.

~

After school, Lola was relieved to find Cate's Land Rover parked outside the café; tears of joy streamed down her face. *Whoever answers prayers, thank you for bringing Cate back.* Checking her makeup in the rearview mirror, Lola fixed the splotches from her tears before walking inside.

"**Luxie**," Cate squealed in delight as she ran over and quickly embraced the teen girl.

Lola laughed as she returned her friend's affections; it was a relief to feel a touch of compassion. "Hey, Cate! I am so glad you are back."

Grasping Lola's hand, Cate led her to a back table where she had two orange-cranberry scones and two steaming cups of apple cinnamon chai tea awaiting them. "I have so much to tell you," Cate began before she was cut off.

"Lola, I need to talk to you in the office" Jacob called out, with a stern expression upon his face.

The sound of Jacob's voice made Lola's expression switch from joy to fear. Noticing this change in her friend's face, Cate gripped Lola's hand before turning to Jacob. "Brother, what did I tell you before I left!"

"Chill the fuck out, *Catarina*! I just need to give Lola her paycheck."

"Fine, but if I find out you have been harsh to her in any way, I swear to God, I will make due on that promise!"

Nervously, Lola removed her hand from Cate's before following Jacob into the office. As soon as both parties were inside the office, Jacob closed and locked the door. Simultaneously, he grasped both of Lola's arms in one hand, holding them above her head. Heart beating at a pace to rival a hummingbird, Lola let her tears fall as erratic thoughts flooded her mind. *Why God?! Why do you hate me? What did I do to deserve this?*

Gazing up into Jacob's eyes, Lola saw a burning passion that ignited terror and curiosity within her spirit. In a sultry and authoritative voice, Jacob stated, "You will *not* tell my sister about any of our interactions. Am.I.Clear?"

With what little defiance she could muster, Lola sarcastically retorted, "Fuck you, Jacob!"

Hearing his little vixen grow some courage, Jacob could barely contain himself, as he pressed harder against Lola's arms while leaning into her ear. "Tsk tsk, *sweetheart.* Why don't we try this again?"

Grimacing in pain, Lola breathed out, "Y-yes, sir."

As soon as those words departed Lola's lips, Jacob ravaged her neck; causing Lola's breath to shudder. Bringing himself to her ear once more, Jacob chuckled darkly as he retorted, "I can't wait to fucking tear you apart," before capturing her lips one last time. Upon releasing her, Jacob walked over to the desk, grabbed Lola's paycheck, and placed it into her hands.

Lola left the office not knowing what to think. Stopping in the bathroom to fix her face once more, Lola finally opened her paycheck; eyes bulging at the sum. Jacob had written a check out to her for **two-thousand dollars.** While she was grateful for the money, at what cost did it come? Folding the check and placing it in her back pocket, Lola squeezed her nails into her palms once more; the burning sensation bringing her much-needed relief.

Dark thoughts took over her mind once more. *Mother was right...I truly am nothing but a slut. Shane can't ever know...he's perfect.* Jacob's voice soon filled her thoughts, along with her own, **Remember, sweetheart, perfect can't handle 'messy'. You and I are the same after all. Just look at your hands! Only I would ever find the beauty in your darkness!**

Feeling the warm liquid surrounding her nails, Lola broke from her thoughts as she gasped in horror at what she had once again succumbed to. Cleaning her palms as gently as possible, Lola made her way back to Cate.

"Hey, girl! I was just about to come and look for you. Jacob wasn't a hardass to you was he?"

Lola contemplated Cate's query; on one hand, she felt she should tell Cate what happened while she was gone, but on the other fear and a secret desire for the darkness within the man who tormented her said she should remain quiet. In the end, the latter option won. Laughing nervously, Lola remarked, "N-no! Sorry, he was just telling me that I did a great job and thanked me for my patience in teaching him about the café. Then I had to pee; turns out I just started my period- thank god for keeping a tampon on hand."

Better judgment tried to tell Cate that something was amiss with her friend's words, however, she dismissed it. "Okay, sweet Luxie. You'd tell me if Jacob was a hardass, right?"

"Trust me, Cate, it's nothing I can't handle. He was fine. I'm fine. I'm fine. Okay?" Lola hated just how easily the lies came to her.

"You sure?"

"Y-yeah … it's just nerves, I guess."

"What's got you nervous, *sweetie*?"

Exhaling in relief that Cate bought her lie and never pushed for the truth, Lola explained, "Well … this is going to be my first trip away with Shane and …"

"And what? Don't just leave me hangin', girl!"

"… and well, I'm beyond nervous. What if he wants to take things to the next level and I'm not ready? What if I'm ready and he's not? What if I give him to myself and he regrets everything? What if …"

Cate looked at Lola with a loving, sisterly expression, "Oh, sweet Luxie. I have seen the way that boy looks at you. You are *literally* his entire world and his everything."

"Really? I mean he's perfect and I'm … well, I'm me."

"Luxie, look at me! Don't ever sell yourself short. You are such a blessing to everyone who meets you. At the end of the day, no one is perfect, so don't fret, sweet one. I can promise you that this trip will be a memory for a lifetime."

Lola embraced her friend deeply, before turning the conversation back to Cate. "Enough about me. When are you going to tell me about your time in Vienna?"

Laughing, Cate remarked, "Fine, fine! Honestly, it was amazing! I got to meet Cade's parents, sister, ex-wife, ex-wife's boyfriend who is Cade's best friend, and his son."

"Woah! How in the world does that even work? How is Cade not pissed that his best friend and ex-wife are together? Lizzie would murder me if Mark and I ever got together."

Laughing, Cate continued, "Honestly, they have this really amazing dynamic. Cade said that he couldn't make Britt happy but knows that Dean will treat her well. It's unconventional, to say the least, but they make it work."

"That's good, I guess. So, what was it like meeting his son? What's his name again?"

"His son is named Logan, and meeting him was pretty nerve-wracking for me. I was so worried that he would hate me and think I was trying to take his mom's place but he gave me the biggest hug and said he's never seen his dad smile so big since he was a little boy."

"That sounds like a win to me."

"You know, it is. Do you know what's crazy? He has the exact same hair color as you."

"Are you for real? I have never met anyone with this shade of red. I mean, I've seen pictures of my dad and Grandma said she had this shade too, but no one my age."

"I'm dead serious! I invited Logan to come for Thanksgiving and I want you and Shane to come too. Cade and I decided to buy a house together and want to host a family dinner."

"Damn, girl! It must be serious if you are wanting to buy a house together already."

"It definitely is. We've both had failed marriages already, so we figured, why waste a good thing."

After another hour of friendly banter, Lola embraced Cate once more before driving home to do some much-needed catch-up on her school work to ensure she had the entirety of the fall break off.

~

October 8, 2000

Five days had passed since Lola's conversation with Cate; guilt tried to plague her mind for keeping what happened with Jacob to herself by living with the notion that no one would believe her anyhow. Interactions with her mother had been slim to none, thus giving Lola's hands and legs some time to heal properly. Lola packed her suitcase for the week before driving to Mark's house, where everyone planned to ride together in the minivan Mark would be borrowing from his parents.

Normally the trip from Parkway to Portland was an easy thirty minutes, however, the group of friends decided to make a day trip to the Willamette River for some hiking and quality time, before checking into their hotel rooms.

Lola had been able to easily reserve the three rooms since her grandparents had set aside certain rooms for her use at any time as a part of her trust. Lola was torn, while part of her wanted to share a room with Lizzie, as they could always do with some sisterly bonding; another part hoped she would get to share a room with Shane and grow their relationship in a new way. Upon arriving at the hotel, Lizzie made the decision for her as the girls were helping each other unpack.

"Sister, there are no parents, so Mark and I can mess around whenever. I love you, but missing a week with my man? Yeah,

I'm gonna have to pass. Besides, it's good for you and Shane to be closer to each other. He's kinda worried about you since you've been working so much; he said you seemed different."

Sighing heavily, Lola hung her head, "Yeah- I know he's been and I know he'd pay for everything, but I just want to make my own money. Besides, I got a really big bonus check."

"What kinda bonus check did you get?"

"It was for two grand!"

Eyes bulging in surprise, Lizzie gasped, "What the fuck? How the hell did you manage that? What did you do, sister?"

Anger seethed through Lola and before she knew it, she slapped Lizzie across the face before yelling out, "Don't you ever insinuate that I did anything other than work my ass off, *Elizabeth*. I don't need your fucking accusations or pity!"

Leaving Lizzie's room in anger, Lola stormed off to the room she would share with Shane. She was thankful the boys decided to watch a movie in Andy's room and could be left alone with her thoughts. Balling her fists in anger, Lola returned to her favorite coping mechanism by finding the familiar divots now entrenched in her palms. *Who the fuck does she think she is? I worked my ass off for that fucking money.*

Looking in the mirror, Lola stared at her reflection, as she dug her nails in deeper and let Jacob's voice crowd her conscience, "*Vixen, what did I tell you? Only **I** will ever understand you.*"

A knock at the door brought Lola from her darkened thoughts; looking down at her hands, Lola sighed in relief at the red sight before her. "Just a minute," she called as she washed her hands before covering her palms with bandages. Making her way to the door, Lola knew Lizzie was on the other side, for neither girl could ever stay away from the other for too long. As soon as Lola opened the door, Lizzie embraced her friend with everything she had. Sobbing,

Lizzie expressed her guilt, "Sister, I'm so fucking sorry! I definitely deserved that slap."

Shaking her head, Lola told Lizzie to come in and stop causing a scene. "I'm sorry for slapping you. I shouldn't have done that. I just get defensive because mom constantly calls me a 'whore' and a 'slut' and I just never expected that to come from you, of all people."

"I know! I don't always think before I speak. Mark calls it endearing, but I was royally fucked."

"I forgive you, sister. Will you forgive me for slapping you?"

"Of course, *baby bear*. Also, please know that I am *not* your mom and I never meant to sound like her."

After a lengthy forgiving hug, the girls decided to go shopping for outfit options for Thursday evening's concert.

~

October 12, 2000

The rest of the week leading up to the concert had gone smoothly for the group of friends; Lola and Lizzie spent every day searching for the perfect pieces to put together unique outfits for the concert. Lola wanted to have a sexy chic look, whereas Lizzie wanted to go as risque as possible; her reason being, "I love it when Mark gets possessive and dominating. I'm telling you sister, every damn time, it's the best sex ever."

"I'm honestly surprised you two aren't pregnant yet," Lola expressed matter of factly.

Shrugging, Lizzie remarked, "You know, it wouldn't be a bad thing. I mean we've been together forever, so why not add a baby in."

The girls parted ways to their respective rooms; Mark suggested Lola and Lizzie should not get ready together or they would miss the concert completely. Turning to Shane, Mark quipped, "Pray for me, brother. I know my beautiful hurricane is going to purposely wear something to make me lose my shit. She's so feisty, but that's what I love about her."

Laughing, Shane offered prayers and condolences before heading into his room to ready himself. Upon opening the door, his heart leaped with both love and lust; the sight of his beautiful girlfriend in nothing but a towel made it difficult for Shane to remain a gentleman. Walking up behind her, Shane wrapped his arms around Lola's waist while placing kisses on the nape of her neck.

Giggling in excitement, Lola turned around to capture Shane's lips, before melting into his warm embrace. "I love you so much, Shay! I am the luckiest girl in the whole damn world."

"*Mijn Bloem*, I'm the lucky one."

Kissing for a few more minutes, Lola eventually broke away, as her nerves were on high alert. Knowing that Shane would notice her change in demeanor, she asked, "Is everything set for the concert?"

"Yeah- Dad is overseeing all of the tech equipment; he could have had anyone from the company do it, but he said it's good publicity for the company if the CEO is present."

Looking deep into Lola's forest green eyes, Shane placed his left hand gently upon her cheek before asking, "*Mijn Bloem*, what's wrong?"

Closing her eyes and leaning into Shane's loving touch, Lola knew she couldn't hide her feelings. "I'm just nervous, is all."

"What's got you so nervous?"

Sighing heavily, Lola turned away as she said, "Don't worry about it. It's stupid, really."

"*Mijn Bloem*, you can tell me anything. You already have my heart, mind, and soul; nothing you can ever say will be stupid."

Letting out a heavy breath, Lola finally admitted her concerns to Shane. "We've been together for a while now, and I'm super nervous to take our relationship to a sexual level. I'm still a virgin and I'm scared to death that things will change once we have sex. I love you with all of my heart and I know I'd be lost without you."

Shane looked into Lola's eyes with such love and admiration before stating, "*Ik hou van je voor Mijn Bloem. Jij bent mijn alles.* (I love you too, my flower. You are my everything.) *Mijn Bloem,* I will wait for you as long as it takes. I don't want my first time to be with anyone else. You are my very heart and soul."

Lola couldn't believe her ears; *Shane is saving himself for me! I really am the luckiest girl in the world.*

Lola kissed Shane again before turning towards the shower, while Shane took out his journal to make note of this special moment. Throughout the week, each moment spent with Lola had been another notation in his journal. *God, I am so thankful that man is gone. Although I can't put my finger on it, I know he somehow changed her. She thinks I haven't noticed her hands, but even they are different. How do I bring this up to her without her brushing me off?*

While in the shower, Lola couldn't help but still revel in the joy she felt knowing she and Shane would only be with each other. Once her body and hair were clean, Lola took the time to shave her legs; laughing as she thought to herself, *Just because I will be wearing stockings does not mean I should have man legs.* Even though this was a happy moment in Lola's usually dreary life, the voices in the back of her head were ever-present to ensure she never truly had a happy moment. The two prominent voices that constantly plagued her belonged to her mother and Jacob.

"You think that boy actually loves you? I loved your father and what did that leave me? A worthless slut of a daughter!"

"Oh, my little Vixen! Remember, every time he touches you, I made you feel that way first. His touch will never compare to mine!"

On and on…back and forth…the taunting voices went before Lola had enough and did the only thing she could do to make them stop… reopen the previous mark on her leg. Relief, as well as guilt, rushed over her body. Life wasn't meant to be this hard at age sixteen, but in Lola's mind, she figured that surely she was cursed.

A loud knocking resonating in the background brought Lola back to reality, as she called out, "Just a minute," before doing one final rinse off. The voice on the other side of the door made Lola laugh.

"My god, *baby bear*! You're already gorgeous, so let's get a move on."

"Alright, alright, *momma bear*! Keep the claws in."

"See, Mark, I'm not the one you had to worry about after all."

On the other side of the door, Mark rolled his eyes as he laughed at his love's prodding quip. Turning to Shane, Mark suggested they walk down to Andy's room before waiting for the girls in the parking lot. "Luxie, hurry your short ass up! There's a new band from Vienna opening and I really want to hear them play."

Calling out from behind the bathroom door, Lola jested, "Damn, Marky-Mark! I guess Lizzie did a good one in pissing you off with her outfit. Don't take that shit out on me; save it for when you two are alone later."

Reaching up to embrace her man, Lizzie seductively remarked, "Don't worry baby, I promise I'll *try* to be a good girl; but who knows, I may have a naughty streak in me that needs to be punished later."

Shane cleared his throat awkwardly in hopes of breaking apart the sexual tension before Mark and Lizzie started going at it like rabbits in his room. "Alright, dude, keep your dick in your pants, and let's get a move on," calling out to Lola, he exclaimed, "*Mijn Bloem*, I love you."

Upon Shane and Mark's exit, Lola walked in the direction of the closet where her shopping bags still sat. Lizzie had made Lola pick out different pieces that pushed her past her comfort zone. "Babe, you're smokin' hot with a fine ass man that loves you. You should feel proud to show off your body."

"I'm not brave like you though."

"Fuck fear! Don't let society tell you how to dress just 'cause you have tits and a vag. Men have all the freedom to dress however the hell they want, so why shouldn't we?"

Looking through the pieces, Lola finally settled a look that would leave her feeling like herself, but also appease Lizzie. Lola decided to go with a teal-colored, plaid miniskirt that was slit up to the waist on the left side and had a built-in pair of black booty shorts; a small faux buckle adorned the bottom of the shorts, leaving a good three inches between the bottom of the buckle and the base hem of the skirt. Lizzie had picked out a black, lace three-quarter sleeve top and tried to convince Lola to wear it sans bra; however, Lola steadfastly objected and agreed that she would only purchase the top if she could wear an opaque black lace haltered bralette underneath. Lizzie relented, knowing that the skirt alone was significantly shorter than what Lola was used to. To complete the ensemble, Lola wore a pair of black thigh-high fishnets embellished with skulls; teal and black fingerless gloves, which covered her palms perfectly; and a stunning pair of black velvet, heeled Mary Jane's with satin ribbons and ruffles.

Giving a quick catcall, Lizzie helped Lola tame her wild curls into a braid that rested over her right shoulder and made sure both of their makeup looked flawless. "Before we meet the boys, I want to go back to my room and grab Mark's red and black flannel, just in case I get chilly."

Looking at Lizzie's outfit, Lola couldn't help but wish for even an ounce of her friend's courage to not care what others thought while being comfortable in her own body. Lizzie had opted for a pair of black booty shorts with the sides completely cut open and replaced with buckles; underneath those, she added a pair of black threadbare leggings; a mesh black top, which specifically accented her breasts, that she wore sans bra; a black spiked choker around her neck, which was her favorite accessory; and a pair of knee-high spiked combat boots.

"When we get back home, you're wearing a bra with that top, yeah?"

"Yes! I'm not stupid. Dad would literally have an aneurism if he saw me in this, and mom would probably cry. Which is why, what they don't know, won't hurt them," Lizzie retorted with a playful wink as she grabbed Mark's shirt.

Upon seeing Lizzie and Lola, Andy rolled his eyes in annoyance, "Took you girls long enough. You know, this is why I sometimes date guys; they tend to take far less time to get ready."

Playfully slapping Andy's arm, Lola stated, "Oh hush, you. Besides, don't let Zaylee hear you talk like that."

"Meh, she knows I like both guys and girls and has been pretty cool with it. She said she's even down for us to find a guy together."

As Mark drove in the direction of the concert venue, Shane interjected, "Speaking of Zaylee, why didn't you bring her along?"

"Ha! You know what her parents are like. They actually called me 'Satan's spawn' the last time I was over just because I'm an atheist and bi. To which I bluntly told them to 'fuck off,' after a fit of laughter. This caused her to get grounded and yeah … anyhow, sucks to be her."

~

"Thanks for having us, Portland! We're Beyond Oregon and hope to play for you again in the future. Now, enjoy Taking Back Sunday and Brand New!"

"Damn it to hell, Luxie! You took too long," Mark belted out.

"Chill, Marky-Mark! I'll see if they have a CD and buy it for you. Deal?" Lola quipped.

"Deal!"

Looking around the venue, Lola was ecstatic. *This is one of the best moments of my life. I'm so lucky to be able to spend it with my boyfriend and best friends.*

Grabbing Lola's hand, Shane led her to an area close to the stage but also away from the crowd; as he had something special to share with her. "Wait here. I need to go check on a couple of things but will be back with drinks, okay?"

"Don't leave me in anticipation for too long, Shay."

"I won't, *Mijn Bloem*, promise," Shane replied as he feverishly pressed his lips against Lola's, before walking away.

With nothing better to do, Lola allowed the music to overtake her. After four songs performed by **Taking Back Sunday**, Shane still had yet to return and Lola was just about to venture out in search of him when she felt two hands grip her waist and a pair of lips on the back of her neck. Feelings of arousal and nervousness at the fact they were in a public setting, Lola giggled as she called out in a chastising manner, "Shane! We are in public; at least wait until we're back in the room."

The hands placed upon Lola's hips squeezed her painfully, as the owner lowered his head to her ear, lustfully speaking, "Wrong name, *sweetheart.*"

Fear gripped Lola's heart as she tried to turn around to face the man of her nightmares, however, his strength would not allow it. The owner aggressively kissed her neck, ensuring a blackish-purple mark would shine brightly; before slinking back into the shadows. Finally managing to turn around, Lola realized she was alone and tried to ask some passersby if they had seen anyone behind her, to which they all denied. Touching the side of her neck, Lola found that it was dry. *What the hell is wrong with me?* Placing her hand on the side of her head, Lola shook her head in hopes of settling her disoriented feelings.

"Sorry I took so long, *Mijn Bloem*," Shane announced upon his return.

Startled by the voice of her love, Lola yelped out. "What the hell, Shane! You scared the shit out of me."

"I didn't mean to, *baby*. I tried calling your name a few times, but you looked lost. Are you okay?"

"Yeah…I'm fine," Lola lied easily as she grabbed her drink from Shane's hand, "I think I just got a little light-headed and thirsty, but I'm better now." Pausing to drink the water Shane brought her, Lola queried, "What took so long?"

"Well, while you and Lizzie were still in the room, Dad called and said he wanted me to check in with the bands about the equipment."

Wrapping his arms around Lola, Shane kissed the love of his life passionately and as if his life depended on it. Breaking apart from their kiss, Shane took a moment to gather his thoughts; he was generally a boy with a peaceful demeanor, so the thoughts which were now flooding his mind, felt very foreign. *I swear I saw that bastard near her. I should have brought her with me, but then her surprise would be ruined.*

A couple of hours passed, as the teens danced and rocked out to their favorite music when **Brand New** took the stage once more.,"***Thank you for having us Portland! To show our gratitude, we want to debut a new song called The Quiet Things That No One Ever Knows, from our upcoming album, Deja Entendu! This goes out to Luxie from Shane.***"

Lola couldn't believe her ears, "Oh my god, Shane! How did you even?"

Laughing, Shane embraced Lola as he replied, "Well, this is part of what took me so long. Dad said the band wanted to offer him some kind of favor as a thank you for providing all the sound and tech equipment at no cost to them. So, he called me and asked if I wanted to cash it in."

Tears of joy welled up in Lola's eyes, as she called out in a voice barely above a whisper, "Shane, I swear, this is the sweetest thing anyone has ever done for me. How the hell did I get so damn lucky?"

As the song came to an end, Shane placed his forehead on Lola's, looking deep into her eyes, as he asked, "Do you want to know what I am always writing?" Enchanted by Shane's blue-green eyes, Lola's response only came in the form of a nod.

"Well, *Mijn Bloem*, I write down all the quiet things I love about you. The things no one else seems to notice. I love your fire and passion. I love how you treat Andy like a real person and not fragile glass, just because he has Asperger's. I love how your forest green eyes burn into me with deep desire. I love that you care so deeply for your family, especially your mother, even though she is such a hateful bitch. I love that you see the best in everyone; especially me. Which makes me want to become a great man and live a life with purpose. I love your wild, curly, red hair, and how your scent intoxicates me. You are my everything."

No longer able to contain her tears, Lola let them freely flow down her face as she greedily captured Shane's lips with her own. *This man loves me more than anything. I don't deserve his love or passion, but he gives it so freely. Cate was right...this truly is a moment for a lifetime.*

17

First Date

October 11, 2014

Morning and afternoon passed in the blink of an eye, and by the time Lola finished speaking, her stomach felt as if it were going to eat her alive. Hearing the sounds of her growling stomach, Logan laughed as he looked at the clock. "Why don't we go into town for dinner tonight? If you're up for it, I think it'd be nice to go on a date before you continue on."

Looking away as she blushed, Lola agreed that a date would be nice; and although she didn't want to admit it to herself, talking to Logan about her life was slowly chipping away at the iceberg surrounding her heart. Feeling a wave of emotions caused Lola to feel overwhelmed. On one hand, she wanted to ask Logan to shower with her, as she desired a deep closeness to him; yet on the other hand, she wondered if he could ever truly love a body as marred as hers.

Seeing the gears turning inside Lola's head, Logan delicately lifted Lola's chin in his hand, before placing a gentle kiss upon her nose and forehead. "*My heart*, don't overthink it, okay? We can be close together when you are ready, okay?"

"Okay."

"Why don't you shower first, while I clean up and start a load of laundry?"

Sighing with relief, Lola agreed as she exited the room. Once showered and refreshed, Lola made her way to the room she shared with Logan to finish getting ready. Looking through her available options, Lola couldn't help but wonder when the last time she went on a date had occurred. *I guess I haven't been on a date since Jacob and I were together the last time, and I hate that I allowed him to taint everything that should be enjoyable. No! I will not allow him to ruin this moment.*

Separating from dark thoughts, Lola decided that her outfit needed to be lighter in hue from her norm, so she opted for a blush-colored, high-waisted, tulle skirt, which fell mid-thigh; a lacy white, long-sleeved crop top; blush-colored strappy, open-toed stilettos with ruffles on the top of the foot, which looked like flowers in bloom; and a pink leather cuffed bracelet with golden studs and accents. With her outfit settled, Lola chose to pull her beautiful curly hair into a high ponytail; leaving a few pieces down in the front, to frame her face. Adding some mascara, winged eyeliner, and her favorite deep red matte lipstick, Lola was ready for her first date in years.

~

Concurrently, in a guest room, Logan readied himself; his heart was deeply elated over the fact that he would finally be taking Lola on a date. *My heart, she has no idea how excited I am. Fuck! I feel just like a teenager. Zio and dad would both laugh if they could see me right now.* Gazing upon his attire options, Logan decided upon a pair of very slim fitting white slacks; a white dress shirt with black pinstripes; black socks, and dress shoes; and a satin blazer, in a rich deep emerald hue, which amplified the deeper blue hues of his eyes and intensified the coppery undertones of his hair. His mother would be quite proud of the fact that he chose not to wear ripped jeans.

Once satisfied with his appearance, Logan sought out the keeper of his heart; finally finding her seated on the porch swing, with a gentle evening breeze blowing through her lovely curls. Walking up behind Lola, Logan tenderly placed his hands upon her shoulders as he leaned over to inhale her intoxicating scent, which always made him feel completely at peace. Feeling Logan's hands upon her shoulders, Lola couldn't help but blush.

Making his way to the front of the swing, Logan helped Lola stand, as he admired her ensemble, before placing a delicate kiss upon Lola's lips. "Lola, *my heart*, you look stunning."

"Do you mean it? I wasn't sure about the color scheme, since it's so much lighter than what I normally wear. It doesn't blend into my complexion too much, does it?"

"*Darling*, if I wasn't a gentleman, I would ravish you right now."

Turning as red as her hair, Lola coughed out in embarrassment, before turning the conversation in Logan's direction. "I must say, Mr. Warren, your attire is quite surprising. I never knew you owned pants without rips. I find this side of you rather dashing. Although, I do adore your ripped jeans."

Logan shook his head as he laughed, "Yeah- my mom bought these for me for Christmas a few years ago and said that I should have a couple of pairs that are 'intact'."

Logan embraced Lola once more before leading her to his car; and driving off in the direction of a small Italian bistro, thirty minutes from the cabin.

~

Time passed quickly as Logan and Lola enjoyed the rustic environment of the bistro, which offered a very homey and romantic feel. After enjoying their meal, the couple decided to walk around the town square before enjoying an evening stroll along the beach. Leaving her heels in the car, Lola opted to walk barefooted across the sand; the feeling of cold sand prickling against her feet was a welcoming sensation to offset Lola's nerves. Feeling her stomach begin to somersault upon itself, Lola grasped Logan's hand in her own, as a few stray tears made their way down her cheeks.

"Lola, are you okay?"

"I'm fine … let's just walk a little while, please?"

Hand in hand, the pair walked on, as the temperature continued to drop and the sea air held a small bite as it blew past them. "Lola, I think we should head back; your hands are like ice." Pausing briefly, Logan removed his jacket and placed it upon Lola before squatting down to lift her on his shoulders.

Laughing, Lola remarked, "Don't you think I'm a little old for a piggyback ride?"

"Nonsense, *love*! It's a long way back and I don't want your little feet to freeze off. Do you trust me?"

"Of course I trust you."

"Good! Now, I want you to feel like you're flying, so close your eyes and hold your arms out while I hold onto your legs."

"Wait, what?" Lola laughed heartily but complied as she felt Logan start running back in the direction of his car. *Is this what being free feels like? Can I really be uncaged?*

As soon as they were back at Logan's car, Logan sat Lola on the hood as he gasped for air. Lola couldn't help but laugh, "You know, Warren, no one told you to run the whole way."

Breathlessly, Logan remarked, "I know … but … you felt happy … right?"

"I really did!"

Placing his body between Lola's legs, Logan looked deep into her eyes and brought his lips close to hers as he retorted, "Then a little side stitch was worth it."

Gulping, Lola felt desire begin to burn within her as she longed for her lips to connect with Logan's. Not wanting Lola to feel overwhelmed, Logan kissed her cheek before suggesting they head back to the cabin and start a nice fire, prior to calling it a night. Lola cursed herself, as once again, she allowed fear and hesitation to hold her back.

18

Initial Impressions

October 13, 2014

Two days had passed since Logan and Lola's first official date, and Lola couldn't help but feel at war within herself. She tried to make note of all of her feelings within her journal, but as they say, *"old habits die hard"* and Lola's palms were evidence of that truth. Knowing the talk with Logan would need to continue, Lola prepared her mind for the next events by going on a three-mile run whilst Logan did whatever he needed to do for one of his many jobs.

~

Once Lola had returned from her run and showered, Logan had lunch waiting for them to enjoy in the enclosed veranda. "How was your run? Did you see anything exciting," Logan asked with genuine interest.

"It was peaceful. I can honestly see why you love it out here," Lola expressed before continuing, "I saw a few red squirrels and a couple of chipmunks, but nothing extraordinary."

"Nonsense, *my heart*, even the smallest things are extraordinary."

Lola laughed while shaking her head. *He always has this way of seeing the world like no one else does or can. Maybe I can too ... if I'm lucky.* Removing herself from her thoughts, Lola quickly ate the last of her lunch, knowing she couldn't continue delaying the inevitable. "Logan, why don't we clean up, make some coffee, and then come back out here so that I can move forward with the story."

"You sure?"

"I guess- I mean, there's not a whole lot else that I can do, so might as well stop stalling."

When they had finished and were comfortably seated, Logan queried, "So *my heart*, what happened after the concert?"

Inhaling and exhaling to steady her nerves, Lola began once more...

~

October 12, 2000

Hearing Shane's loving words and the deepening of each kiss awakened an intense sexual desire within Lola; so much so, that as soon as **Brand New** exited the stage, Lola broke their kiss while urging Shane to find their friends so they could all call it a night. As if providence itself were smiling upon Lola for the first time in her miserable life, Lizzie was the first to find them.

"Hey, you horny fuckers! Let's get ready to head back. Mark's already got the van waiting."

Always having Andy in his mind, Shane asked of his whereabouts, which caused Lizzie to laugh uncontrollably, before responding, "Oh, he's already in the back of the van with one fine ass blonde guy. I think Andy said his name was Luke, Luka, something like that. I mean it was hard to understand since they had their tongues down each other's throats."

Lola chuckled and shook her head as she grabbed Shane's hand. "You know, Shay, Andy has really come a long way this year."

Pondering for a moment, Shane remarked, "Now that I think of it *Mijn Bloem*, you're right. I think since all of us are in relationships, he may be tired of fifth wheelin'. Dating Zaylee has been really good for him."

The drive back to the hotel felt unbearably never-ending, for the group of teens, who were all ready to undress their respective partners.

~

In the light of the elevator, Lola looked at Shane as if she were seeing him for the first time. *I thought I loved Shane before, but tonight, it's as if my love for him grew exponentially. God, or whoever is there, thank you for bringing Shane into my life. I don't think I could make it through my living hell without him.*

As soon as the elevator doors opened, Shane delicately grasped Lola's hand, leading her back to their hotel room. Once their door was shut, Lola pushed Shane against it while hoisting herself to wrap her legs around his waist before devouring his lips. After kissing for several minutes, Shane broke away as he breathlessly chuckled, "Well, *Mijn Bloem*, I think it's safe to say that you loved your surprise."

Laying her head upon Shane's chest, Lola sweetly replied, "I loved it more than anything, Shane. You are far too good for someone as dark as me."

Turning Lola around to where her back was now against the door, Shane playfully growled, "No more of this darkness talk, *Mijn Bloem*, you have so much light in you. Your name even means 'light', so stop doubting yourself and kiss me."

The passion and lust Lola and Shane felt for each other at that moment was explosive; the need to feel each other close, the way God intended, was so overwhelming, that before they knew it, the pair were standing before one another in solely their undergarments, just as they had many times before. Gazing into Lola's eyes, Shane asked, "Luxie, *Mijn Bloem*, are you sure you're ready? I know this is the first time for both of us, and I want you so bad right now. But, if you want to wait, I will wait until you're for sure ready. I only ever want my first experience of making love to be with you."

Looking back into his eyes, Lola thought to herself, *Could he be any more perfect?* before replying with vigorous sincerity, "Shay, I want you so badly right now that I can't hold back anymore. I **need** to feel you. I am so happy that we can experience this level of love only with each other. All I ask is that you please be gentle."

Kissing her passionately once more, Shane then carried Lola to their bed, where he trailed delicate kisses up and down her body. Unable to take the desire burning within the pit of her core any longer, Lola ripped away at her bra and panties, as she called out in frustration, "There's still too many fucking clothes in the way!"

Using all of her willpower, Lola did the best she could to not allow the voices room to ruin the beautiful moment unfurling before her, and how glad she was, for that night, as Shane and Lola became one, it was as if their desire had set the world around them on fire.

~

October 15, 2000

The remaining days passed all too quickly, and before the friends knew it, reality came knocking to announce the end of their Portland trip. Lizzie demanded that Shane sit in the front with Mark so that she and Lola could have some much-needed sister time. Andy, in typical Andy fashion, decided to tune the group out with music and headphones; he and his fling for the week had kept one another busy, fulfilling their sexual desires, and he was in desperate need of solitude.

As soon as Mark pulled back into his driveway, Lizzie made it known that Lola would, in fact, be staying the night at her house; thus causing Shane to playfully pout. With a firmly, pointed finger and a scolding tone, Lizzie spoke with authority, "Don't you dare give me that look, *Shane Michael Carson*! You've had my sister for most of this trip. Y'all can have sexy time later, once we're all settled in. But for now, this will be my time with my baby bear. Am I understood?"

The ferocity in Lizzie's voice caused both Shane and Mark to look upon her in fear, while Lola who was by now used to Lizzie's theatrics, only burst out laughing. Finally gaining some composure, Shane remarked, "Geez, Lizzie! Calm your tits!"

Mark shook his head in love and disbelief, as he wrapped his arms around Lizzie and spoke. "Reign it in, my *beautiful hurricane.*"

Time at the Sommers' house was something Lola needed to help ease herself back into reality before she crossed the threshold of hell, also known as her home, once again. Kissing their boyfriends once more, the girls placed their belongings in Lola's car, then drove off in the direction of Lizzie's house.

~

November 15, 2000

Life for Lola, for the most part, had returned to normal; while doing all that she could to avoid her mother, Lola eased back into school and work without a hitch. As Lola entered the café after school, Cate greeted her with a warm embrace, "My sweet Luxie, I have some exciting news to share with you once we close tonight."

While Cate had been in Vienna, Jacob decided to close the café on Wednesdays, as they were not financially lucrative, however, Cate being a woman of defiance, didn't care what her father or brother felt or thought; this was **her** café and she would be damned if she gave them any more control than what she had to.

Calling Jacob with her decision, Cate was able to do the unthinkable and reach a compromise with her twin. "Jacob, I know you know the numbers, but I know the people in this town. I'll have reduced operating hours on Wednesdays, but I will be open. Besides,

I'm not going to cut Luxie's hours like that."

An eye roll and a grunt of "Do whatever the fuck you want, Catarina," was a sign of victory in Cate's mind.

~

When the duo finished their tasks, Cate asked Lola to sit in their favorite corner, so she could tell Lola her good news, "You remember how I said Cade and I were looking to buy a house?"

"Yeah. Did you finally find one?"

With a squeal of delight, Cate remarked, "We did! It is the cutest little 1950s style bungalow; my father would hate it, which means I love it even more!"

Lola couldn't help but laugh at her friend's defiance, before carrying on with their conversation, "I'm so happy for you guys. Are you moved in yet?"

"We're almost done. My goal is to be finished in five days, which will give us three chill days before Thanksgiving. Cade is having Logan come for Thanksgiving. Cade and I really want you and Shane to meet Logan and see our home."

"That would be awesome. We'll have lunch at Shane's house that day, so we can come after that to help with any setup." Lola paused for a moment, as a nerve-wracking thought entered her mind, causing her palms to grow sweaty, "Uh … is Jacob going to be there?"

Cate chuckled as she replied, "Of course, *sweetie*, he's my twin. Besides, I need all of my people at this dinner."

When those words left Cate's mouth, Lola's heart was filled with a mixture of dread and excitement. Her body became flustered at the memory of Jacob's strong hands roughly caressing her; his dark dominance overpowering her, causing her to bend and submit to his every whim. Noticing the change in her friend's demeanor, Cate inquired, "Luxie, are you okay? You look a bit flushed."

Internally face-palming herself, Lola nervously replied, "Y-yeah … Just thinkin' about some stuff with Shane."

Cate laughed as she threw Lola an all-knowing smirk. Lola chastised herself for even allowing her thoughts to grow excited over the torment Jacob has caused her. *Jacob hasn't been back since Cate returned, which I am thankful for. I hate that he ignites this dark spark within me. What the fuck is wrong with me?! I can't have these weird feelings, especially now that Shane and I are lovers.*

~

November 23, 2000

Thanksgiving arrived and with it, Lola found herself feeling a mixture of elation and dread. Anytime she would try inquiring about Cade's son, Logan, Cate only provided generic answers as she wanted Lola to be able to formulate her own opinions of Logan. After lunch with Shane's parents and Andy, Shane and Lola arrived, only to find Cate in quite the stupor. Quickly embracing her friend in a hug, Lola asked, "Cate, what's going on? Why are you so stressed?"

"Logan called last minute and let me know that he's bringing his girlfriend, Avia. She's a sweet girl, but I don't know if we'll have enough … If this isn't perfect, J is going to give me shit. Gallagher events have to be perfect!"

Embracing Cate once more, Lola spoke with an authority that shocked her, "*Catarina Adeline Gallagher*, look at me! Everything is going to be just fine. You've prepared enough for a small army. Now, why don't you go for a cigarette - and yes, I know about your stash. Then, you can come back and I will help, okay?"

"Okay-"

Before Cate could continue her statement, Jacob entered the room and Lola's senses instantly became erratic and elated. *Damn it, why the hell does he have to look and smell so good?!*

Turning his attention to Cate, Jacob remarked, "Hey, sis" as he lovingly embraced his twin sister. Returning his affections, Cate felt at peace. "You look stressed, Catarina. What do you need me to do?"

Shaking her head in laughter, Cate bemused, "You know I hate being called by my first name. I'll let it slide this once **if** you help me out by handling the place settings. Everyone has a name card; I had to make a new one for Logan's girlfriend. I don't care where everyone sits, just make sure everyone has a seat."

Turning his attention to Lola, Jacob looked her up and down as he inspected her ensemble. Lola, knowing Jacob would be in attendance, opted for something a bit more subdued than her normal outfits; however, the outfit she chose, only peeked Jacob's interests even more.

Lola had chosen a mock-neck, cream-colored three-quarter sleeve length sweater, which tastefully revealed her midriff, that she wore underneath a mid-length, taupe three-quarter sleeve cardigan; a beautiful burnt sienna, high-waisted leather midi skirt; and black studded ankle booties.

Before exiting the room, Jacob seductively greeted Lola, "Well, hello there little *Vixen*," causing a blush to creep upon Lola's fair complexion.

The interaction between Jacob and Lola did not go unnoticed by Cate, as she firmly gripped Lola's arm while dragging her in the direction of the pantry. "What the hell was that about, Luxie?"

"What was what about?"

"You know damn good and well what I'm talking about! What the hell is going on between you and my brother? Did something happen while I was away? You'd best be honest with me because if something did, I swear to God, I will kick J's ass!"

Lola knew she should use this moment to be truthful, however, she already found herself far too embedded with her inner darkness. Even though she knew it was wrong to feel some sort of attraction to Jacob, she couldn't help but fall further in. The web of lies was the only thing holding Lola's sanity in place, so she felt it best to remain ensnared. Laughing nervously, Lola remarked, "Oh my God, Cate. Are you for real? How many times do I have to tell you nothing happened? I honestly think the stress of today has gotten to you."

Hugging her friend, Cate instantly felt relief; being Gallagher wasn't a fate she would **ever** wish upon her dear friend. For being Gallagher came with invisible bondage held by none other than Maximillian Gallagher.

"*Mijn Bloem*, are you in here?"

"Hey, *baby*! Yeah, I'm in here with Cate."

Finally reaching the love of his life, Shane exhaled deeply as he tightly embraced Lola's small body. Jacob being in attendance had Shane's nerves on edge, and he needed to hold Lola close, in effort of calming himself.

"Alright, lovebirds, I'm going to find Cade and see if he has heard from Logan. Please keep your clothes on and save any sex for when you get home," Cate jested before leaving the pair in peace.

Turning his focus back on Lola, Shane kissed her passionately before stating, "*Mijn Bloem*, I don't like that *klootzak* (bastard) being around."

Guilt crept her way into the forefront of Lola's mind; knowing the feelings she had experienced earlier were nothing but a deceptive snare, which she had once again found herself entangled. Dropping her hands to her waist with fists balled, in order to feel the comfort of her favorite coping mechanism, Lola did her best to comfort Shane. "Shane, can we please not do this now? You know that we're here for Cate. I get that you don't like her brother, but we just need to get through this, okay?"

~

While Shane and Lola found themselves occupied in the kitchen, debating the importance of Jacob's presence, Logan found himself sitting in the driveway of his father's house, fighting with his girlfriend, Avia Marinova. The two-hour drive from Vienna to Parkway had been less than pleasant, as the young couple had either fought or given each other the cold shoulder for the majority of their trip. Logan loved Avia with all of his heart, but he couldn't help but find himself doubting her affections.

"Avia, let's just get through this fucking dinner because I'm about over your shitty attitude."

"Logan, do you even realize what I had to go through to get my dad to let me come?"

"Honestly, I don't give a fuck. No one said you had to come. I merely made an offer. Had I known you'd be a bitch the whole way, I'd have kept my damn mouth shut."

"You know what, fuck you Logan Asher Warren. I'm getting out of this piece of shit car so we can just get this stupid dinner over with."

"You know, maybe if you would fuck me every once in a while, I might not be such an asshole."

Tired of being berated for the second time that day, Avia turned and slapped Logan across the face. "I put up with enough from my dad. I will not tolerate my boyfriend speaking to me in this manner. Just wait until I speak with your mom tonight."

"Avia, babe, I honestly don't give a fuck. Now, get your ass out of my car."

Fighting back her tears, Avia smoothed out her dress before allowing Logan to take her hand in his, to lead her in the direction of the front door. Before knocking on the door, Logan turned to gaze down at Avia, as he spoke with heartfelt intentions, "Look, Vee- I'm sorry I was a complete asshole. I know your dad's a dick and we have some things we need to discuss when we get back."

With a heavy sigh, Avia simply nodded her head.

~

As Cade opened the door, he lovingly embraced both Logan and Avia, "Hey, son! I'm glad you made it. Are you guys staying tonight? We've got a couple of rooms set up for you guys, or you can share."

"Hey, dad! Yeah, we'll stay the night. Where's Cate?"

Making his way in the direction of his lovely, raven-haired girlfriend, Cade told Logan and Avia to follow him. "Cate, *baby*, are Shane and Luxie ready to join us? Also, where's your brother?"

Calling out from the dining room, Cate replied, "Just have Logan and Avia go ahead and sit here at the dining table wherever J placed their name cards. I'll have Shane and Luxie join in a minute and also see if J is off of his call with our father."

~

Once everyone was accounted for, Cade began introductions around the room. Avia, normally a loving and peaceful girl, still had her mood soured by the events of the day, inadvertently spoke her thoughts, as she sneered while gazing about the room, "Ugh, whatever! Can we just hurry up and get this over with? I've got stuff to do."

Walking into the room with a final dish in hand as she trailed behind Shane, Lola couldn't believe her ears. *Who the hell does this bitch think she is? How dare she come into Cate's home and insult her, after Cate has literally slaved away all day?* Turning to Shane, Lola retorted, "*Wat een paarderlul!* (What a horse's ass!)"

Taking the dish from Lola's hands, Shane placed it upon the table as he nervously chuckled; he never was one for assumptions and name-calling, unless it were his nemesis, Jacob. Turning to Lola, he whispered in her ear, "*Mijn Bloem*, you should know better than anyone to judge things as they appear. You don't know this girl and you don't know what happened before she arrived."

Knowing Shane was right, Lola's sole response was a very prominent eye roll, before turning to find her seat. Shane saw red as he realized exactly where Lola would be seated. "Cate, do you mind if I switch seats with Jacob?"

Sighing heavily and on the verge of tears after a very hurtful conversation with her father, Cate hung her head while wearily replying, "Look, Shane, I'm sorry but you're just going to have to sit between Avia and Logan. We just need to get this shit show over with." Not wanting to cause Cate any further stress, Shane did the only thing he could do at that moment … comply.

Apprehensively, Lola found her seat, which conveniently was right beside Jacob at the very end of the table, isolated from the other guests. With a deviously seductive smirk, Jacob lustfully whispered in Lola's ear, "Well, well, well, *Vixen*. Isn't this just the nicest of surprises?"

Throughout the meal, Lola did her best to ignore Jacob, while trying to observe the interactions of the other guests. Although Shane had chastised her for her earlier assumptions, Lola still couldn't help but feel Avia was the rudest creature she ever had the misfortune of encountering.

Lola's anger was getting the best of her, so as a means of distracting her thoughts, she watched the interactions between Shane and Logan; the teen boys appeared to be having a wonderful conversation about only God knows what. Lola found herself disliking Logan, as he never once stood up for Cate. *The nerve of that asshole, just letting his girlfriend act that way.*

Jacob, noticing the gears turning inside of his little vixen's mind, knew that this was something to use to his advantage; his goal had been to get Lola alone, as he longed for the touch of her delicate skin and the taste of her cherry lips. Leaning into Lola's ear while resting his hand upon her bare thigh, Jacob remarked, "*Vix*, you seem tense. Is your precious Shane not relieving your stress just right? If you want, I can show you how a real man treats your body. Just think back to all of those nights in the office."

Trying to remain composed, Lola moved her hand in hopes of hitting Jacob underneath the table while he had struck up a conversation with Cade. Jacob, however, grabbed Lola's hand and pinned it under her thigh as he whispered, "My, my, my … still with the fire, I see. You should know by now that this rage you have, only succeeds in turning me on even more." As those words left his mouth, Jacob began caressing Lola's thigh once more, before slowly making his way under her skirt, and into her lacy panties.

Jacob's actions caused Lola's breath to hitch and her body to shiver in desire. Chuckling darkly, and knowing Lola was on the edge of her release, Jacob told her, "I will make you yearn for me once more, my little *Vixen*."

Feeling the heat rising in her face and her body nearly coming undone in front of her boyfriend and everyone else present, Lola thanked whoever answered prayers when Cate called her name. "Luxie, *sweetie*, are you okay? You seem a bit flushed. Should I turn the heat down?"

"I-I'm okay … Cate. Just have a bit of a headache is all," Lola expressed wearily, hating that she once more found ease and comfort with the lies she told. Turning in Shane's direction, Lola asked if he would be willing to take her home.

Jacob leaned into Lola one last time as he said, "How sad it is that our fun has to end right now. I promise you though, *Vix*, I will make you yearn for me next time. You'll be mine."

~

Riding home in silence, Lola allowed her thoughts to overtake her. *I can't believe I allowed Jacob to violate me at dinner, right in front of everyone. Although, it seemed like no one even cared enough to notice. Mom really is right, I'm nothing but a useless whore.*

When Shane pulled his car into the driveway, Lola looked at him with pleading eyes, "Shay, will you please stay the night with me? Mom's gone, which is a blessing, and honestly, I just don't want to be left alone tonight."

Inhaling deeply to calm the fire within his heart, Shane firmly stated, "I will, but only if you tell me what the hell was going on at dinner. I love you, Luxie, and if that asshole is harassing you, we need to go to the authorities."

"Shane, *baby*, it's nothing, I promise. How many times do I have to beg you to trust me?"

"Well, then what the hell was so funny down there? You two looked awfully cozy."

"Are you shitting me, Shane Michael Carson? He made some jokes and was being funny. What the hell do you want from me? Jacob is Cate's brother. Am I just supposed to sit there and be rude?"

Sighing in defeat, Shane apologized for overreacting; he hated who he was when jealousy took control, which only seemed to happen when Jacob was present. "*Mijn Bloem*, I'm gonna give my parents and Andy a call, to let them know my plans for tonight. Why don't you head on in?" Lovingly, Lola kissed Shane's lips in an effort to ease the pangs of guilt in her heart.

While Shane was on the phone, Lola started a shower in the hopes of scaling off Jacob's invasively volatile touch. With her eyes closed, Lola allowed the unwieldy tears to fall, as the water's warmth cascaded around her. *How the hell could this have happened again? Why do I keep lying? Not once, but twice tonight someone has thrown me a lifeline, and what does my stupid ass do? I reject it.*

Feeling a gentle kiss upon the back of her neck and loving arms embrace her, Lola wearily remarked, "How do you always manage to do this, Shay?"

Smiling as he lightly peppered kisses on the back of her neck, Shane asked, "Do what, *Mijn Bloem?*"

Melting into her beloved's touch, Lola exclaimed, "How do you always manage to calm the storm inside of me?"

Running a hand down Lola's body and speaking between kisses, Shane replied, "The same way you do for me, *Mijn Bloem.* I am yours and you are mine. Together we are one."

Lola leaned her body forward in hopes of causing more stimulation and friction under Shane's touch, for she needed to release the darkness within her. *If only I can have a small fraction of Shane's love and light, I know I'll be just fine.* Calling out as her body reached its breaking point, Lola begged, "Shane, I need to feel all of you in me now." Needing no further prompting, Shane gave his all to the keeper of his heart and soul.

~

November 24, 2000

The following day, Lola arrived at the café in hopes of apologizing for her early dismissal. "Do you forgive me, Cate?"

"Oh, my sweet Luxie, there's nothing to forgive. I'm honestly just glad that you are feeling better."

"So, how did the rest of the night go?"

"Well, as soon as you and Shane left, J's phone started ringing. Our father just had to call *again* and ruin the evening even more …" Cate trailed off, not wanting to relive her father's harsh words from the night before.

"What did he want?"

Sighing exasperatedly, Cate said, "He told J that he needed to go back to Vancouver to finalize the documents for some new business opening in Seattle. You know, his mean, old ass is supposed to be retired, but with the way he keeps an iron grip on everything, you'd never know."

Lola couldn't help but exhale in relief at her friend's statement. *I guess prayers can be answered. I can finally breathe now that Jacob is gone.*

Not wanting to proceed with a bitter conversation, Cate queried, "So … what did you think of Logan?"

"Can I be honest, Cate?"

"Always!"

"Well, if I'm being honest, I think he's a complete douche. Oh, and don't even get me started on his girlfriend. First impressions are everything, and let's just say, I don't have a very fond one of Logan."

With sadness lacing her words, Cate exclaimed, "Luxie, he really is a good boy and Avia is actually very kind. There's some stuff that's going on that isn't my place to tell. Logan is the closest I'll ever come to having a son. I'm sorry yesterday was a complete fiasco, but can you please promise me one thing?"

"What's that, Cate?"

"Please promise me, that when you meet Logan and Avia again, you'll give them both a real chance."

Allowing Cate's plea to soften her heart, Lola sighed, "Fine. I'll give them both another chance. After all, like Shane said, it seems we're all going through some shit at one point or another."

19

Back to reality

October 13, 2014

As Lola finished speaking, Logan couldn't help but laugh at his teenage self. "I remember that Thanksgiving *very* vividly and … yeah … I was a total shithead. I honestly don't blame you for detesting me after that first dinner."

Lola, looking away bashfully, softly stated, "Yeah … b-but I'm honestly glad that I listened to Cate and gave you a second chance."

"Really? Is it my dashing good looks or witty personality that won you over, *babe*?"

Rolling her eyes, Lola playfully jabbed, "Well, if I didn't give you a second chance, I wouldn't have found my best friend!"

Lola's statement caused Logan to grow somber, as he excused himself from the room. *The fucking friend zone for life. I know I have to be patient with her, but it's just so fucking hard when I love her so damn much that it hurts.*

Seeing the change in Logan's expression brought an overwhelming sense of guilt upon Lola, as she called out to him. "Logan, wait! Are you okay? Did I say something wrong?"

Stopping in his tracks and placing his hand upon his chest, Logan took a deep breath before replying. "Lola ... I love you so damn much ..."

Interjecting, Lola expressed with great remorse, "Logan, I know you do and whether you want to see it or not, I *truly* care about you. Just please be patient with me. I know that I'm asking a lot. Don't you think I realize just how fucking selfish I sound?"

Silence stood between Logan and Lola as the pair gazed upon each other. Logan's ocean blue eyes reflected the tsunami of emotions raging inside of him. Breaking the emotional barrier, Lola made her way over to Logan and buried her head into his chest as she sobbed her apologies for being selfish and making him hold on. In turn, Logan did the only thing he could do- hold on to the keeper of his heart; all while internally scolding himself. *Damn it all to hell. God, what's wrong with me? I hate that I can't let her go. She holds every ounce of me and it fucking sucks giving her everything of me, but not knowing where I stand in her eyes.*

Finally finding the courage to break away from Lola's grasp, Logan picked her up and carried her inside before gently placing her on the sofa; he planned to simply set her there before going on a walk to calm his own emotions. Lola, however, didn't want Logan bearing the weight of her guilt, so she grasped his hand as she pleaded, "Logan, wait. Please just wait."

Looking down into her eyes, Logan sighed, "What now, Lola? I think we, no...**I**...need to cool down. I'm about to lose my shit and I need to have a moment to process. Besides, I believe it's about time we start thinking about going back to Parkway."

Never letting Logan's gaze falter from her own, Lola silently pleaded for him to just be still, as she internalized her next movements. Deciding to finally throw caution and hesitation out the window, Lola pulled Logan down to her, forcing both of their bodies back onto the sofa, kissing him as if her life depended upon it; he was the oxygen she needed.

Logan was completely caught off guard by Lola's sudden act of boldness. He'd waited nearly two years to kiss Lola again, and this feeling was far better than he remembered, or could even imagine. *God, if this is a dream, please don't let it end.*

Breathlessly, Lola eventually broke their kiss as she stared into the ocean before her; Logan's rose-red hair hung slightly over his eyes, which were still a stormy sea. *I want to give my everything to this man, but how can I when so much is still unsaid and unknown. Fear is a constant demon plaguing my mind and soul. God, I want to trust him with every fiber of my being, but my sad reality is that fear and deception outweigh trust every single time.*

The minutes slowly ticked by as Logan and Lola continued to look upon each other passionately; each one soaking in the beauty of the other, but also not wanting to face their reality. The reality where this kiss, so filled with orgasmic intensity, probably should have been denied. The reality in which uncertainty is the most recognizable player and a plethora of questions remain unanswered.

Finally, Lola exhaled the breath she had been holding in and spoke, "Logan, I care about you so fucking much. I know that I can't be everything you want *and* need at this point in my life, but I do not regret that kiss for one single minute. I **know** I feel something for you. However, as much as I freaking hate it, this process that Dr. Indigo has me on has to happen for me to truly be healthy."

Pausing to give Logan room for any thoughts or objections he may have, Lola took his silence as a nod to continue talking. "I'm scared shitless every day that I'll never be able to fully escape the terror looming in my mind. I'm so worried that I'll give into my weaknesses and the voices once again and you'll find me just like you did two years ago. Do you even know just how much the consequences and guilt have screwed my mind over; knowing that I was so weak and caused a tidal wave of torment in my wake?"

Tenderly brushing the hair from Lola's tear-stained face, Logan finally found the words to speak. "I get it, *my heart*. I really do. What happened fucked me up for a long time, but you're back with me now and that's…that's something he can't take away again." Wavering slightly, Logan continued, "I'm glad you don't regret our kiss, because *baby*, you're my world and my everything. Like I told you before, I've lived **life without you** and it fucking sucks."

~

October 14, 2014

The drive back to Parkway was filled with silence, for what else could be said that hadn't already occurred during the moment of passion back in the cabin. The real world came crashing in hard, with neither Logan nor Lola truly knowing what to say. Focusing her attention out the window, Lola's mind overwhelmed her as she did her best to ignore the burning desire for unhealthy stress relief. *You know, if you just give in, you'll feel better. Don't you realize that nothing else helps extinguish your selfishness and the burden you put on everyone around you? Just fall into the darkness and let it surround you. I mean, after all, what could it really hurt?*

Unable to take the self-induced ridicule any longer, Lola sobbed out in response, thus causing Logan to stop the car. "I can't! I can't- even though I want to!" After pulling safely off the road, Logan turned to Lola, touching her arm in what was meant to be a comforting manner, while doing his best to assure her that everything would be okay.

Stepping out of the car, in hopes that the fresh air would soothe her nerves, Lola bitterly remarked, "Logan, it's not okay. The truth is, nothing will ever be okay."

~

Upon arriving outside of the café, Lola bolted from Logan's car before making her way to Logan's apartment; she needed to remove herself from the situation at hand, even if only for a little while. Having reached her breaking point earlier, Lola knew that her only hope was a face-to-face meeting with Dr. Indigo.

Logan did his best to keep pace with Lola's swift movements while having his pleas for her to, "Stop," fall upon deaf ears. Breathlessly, Logan entered his home and was deeply dismayed to find Lola packing the remainder of her belongings. "Lola, what's going on? Please talk to me."

Anger and frustration brewed within Lola's forest green eyes, giving them an almost blackened appearance, as she fumed, "Logan, I've been talking to you. Don't you fucking get that?! I need to leave…"

"*My heart*, please stay. Talk to me. I can help," Logan helplessly interjected.

"Damn it, Logan. You still don't get it. I **need** to leave right now. I am drowning in my own thoughts and if I don't go see Dr. Indigo in person, well …" Lola paused in hopes of retaining some manner of control over the situation, "… I'm afraid that I'll give in to the haunting of my mind and open the flood gates. My life literally depends upon me leaving at this moment."

Sighing heavily as tears flowed down his face, Logan knew he couldn't stand in Lola's way if he wanted to lovingly hold onto her for the rest of her life. So, instead of trying to stop her, Logan pulled Lola into his arms before kissing her passionately. *I don't care if she pulls back; I need to feel her kiss just one last time.* To Logan's relief, Lola returned his kiss with as much intensity as he gave, before pulling away.

20

Dr. Indigo

October 14, 2014

After filling her car with gas, Lola sent Dr. Indigo a quick text message to let her know she would be stopping by her office first thing in the morning. When she was back on the road, Lola felt the pangs of Shane's absence, as she rhetorically asked herself, "How the hell did it all come to this?"

Walking through the door of her apartment, Lola allowed the emptiness to envelop her in a loving embrace. Having been with Logan for over a month left Lola feeling immensely drained and overwhelmed. Not bothering to change her attire, Lola crashed onto her bed with hopes of sleep overtaking her. Yet, sleep felt empty and hollow at best; no warmth or love surrounded her. The only thing cradling Lola that night was the cold and empty darkness of solitude.

~

October 15, 2014

Lola awoke at six o'clock the next morning, ensuring she had enough time to shower before making the trip to Dr. Indigo's office. Not having the motivation nor care to dress up, Lola quickly threw on a long, merlot and white-colored sweatshirt; some light washed, skinny jeans; and a merlot-colored pair of **Vans**.

Standing outside of her therapist's office, Lola began to feel her uneasiness and stress lift. *Even though I hate to admit it, Dr. Indigo did help save my life. I guess it makes sense I feel kinda peaceful here.* Lola couldn't help but smile a bit as she willingly made her way into Dr. Indigo's office.

"Good morning, Lola." Dr. Indigo warmly greeted, before asking her to have a seat. "How have you been since our last session over the phone? I must say, I am surprised to see you back in my office so soon. Were you able to complete some of the tasks I set out before you?"

Dr. Indigo's queries were met with silence, as Lola just sat and stared, not wanting to answer. Dr. Indigo allowed Lola to sit in silence for ten minutes, before speaking once more. "Lola, you sent me a text stating that it was an emergency. I know that you are here for a reason, but I can't help you if you don't open up and share with me. If you're going to just sit here, then I'm afraid I'll have to reschedule to make room for other patients."

With an immense roll of her eyes and a heavy sigh of frustration, Lola retorted, "Fine! To answer your first question, if I'm being honest, I've been pretty shitty the last few days."

Looking at Lola, Dr. Indigo prompted, "Please tell me about your getaway with Logan? Did this little adventure help bring the two of you closer together?"

Rage began to fill Lola's heart as she belted out, "You *really* want to know how that stupid trip went? Well, I'll tell you … It fucking hurt. It caused so many painful memories to come up. From what happened to Andy to the Thanksgiving dinner at Cate's house. Do you even know what happens to be the next thing I have to tell Logan? It's about Shane and my deepest regret. I can't do it, Dr.

Indigo … I just can't!"

"Lola, when you're ready, will you please tell me why you can't tell Logan?"

Glancing up at Dr. Indigo with tear-soaked lashes, Lola bitterly retorted, "I can't tell him because the reality is … well … the reality is that everything goes downhill from there."

Looking at the woman before her, Dr. Indigo empathetically exclaimed, "Lola, I know this is hard, but this is something you have to do. In fact, you agreed to this as a part of your release from the clinic. You have made amazing steps forward and can't go backward now." Pausing to make a few notations, Dr. Indigo asked Lola to discuss the events of her trip with Logan and any further developments in their relationship, be they platonic or otherwise.

In her heart, Lola knew Dr. Indigo was right. *There's no point in denying it … I just need time to make it over this hump. I just hope my deepest regret isn't something Logan will hold against me.* Taking a few breaths as she dried her eyes with a tissue, Lola bashfully recanted the events from her date, as well as the little moments in between. "Well … I think … we have been starting to grow closer every day. It feels like my icy walls are trying to break down and that scares the hell out of me."

"Why does this scare you, Lola?"

"W-we haven't had s-sex yet, but I did kiss him."

Making a few notations, Dr. Indigo asked, "Lola, I have two questions I'd like for you to give ample consideration and thought too, as we break for lunch. First, are you wanting to move into a sexual part of your relationship with Logan? Second, who initiated the kiss? You say you kissed Logan, but are you meaning you were the initiator or the receiver?"

~

Following lunch, Lola found herself enjoying a nice stroll around downtown Portland. As she pondered the answers to Dr. Indigo's questions, Lola found herself outside of her favorite coffee shop in Portland, **Brewed Awakening**. *I love this little shop, it gives me similar vibes to the good times I had with my friends at **Cate's** and **Marty's**.* Upon entering, Lola allowed the comforting smell of freshly ground espresso beans to captivate her senses. Glancing at the menu, Lola was pleased to learn her favorite item, a caramel apple mocha, was finally back in season. With coffee in hand and answers in mind, Lola turned in the direction of Dr. Indigo's office to continue their session from this morning.

Now seated across from Dr. Indigo once more, Lola held her coffee as the warmth of the cup provided her the small amount of courage she needed to press on. "To answer your first question, Dr. Indigo, if I'm being honest … well … I want to climb him like a freakin' redwood! Every damn time he grazes my arm, kisses my cheek, or hell just glances in my direction … I want to say, 'Fuck it,' and bring our relationship to that level, but then … umm … I just hold back, I guess."

"Lola, what do you think is holding you back?"

Thinking for a few minutes, Lola replied, "Well, I guess it's the fact that I know his love for me is so pure and so real, that fear clouds my thoughts. I think the appropriate word would be that I'm terrified. And before you ask, I think I'm terrified to experience loss again. So for me, it's just easier to keep him at arm's length."

Writing down Lola's words, Dr. Indigo exclaimed, "Alright Lola, that's very perceptive of you. I see that you are making great progress in trying to recognize the need to think of another's feelings. I do have another question that I'd like to ask before we discuss the second one I left you with."

"Uh … okay, what is it," Lola asked, although, in the back of her mind, she knew what was coming. After all, isn't this the exact reason she left so hurriedly to see Dr. Indigo?

"Lola, would you please tell me how you have been handling any urges to harm yourself? If I recall, you had a pretty traumatic dream shortly after returning to Parkway."

Bringing her coffee cup to her lips with shaky hands, Lola took a quick sip, allowing the warm liquid to give her courage. With a heavy sigh, Lola said, "If I am being honest, I struggled on the way back from the cabin. The reality of all of my faults, weaknesses, and selfishness hit me like a ton of bricks. It hit me so hard that all of the old areas where I found temporary relief began to itch and burn."

Continuing to document the session, Dr. Indigo inquired, "Knowing these things have come to your mind, what did you do, Lola?"

Lola recanted both the moment in the car, as well as the moment where she just packed up and left. "Dr. Indigo, I feel so weak. I was so scared that if I had stayed, something bad would have happened. It's been two years and I don't know why I'm not any stronger or braver."

Setting her pen and notepad upon her desk, Dr. Indigo clasped her hands together as she firmly but lovingly stated, "Lola, what makes you think that you are weak? You recognized that you were in a situation that was causing both your brain and body to go into survival mode. Instead of faltering to old habits, for the first time since we started our sessions, you chose to reach out to me. Lola, that is a sign of true strength. You have come so far since our sessions first began."

Smiling through teary eyes, Lola thanked Dr. Indigo for her encouragement and reassuring. "I just hate the fact that I practically flipped out on Logan."

"Did you communicate with Logan as to what was happening and where you were going?"

"Yeah. I told him that my life depended upon my leaving and

coming to see you. He seemed like he understood and kissed me."

"Alright Lola, why don't we make our way back around to the second question I had asked, considering there are now two kisses present. How did you feel after each one?"

"Well, the one at the cabin … I may or may not have initiated," Lola playfully jested, before admitting, "Okay, okay … I did initiate it. I guess I just felt desperate and sorrowful."

"How so?"

"I could see the pain I was causing Logan by not being what he needs right now. I felt so desperate because I needed him to know that even if I can't tell him that I love him, I *do* feel something for him."

"What about the kiss he initiated? Was this one similar to yours or different?"

"The one he initiated … hmm … the best way I can describe it would be that I could feel his heartbreaking at the thought of losing me again. I really feel so selfish for putting him through all of this torment."

"Lola, recognizing that you need to take care of yourself is neither selfish nor weak. It is a sign of true strength. I can assure you that Logan understands this as well. Now, do you have any notion as to when you will be heading back?"

Chewing on her lower lip while in thought, Lola replied, "Probably not until next week. I need to check in with work and above all else, I just need time to myself. The part about Shane's death is something that is so hard for me to think about … let alone speak on … so, I just want time to process and prepare."

"I think this is a very wise decision, Lola. Even though it may not seem like it, talking about these things, especially with Logan, will help you to heal and move forward. Let's go ahead and schedule an appointment one week from today. Never hesitate to call or text me when you are struggling."

Thanking Dr. Indigo for her time, Lola drove back to her apartment; whereupon entering, she realized just how much she had enjoyed being with Logan. At that thought, almost as if by instinct, Logan called. Looking at her phone, Lola hit decline for she was far too drained from today's session to even consider entertaining another conversation. Sending a quick text which read, *I'm okay. I arrived last night. Sorry for not texting. I talked with Dr. Indigo for several hours today and I'm spent. No energy or desire to talk. I'll be back next week ~xxx~*

After sending the message, Lola turned her phone on silent as she settled into bed. Drifting off to sleep, Lola realized just how much it sucked to be back in reality. *Why couldn't we be as somewhat happy as we were in those little moments?*

21

A is for…Diagnosis

October 17, 2014

Two days had passed since Lola's last session with Dr. Indigo, and while Lola thought that she wanted solitude, each morning she awoke with a heavy and lonely heart; feeling cold both inside and out. Cold from the emptiness of a lonely bed, but also from the void in her heart…the void Logan so desperately wanted to fill with his love and safety. Sadly, Lola still couldn't bring herself to allow Logan to fully enter her heart. Sometimes, it seemed that loneliness was easier for Lola to handle because when it's only yourself, there's really no one to hurt or disappoint. Although, according to Dr. Indigo, this wasn't truly living.

Mustering all she had, Lola forced herself to leave her bed and go out amongst the world. *Seeing as how I'm home, I might as well check in on the company. I know Dr. Indigo has practically forbidden me from stepping foot in there, but it would be nice to see Jade and Daisy face-to-face. I should probably make a formal introduction to Marina too.*

After college, **Swan Industries** had fallen onto Lola's shoulders, as she was the last remaining Swan heir. The thought of being a Chief

Executive Officer, or CEO, still baffled Lola's mind, as she merely saw herself as a figurehead. In her eyes, the true CEO was her dear friend, Jade Rhianne Evans. Jade had originally started out as Lola's assistant, after immigrating from England. Over time, Jade had become far more than an assistant to Lola, thus quickly promoting to Chief Financial Officer, or CFO. When Lola was admitted into the clinic for treatment, it had been Jade who kept the board of directors in their place, not allowing them to usurp Lola's authority.

Quickly changing into a white dress shirt; a black pair of high-waisted, slim-cut dress slacks; a sapphire blue blazer; and her favorite pair of black strappy stilettos. Lola chose to put her curly hair up halfway, before applying a quick coat of mascara and her favorite deep red lipstick. Satisfied with her appearance, Lola drove off in the direction of her company. *Dr. Indigo may scold me for this, but I feel it's important. Well, as they say, "It's better to ask for forgiveness than permission,"* Lola couldn't help but laugh at her thoughts.

~

Parking in the spot reserved for her, Lola couldn't help but sadly smile as she reminisced on the memories of visiting her grandfather at work. All of her life, Lola knew **Swan Industries** would be passed on to her, however, she had always thought her grandfather would be there to train her. *I know Grandpa's been gone nearly 14 years, but Lord, I miss him and Grandma so much. Who knows how my life would've turned out had they not died that night?* Not wanting to delay the inevitable any longer, Lola exited her vehicle, heading to her intended destination.

Knocking on the door to the office placed just outside of hers, Lola heard the chipper voice of who she knew to be her assistant, who happened to be preoccupied with several files. "Good morning. Please come in and I will direct you momentarily."

Sitting at the seat in front of Marina's desk, Lola couldn't help but stifle a laugh as she queried, "Hello, Ms. Vasquez. Could you please tell me how things are coming along with the **Carson Tech** merger?"

Startled, Marina finally turned her attention to the person seated before you, as she quickly stuttered, "M-Ms. Swan, I mean Lola, g-good m-m-morning."

Laughing light-heartedly, Lola exclaimed, "No need to be nervous, Marina. Good morning to you as well."

"I had no idea you were coming in today. Please forgive me," Marina begged.

"Nothing to forgive, my dear. Besides, you can't effectively do your job when I don't fill you in on my whereabouts," Lola jested with a playful wink.

"Yes, ma'am," Marina stated, before sheepishly inquiring, "If I may be so bold, what brings you in today? Jade and Daisy had said that you were still on sabbatical."

"That is correct. I actually came here for two reasons. The first being that I feel any boss worth their salt, should know who their employees are. It is a pleasure to officially meet you in person, Marina."

"It's a pleasure to meet you too, ma'am."

"As for the second reason, I'd like for you to tell me when Jade and Daisy are free today."

Glancing at the schedules of both ladies, Marina remarked, "It looks as if both are free between 2:00 and 4:00 this afternoon."

Clasping her hands together, Lola exclaimed, "Perfect! Please schedule a reservation for four," noticing the puzzled look upon her assistant's face, Lola chuckled, "Yes, Marina, you are to join us as well. Now, as I was saying, please schedule a reservation for four at *Étoile Bleue*."

"Should I let Daisy and Jade know that they are meeting with you?"

Pondering for a brief moment, Lola stated, "No. I think it would be best for this to be a surprise. See you this afternoon, Marina."

~

Seeing as she had four hours to kill until her lunch, Lola decided to give her friend, Louisa Johnson, a phone call to see if she was free for coffee at **Brewed Awakening**. Louisa had been an important part of Lola's life during her time at the clinic, eventually becoming an amazing friend and confidant. With no luck of reaching her friend, Lola knew this must be a sign. *I have put off my letter writing and journaling long enough, so I may as well treat myself to another coffee and get this over with.*

In her heart, though, Lola wanted to call Logan, even if it was just to hear the comfort his voice had to offer; however, this was a phone call she chose not to make. *As much as I want his closeness and comfort, I know I need to save it for when it's time to have the discussion about Shane.* Wiping the stray tear from her eye, Lola entered the coffee shop to complete her task at hand.

~

Returning to her car, Lola decided to check her phone before driving off in the direction of the restaurant. Finding two text messages, although neither were from who she secretly wished to hear from. Louisa sent a message apologizing for missing Lola's call; she said her and her husband, Dr. Kaleb Johnson, were on a vacation and wouldn't be back until the following week. Lola wished them well and sent her best regards to their children as well.

The other text, being from Lizzie, was one Lola had honestly expected before now, and dreaded it nonetheless. Lizzie was not happy with Lola's lack of communication after her return. Instead, she had to hear from Logan that Lola up and left and that he was heartbroken and devastated. Lola sent a reply apologizing to Lizzie and letting her know she would call her after her business lunch with Daisy and Jade.

As she drove to the restaurant, Lola couldn't help but think of her fondness for her two work companions. *The thing I love about Jade and Daisy is that neither really question me about everything that I have gone through. I can just be Lola. I mean, they know that I obviously had some struggles two years ago and needed a sabbatical, but they have never once questioned anything. It's hard enough being a female CEO of a Fortune 500 company ... add mental health issues into the mix, and yeah ... you're pretty much fucked. Too many board members already saw me as a weak liability ... fucking Jacob ... Had the board really known what happened, it would have just given them another damn reason to try to get rid of me.*

~

Upon entering the restaurant, Lola smiled as she saw Jade, Daisy, and Marina chatting happily at a table in a nice, sunny area. Daisy Rae White had only been a part of **Swan Industries** for a short amount of time, before Lola's sabbatical. However, from what Jade told her, Daisy was one hell of a marketing genius; which suited her well as the Chief Operations Officer (COO). During one phone report, Jade informed Lola of Daisy's ideas and perspectives to help keep the hotel industry, as well as the annual charity gala for **Lorriene Swan Center**, relevant for modern-day families. With both ladies by her side, Lola knew in her heart that her grandfather would be proud. She never really wanted to run the company; hell, she was 30-years-old and still had no clue what she wanted to do with her life. Right now, all she knew was that she wanted to have more good days than fucked up ones.

Reaching the table, Lola called out, "Surprise, girls!"

Jade and Daisy quickly embraced the woman standing before them. Once greetings were made and lunch was ordered, Lola asked for a rundown of the analytics and financial projections going into the winter quarter. Lola also asked for any news relating to Carson Tech, which Marina was happy to declare that she was at least able to finally schedule an in-person meeting with Andre Bennett. "Marina, I must say, Jade was not lying when she told me of your persistent nature. It will serve you well with Andre's hardass nature," Lola beamed with pride.

With the boring "shop talk" out of the way, the real girl talk began. Turning to Lola, Jade asked, "So, how's your time in Parkway been?"

Daisy interjected, "Yes, girl! Spill the beans will you. I mean, you're back earlier than projected. Not that we're complaining though."

Laughing, Lola remarked, "Oh, girls! You crack me up so much. You know, going back home was hard at first, but it was nice to spend time with Logan. He took me to his family cabin in Pinecrest."

With squeals of admiration from the three ladies surrounding her, Lola shook her head while she laughed at their childlike exuberance. Daisy quipped, "Ya know, if it's the same Logan I think it is, his ginger ass is fine! Did you get closer to him?"

"Daisy, I didn't know you knew Logan. Are you familiar with some of his photography?"

With a silencing glance from Jade, Daisy wearily replied, "Y-yeah. He's a great photographer."

"He really is! You should see these images he captured for me while we were gone," Lola boasted proudly as she showed off the pictures Logan took for her, while responding to Daisy's question. "To answer your question, Daisy, I would say, 'yes and no.' I mean there were two *very* passionate kisses, but I had to come back here to Portland. I am staying here for about a week, maybe two, because I feel like we both need a little time apart."

Looking at Lola's eyes, Marina observed, "Lola, your eyes say it all."

Laughing, Jade exclaimed, "Marina, you're right. Lola, it's so obvious that you **love** Logan."

As the blush upon her face betrayed her innermost feelings, Lola stated, "Now, now girls. I don't know *if* I love him, but what I do know is that I do care for Logan deeply. Maybe one day I can love him, but for now … well, I'm honestly just glad that he's a part of my life."

Deep in her heart, Lola knew she was withholding the truth from her friends, but it was nice not having more people to have to worry about the possibility of her hurting herself. Lola also knew that she was lying to them, as well as herself, concerning the real reason she came back to Portland so soon. The truth was, Lola couldn't handle the heartbreak and disappointment in Logan's eyes once again, especially after what had happened two years ago. Gazing out at the skyline as she pushed her food around the plate, Lola retreated to her thoughts. *It's nice to just be "normal" every once in a while. I want to let myself love Logan and accept his love in return, but you aren't supposed to hurt the ones you love; nor are you supposed to cause them sorrow the way I did. He claims to forgive me, but how the hell can I believe that, when I don't even forgive myself?*

~

Once her lunch date had come to an end, Lola made her way back to her apartment. Waiting outside her door was a beautiful bouquet of flowers, containing red poppies and white tulips. Carefully picking up the bouquet, Lola's eyes filled with tears and she breathed a sigh of relief upon seeing Logan's name. The message on the little card was bittersweet; *"My beautiful Lola, I don't know why you left me again. I love you and will be here waiting. Please come home soon. Always yours, Logan."*

Lola felt more selfish than ever; how could she not? It pained her to know that no matter what she did or would do, in the end, Logan would always be hurt. Dr. Indigo told her countless times of the importance of recognizing the moments causing her pain; and while it was best to remove herself from the situation, Lola also had to come to terms with said moments, if she truly wanted to have a life worth living. Taking the flowers inside, Lola placed them in a vase on her counter before going to bed.

~

October 22, 2014

The remainder of Lola's week in Portland mundanely crawled by, leaving her feeling cold and lonely. Each day, Lola did her best to follow some semblance of a routine in hopes of focusing on her well being; but as always, her mind had other notions. *You don't honestly think that Logan will wait for you forever, do you? I mean seriously, how the hell can he love someone as fucked up as you. You know the only one who ever truly loved you and your darkness was Jacob; he helped you embrace the crazy. I mean, after all, isn't that all you'll ever be? Nothing but bat shit crazy!*

Each thought was a bitter attack. Lola did her best to remember what Dr. Indigo had told her, "Love doesn't hurt. Love doesn't take away the things and people who are important and special to you. Love uplifts you." With shaking hands, Lola faced her reflection in the mirror while shouting, "Jacob wasn't love…he's the opposite, in fact. Jacob is nothing but toxic death."

Before returning to Parkway, Lola arrived at Dr. Indigo's office for her scheduled session. While Lola knew the regular phone sessions would happen once she returned, she couldn't deny the serenity she felt inside of Dr. Indigo's office. "Good morning, Lola. Please have a seat and tell me how your week in Portland was," Dr. Indigo warmly greeted.

"It was good, but also kind of scary. Also, even though I know you wanted me to wait on going back to work, I did stop by the office … but only to meet Marina and to schedule lunch with her, Daisy, and Jade."

"Lola, I think that was fine. The point of you not fully returning to work, is to keep your stress level down. Now, will you please elaborate on what made your time here feel scary."

Thinking for a moment, Lola stated, "I guess it was the loneliness."

"Is that not what you wanted by coming back here?"

"I-I mean, I thought it was. Ya know, I was alone in my apartment for three months before calling Logan. Hell, I was content with the loneliness … but now …" Lola trailed off, picking at her nails before she continued. "Now that he's back in my life, the loneliness seems to invade my mind with cruel thoughts?"

Making notations, Dr. Indigo asked, "Was there anything that triggered the cruel thoughts?"

Lola told Dr. Indigo about the flowers and card Logan had delivered to her apartment; along with how her mind began bombarding her with the claim of Jacob being the only one to ever truly love or understand her.

"Lola, I want to start off by thanking you for sharing these things. I am extremely proud of the progress you have made in recognizing the signs of what love really is and isn't. Now, from what we have discussed in the past, regarding Jacob, it would seem that he is in fact incapable of truly loving anyone."

"But Dr. Indigo, isn't that the same thing as my condition?"

"Lola, while there are some underlying similarities between your condition, *Alexithymia*, and *high functioning sociopathy*, which is what I believe Jacob has - remember, I cannot officially diagnose him. I can clearly state that *Alexithymia* is vastly different."

"How so," Lola asked in hopes of easing her mind.

"Well, Lola, you already know that you have a hard time under-standing and identifying the emotions felt within yourself, and stressful situations cause you to take these misunderstood feelings out on yourself in a destructive manner. Jacob, on the other hand, does not have the ability to feel anything. Instead, he utilizes his charm and intelligence as a means to maintain constant control and stimulation. His lack of empathy and his addiction of you are also signs of a high functioning sociopath."

"So, you're saying that while our conditions are kind of alike, we're also worlds apart?"

"Precisely, Lola."

Breathing a much needed sigh of relief, Lola expressed her gratitude to Dr. Indigo for once again providing her with reassurance. As she stood to leave, Dr. Indigo asked one final question. "Are you now prepared to talk about what happened to Shane?"

Shrugging, Lola replied, "Honestly, not really. I know that I have to at some point, so I may as well just get it over with."

"Lola, one parting word of advice. Make sure you take your time with this. It would seem that Logan is very patient with you. Don't hesitate to contact me with any difficulties or concerns you may have." Lola thanked Dr. Indigo for her time before driving back to Logan.

22

Reminiscent

October 23, 2014

The session with Dr. Indigo took longer than anticipated, so Lola made the decision to return to Parkway early the following day. The journey was quiet as Lola gathered her thoughts; she feared it would be Logan who left in the future. Having experienced the pain of one man being pushed past his breaking point, Lola knew this was a very real possibility. Placing those fears on the back burner as a problem for future Lola, she chose to focus on the task at hand … learning to fully heal.

Pulling into the driveway behind the café, Lola took a few minutes to collect herself before unloading and entering Logan's apartment. *This place never felt like home, but he does, and that terrifies me.* As she opened the door, Lola saw Logan with his back to the door, headphones on, notepad in hand, and the strangest sight of all, a guitar strapped across his chest. *I never knew he was musical. I guess there's still so much I don't know about him.*

Quietly making her way to the bedroom, Lola put her things away before going back to where Logan was and wrapping her arms around his waist, as she inhaled his comforting scent. He was her safe space and comfort. Feeling tiny arms wrap around him, Logan turned with great surprise as he exclaimed, "*My heart*, you're back! Why didn't you call to tell me you were on your way? Let me put this stuff down and we can talk."

Chuckling, Lola said, "Yeah, Warren, what's with the guitar? All these years we've been friends and your ass fails to tell me that you play an instrument. What's up with that?"

Sheepishly rubbing the back of his neck, Logan replied, "Wel-l, ya know, it's just a minor hobby. I'm honestly not even that great." Logan chuckled as he thought to himself, *I'm honestly a great fucking musician. I was just hoping to finish this song, before she came back, so the guys will get off my ass.* Looking at Lola, Logan asked once more, "Why didn't you give me a call?"

Hanging her head, Lola stated, "I'm sorry, I just needed some time to gather my thoughts."

Logan took a deep breath as he drew Lola into a longing embrace. Allowing herself to become enveloped in Logan's warmth, Lola expressed with sincerity, "I'm sorry for leaving the way I did and causing you pain. I needed to gather my thoughts and everything felt like it was crushing me."

Lifting Lola's chin with his hand, Logan gazed into the earthy orbs his heart desired, as he said, "*Baby*, it's okay. I'm just happy that you're home now."

Home … Lola's mind focused on that single word. *What does home even mean? Is it a person? A feeling? A place? Whatever it is, it sounds so out of reach.* Looking back at Logan, Lola thanked him for the flowers, "They really did put a smile on my face."

"Well, *my heart*, I'd do anything to put a smile on your face."

~

Morning and afternoon passed with the pair quickly returning to the familiarity of one another. Logan was elated to know that

Lola was back again and that she would be in his arms each night, bringing him a sense of peace no other could. Lola was happy to feel safe again in both the sea of Logan's eyes and the warmth of his embrace … even if it was only for a moment. When evening rolled around, Lola found herself exhausted and told Logan she would be heading to bed. As they lay together in each other's arms, Lola wistfully exclaimed, "Tomorrow. Tomorrow I'll be ready."

Running his fingers through her curls, Logan asked, "Ready for what, *my heart?*"

Exhaling, Lola stated, "Ready to finally tell you everything about Shane, his death, and my deepest regret."

"Are you sure?"

"Yes and no. I don't think I'll ever be ready to relive the hurt again, but I'm ready to move forward with my life." As the final words of Lola's statement passed her lips, she drifted off into a peaceful slumber.

~

October 24, 2014

The next morning, Logan awoke at 5:00 a.m. to prepare for his day. He had several tasks at hand and hoped to finish them early in an effort to maximize his time with Lola. Before going to *Cate's* to help her out, Logan gave Pierre a quick call to fill him in on the progress of the song he started in Lola's absence. *All this heartache fucking sucks, but man, it sure does make decent writing material.*

Logan returned around 10:00 a.m. and smiled as he saw Lola still sleeping. Tossing a fluffy pillow at her, before pouncing on the bed, Logan belted out, "OUT OF BED, SLEEPY HEAD!" Lola awoke with a fit of giggles as she surrendered to Logan's playful antics.

Returning his tone to its more neutral sound, Logan asked, "Lola, would you like to take a walk as you tell me what all happened?"

"Umm … sure. I guess that'll work."

Logan suggested the walk because from his keen observations, Lola seemed to be most content when surrounded by the serenity of nature. Lola quickly threw on a pair of red skinny jeans, a cream-colored sweater, brown hiking boots, and a navy blue puffy coat with faux fur trimming. Once they were on the forest path behind the café, Lola grabbed Logan's hand as she spoke, in hopes of gaining a tiny fraction of his courage.

~

December 2000

After the dinner at Cate and Cade's house, Shane found himself deeply burdened. Even though she had never admitted it, Shane knew something had happened with Jacob. After a lengthy conversation with his parents, filling them in on the abuse Lola was experiencing at home, Shane was able to convince them to let him and Andy get an apartment with Lola. "*Moeder en vader* (mom and dad), we will be graduating after next year and going to college. You already know that we're responsible and I wouldn't even think to ask if it wasn't important. I'm just really concerned for *Mijn Bloem's* safety."

Mona thought for a moment, she truly loved Lola as her daughter, but she also knew the struggles of being a teenager. "*Mijn lieve jongen* (My sweet boy), has she not considered calling CPS?"

"Mom, she doesn't want Lizzie's parents to suffer anymore. I mean, if Luxie knew you guys had even an inkling of what was going on, she'd be mortified. I never ask for anything, just please consider it. If not for me, then for her safety and well-being."

After a deep and lengthy, prayer-filled conversation, Mona and Jordan relented to their son's request. They had obvious conditions and expectations, as any parent would; in their hearts, though, they knew this was the right thing to do.

~

July 2002

Time moved quickly for Lola and Shane. The couple, along with their friends had finally graduated high school and were preparing to start university in the fall. Mark decided to take a job with both ***Swan Industries*** and ***Carson Tech*** as an independent contractor. He wanted to go into Cyber Security.

Lizzie, always having a love for kids and science, decided on becoming a high school biology teacher.

Andy, Shane, and Lola were all going into business management. Jordan wanted Andy to enter the program because he was just as much of an heir to ***Carson Tech*** as Shane was. Shane was happy when Andy told him the news, "Brother, you have no idea how excited I am that we'll be working together in the future."

It had been nearly two years since Jacob's last appearance in Parkway, and while Cate's heart was deeply saddened, both Shane and Lola felt relief. Being out of Anne-Marie's house had done wonders for the state of Lola's mind. Shane kept her grounded and at peace, so much so, that she even started attending church services with him. While she still wasn't sure what she believed or if God was even real, Lola did have to admit that just being with Shane was enough to fill her heart with happiness.

~

July 19, 2002

Lizzie's eighteenth birthday arrived with a bang. Since Lizzie was Luke and Patricia's miracle baby, they always made a big to-do celebrating her life. As she did every year, Lizzie wanted her and Lola to have their parties together, since they were born two weeks apart. Although Lola appreciated the gesture, she again declined, feeling there's no real reason to take the spotlight from Lizzie.

Lizzie grew impatient as the evening progressed. "Mom, where is Mark? It's not like him to just miss my birthday. I didn't even get a birthday call or anything."

Even though she was well aware of Mark's whereabouts, Patricia agreed to keep her lips sealed. Lovingly embracing her daughter, Patricia spoke, "Just be patient, sweetheart. You know Mark always goes over the top when it comes to any celebrations involving you." Chuckling and feeling a bit relieved, Lizzie nodded her head in agreeance as she hugged her mother one last time before going to mingle with the rest of the guests.

At precisely 11:50 p.m., Mark arrived with a large entourage. While Luke had distracted Lizzie by talking to relatives who had flown in for her birthday, Mark had phoned Patricia to let her know that everything was ready and to send out Lola, Shane, Andy, and fourteen other guests. Once everyone was lined up single file, with Mark bringing up the rear, Patricia nodded to Luke, signaling the time had come.

Making his way to the small platform in the backyard, Luke clinked a glass, gaining the attention of all in attendance. Being a sensitive man, Luke always became overwhelmed when speaking about his pride and joy- his precious miracle daughter. With teary eyes, Luke spoke, "Before we call it a night, I just want to say 'thank you' to all who have come out to celebrate our precious baby girl."

Lizzie couldn't help but smile and shake her head at her dad. Luke continued, "Now if everyone will turn their attention to the back door, we have one last surprise in store for Lizzie."

When Luke finished his announcement, Patricia turned on *Wherever You Will Go,* by **The Calling** as each person in the row began to approach Lizzie while holding a vase of daisies. Hearing the music, Lizzie's heart skipped a beat while tears streamed down her face. Finally making his way in front of his beloved, Mark gave her the last bouquet before giving her a quick kiss on the cheek.

As the music faded off into the background, and the vases

adorning the back of the platform, Mark grabbed Lizzie's hands before speaking, "Happy birthday, my *beautiful hurricane*. You are mighty and fierce, but also beautiful and peaceful. You have brought so much love and joy into my life." Getting down on one knee, Mark said, "*Baby*, I know we're only 18, but I can't live my **life without you**. Will you marry me?"

For the first time in her life, Lizzie was speechless. All day she'd been quite upset, thinking Mark had forgotten her birthday; but as always, he had some grandiose gesture of love planned. Finally able to compose words and thoughts, Lizzie cried out, "Yes, Mark! A million times, yes!"

~

August 2, 2002

Lola's eighteenth birthday arrived two weeks later. Not being one for a big celebration, Lola requested her friends join her and Shane for a camping trip at the waterfall she and Shane visited a couple of years ago. So much had happened in those two years, Lola felt it would be nice for everyone to do something peaceful before going off in different directions for college and work.

Before leaving for the waterfall, Cate gave Lola a call to wish her a happy birthday. "Happy birthday, sweet Luxie. I hope your day is blessed."

"Thanks, Cate. I really appreciate you calling me. How's everything at the café?"

"It's all good here, so don't worry. Oh! Before I forget, I have good news."

Lola felt her stomach drop at the mention of "good news," because the last two times Cate proclaimed that, Jacob was involved. Not wishing to be rude, or hurt her friend's feelings, Lola nervously inquired, "Uh … what's up?"

"Well, Cade finally convinced Logan to not miss out on college.

Logan was thinking about taking a gap year since his mom had a baby back in February, two days after his eighteenth birthday."

"Woah, that's awesome! What did she have?"

"She had a little girl, who they named Eloise Elise."

"Aww, that's so pretty. Why did Logan want to take a gap year though?"

Cate went on to explain, "Logan wanted to help his mom, but she had apparently told him in a very matter-of-fact tone that he wouldn't be missing college in any way, shape, fashion, or form. If he continued to press the issue, she would be calling his uncle. Logan finally relented to go but told his mom, he would make the drive to campus only on class days, at least until Eloise turns two so that he could be there for her. From what Cade says, these types of conversations are common between Logan and Blue."

Lola laughed heartily, "Well, Cate, now I guess you'll get your wish for me to finally give him another chance to be friends. If Shane and I see him on campus, we'll make sure to show him around. Anyhow, we're about to roll out, so I'll see ya when we get back."

~

September 17, 2002

Nearly a month and a half after Lola's birthday, the group found themselves celebrating Shane's eighteenth birthday. One would think with Lizzie, Lola, and Shane having their birthdays so close together, there would be one big celebration; however, everyone enjoyed letting their friends have their own special day.

That day, Lola found herself very stressed, as she had no clue what to get Shane for his birthday. Shane kept reassuring Lola that her love and commitment were more than enough for him. Gazing into her eyes as he held her hands, Shane stated, "Besides, I want to treat you tonight. My parents made reservations for the two of us at *Étoile Bleue*."

"Oh my gosh, are you serious? I remember when we tried to reserve a table for prom and had no luck," Lola recalled.

"Dad always says it's the perks of being the CEO of a tech company. People always want to be associated with his name, so they typically make a way for him." Shane expressed with slight chagrin, before continuing on. "So, *Mijn Bloem*, wear something exquisite tonight."

~

Looking through her formal attire, Lola chose to wear a lovely, sheer chiffon, long sleeve, tea-length dress in sage green; with a nude slip underlay. The bodice of the dress was inlaid with small floral appliques, which flowed down to the sleeves. Lola paired the dress with a pair of pale gold, crystal-embellished, mesh pumps. Adding a new lip color and putting her hair into a low chignon, with curly wisps framing her face, giving the whole look a romantically ethereal feel.

Walking out into the living room, Lola felt her nerves at an all-time high. *Shay said something exquisite, so I just hope this is alright. Is it too formal? Is it not formal enough? Ugh ...*Hearing a loud gasp, Lola turned her attention to the other side of the room, where her eyes met Shane's blue-green ones. To say he was in awe would be an understatement. Swiftly making his way to his beloved, Shane wrapped his arms around Lola before hungrily capturing her lips. After several moments, the young couple breathlessly broke apart. "*Mijn Bloem*, I have no words...you are just...wow!" Shane spoke with tears of love dotting his eyes.

"Are you sure? I'm not over or underdressed am I?"

"Nonsense. Now, let's go to dinner before I cancel our reservations and take you here."

With a playful giggle and a blush across her cheeks, Lola stuttered out, "O-oh stop, you. Behave." Taking in Shane's appearance, Lola smiled. He had chosen a slim-fitting, tweed, three-piece navy blue suit, cream-colored dress shirt, navy tie with small cream polka dots, and a pair of cognac-colored dress shoes. "I must say, Shane Michael Carson, you look devilishly handsome. Happy birthday, baby!"

~

After a lovely meal, Shane got down on one knee while holding Lola's left hand in his. "Luxie, *Mijn kostbare bloem* (my precious flower), you are my everything. I am nothing without you and everything with you. You have shown me how to really love and how to forgive myself during my darkest moments. Your compassion knows no bounds. We have been together for two years and in that time, my love for you has only grown. You are my only one … will you marry me?"

Time seemed to stand still as every eye in the restaurant turned to gaze upon Shane and Lola. With tears falling down her rosy cheeks, Lola nodded in reply as she meekly called out, "Yes, Shane." The couple kissed passionately as everyone privileged to witness the proposal cheered them on.

~

October 24, 2014

Lola absentmindedly grasped Logan's hand in hers, as she stilled her voice. "Do you mind if we walk quietly for a moment," Lola asked. Logan stated that he didn't mind, in fact, it made his heart happy to see the flickers of joy in Lola's eyes as she reflected upon the sweet memories of her past. Walking silently for a good twenty minutes, the pair came across a fallen tree. "Logan, is it fine if we sit down and watch the sunset through the tree line before I ask you a very important question?"

"Of course, *my heart*; anything you want. After all, this time is about you."

As they sat, Lola gazed into the sky while still holding Logan's hand. *Lord, I need all the strength I can to make it through this. Please give me the right words to explain this.* Exhaling deeply, Lola squeezed Logan's hand as she avoided looking into his eyes, and asked, "Logan, do you know what the saddest sound in the world is? It's the sound that echoes across the planet yet, it's also the sound that no one can hear."

Pondering for a few moments, Logan truthfully replied, "No, *babe.* I'm sorry to say that I don't."

Sighing heavily, Lola expressed remorsefully, "I figured. Many have experienced it, but none like to think about it or focus on it …"

Lola trailed off while closing her eyes, as a gentle autumn breeze kissed her cheeks. After a few minutes of silence, Logan bravely asked, "Lola, what is it? What's the saddest sound in the world."

Eyes still closed, as tears pooled in the corners, Lola dismally stated, "It's the sound of a breaking heart. A heart that dies as what made it whole is ripped away so suddenly and tragically."

23

Liefdesverdriet

October 26, 2014

Two days had passed since Lola's thought-provoking question, and while Lola had wanted to power through this section of her story, it was Logan who made the conscious decision to reflect upon what he has learned so far. Lola graciously complied, feeling it only the right thing to do since Logan had been more than patient with her.

That afternoon, Lola asked Logan if he was ready for her to continue. As he wrapped his arms around her in a loving embrace, Logan said that he was. Allowing Logan to hold her for a few minutes, Lola broke away before speaking, "I'm glad. Now, if you are ready, I'd like to take you somewhere. Grab two cups of coffee from the café, and meet me at Averie."

Once they were in her car, Lola pulled out onto the main road, as Logan stared out the window wondering where they were headed to. After a few minutes of driving, Lola asked, "Logan, do you remember when I asked what the saddest sound in the world was?"

Turning to face Lola, Logan acknowledged, "Yes, *my heart*. You said it was the sound of a breaking heart."

Smiling bittersweetly, Lola continued, "The only other sound that is the hardest to hear, is that of a repairing heart. A heart once torn so far apart that it splintered, and trying to be repaired fragment by fragment."

Cautiously, Logan asked, "Where are we going?"

Lola replied, "You'll see soon enough. With everything that has happened, I almost forgot what today is … so … I guess it's just fitting."

~

September 2003

Another year had passed quickly for Lola- she was excelling in all of her classes, reveling in being able to call Shane her fiancèe, and taking her duties as Lizzie's designated maid of honor very seriously. While Shane and Lola were planning to wed in 2006 after graduating from college, Mark and Lizzie were eager to marry as soon as possible. Luke and Patricia were able to convince their headstrong daughter to have a year-long engagement, in order for them to save as much money as possible. Although they began saving since the day she was born, they wanted her and Mark to have the experience of their dreams and not worry about any costs. In the end, Mark told Lizzie that her parents had a point and the two agreed upon October 11, 2003, as their wedding date.

~

September 29, 2003

In true soul sister fashion, Lizzie and Lola were about to embark upon another one of life's journeys together. For about a month both girls found themselves feeling slightly under the weather; Lizzie equated it to prenuptial nerves, while Lola assumed hers was from her heavy class load. Shane grew concerned, and while Lola was able to reassure him she was fine, Lizzie was not so fortunate; Mark made Lizzie schedule an appointment with her doctor. "Lizzie, our wedding is coming up, and what if something's majorly wrong?"

Rolling her eyes in annoyance, Lizzie retorted, "Why can't you just let me be?"

"Please, *babe*. Please just make an appointment to ease my mind. You can even take Luxie if that'll help."

Laughing at this rare stubborn side of her usually mellow man, Lizzie kissed Mark before agreeing that he was probably right.

The date of Lizzie's appointment arrived, and both she and Lola found themselves in the waiting room of their family doctor. Lizzie demanded that if she had to get checked out, Lola should too. "*Baby bear*, if it's your class load, the stress could give you an ulcer. Why don't you let Dr. Rose check you out?"

After a brief stay in the waiting room, the girls were called back to their appointment room. Most physicians wouldn't allow them to go back together, however, Dr. Rose was a compassionate lady, having known the pair were a lifelong package. "Good afternoon, girls. What seems to bring you both in?"

Each girl took turns explaining their symptoms to Dr. Rose, while she made minor notations. "Now, girls, I think I know what's going on but I'll need to ask you each a couple of questions."

In unison, Lizzie and Lola agreed to Dr. Rose's questioning. "First off, would you each mind telling me when your last period was?"

Sheepishly, Lizzie admitted that she honestly didn't know and assumed her cycle was sporadic due to the stress of the wedding, "The last one I'm pretty sure I had ended right after Lola's birthday because the week after, we all took that trip to Seattle for a belated birthday celebration."

Reality slapped Lola in the face as she blurted out, "Shit! You're right. Oh, fuck! That's the same trip we all got high and drunk on, isn't it?" Realizing she blurted out profanities and illegal activities in front of her childhood doctor, Lola sheepishly replied, "Ugh- sorry,

Dr. Rose. You won't say anything, right?"

Dr. Rose chuckled as she reassured both girls that doctor/patient confidentiality was in full effect, and now that both girls were over the age of 17, she was no longer legally obligated to inform any parental figures. "So, on this Seattle trip where 'indulgences' occurred, were either of you sexually active? If so, did you use protection?"

Lola's face paled, while Lizzie laughed hysterically. Lola admitted that she wasn't sure if she and Shane had used protection that night, even though they normally do. Lizzie on the other hand stated, "Dr. Rose, Mark and I have never used protection. We've been doin' it since Sophomore year. We've always known we would be together forever, so ... yeah, if we get pregnant, it's a happy accident."

Wide-eyed, Dr. Rose clapped her hands together as she exclaimed, "Umm ... well, why don't you girls follow me to the restrooms? I'll get two pregnancy tests and go over with you both how to use them."

After going through the directions and waiting the required five minutes, both tests came back positive. "Now, girls, from my calculations, I am going to presume that you are both approximately seven weeks pregnant. Lizzie, you could be further along, if you have been sexually active this long without protection. Make sure to schedule your appointments with Judy at the front desk."

Once they were back in Lizzie's car, both girls cried; Lizzie cried tears of joy, while Lola cried tears of concern. "Lizzie, I'm never getting drunk or high again. Shit! Shane and I planned to finish college, get married, then after a couple of years have kids. What the hell are we gonna do?"

Lizzie held Lola's as she softly spoke, "Sis, look at me, okay?" Once she had Lola's full attention, Lizzie said, "These babies, they're blessings from God. I mean, how sad would it be for us to not go through this life step together?"

Rolling her eyes at Lizzie's mention of *God*, Lola said, "I don't know about God, but yeah … I guess you're right. I mean, we are a package deal after all. Anyhow, when are you telling Mark?"

"I'm telling him as soon as I get home. When are you telling Shane?"

Nervously, Lola gulped, "Yeah … about that … I'm going to wait until after you and Mark come back from your honeymoon."

"Lola Luxe Swan, what the hell are you thinking?"

"Look, Elizabeth Renee Sommers," seeing Lizzie cut her eyes, Lola smirked, "You want to use full names, well- I can too. Anyhow, as I was saying, I'm waiting until after y'all get back to tell Shane. I want to focus on your wedding and besides, Shane and Andy are going camping shortly after. If I tell Shane now, you know he's gonna cancel and Andy has really been looking forward to it."

"How's Andy doing by the way?"

"He's alright, I guess. I know having both Zaylee and Luke, or Luka, god I can never remember his name, end things with him must've hurt, but he doesn't show it."

Sighing in defeat, Lizzie promised, "I don't agree with your choice, but I won't even tell Mark. Let's just hope this doesn't bite you in the ass."

~

October 2003

Mark cried tears of joy when Lizzie announced her pregnancy, he couldn't wait to be a husband and father. Much to their relief, both sets of parents also took the news very well and were extremely supportive.

Aside from a small bridal shower, neither Mark nor Lizzie felt the need to have a quintessential "last night of being single" with a drunken haze. There had been several reasons, but the most important was Lizzie's pregnancy and the fact that Lizzie gave Shane a foreboding warning. "Shane Michael Carson, you listen to me and you do it well. I swear that if there is even a hint of debauchery, I will hunt you down and burn your car."

Shane shot Mark a look pleading for help. Shaking his head as he laughed pitifully, Mark clasped a hand on Shane's shoulder, "Ya know, brother, I'd like to say this is pregnancy hormones … but … yeah, who the hell am I kidding? We **all** know this is just Lizzie, being Lizzie."

Reassuringly, Shane told Lizzie, "Don't worry, Lizzie. Alright? You should know by now, that's not my style. We're just gonna go hiking and maybe catch a movie afterward. Besides, why would I want to see some random chick flaunting her tits and shaking her ass when I get to come home every night to *Mijn Bloem!*"

~

October 11, 2003

Wedding day had finally approached with jubilation resonating in the air. Lizzie and Mark couldn't have picked a more perfect day to wed, with the temperature settling in the mid-70's. As the sun set down into the horizon, Lola dancing closely with Shane became lost in her thoughts. *I can't believe this little one is growing inside of me. I know I freaked out at first, but honestly...I think I'm kind of excited now. I think I will finally tell Shane in November. I wonder if we should move to Swan Manor? I think I would like to see our baby growing up where I did.*

Shane looked down at Lola with wonder in his eyes as he marveled, "*Mijn Bloem*, you are positively radiant. I have never seen you look more magical than what you do, in this **golden hour**."

Lola's heart leaped with love and a small twinge of guilt at Shane's expression of love. *Ugh...bestill my heart. I want to tell him, but this isn't the right moment; I'm going to have to stick with my plan.*

~

October 15, 2003

After their wedding, Mark and Lizzie left for their month-long honeymoon adventure in New Zealand; they wanted to maximize their time alone as much as possible, while Lizzie still had the energy.

Shane and Andy packed for their two-week-long camping trip; while the original goal was for them to only camp for a weekend, Shane felt it wise to maximize time to reconnect with the brother of his heart. Still leaving Shane in the dark about the life growing inside of her, Lola was secretly happy to have solitude for a couple of weeks, as her pregnancy left her feeling physically drained. *I'm so tired all the damn time. I thought that nearing the second trimester meant I'd get more energy. I honestly don't know how much longer I can go without telling Shane.*

Shane bent down and lovingly nuzzled into Lola's neck, speaking enticing words whilst placing delicate kisses upon the sweet spot on her neck. "*Mijn Bloem*, I can barely go a day without you, how the hell am I supposed to go two full weeks without your sexy body and your intoxicating presence?"

Lola shivered as she panted out, "Shay, you're … going to have … to stop. Andy's waiting in the car." Shane chuckled as Lola playfully jested, "Shay, my love, I am sure you will manage just fine. Besides, this time will be good for you and Andy to reconnect."

"You're right as always, my love. Can you please just come to see me at the campsite on the twenty-sixth? It gives Andy and me most of the trip to hang out, and then I can have three, *very needed*, days with you."

Lola readily agreed before kissing Shane goodbye, allowing another opportunity to tell him about the baby slip through her fingers. Stubbornness can be a fickle fiend, for once she has a hold of your mind, it is damn near impossible to relinquish her deathly grasp.

~

October 26, 2003

While the first week of being by herself had been serene, the beginning of the second week brought an old, unwelcome friend- her thoughts. The guilt of denying Shane knowledge of her pregnancy began to eat away at her. *You're so selfish, you know that right? I mean, can you be any more like your mother? You may look like your father, but in your core, you're all Anne-Marie. Shane's going to hate you for keeping this a secret. Honestly, what does he even see in you anyhow?* Finding the faintly scarred areas on her palms, Lola allowed her nails to find comfort as the warm liquid slowly seeped under her nailbeds.

The ringing of her cellphone in the background brought Lola back to reality; quickly washing her hands and bandaging them before answering the call with a breathless, "H-hello?"

"*Mijn Bloem*! Damn, it's good to hear your voice! Are you okay? You sound winded."

Lying easily, Lola simply reassured Shane that she had just come in from a run and was trying to catch her breath. Shane chortled, "Don't overdo it, otherwise you'll be too tired to come see me!"

Bemused, Lola retorted, "Now, now, Mr. Carson … who said I was even coming?"

Flirtatiously, Shane stated, "You will be later!"

Although none were around her, Lola felt her cheeks warm as a blush crept upon them, "Shane! Oh my god … you! Control your hormones, boy."

Shane belted out with a belly laugh, "*Mijn Bloem*, you know I have to give you a hard time. But in all seriousness, when will you be here? Andy and I are grabbing some extra supplies so that I can cook dinner tonight."

Lola reassured Shane that she would be arriving in a few hours.

"I'm just about to finish packing. So, what have you guys been up to?"

Shane hemmed and hawed before uneasily replying, "Wel-l … we've done some fishing and may or may not have done some hunting."

Never being one to feel overly comfortable with the idea of guns, Lola worriedly asked, "Umm … Shane, is that really a good idea? I didn't even know you knew how to shoot a gun, let alone owned one."

After Shane reassured Lola that he and Andy took a refresher course when planning their trip, Lola disapprovingly relented before setting out in his direction. Sighing to herself, Lola knew she couldn't really be too mad at Shane for not sharing this small tidbit with her, when she kept a far bigger secret from him.

~

What should have been a two-hour drive, took Lola four, as she cursed herself. *Fucking pregnancy problems. I can't believe **now** is the time this child decides to cause a revolution in my body. All of this puking nonsense should have happened in the early part of the first trimester, not magically starting near the end.*

Parking her car by Shane's, Lola quickly grabbed her bag, along with a flashlight and backlit compass, before heading down the three-mile path where Andy and Shane had set up camp. Shane had told her the path shouldn't veer, but bringing a compass and flashlight was always a wise idea, especially in the dark of night.

Apprehension filled Lola's gut as she slowly walked along the darkened path. Not normally one to spook easily, Lola found herself jumping at every little twig snap, leaf rustle, or minor breeze. *Lola Luxe Swan, get yourself together. Everything is fine. You'll be there soon.* The closer Lola came to the campsite, apprehension became gut-wrenching fear that she couldn't shake. In the distance, she heard what sounded like panicked yelling of Shane's voice, "What the hell, man? Look, just put the gun down."

Hastily, Lola quickened her pace, calling out Shane's name before tripping over a leaf-covered tree root. As Lola's body crashed to the ground, her entire world crumbled around her; for in the distance, as clear as a church bell on Sunday morning, a gunshot rang out. *No, no, no. Get up, you stupid idiot.* Lola chastised herself as she stood to run again.

Finally arriving at the edge of a clearing, the warm amber hues of the campfire became the backdrop for a horror story. Approximately 10 yards in front of Lola, Andy stood holding a **Smith & Wesson M&P**, looking down in disbelief; while to her left, Shane's body lay bleeding out. In what felt like an out-of-body experience, Lola swiftly made her way to Shane, who was barely clinging to life.

"Shane … oh my god … fuck! There's so much blood," Lola choked out in sobs. "Please *baby*, stay with me. I have to tell you …"

With a feeble voice, Shane interjected as he lovingly touched Lola's face, "*Mijn … Bloem …* I l-love … y-you. H-he-help … An-d-d-y."

Lola begged for Shane to listen to her, she had to tell him the truth of her pregnancy, because maybe the news would give him a tiny bit of hope to cling to. Sadly though, Lola's pleas would only be heard by the wind, as she cradled the love of her life in her arms.

~

October 26, 2014

Standing in front of a beautifully adorned, white granite head-stone, Lola turned to Logan and did the only thing she could do; she grabbed onto his jacket as if it were a lifeline and released the flood of tears that welled up within her. Logan did the only thing he could think to do; he embraced Lola as the torrential tears soaked his shirt. His heart could never deny her, especially when she was finally opening up about the greatest tragedy in her life.

After several minutes of intense sobbing, Lola asked Logan to wait for her in the car while she spent a few moments alone at Shane's gravesite. Upon returning to her car, she asked Logan if he minded driving back to the apartment, "Now, Warren, don't get any ideas. Averie here is my baby, so this is a one-time deal."

Forcing a chuckle through the heavy ladened atmosphere, Logan jested, "We'll see about that, *babe*."

As Logan drove, Lola found her voice once more, "October 26, 2003, was the day I started dying. At that time, everyone was so confused because Andy wouldn't ever hurt anyone, especially Shane. Knowing what I know now though ... yeah ..." Trailing off as she gazed out the window, Logan knew what Lola was going to say; and while he wanted to allow the justice-seeking beast within him to take over, he knew the monster must be kept at bay.

When Logan pulled into the parking space by his car, Lola grabbed his hand just as she spoke, "I used to hate myself every day for not telling Shane about the pregnancy, in fact, it's still my deepest regret. When I first told Dr. Indigo what happened with Shane, she told me that there was more to living than just being alive. I didn't understand this for quite a while, so I finally asked her what she meant ..."

Hearing the hesitation in Lola's voice, Logan questioned, "What did she mean?"

"She told me that just because I wake up each day, it doesn't mean that I am actually living my life."

Thoughtfully, Logan proclaimed, "So ... you're just barely getting by."

"Yeah. She then said, 'When you don't allow yourself to express and to feel, you become an empty husk and shell of a person. And Lola, you are so much more than that.'"

Knowing he should probably wait, Logan acted upon impulse as he reached across the center console before capturing Lola's lips in a gentle kiss. A hitch in Lola's breath signaled that she was caught off guard, but instead of pulling away as better judgment told her, Lola chose to passionately return Logan's kiss.

24

Vindictive Condemnation

November 5, 2014

Nearly two weeks had passed since Lola told Logan about Shane's death, as well as the passionate kiss which occurred in Lola's car. Unspoken words hung in the air like the first snow of the season waiting to fall.

With the holidays looming around the corner, Lola wondered where she would go this year; while she played around with the idea of asking Logan if she could join him, Cate, and Cade when visiting the rest of his family in Vienna. However, propriety and protocol deemed self-invitation as rude. Eventually gaining the words she needed, Lola queried, "Uh … I know it's still a ways off, but what're your plans for the holidays?"

Logan wanted nothing more than to spend Thanksgiving and Christmas with the keeper of his heart, but with his mother's very choice feelings concerning Lola, Logan knew that this simply wasn't the year to press his luck. Cautiously, Logan responded, "Well … most likely, dad, Cate, and I will join the rest of the family at the cabin. As much as I'd love to bring you, *babe*, my mother would flip shit! How about we plan on doing something special for my birthday or something like that?"

To keep her disappointment at bay, Lola smiled at the thought and stated that she already had a standing invitation at Mark and Lizzie's and was wondering if he would want to go with her. Kissing her lips sweetly, Logan smiled, "I'd honestly love that. Why don't you see if Mark and Lizzie want to do something in between?" Lola squealed with delight as she pecked Logan's lips, before giving in to the lust burning within her.

Breathlessly exhaling, Logan gazed into the evergreen orbs beneath him, "God, I love you so damn much," before leaving to meet up with his dad.

Ever since the passionate kiss in her car, Lola found herself willingly seeking out Logan's kisses; although, the weight of his loving adoration still stung bitterly, as she was still unable to bring herself to offer sentiments in return. After a phone conversation with Dr. Indigo regarding the current events, Lola did her best not to focus on her inabilities, but instead focus on her progress. "Lola, the fact that you are seeking out physical affection with Logan is an amazing advancement from where you were even a month ago."

~

November 27, 2014

Thanksgiving for Lola had been eventful, and it had done her heart good to spend time with her family; Luke and Patricia offered affectionate embraces while trying to fill her in on news of her mother. Even though it had been several years since Anne-Marie had abused her, Lola still couldn't bring herself to taint Luke and Patricia's image of the woman they loved so dearly as a daughter. Lizzie hated Lola's self-sacrifice, even going so far as to threaten finally revealing the truth to her parents. "Elizabeth Renee Keane, you will do no such thing. I don't know who the hell you think you are, but it's not your place to tell them," Lola stated firmly.

"Sister, they have a right to know," Lizzie protested.

"**You** think they have a right to know, but have you ever thought about what that knowledge would do to them?"

"Well, no but …"

"Exactly! You didn't fucking think, Lizzie. Your parents are old and dropping a bomb like that on them would destroy their world. I know you mean well, and I love you for it, but for everything that is good in life, I am *begging* you to finally just drop it." Taking a deep breath, Lola closed her eyes in an effort to calm herself. "Lizzie, I don't mind bearing the weight of what happened. I'm in a good place now, so yeah …"

Knowing Lola would never relent, Lizzie submitted; after all, she would never want any heartache to destroy her parents. They suffered enough with what little knowledge they had been given regarding Lola's hospitalization

~

November 29, 2014

Lola allowed an additional two weeks, giving herself a full month of just living, before readying herself to proceed with her story. After a second date consisting of dinner and a movie, Lola asked Logan to join her on the couch, as she was ready to move forward. With two glasses of warm apple cider and the Lussekatter Logan brought home from his grandmother, the pair cuddled up on the couch with a thick, fuzzy blanket.

Taking a bite of the delicious bun, Lola couldn't help the small moan that escaped from her lips. "Oh my god, Logan! This is one of the most amazing things I have ever eaten. What is it?"

Chuckling, Logan filled her in, "Well, *my heart*, that is a traditional Swedish Christmas bun called, Lussekatter. My grandma …"

Lola interjected, "The one that you said is your mom's mother and from Sweden?"

"Yeah! Well, anyhow, she makes them every year. Grandma always makes extra because most of the Lussekatter and Polkagriskola, which is a peppermint topped toffee, go to my *Zio*, in L.A. Out of the two, the Lussekatter is definitely my favorite."

"I love toffee! Maybe you'll be able to bring some Polkagriskola after Christmas." Logan nodded his head in agreeance before calmly waiting for Lola's cue she was ready to speak.

~

November 20, 2003

In the weeks following Shane's death, time simultaneously stopped while moving in overdrive. Most cases, such as the one being built against Andy and labeled as second-degree murder, often took anywhere from months to years to even begin progressing forward; however, for Andy Bennett, it seemed fate had other plans.

Andy held onto his plea of innocence, and those who knew him well knew that there was no way Andy could ever harm anyone; however, the evidence stacked against him looked bleak. Jordan and Mona were in an unusual predicament- should they choose to support District Attorney (D.A.) Sierra Holden's case against Andy, or should they believe their second son's claims of innocence and pray that one day the real murderer would be convicted? In the end, far against public opinion, Jordan and Mona chose to believe Andy; they knew him better than anyone else, and if he claimed his innocence, then in their eyes, that's exactly what he was.

Sparing no cost, Jordan hired Attorney Ronan Harper, as Andy's defense attorney. At age 29, Ronan was the youngest attorney to make partner at his father, Luis' law firm, **Connor, Montgomery, & Harper**. Calling Ronan into his office, Luis told him, "Son, I'm going to level with you. The only reason I'm giving you the **State of Oregon vs. Andy Bennett** case is because I believe in you. That being said, this is a make it or break it moment for your career and a true chance to prove you truly earned your place as a partner and didn't advance because of nepotism."

"Geez, dad. No pressure, huh?" Ronan gathered all of the documentation provided by the police and went to check the crime scene for himself. Ronan was able to find what he hoped would be the saving grace of this case; he hated to see his client's life thrown away.

Although Ronan tried to petition for more time, Judge Barton refused, so Ronan did the best he could with what little he was presented with. The day before the trial, Ronan called Andy's friends, Andy's therapist, Dr. Derek Winters, the school faculty and administrators, and even Shane's parents, into his office in hopes of providing the jury with ample character witnesses, who would prove his client had been arrested under false pretenses.

The day of the trial arrived, and with it brought a severe thunderstorm, the likes of which rarely appeared. Walking up the courthouse steps, as reporters tried to flag her down for an interview, Lola bitterly thought, *Even nature knows this case is a farce.* Once inside the courthouse, she made her way in search of Ronan.

Having no luck, Lola decided to rest on a bench; her pregnancy was extremely hard on her body, which she simply wrote off as stress. Guilt still resided in the forefront of her mind, for she hadn't even had the ability to inform Jordan and Mona that she was carrying their grandchild. *How the hell can I tell them now? Oh yeah, by the way, I'm pregnant with your grandchild. What's that? Why are you just now finding out after your son's death? Welp, that's because I am a selfishly stubborn bitch who chose not to tell your son....Yup...that sounds about right.*

A minor cramping feeling began to resonate within her lower belly, and while she should have addressed it, Lola chose to ignore it and instead hone in on the voice calling out her name. "Miss Swan?

Miss Swan?"

"Yes, that's me," Lola answered as she looked at the man before her. He stood at approximately 5'10, with a medium, sunkissed golden complexion. He also had warm black wavy hair, which was smartly parted to the right, and the brightest emerald green eyes Lola had ever seen; eyes which spoke of determination to prove Andy's innocence.

Looking at the grieving young woman before him, Ronan greeted her promptly. "I am sorry we've not had a chance to go over your statement until just before the trial. Are you sure you are okay to take the stand?"

Steadfastly, Lola replied, "Yes. I know in my heart of hearts that Andy is innocent. Someone framed him and Shane deserves real justice, not his brother being crucified.

~

Witness after witness took the stand, all providing unblemished accounts of Andy's character. Everyone in the courtroom felt hopeful that this farce of a trial would be dismissed. Standing once more, Ronan addressed the judge, "Your honor, before calling the last witness on our list, the Defendant would like to speak on his own behalf."

Judge Barton allowed Andy to take the stand, and once he was seated, Ronan began his questioning. "Mr. Bennett, if you would, please recall for the court the events leading up to the incident in question."

Taking a few deep breaths, Andy told the court everything about the camping trip and all of the events that had occurred, prior to Shane being shot. "Everything was going well, we were just hanging out and waiting for Luxie to arrive when we heard something in the distance. Shane and I stood to check it out but found nothing, so we sat back around the campfire. A few minutes later, I needed to take a piss, so I told Shane I was going to find a tree to mark. He laughed and said he'd be waiting on Luxie …"

Hearing his client pause, Ronan queried, "Mr. Bennett, it's alright if you need a couple of minutes. Just take your time."

From the side, D.A. Holden belted out, "Objection, your honor! Defense is leading the witness."

Judge Barton, tired and ready for the Thanksgiving holiday, affirmed, "Sustained! Witness will proceed with speaking, while the Defense will refrain from pampering the witness. Mr. Harper, it would serve you well to remember your job."

Anxiety flooded Andy's body as he began to bounce his right leg up and down, a calming technique recommended by Dr. Winters when vocalization exercises were not feasible. D.A. Holden, made sure to make note of Andy's twitchy mannerisms, as she was finally ready to sink her claws into him with her round of questioning. *This case should be open and shut, it's an easy win. Besides, next year is an election year and this case will look good under my repertoire.*

Finally able to calm himself, Andy continued, "As I was taking a piss, I heard Shane yelling out and I quickly zipped up and ran back in his direction. When I got there, there was a figure in all black pointing a gun at Shane. I hate that I froze, but I was scared shitless."

Feeling sorrowful for his client, Ronan stated, "No further questions, your honor."

Turning to D.A. Holden, Judge Barton asked, "Does the State wish to question the defendant before he steps down?"

With her award-winning smirk and a glint of victory in her steely gray eyes, Sierra Holden stood preening her black bobbed hair as she asked, "Mr. Bennett, you claim on the night in question, that a mysterious black figure was present in the woods. How do you expect the court to believe this, when the police found no evidence of any other footprints except for those who were questioned the night of Shane Michael Carson's murder?"

Firmly, Andy stated, "I know what I saw! I'm not fucking blind, you worthless cow."

Clanging his gavel on the bench, Judge Barton turned to Andy as he bellowed, "Mr. Bennett, need I remind you that you are in **my** courtroom! You will show respect to **all** members of this court. Now, I have shown you mercy by letting your foul language slide. However, if there is one more disrespectful display, I will hold you in contempt and have the jury deliberate at once. Do I make myself clear?"

Biting back the bile in his throat, Andy enunciated, "Crystal, your honor."

With a nod from the judge that she was now able to continue, D.A. Holden asked, "Mr. Bennett, who's idea was it to go hunting?"

"It was Shane's. He hadn't been in years and thought it would be nice to finally make use of the hunting license he renewed every year."

"Alright, Mr. Bennett, next question. Are you 21 years of age yet?"

"No ma'am."

"Would you mind stating for the court how old you are then? Also, please inform the court how old the victim was."

Sighing in frustration, Andy retorted, "I don't see what this has to do with anything...," before a stern look from Judge Barton caused Andy to change his tune. "I'm 19 and I'll turn 20 on April 25, 2004. Shane had just turned 19 on September 17 of this year."

"Interesting. Mr. Bennett, if you and the victim are both under the age of 21, why did police find several beer cans at your campsite?"

"We brought some beer from our place. A couple of college buddies left a few cases after a party and we figured why not bring them."

With a triumphant look upon her face, D.A. Holden nonchalantly concluded, "Well then, Mr. Bennett, isn't it safe to say that maybe due to being under the influence of alcoholic beverages, that you most likely imagined this mysterious figure in black? This presumption stands to reason, as stated previously, the police never found any unaccounted footprints."

Paling at the blatant disrespect of his client and unnecessary accusations being thrown, Ronan bellowed out, "Objection, your honor! District Attorney Holden is badgering my client and leading them. I would also like to present Defense exhibit A to the court."

Having already decided the outcome in his mind, Judge Barton proclaimed, "Objection overruled, however, as for the evidence, I will allow it … for now. Would both counsels please approach the bench? Mr. Bennett, you are free to return to your seat, but please know the D.A. reserves the right to call you back to the stand."

Presenting his evidence to the judge, Ronan explained how he had gone on his own to the crime scene and found a partial footprint that had been carefully covered by a low-hanging fir branch. Examining the photograph before passing it on to D.A. Holden to review, Judge Barton remarked, "Mr. Harper, while I would like to allow your 'evidence' in the court, I am afraid it is merely circumstantial and therefore inadmissible in court. You are both now free to return to your positions."

Returning to sit by his client, Ronan couldn't even look Andy in the eye. This was the one piece of evidence he hoped would at the very least get the case dismissed on the grounds of lack of evidence. *It looks like I'm going to have to call Shane's fiancée, Luxe, to the stand. God knows I was trying to avoid this since the poor thing has suffered enough as it is.*

Once both counselors were now seated, Judge Barton exclaimed, "The court has heard enough, and now the jury will deliberate-"

Cutting off a judge is never wise, but Ronan was not yet ready to give up on his client. "Your honor, the defense has one last witness to call."

"Mr. Harper, you are about to be held in contempt. If the witnesses and the case you have presented do not sway the jury in your favor by now, then it is highly unlikely one last witness will." Turning to the bailiff, Judge Barton remarked, "Bailiff, please see the jurors to the deliberation room. Court will resume once a decision has been reached,"

~

"All rise! The Honorable Judge Barton is now entering the courtroom," the bailiff bellowed out before asking everyone to be seated. After two hours of deliberation, the jury had finally reached a verdict; to say that everyone was on the edge of their seats, was an understatement.

Walking over to the jury, the bailiff grabbed the verdict card, handed it to the judge, then back to the lead juror. Judge Barton queried, "Has the jury reached a verdict?"

"We have, your honor."

"What is the verdict?"

"We, the jury, find the defendant, Andre Roman Bennett, guilty of the second-degree murder of Shane Michael Carson."

25

Confliction

November 29, 2014

Exhaustion fell upon Lola as she drew the conversation to a close. Allowing her head to rest on Logan's shoulder, Lola muttered, "Everyone was flabbergasted beyond belief, ya know. I guess that's something good that came from this whole mess … truth."

Logan allowed Lola to rest upon his shoulder until he felt the tingling pricks of sleeping nerves, and the small puddle of drool saturating his shirt. Chuckling, he said, "Alright, sleepyhead; it's time to move you to bed."

As Logan gently covered Lola with the comforter, he weighed several options in his mind. *Shit! How do I go about this whole fiasco? What the fuck do I even say to that? I mean, do I admit that she's right and that truth came from the most horrific moment of my life? Or, do I just stow any emotions regarding this away until later? I get that truth did come about, but how can I be happy about that revelation when...*

With tears falling from his eyes, Logan kissed Lola upon her forehead before grabbing his guitar and notebook and sitting just outside the apartment in hopes that strumming a few chords for **Momentary** would take the edge off of his nerves. Pierre had called a few weeks prior saying they all loved the title name and would offer Logan any help if he needed it for chords and lyrics.

~

January 2, 2015

Braving through the hecticness of Christmas and New Year's Eve, Logan and Lola found themselves preparing for a quiet dinner at Mark and Lizzie's. When Lola announced at Christmas dinner that she would be bringing a special friend very soon, Raelee squealed with delight. "*Auntie Bear*, I hope he makes you smile and not cry like the man with scary white eyes."

Gently reassuring the ten-year-old girl that her new friend, Logan, was much nicer, Lola proposed, "If I remember correctly from what Cate has said, Logan has two sisters that are close to your age. Maybe if things work out well, you make a couple of new friends?"

Giddy with the thought of new friends, Raelee stated thoughtfully, "I wonder if they like ballet. If not, I hope they're nice and enjoy playing dress up and stuff," before pirouetting out of the dining room in the direction of the room Mark had designed as an in-home ballet studio.

Looking at Lizzie, Lola asked, "Sister, is Baby Rae okay? Does she have friends at the studio?"

Concern filled Lizzie's voice as she relayed, "She's had a few struggles with some of the girls ostracizing her because the director continually places Rae in lead roles. They have also made rude comments about her weight, trying to call her anorexic. I mean, what the hell? Do you remember us being so catty at that age?"

Lola shook her head, "Honestly, no. But then again aside from each other, we never hung out with girls our age … just Shane, Mark, and Andy."

Lizzie stated, "I've asked the director not to put Rae in the spotlight as much, but she's determined that Rae will one day become a principal dancer. She said, and I quote, 'Mrs. Keane, one as naturally gifted and dedicated as Raelee, is meant to do great things in this profession. I would not be a good teacher if I didn't foster her talent.' So … yeah."

When Lola relayed Raelee's struggles to Logan, she asked him about his sisters. "Do you think, maybe if I get to meet your family, Raelee could come with us? Lizzie said she just wants Raelee to have a couple of good friends, even if they live a couple of hours away."

"*Babe*, I'll talk to my mom when it's time, but I think that's a great idea. My mom … ugh how do I put this … well … she isn't your biggest fan," Logan tried to state his mother's disdain for Lola as delicately as possible.

While most women would have been upset by this revelation, Lola agreed, "Logan, I'm not surprised. Hell, most days, I don't even want to be around me. I can't even imagine as a mother, if I had a son, him bringing home some fucked up bitch like me."

Grabbing Lola's hand in his, Logan moved a curl out of her eyes as he chastised her for putting herself down once again before inquiring, "Speaking of being a mother … If you don't mind my asking, what happened to your baby? Did you give it up for adoption?"

With an expression etched in contrition, Lola lamented, "I was hoping this wouldn't come up … but I guess it's the next event in my miserable life. Let's get through tonight and I promise I'll tell you everything in a couple of days. Deal?" Logan readily agreed as the couple made their way to his car.

~

Dinner at the Keane home was one filled with love and friendship. Mark and Logan spoke to one another as if they had known each other for years, while Raelee was excited to show off her new skills for being *en pointe* to an eager audience. After showcasing a portion of her solo from *La Sylphide*, Raelee pointedly asked, as children often do, "So, Mr. Logan, when are you gonna marry my *Auntie Bear*?"

Logan couldn't help but double over in laughter as Lola's drink spluttered from her mouth. Wiping the joyous tears from his eyes, Logan said, "Well, Miss Raelee, I would say that all depends on your Auntie," while tossing a flirtatious wink Lola's way.

Grabbing Lola's hands to stand her up, Raelee had them spin together, "Oh, *Auntie Bear*. I hope to have a handsome man look at me in love like Papa looks at Momma or Mr. Logan looks at you. I would feel like the most magical girl in the whole world."

~

January 5, 2015

The days following dinner with the Keanes, found Logan and Lola stealing glances at one another whenever they were in the same room; or casually allowing their hands to linger a little too long.

Lola awoke that morning and knew the time had finally come to tell Logan what happened with her baby. Lola prepared for a run, in hopes this would take the edge off of her nerves. Sensing her presence had been removed from the bed, Logan awoke, "Morning, *babe*. Where are you going?"

Lola filled Logan in on her plan before asking, "Why don't you come with me? I'm only going for a half, so it shouldn't take too long."

"What the hell is a half?"

Lola chuckled in amusement as Logan's eyes bulged from their sockets, "A half means the length of a half-marathon or 13.1 miles."

"Are you trying to kill me?"

"Oh, come on and stop being such a baby. Running is good for your body, especially after overindulging during the holidays," Lola pointed out.

"So is sleep, and I think … Hey! Don't steal my blankets," Logan yelled as he laughed at Lola's antics.

"How about we strike a deal? You come with me for a small run, like 5k length, and then we'll come back for lunch and I'll tell you about my baby," Lola proposed.

"You're not giving up are you," Logan asked before playfully pouting in agreeance.

~

As they made their way back into the apartment, Lola couldn't help but laugh at Logan's breathless expression. "You know, Warren, when you ran across the beach with me on your shoulders, I thought you were out of breath because of my weight. Now I know the truth! You're just out of shape."

Flexing his arms, Logan boasted, "*My heart*, look at these guns and tell me I'm out of shape."

Lola couldn't help but laugh at Logan's playful antics before getting lost in her thoughts while preparing lunch. *You know, I didn't realize how long it had been since I really laughed. This time with Logan has shown me that I can still be witty and funny; which is something I thought Jacob stole from me. I just hope Logan doesn't change his feelings for me when he learns the truth about the baby.*

Sitting down at the table with soup and salad for lunch, Lola asked if Logan was ready to listen; once he gave the signal, she began.

~

December 1, 2003

The cramping in Lola's lower belly only intensified in the days passing Andy's trial and conviction. Her fall, the death of her lover, the incarceration of one of her dearest friends…all things that added extra stress onto her already naturally gaunt body. No longer able to bear the pain, Lola called Dr. Rose to see if she could be seen that afternoon, who just so happened to have an afternoon cancellation.

"Good afternoon, Luxe. I'm surprised to see you here. I heard about …" Dr. Rose began to offer her condolences before being abruptly cut off by Lola.

"Look, Dr. Rose, I know what you're gonna say and please … please just save the pity. I just want to discuss this pain in my stomach."

"Of course, Luxe. My apologies for starting our appointment in an unprofessional manner. Now, have you had any spotting or bleeding recently?"

"I've had some minor spotting since the trial. Is that bad?" Lola asked, slightly concerned.

"Not necessarily. Approximately 25% of women do experience some form of spotting early on in their pregnancies. Why don't we do an ultrasound to see how baby is developing, okay?"

Lying back upon the exam table, Lola lifted her top and rolled down the waistband of her skirt for Dr. Rose to apply the blue jelly-like substance, as she spoke. "Now, Luxe, if my calculations were accurate, you should be around 16 weeks pregnant as of yesterday. Want to know some fun facts about baby's development at this point?"

Nonchalantly, Lola replied, "Sure- why not?"

"Wonderful!" Dr. Rose bemused before continuing, "At 16 weeks, baby will be around three or four ounces in weight and four or five inches in length. Baby's eyes should begin working. Baby can start recognizing your voice too."

Bringing Lola's attention to the monitor, Dr. Rose pointed out the tiny baby in Lola's womb. While most mothers felt jubilation at the sight of the tiny life housed within them, but not Lola; the only thing she felt was numbness. Dr. Rose spouted off several other facts before stating, "Baby's heartbeat should be nice and strong as well. Speaking of the heartbeat, let's see if we can find it!"

Hemming and hawing for several minutes as she moved the doppler around Lola's belly, Dr. Rose found herself greatly dismayed. *God, hasn't this poor girl suffered enough? Must I really tell her this...* Clearing her throat to mask the tears, Dr. Rose asked Lola to sit up while she had a talk with her, before momentarily exiting the room.

Returning with a box of tissues in hand, Dr. Rose sat beside Lola, passing her the tissues as she dismally affirmed, "Luxe, I don't know how to sugar coat this, so I'm just going to be blunt. It looks as if your baby has passed. The cramping you have been feeling is your body's natural way of removing the baby."

Tears streaming down her face, Lola asked, "When?"

"It's hard to say, but if I had to guess, it would be around the time you began cramping."

Wiping the tears from her eyes, Lola confided in Dr. Rose, "This is what I deserve for not telling Shane about the pregnancy to begin with. I knew he was too good for me, even his child couldn't stay."

Standing to leave, Lola thanked Dr. Rose for her time as she took the pamphlet explaining the symptoms that would continue to occur in her body as it completed this process.

~

May 6, 2004

Through everything that had occurred in her life, by some miracle, Lola had managed to stay on top of all of her course load. When grief came knocking at the door, the only thing Lola could do to survive was to board up the door. However, when the knocking became too persistent, she found solace in her old coping mechanisms once more.

There were days Lola found herself longing to experience the things Lizzie was with her marriage and pregnancy; this was the first time in their history where they weren't on the same page. Other days, Lola couldn't help but feel relieved at the fact that she didn't have to do this on her own. The back and forth added a new player into the mixture of her already messed up mind- Confliction.

~

Having breezed through her finals that week, Lola decided to pick up a couple of weekend shifts at **Cate's**; while she could have found a job at any place in Portland, Lola longed for the comfort of the one friend who wasn't either incarcerated or pregnant. Pulling her car into the parking space, Lola was pleased to find business was booming. *The more people there are, the less I have to be left alone with my thoughts.*

Before stepping out of the car, Lola tossed her curly hair into a high ponytail and applied some cherry-flavored lip gloss. Upon entering the cafè, a boisterous laugh resonating through the building made Lola's blood freeze. Panic filling her chest, Lola willed her lead-filled legs to the lady's room, where she would be ready if the bile rising in her throat made due on its promise to expel from her mouth. *You've gotta be shitting me right now! Why is he here? Hell, why am I freaking out? It's been almost four years. You're better than this, Lola Luxe Swan.*

The opening of the bathroom door shook Lola from her thoughts. "Luxie," Cate squealed as she embraced her friend.

"H-hey, Cate," Lola choked out.

"Did you just get here? I'm sure you saw how packed it is today. Not that I'm complaining but it's already one in the afternoon and it's the first chance I've had to go pee since we've opened. Sales have been up like crazy, so I even had to call J in for help. Well, I'll see ya out there."

Giving herself one last look in the mirror, Lola checked over her outfit as she prayed it would be downplayed enough to keep Jacob's eye off of her. She had chosen a pair of black khaki shorts that stopped mid-thigh and had a cute, braided white belt to accentuate her already slender waist. Smoothing down her black cropped, tight-fitting tank, Lola was grateful she had thought to bring a purple flannel shirt as a form of cover-up and modesty, which she rolled at the elbows. *Let's get this day over with.*

~

All throughout her shift, Lola felt Jacob's icy gaze rove over her body; four years ago this gaze would have rendered her weak in the knees, but today she was stronger and a bit more jaded. Anytime Jacob came in her vicinity, Lola made sure to find a customer or task that needed tending to in the opposite direction.

In Lola's mind, the day had been quite successful in her efforts to avoid the man who tormented her … right up until she made it to her car; there, she found Jacob waiting. With daggers lacing her words, Lola seethed, "What the fuck do you want, Jacob? It's been a long ass day and I don't have the energy to deal with your shit."

Putting his hands up in defense, as a sign he meant no harm, Jacob cautiously spoke, "Look, *Vix* … I mean Lola. I just wanted the chance to talk with you."

Seeing sincerity in his diamond eyes, Lola felt her resolve try to crumble. Glancing at her watch, Lola firmly articulated, "You have five minutes to make this worth my while and if it's not, I'm going to get Cate. I don't have time for your sick ass games, Jacob."

Knowing this was his one chance to make things right, Jacob sputtered nervously, "I just wanted to say I'm sorry."

Laughing maniacally, Lola retorted, "You're sorry! Your ass is sorry? For what? Tormenting me? Sexually assaulting me? Making me lie to everyone around me?"

"Yes, all of that and for -," Jacob began before Lola cut him off with venom dripping in her words.

"Almost four fucking years and now you decide to come apologize? Why? What's the catch?"

Closing his eyes in an effort to remain composed, Jacob pinched the bridge of his nose, "I know and I can't change it, alright! I wanted to come sooner, but as I know Catarina has filled you in, our father is less than accommodating; he's had me traveling extensively. I wanted to show my condolences when I heard the news of Shane passing but then I figured you might think I was trying to take advantage of you in your time of need."

Feeling her walls crumble, Lola looked at her watch one last time as she muttered out, "Five minutes are up, Jacob," before entering her car. Watching him walk away, Lola broke down for the first time in months. The weighty door she built was swept away in the undertow of her repressed emotions.

~

May 12, 2004

Six days later, at 39 weeks gestation, Mark and Lizzie welcomed a beautiful little girl named Raelee Sommer Keane, into the world. Lola had been one of the first people in the recovery room, after Mark and Lizzie's parents, and as she held her niece, she couldn't help but feel bitter. *I should be experiencing this joyful moment too. I can't fault Lizzie for being happy but it hurts like hell knowing that I'll never hold my baby in my arms or kiss my lover again.* Giving Raelee a peck on her forehead, Lola passed the precious babe back to Lizzie, before embracing both parents and offering her congratulations.

Leaning back in the driver's seat, Lola felt the heaviness trying to fully consume her. Needing some sort of distraction, Lola reflected upon the conversation with Jacob that was constantly in the forefront of her mind, no matter how she tried to ignore it. *I wasn't prepared for an apology. Fuck! Even his eyes showed sincerity. Should I believe him or should I be cautious?*

Everything within Lola told her that she should remain cautious, however, she never was one to err on the side of caution. Knowing she would probably regret this decision later, Lola wiped a stray tear from her eyes as she picked up her phone.

"Hello?" Came the voice on the receiving end.

"H-hey, Jacob. Uh … it's Luxie. I mean yeah, you probably guessed that" Lola nervously spat out.

Chuckling, Jacob said, "Hey there, Lola. What can I do for you?"

"Well, I gave some thought to what you said last week, and I was wondering if you could meet me at this new coffee shop in Portland called **Brewed Awakening**. Plus …" Lola trailed off as tears threatened to break way.

"Sure thing. Catarina has the cafè under control and all of my other businesses are under control, so I'm free all afternoon."

One hour later, Lola found herself sitting at a patio table across from Jacob, sipping her iced vanilla latte. "Thank you for meeting me here."

Jacob returned the thanks for being invited, before Lola continued, "Like I said, I've given a lot of thought to what you said, and I've decided to forgive you. I have so much going on in my mind as it is, that hating you is the least of my worries. Today has just been …"

Lola found herself rambling, "Shit! You probably don't want to hear about my day. I'll just wait until I can talk to Cate. So, thanks for meeting me. I guess I'll see you around."

When Lola stood to leave, Jacob gently grabbed Lola's hand, "Like I said, I'm free all day. I know I'm not Catarina, but she has said that I have a great listening ear. If you want, we can walk around at the South Waterfront part of the Willamette River; it's not too far from here after all."

~

As Jacob and Lola walked along the waterfront, Lola unloaded every emotion and painful memory she had experienced in the last year, even telling him about the baby; something she still had yet to tell Cate. Jacob said, "If I may speak, do you think that maybe you feel jealous of your friend, Lizzie? You probably feel like she's flaunting all of her achievements, while you are left desolate."

Smiling to herself, Lola had to admit that it felt freeing to empty her emotional vault. Grabbing Jacob's hands in hers, Lola stared into the icy eyes before her, biting her lower lip, she breathlessly proclaimed, "Cate's right, you really do have a great listening ear. Thank you for today, Jacob," before she stood on tiptoe to capture Jacob's lips with her own. Jacob hungrily returned Lola's kiss as a glint of chicanery glistened in his eyes.

And thus began the beautifully, haunting relationship between the broken girl and an enchantingly ophiomormous man.

26

Incandescently Arduous

January 5, 2015

While cleaning up the lunch dishes, Lola turned to look at Logan, "For so many years, I have had this confliction deep within my soul."

Striding over to her, Logan wrapped his lanky arms around Lola's waist, inhaling her scent. "What do you mean exactly?"

As flutters arose in her stomach, Lola focused on the tasks at hand. "Well, I've always felt conflicted about the guilt I have for not telling Shane about the baby and then losing the baby. Like, maybe I could have done something different, ya know? Then, the other part sets in, where I feel relieved that I didn't have to raise a baby with everything I was going through. As fucked up as it sounds, now that I'm older, I can understand why my mom left. But ..."

Running the tip of his nose along the side of Lola's exposed neck, Logan reassuredly reminded Lola that she wasn't her mother. "*My heart*, you would never abuse a child. Even when you mentioned feeling pain in your heart holding Raelee, you still loved her. May I ask a question?"

Trying her best to focus on something other than the desire for Logan burning within her, Lola stuttered out, "Y-y-yeah, sure!"

Chuckling as he placed a delicate kiss behind her ear, Logan asked, "Do you think you'd ever want kids?"

Placing her hands upon Logan's arms, Lola pondered before answering, "Hmm … you know … I don't think I'd be opposed to the idea of children if the circumstances were right with the right person."

Nibbling on her earlobe a bit, Logan lustfully whispered into Lola's ear, "I'll **gladly** be your baby daddy!"

Swiftly turning to face him, Lola brought her hand across Logan's cheek as she fiercely reprimanded him; her face turning crimson. "Logan Asher Warren," she sputtered before quickly escaping to the bathroom.

Bringing his hands to his mouth, Logan bellowed, "Totally worth it, *babe!*"

~

February 14, 2015

While February 14 merely signified Valentine's Day, for the vast majority of the populace, for Logan it was also the date of his birth. After an early morning birthday call from his mom and sisters, Logan phoned his uncle, Antonio, to ensure he was still good to use the private jet and everything was set for later that evening. "I don't know how I can ever repay you for this, *Zio* … I know, I know … Anyhow, I'll let you know once we land … Lola's birthday is in August, and everything keeps going well between now and then, I'll introduce her to mom, Dean, and the girls first … Talk to you soon, *Zio*."

Turning to Lola, Logan asked if she was ready to drive to the private plane hanger at the Portland airport. "Woah," he exclaimed in awe, "I don't think I have ever seen your hair straight."

Rolling her eyes in annoyance, Lola sassed, "And for good reason, so don't get used to it, Warren; this shit took over four hours yesterday. Besides, I'm gonna style it when we get on the plane. I hate having my hair down past my ass."

Gathering her weekender bag and purse, Lola placed her hands on her hips as she asked, "Are you finally going to tell me where we're going?"

"No-p-pe!" Logan quipped, drawling out the "p" sound with a pop of his lips in an effort to playfully mock Lola. "Besides, I want to see your eyes light up when we arrive. Now, move your sweet, little ass so we can get this show on the road."

~

Once everything was secured and the captain had given the signal that it was fine to move about the cabin, Lola set out in search of an outlet for her flat iron. Lola decided that since it was Logan's birthday, she would do something special with her hair. Glancing in the mirror, Lola tried to recall the last time she had done something special with her hair. *It was definitely over two years ago ... maybe the last time Jacob and I went out? It's funny how you forget the tiny details when you live your life as an eccedentesiast. Well, enough of that! I hope Logan likes the style I have in mind.*

Two hours later, the captain announced that they would reach their destination in approximately thirty minutes, "Clear skies and sunny, folks. If you can, please return to your seats." Taking note of her cue, Lola packed her flat iron back in its heat-resistant pouch before tapping Logan on the shoulder to announce her return.

Seeing the fiery beauty before him, Logan felt his jaw drop. Lola giggled at his reaction and tossed him a tissue while fastening her seat belt. "Close your mouth, Warren, you're drooling."

"Lola, *my heart*, you look…wow! I don't think I've seen your hair like this since…" Logan thought for a moment before recalling the memory. "Ah yes, it was the last charity gala, four years ago."

Hiding her face in embarrassment, Lola called out, "Oh, god. That entire night was a shit show.

Smiling, Logan protested, "That's not the way I recall it. The theme was 'Old Hollywood' and you shone like the star you are. From the Hollywood waves, which you have now, to the long sleeve, velvet dress with a low back. The emerald green hue amplified everything about you."

Lola belted out in laughter, "Is that why Naja slapped the shit out of you?"

Shrugging nonchalantly, Logan said, "Totally worth it, *babe*."

Lola playfully swatted at Logan before remarking, "You know that dress belonged to my grandmother, Lorriene. She was the one who originally started the charity galas to raise funds for the **Center**. I always loved seeing it hang in her closet and she told me one day that I would get to have it for my own."

Getting lost in a light-hearted conversation, the descent to their destination swiftly passed by. Thanking the crew for their kindness and service, Logan and Lola stepped off the plane before walking in the direction of the private garage, where Antonio had a car ready for Logan to borrow. Taking a black satin scarf from his bag, Logan told Lola she would need to be blindfolded in order for the surprise to maintain its full effects.

"Really, Logan. Why must I be blindfolded? I promise not to peek," Lola protested.

"Don't be a spoil sport, babe. Besides, it's my birthday," Logan countered.

Scowling with obstructed vision, Lola sneered, "Ya know, just because it's your birthday doesn't mean it's okay to blindfold me."

Knowing Lola wouldn't be able to slap him for his upcoming flirtatious remark, Logan seductively said, "*Babe*, you know, you don't even have to wait until your birthday to tie me up."

"Logan Asher Warren! We are in public. Are you trying to make me die from embarrassment?" Lola recoiled. Logan loved seeing the playful feistiness that had begun surfacing in Lola as the days went by.

~

"Logan, can I please remove the blindfold," Lola meekly asked before stating, "I'm feeling a bit claustrophobic. I promise if you want me to keep my eyes closed, I won't peek. I just don't think I can handle not being aware of my surroundings anymore ... it's getting a bit ... overwhelming."

Cursing himself for making Lola feel anxious, Logan told her it was fine and she could definitely look around to gather her bearings. "I'm sorry ..." both belted out simultaneously, before laughing.

"Lola, I'm sorry. I didn't mean to make you feel so anxious. I was honestly just trying to be playful," Logan stated sorrowfully.

Letting her eyes readjust to the sunlight, Lola gently placed a reassuring hand on Logan's right arm, while he kept his left on the steering wheel. "Logan, you don't have to apologize. I went along with it initially because I knew your intent was pure. Besides, since it's your birthday, I wanted to play along. My mind, however ..."

"Lola, you don't have to go on if it's too uncomfortable," Logan offered reassuringly.

"I-I can't go into everything yet, b-but after a little while, my mind started to relive some of the really messed up shit Jacob did to me when I was blindfolded." Lola wearily tried to explain before clearing her throat as she fidgeted with her leggings. "But, enough of that, okay? It's your birthday.

~

Pulling up in front of a glamorous hotel, Lola asked in awe, "Logan, is *this* **The Roosevelt**? Are we in L.A.?"

Handing the keys to the valet, Logan chuckled, "How did you guess?"

"Really, Logan! I grew up a hotel heiress **and** I am the CEO of a hotel conglomerate. It's my job and familial duty to know the biz," Lola stated matter of factly as she entwined her fingers in his. "I've always wanted to come visit this place, well and L.A. in general. The architecture of *The Roosevelt* is supposed to be second to none. Plus, if we have a chance, I'd like to scope out some areas to maybe expand *Swan Hotels* in California."

Giving Lola's hand a gentle squeeze, Logan said, "I thought you weren't supposed to be working."

Scrunching up her face as she stuck out her tongue, Lola retorted, "Killjoy!"

~

After settling into their suite, Logan and Lola began to ready themselves for their night on the town. As she carried her garment bag and makeup case in the direction of the bathroom, Lola sighed, "You know, I really wish you would have told me what you wanted for your birthday."

Logan declared, "Lola, beautiful keeper of my heart, how many times do I have to tell you that all I want is to just spend the day with you. Just to enjoy one another's company is more than enough-"

Interjecting, Lola shrugged, "Umm … okay, if you're sure. If you change your mind, just let me know," before turning heel into the bathroom.

Watching her leave, Logan put his hand to his chest in an effort to control his racing heart. *What I really want is to make love to you, but I know you're nowhere near ready for that.* Logan pushed the notion from the forefront of his mind, as he started to get ready.

Normally, he would opt for some shade of blue or even green, as those were his two favorite colors; however, for this evening, Logan chose an ensemble in Lola's favorite color palette, thus making it perfect for Valentine's Day. After slipping into a pair of charcoal, slim fit slacks, Logan put on a cream-colored dress shirt; foregoing the tie in favor of leaving the top two buttons undone, for a more relaxed look. Completing the look, Logan added a velvet, slim-cut blazer in rust red, and black patent leather dress shoes. Stepping out onto the balcony, Logan gave Antonio a call to quadruple-check his reservations.

~

While in the bathroom, with her garment bag opened, Lola contemplated the two outfit options she had chosen to bring along. Finally settling for the black, wide-legged pants, which would be paired with a black, satin, v-cut bralette, and sangria colored, satin blazer with matching clutch; Lola saved the sparkly, silver mini-dress for another evening.

The outfit she chose was one she had only worn a handful of times, and while removing the jacket made her uncomfortable, she was sure Logan would like the overall look. Completing the look with subtle makeup, save her signature deep red lipstick, and a pair of strappy black, open-toed heels, Lola exhaled as she gazed upon her reflection. *I am thankful for the cooler weather. It sure does make it easier to hide all of the scars.*

Apprehensively walking into the bedroom, Lola scanned the room for Logan before spotting him on the balcony. As she began walking in his direction, Logan opened the sliding door, "Seriously, *Zio*, you and *Zia* are the best ...," his voice trailing off as he took in the beauty before him. "Uh-hh, I'm gonna have to let you go, *Zio*," Logan stuttered out before taking two long strides over to Lola.

Wrapping his arms around her waist, Logan huskily breathed out, "My god. You just get more and more beautiful each time I see you."

"Oh, hush you. You act like you haven't seen me practically all day."

"I have two years of not seeing you to make up for," Logan

reminded, while placing a gentle kiss on Lola's lips, before leading her out the door of their suite and down to the valet for their car.

While driving to their destination, Logan decided to go ahead and fill Lola in on where they would be having dinner, in hopes that he could make up for blindfolding her earlier. "The place where we're heading to for dinner is owned by my *Zio*, Antonio. He purchased it shortly after he married my *Zia*, Cynthia, and gave it his special nickname for her."

"Aww!" Lola exclaimed in adoration, "That's so sweet. What did Antonio name the restaurant?"

"**Bel Fiore**. It's Italian for beautiful flower; which is what Cynthia reminds him of."

Lola beamed with delight, "Your family sure does seem to filled with hopelessly romantic men. You, your dad, and now from the sounds of it, your Uncle."

Pulling up for the valet, Logan handed over the keys as he grabbed Lola's hand, "I honestly don't think it's a bad thing, *my heart*."

Playfully pinching Logan's arm with her free hand, Lola jested, "Never said it was, Warren."

~

Cynthia Moretti ensured the VIP section was reserved under Logan's name, and made Antonio swear that he wouldn't go anywhere near the restaurant. "Listen, *my love*. You need to let Logan do this on his own and when *he* thinks it's the right time for us to meet his Lola, then he'll let us meet her. Now," she commanded, "if you know what's good for you and I'm very good for you, you will promise me you'll stay home. Otherwise, it's the couch for you."

Groaning like a rich teenage girl who's father just cut up her credit card, Antonio relented. Cynthia pecked him on the cheek before calling out as she turned in the direction of their bedroom, "Now if I remember correctly, it's Valentine's Day and I am married to a very sexy, beast of a man. If you see him, please send him after me so that he can unwrap his gift. It may or may not be in his favorite color.

~

Ensuing their amazing dinner, Logan and Lola found themselves back in their suite, where lusty emotions were at an all-time high. Lola was unsure if it was the overall sexual tension that had been growing between her and Logan since their last kiss, the romantic atmosphere of the entire trip, or a combination of everything, but all she knew was that her insides felt like they were on fire.

Stripping away her jacket and removing her heels, Lola strode over to Logan as she seductively proclaimed, "I finally figured out what to get you for your birthday!" On the outside, Lola may have oozed confidence; but on the inside, her mind was trying to extinguish what little courage she had.

Logan's breath hitched as Lola grazed her hand upon his groin, before devouring his lips. Letting the pent up emotions take the lead, Logan broke their kiss just long enough to swiftly wrap Lola's legs around his waist, walking her to the bed. Laying her back, Logan removed his jacket and shirt before positioning his body above Lola's as he recaptured her lips. As tensions swelled and clothing lessened, Lola breathlessly called out Logan's name.

For most men, the woman they love calling out their name in a breathy moan would have sent them over the edge. Logan Asher Warren, however, was not most men. Lola calling out his name was a much needed wake up call. *God, You know I want this. Please give me the strength to let her know I'm not rejecting her because I don't want her. In fact, it's quite the opposite. I love her far too much to take advantage of her in a healing state.*

"Lo-l-la, w-we n-nee-d to stop," Logan ardently exhaled.

Feeling utterly embarrassed, Lola grabbed a pillow in hopes of hiding her face. "I'm so sorry, Logan." She mumbled out behind her pillow.

Helping Lola sit up, Logan swept her lovely rose-red hair from her face, doing his best to reassure her. "Lola, I didn't stop because I don't want you."

On the verge of tears, Lola fretted, "Y-you didn't? Did I do something wrong then?"

Wiping a stray tear that made its way down Lola's cheek, Logan sympathized with her worries. "No, not at all. I stopped because I worry we're moving too fast. I love you with all of my heart and don't want to take advantage of you while you're still healing."

Meekly, Lola said, "You're right. I'm sorry for acting on impulse."

Kissing Lola on her cheek, Logan assured her that in the future, when the timing is right, he will gladly stop holding back before standing a bit uncomfortably, "Now, if you'll excuse me … umm … I've got to go … umm … take care of something in a very icy shower."

Slightly confused, Lola asked, "What do you …" before it dawned on her what Logan meant, "… oh my god! I'm so sorry." She called out as she once again buried her embarrassed face in the pillow.

~

February 15, 2015

At two in the morning, Logan found himself very restless. Looking over to the beauty next to him, Logan slipped out of bed, putting on a pair of track pants and a plain black tee, before sending a quick text message to see if Antonio was awake and if he could stop by. Antonio responded, reminding Logan that he was welcome any time of day and never needed to ask.

The drive to Antonio and Cynthia's was grueling at best, as Logan continued to chastise himself for his earlier response. *What kind of idiot is 31-years-old and turns down sex with the most beautiful woman in the world? This fucking idiot, that's who. Logan, you really are one stupid son of a bitch, aren't you?*

Cynthia and Antonio greeted Logan warmly, as they showed him to the living room. Looking around, Logan remarked, "It's been a while since I've been here and it seems like nothing's changed."

Cynthia turned in the direction of the kitchen to get water for the three of them, while Antonio gestured for Logan to sit in the arm chair adjacent from his own. "Now, *nipote*, what's going on?"

Sighing heavily, still very discontented with himself, Logan explained everything in great detail to Antonio; who listened earnestly. Antonio chuckled, as Cynthia came up to wrap her arms around his neck. "*My love*, I'm going to head to bed. Don't worry, Logie, I'd bet my life that she's having the exact same feelings and struggles as you are."

Kissing his wife "good night", Antonio turned to Logan as he stated, "Your *Zia* is right." Before he proceeded to tell Logan the details of his earlier years prior to becoming enamored with Cynthia.

Glancing at his phone, Logan noticed that four hours had swiftly passed. Trying his best to stifle a yawn, Logan wished his uncle well. Antonio grabbed a small box from the kitchen island as he led Logan to the door. "Happy birthday, *nipote*. I hope this is something you'll love and can bring you some peace of mind, while you're **Loving Lola**."

~

As he sat in the driver's seat outside of the hotel, Logan opened his gift prior to returning to his suite. A joyful smile spread across his face; he couldn't wait to tell Pierre, Pablo, and Shaw what Antonio had gifted him … well, all of them.

Back in his room, Logan stripped down to his underwear as he crawled into bed. Finally feeling at ease with his decision, Logan drifted off to sleep as he held onto the keeper of his heart.

27

Euphorbia

February 16, 2015

While still in sunny Los Angeles, Logan and Lola found themselves easing back into their casual banter; the embarrassment of their missed connection tucked safely in the back of their minds. As she prepared to check out a potential location for expanding **Swan Hotels**, Lola's phone rang. Seeing the name of her assistant flash across the screen, Lola stepped out onto the balcony to take the call privately; while not disturbing the call Logan was on.

"Good morning, Marina. How's everything going?" Lola warmly greeted.

Nervously pacing around her office in Portland, Marina nervously spluttered, "Umm … everything's oka-y, I guess."

Cocking her head in mild confusion, Lola inquired, "I'm not following, Marina. You're going to have to elaborate for me."

Exhaling deeply, Marina exclaimed, "I may or may not have messed things up in regards to Mr. Andre."

Feeling dread in the pit of her stomach, Lola did her best to remain calm so as not to frighten the dear girl who boldly entered the bear's den. "Alright, Marina, why don't you let me know what happened.

Okay? As I have stated many times, Andre is nothing but a hardass. There's a lot of things that have happened that I can't really talk about, but I'm sure you're just fine."

"If you're sure, Lola," Marina stated as she caught her breath before informing her boss in grave detail the entirety of her interactions with Andre Bennett.

~

February 2, 2015

The morning of February 2 started off as any other morning would for Marina Isobel Vasquez. Ever since Lola had agreed to give her a promotion on the condition of brokering the deal between **Swan Industries** and **Carson Tech**, Marina spent countless hours gathering research to show Andre Bennett why it would only maximize profits for both companies in the long run.

Smoothing down her black suit, Marina stepped out of her aquamarine 2008 **Lexus ES 350**; gathered her presentation items, and entered the front lobby of **Carson Tech**. Finding the front desk clerk busy at work, Marina politely drew his attention as she made notice of his nameplate. "Good morning, Trevor. Would you be able to tell me if Mr. Andre is currently available?"

Looking up from his computer screen, Trevor instantly became enchanted by the sapphire-eyed beauty before him; from her rich olive complexion to her divine chocolate curls, he knew it was a lost cause. Realizing he had been quite impudent in his staring, Trevor meekly cleared his throat before asking, "Uhh … I'm sorry miss, what was the question?"

Chuckling politely, Marina repeated, "It's okay, Trevor. I was asking if Mr. Andre was available."

Professionalism setting in, Trevor inquired, "What's your name? I'll pull up his calendar to see if I can find your appointment."

Sheepishly, Marina replied, "My name is Marina Vasquez. You

won't find my appointment though, as I don't have one."

Sighing heavily, Trevor looked back into the sapphire eyes standing above him, "I-I-I wish I could help you, Miss Marina. Without an appointment, even someone as alluring as you, won't get in."

The deafening sound of heavy footsteps resonated through the empty lobby caused Trevor to immediately make his way to the front of his desk, as he held onto some important looking files with shaky hands. "G-g-g-ood m-m-morning, Mr. Andre. Here are the files you asked to be ready upon your arrival. Miss Marina here would like a moment of your time."

Marina gave Trevor a small smile as she delicately approached Andre Bennett. "Good morning, Mr. Andre…" She sweetly began, only to receive a curt glance before Andre marched swiftly to his private elevator.

Not one to be easily scared away, Marina turned to Trevor as she pledged, "Trevor, I think you and I are going to become fast friends. I'll be here all day, every business day until Mr. Andre gets bored of me and finally relents!"

"Miss Marina, I wish you all the best. Braver men have tried and failed."

"See, my dear, sweet Trevor, that's where I'll succeed. Men may have tried and failed, but I am far from being a man," Marina winked as she returned to the plush lobby bench.

~

February 12, 2015

Ten full business days had passed, and Marina made true to her vow to Trevor. Every single time Andre Bennett passed through the foyer of his office building, there sat Marina Vasquez with her presentation promptly in hand; and each time she greeted him in her sweet, lively demeanor. Most businesses would have had Marina physically escorted from the building, but Andre was quite curious to see how long her determination would hold through.

By the close of business on the tenth day, as she stood to leave, Marina overheard Trevor answer his phone. "Yes, sir … Are you sure? S-s-sorry, sir … I figured as much, sir … Right away, sir."

Hanging up the phone, Trevor wrote something on a slip of paper and folded it in half, before striding over to Marina. "Miss Marina, Mr. Andre said that if you can show up tomorrow at 8:00 a.m. with the meaning of the word enclosed on this paper, he will grant you your presentation."

Unfolding the paper, Marina saw the word **_Euphorbia_**. Glancing back at Trevor with inquisitive eyes, Marina asked, "What's this?"

Turning away, as the sparkling sapphires staring back at him would cause his countenance to falter, Trevor called back, "As much as I would love to help, my hands are tied, Miss Marina. I've got faith in you though. You sure are the most persistent girl I've ever met, and if I wasn't already engaged to my sweet Tilly, I'd ask you out in a heartbeat."

As Marina drove in the direction of her apartment, she chose to give her _Shavta_ (grandmother) a call; in hopes that the older woman might give her some insight into this very daunting situation, she now found herself in.

~

February 13, 2015

The conversation with her grandmother had been precisely what Marina needed to renew her focus and hone in on the answer to the question at hand. After much discussion about all of her cousins back in Seattle, Washington, the older woman told her that whether Trevor realized it or not, he had inadvertently provided her with the answer she needed. "My little, _Sheifale_ (lamb), think of the qualities we spoke over you in childhood; there you'll find your answer."

Arriving promptly at 7:45 a.m., Marina greeted Trevor warmly, who informed her that Andre was already waiting in his office, which she would find on the 25th floor. As the elevator slowly inched to her destination, Marina smoothed down her houndstooth patterned pencil skirt in hopes of calming her nerves. *You've got this, Marina. You've come too far to turn back now.*

The final ding of the elevator blatantly resonated as if to announce Marina's impending defeat, instead of her arrival. With gold heels clicking across the floor, Marina felt her courage begin to waver, as she overheard the employees whispering. Finally, outside of Andre Bennett's office, Marina reiterated her earlier pep talk before placing a delicate knock on the door.

"Enter." The baritone voice commanded from the other side of the closed door.

Walking into the office, Marina forgot to close the door as she took in her surroundings; where she noticed that it was very much the romance novel cliché office, all the way from the brooding color palette to the oversized leather sofa. Seated behind the mahogany-colored desk, Marina finally had the opportunity to fully analyze Andre Bennett's features. He had a perfectly chiseled jawline; coiffed honey-blonde hair, with subtle champagne undertones; and green eyes the likes of which Marina had never before encountered. The eyes which fixated her started off as a clover shade, but the longer she stared, Marina saw the rich emerald rings and flecks of jade.

"Ms. Vasquez, if you have finished with your gawking, I'd like to move forward. I am a busy man after all!"

Andre's abrasive tone brought Marina back to reality, as she belted out, "Persistence," before regaining her composure. "The answer you are looking for is persistence. *Euphorbia* is a plant symbolizing such."

"Well done, Ms. Vasquez."

"Thank you, Mr. Andre; it is one of my best qualities after all,"

Marina playfully boasted with a flick of her hair.

"That opinion remains to be proven factual. You have one hour to impress me," Andre pointedly remarked.

During Marina's presentation, a crowd began to form, as all were curious about the young woman who boldly outlasted the icy tactics of their employer. As the final word passed from her lips, a rousing cheer came from those in view of Marina's beautiful oration.

"Back to work," Andre barked before commanding Marina to sit in the chair in front of his desk.

Andre leaned forward, clasped his hands together while strumming his fingers, deep in thought. Fifteen minutes of eerie silence passed, with Marina feeling utterly unnerved when Andre finally spoke. "Ms. Vasquez, while that was a roving performance; apparently garnering the attention of my entire staff, I must deny your proposition.

Dumbfounded, Marina spluttered, "W-what? Did you not see the projections?"

"Oh, I saw them alright, and while they might make me a profit … I see no real reason to provide products solely to **Swan Hotels** or even **Swan Industries** in general."

Enraged that countless hours of work would now be flushed away, Marina gathered her belongings before she bitterly spat out, "Andre, or should I say, Andy, you need to grow up!"

Noting the look of shock upon the face of the man before her, Marina continued, "When I said I did my research, I meant it. Yes, shit happened to you, but you need to learn to move on and stop holding on to what you missed out on before and see that you are missing so much more by being jaded now."

No employee dared to utter a word as Marina stormed off in the direction of the elevator, for they had never witnessed their hard-nosed boss being rendered speechless.

"Back to work, before I dock your pay!" Andre boomed as he slammed his office door, shattering the glass. "Mother fucker!" He cursed as he angrily phoned Trevor demanding a crew come fix the door before the end of business the following day.

~

February 16, 2015

Having listened intently, Lola responded as Marina's voice trailed off at the end. "Andy definitely is a tough one. I will say, I am proud of you for sticking with this and for your determination. How do you-"

"One moment please, Lola. There's someone at the door," Marina politely interjected as she set the phone on her desk. Signing for the delivery, Marina returned to her phone.

"Okay, I'm back. Sorry for interrupting."

"That's alright, Marina. Is everything okay?" Lola inquired.

"Umm … I think so," Marina replied hesitantly, "I just received the strangest bouquet of flowers."

"Is there a card?" Lola asked although she was more than certain as to who the sender was.

Marina responded that there was in fact a card, as she placed her phone on speaker. "The card says that the flowers are scarlet geraniums, amaryllis, and purple hyacinths. Oh! It's from M-Mr. Andre," Marina stuttered out at the end.

Beaming brightly, Lola stated, "Ah! I expected as much. Does he give you the meaning, or does he expect you to look it up as he did with his challenge?"

Marina was silent for a couple of moments before she responded, "He provided the meaning. The card says, 'Please forgive me (purple hyacinths) for my pride (amaryllis) and stupidity (scarlet geraniums).' Then, he asks if I am willing to forgive his impudence if I would be willing to meet him for dinner tonight at the new restaurant Naomi and James Grey just opened here in Portland, **Mon Étoile**; from what I hear it's supposed to be even more exclusive than **Étoile Bleue**."

With final parting words, Lola offered, "I would accept but in a very 'Andy' way. You're a clever girl, so I know that I won't need to spell it out for you. Also, I would recommend picking up a book on the language of flowers. I have a feeling that it will suit you well in the future."

With determination in her mind, Marina let Jade and Daisy know that she would be leaving early for today, before making her way downtown in search of a vintage book store where she was sure to find what she needed.

~

Morning quickly turned to evening and for the first time in his life, Andy Bennett found himself nervously awaiting his dinner guest's arrival. He had been quite surprised earlier that afternoon when Trevor phoned up from the lobby stating there was a delivery of a single sprig of *Liatris* and a *Fern* frond wrapped together with a blue ribbon, and an unsigned card reading "See you tonight at nine."

Andy didn't have to suffer through his nerves for long, as the maître d' escorted Marina to his table. Marina was a vision in a modest, short-sleeved, cocktail length, lacey dress in the same sapphire shade as her eyes; she kept her attire simple with nude makeup and heels; pulling her curls halfway up, allowing the rest to cascade down her shoulders.

Standing in a gentlemanly manner, Andy greeted Marina warmly as he pulled out her chair. "I must say, I am quite impressed with the response you sent," Andy expressed honestly.

Marina chuckled softly, "I may or may not have been given some 'insider info' on the best way to respond."

Playfully rolling his eyes, Andy simply muttered, "Fucking Luxie."

After enjoying their meal, as they awaited dessert, Andy spoke. "I want to thank you for joining me tonight, Ms. Vasquez-"

"It's Marina. Please just call me, Marina," she warmly expressed.

"Thank you for joining me tonight, Marina. I am glad that you are, as your message said, sincerely willing to try again. Now, I have given your proposal significant thought over the last few days and I will accept **but** only on one condition!" Andy firmly stipulated.

Nervously, Marina inquired what the condition was and the revelation was not something she was prepared for. "Thank you for the lovely evening, Mr. Andre," Marina uttered as she left the restaurant. The outcome of the evening had not been something she had expected and she now found herself feeling overwhelmingly confused.

28

Withered Poppies

February 2015

For Logan and Lola, the month of February was quite eventful. After Marina's dinner with Andy, who preferred Andre these days, because as he pointedly reminded Lola, "That boy died right along with Shane. You and I both know that nothing was ever the same without him;" Marina informed Lola that Andy would only accept the proposal on the condition that she, Marina, come to work for him. With much thought and consideration, Lola told Marina she should pursue this opportunity. Jade and Daisy were sad to see their friend move on but were excited knowing she would keep her new boss in line. Thus, Marina found herself the head of the Swan-Carson partnership.

Lola returned to Parkway on February 18 alone, although that had never been the original plan. While Logan and Lola were en route to the air hanger, Logan received a phone call with exciting news from his friend Shaw. The call ended as Logan parked in the back of the hanger, in guest parking. Turning to Lola, he hesitantly began, "I'm going to have to stay for a little while longer. I'm thinking two weeks at the most."

Clearly confused and rightfully so, Lola inquired, "Why?"

A huge smile broke out across Logan's face as he relayed the reasoning to Lola. "One of my best friends, Shaw Owens, was who just called. He called to tell me that he and his wife, Avia, just brought their newborn daughter home-"

Lola interjected, "Avia? Is that the same Avia that is your ex, and the one you brought to Cate's house like 15 years ago?" Seeing Logan nod his head, Lola queried, "So … how'd they end up together? Isn't that a little odd?"

Trying to remain patient, Logan exhaled his frustration, "Lola, if you'd let me talk, I'd really like to share this with you. It's important to me."

"S-s-sorry," Lola meekly muttered.

Ignoring the sadness in Lola's face and tone, in hopes of remaining focused on the joyous news, Logan continued. "Yes, Avia was my high school girlfriend. Yes, she's married to Shaw now. No, I won't go into the details of that right now. It's way too much to tell and frankly, irrelevant to this conversation. If you promise to listen, I promise to fill you in on the minute details later. Okay?"

Noting Lola's sheepish nod, Logan stated, "Avia and Shaw got married right after high school, which was in 2002. They tried for years to have kids but weren't able to conceive until 2009. Avia gave birth to their son, Zelig in 2010. They wanted another baby, but their doctor advised against Avia giving birth again, so they found an adoption agency and it was lined up that they would adopt a baby girl. When Shaw called, he said their daughter was born on February 15 and they were just now bringing her home."

Hearing the pause at the end of Logan's spiel, Lola apprehensively remarked, "I-I like the name Zelig; it's really unique."

Logan chuckled, "Yeah, it is. If I remember correctly, Avia said his name means "miracle" because they never thought they'd have kids."

The thought of returning to Parkway alone made Lola quite anxious; and although she bore a brave face, fear began crouching at the door of her mind. Gripping Logan's hand, Lola expressed, "Do you think I could stay here with you?"

Every part of Logan's being wanted to scream "yes," however his resolve told him Lola meeting his friends now wouldn't end well for anyone. Besides, this moment was about Shaw and Avia, not him.

Bringing Lola's hands to his lips, Logan spoke, barely above a whisper. "*My heart*, as much as it pains me, I can't have you do that. I love you with everything I have, but I also know that right now isn't the time to have you meet my friends and their families ..." Logan paused to choose his next words carefully. "It's just that after ... everything ... they already question my sanity."

Willing the tears to stay in place, Lola wearily left the car as she said, "I get it, Logan. You don't have to explain. I hurt a lot of people and ... that's the cross I bear. I-I'll ... s-s-see you when you get back."

Hearing the hurt in Lola's voice, Logan's heart shattered. Quickly leaving the car, Logan blitzed over to Lola as he caught her in a hug from behind. "It's only for a couple of weeks, okay? Why don't you go stay with Lizzie? I don't want you to be alone."

Turning to face him, Lola melted into Logan's embrace as the flood gate she had done so well to dam up finally broke free. *Why must I be this way? Why can't I just be happy for him? Instead, I'm too worried about myself...* A deepened kiss upon her lips brought Lola from her thoughts. Logan breathlessly broke away, reminding Lola he loved her, before returning to the vehicle and heading off in his intended destination.

~

March 5, 2015
The morning of March 5 signified two things in Lola's mind- the first being, she would pick Logan up from the airport soon; the

second, this officially marked six months of being back with the people she hurt the most. During her morning phone call with Dr. Indigo, Lola expressed that she felt quite annoyed that she hadn't been able to just blitz through everything that happened.

Dr. Indigo reassured her, "Lola, this is real life, not some fictional story in a book. In fiction and fantasy, authors are limited to time constraints. Your life is very real, and with reality comes the need to process new and/or emotional information. Healing takes time. I'm going to pose a question to you."

"Okay?"

"Lola, if you were to just give Logan the highlight reels of the basic events, do you think he would truly understand you?"

Pondering deeply, Lola finally spoke after several minutes. "Well, I guess he'd probably have more questions that would be thrown at me than what I can handle answering."

"That's correct, Lola. Now, can you please tell me how the letter writing has been going? I haven't asked in a while, so as not to nag. However, this step is crucial to your recovery"

Sighing wearily, Lola truthfully admitted that she found herself in a stalemate. "I have literally been trying to work on the same one for six months. I have started so many drafts that I've lost count. You'd think it'd be easy for me to write one to my dead father, but …"

Making a few small notes, Dr. Indigo queried, "What makes this one so hard to write?"

Teary-eyed, Lola bitterly stated, "Everyone tells you not to speak ill of the dead but you want me to be honest in my letters. How can I be honest when I'm so fucking mad that he's gone. I've got all this anger at him and I can't even get it out because then I'd just sound like a crazy bitch yelling at a dead guy … a dead guy who didn't ask to die from cancer."

Silence filled both ends of the line, as Dr. Indigo gave her patient the time she needed to calm her nerves. Several minutes later, Dr. Indigo gently reminded Lola that the point of writing the letters was to be able to have a safe space to get the hurt and anger out. "To the people who are still living, it's your choice whether they see their letter or not. It's for no one else other than yourself."

"I guess you're right. I'll think of something. Anyhow, Logan's here so I'll talk to you later, Dr. Indigo," Lola stated before ending the call. Putting on her best happy face, Lola waved to Logan as he approached.

The fifteen days without Lola were agony for Logan; while he had enjoyed getting to meet his newest niece, Celeste, as well as being with his brothers, his heart still felt empty. Being surrounded by the Oliviers' and Owens's children made Logan's heart long for the hopes of one day being a father. While he had joked about having no qualms with impregnating Lola or being her "baby daddy," one must remember that there is always a level of truth in jest.

~

When Logan was settled back in his apartment, Lola filled him in on her time with Lizzie. "It was so amazing seeing Baby Rae dance! Even though she's attending classes four times a week at the studio, she's practicing everyday, on top of being a straight-A student. Honestly, I've never seen anyone so dedicated."

Never having been one to take a particular interest in ballet, Logan surprised himself by asking, "When's her performance? You said she got the lead in *La Sylphide*, right?"

Lola's eyes widened in astonishment. "I can't believe you remembered! Her performance is in June. I'll ask Lizzie to save us a couple of seats."

After some playful banter, Lola told Logan she was going to sit in the new gazebo Cade had recently built. Feigning offense, Logan whined and acted as if she were cutting him deeply, "Awe- come on, Lola! Didn't you miss me?"

Lola shook her head as she laughed, "Oh, hush you! I did miss you, but … well, I've got something really important I need to do. I may go for a drive as well. If I do, I'll text you, so don't worry."

With pen, paper, and a bottle of water in hand, Lola ventured down the gravel path. While Lola and Logan had been away, Cade surprised Cate with plans for a gazebo to be built just outside the entrance to the forest; there would be a variety of flowering plants growing as well. Cade's hope was that this would be a cheerful place for Cate, who still found herself overwhelmed with guilt for everything that occurred between Jacob and Lola.

~

Sitting in the gazebo for around an hour proved to be just the space Lola needed to pen down all of her thoughts. Throwing propriety out the window, Lola wrote down everything she had felt and thought in the letter to her father. Folding the papers, Lola placed them neatly into her back pocket before sending Logan the text she promised.

Driving in the same direction she had gone with Logan a few months prior, Lola made a small pit stop before she pulled up in front of the cemetery once more; opting to again leave her car at the entrance. The lengthy walk down the perfectly kept rows of brightly polished headstones gave Lola the courage she needed to stand before her father's headstone.

Standing in front of the weathered granite marker, Lola wiped it down as she read the words written across it. *"Jackson Archer Swan II; beloved son, friend, fiancée, and father. All of these labels he loved, but the one he treasured most was … Father."*

Although Lola had seen those words countless times throughout the years, today they seemed to show her father in a different light.

Taking a seat, Lola opened the thick letter and slowly read out all of the words she had buried deep within her heart.

Drawing her letter to a close, Lola picked up the bouquet of red poppies she had stopped for, replacing the withered stalks remaining in the vase. "My anger and hurt are just like these withered poppies. Nothing but dead memories serving no true purpose but to show the empty husk of what once was." Standing to leave, Lola closed her eyes and for a brief moment, it was as if time stood still, opening the heavens solely for Lola, and she could swear she saw her father standing before her, the ghost of a man whose image she bore, and embrace her in a hug that only a father could give.

"I love you, daddy." Lola choked out as the wind picked up, leaving her alone once more.

29

Habromania part 1

March 7, 2015

When Lola returned from her father's gravesite, she found herself quieter than usual, causing mild concern for Logan. While he tried to think nothing of it, curiosity and concern got the best of him by the second day.

"Lola, *my heart*, are you okay? You're not hurting yourself are you?" Logan asked as he gently pulled Lola into a hug.

Not feeling overly affectionate at the moment, Lola let her arms hang by her side as she sighed heavily, "I'm fine, Logan. Okay? There's just something ... I can't really explain without sounding crazy. Just give me a couple more days."

Lola watched as Logan stepped back with hurt-filled eyes and threw his hands up in defense as a sign he meant no harm, before calling out, "I'll give you some more time. I didn't mean to sound offensive."

"I'm s-," Lola began before Logan cut her off.

"I know ya are. I'm gonna go spend some time with my dad. I haven't seen him since Christmas, so I'll be back in a couple of days. Alright?"

With nothing left to say, Lola quietly watched as Logan left her alone with her tempestuous thoughts.

~

March 9, 2015

By the time Logan had returned from Cate and Cade's home, he and Lola found themselves desperately missing one another. As Logan entered his living room, a smile widened across his face as he saw his nature photography proudly on display. Following the sound of a hammer, Logan walked down the narrow hall to his bedroom. Turning to grab another frame, Lola jumped in surprise as Logan came into view; he couldn't help but chuckle at her resemblance to a cartoon character.

"L-Logan! Oh, my gosh. You scared the crap out of me!"

"Nice to see I have such a shocking effect on you, *my heart*," Logan preened.

Rolling her eyes, Lola closed the gap between her and Logan. "I hope you don't mind that I took your film rolls and had these beauties developed."

"I never thought about displaying them, to be honest. I think it looks nice. Not that I'm complaining, but what brought this on?"

Nervously looking at her feet, Lola replied, "I was feeling … I guess … guilty." Lola waited for Logan to interject, but continued when there was only silence. "I was feeling guilty because I couldn't express what I wanted. It's part of my condition. Can we sit and I tell you about it?"

Logan nodded in agreement as the pair sat down on the bed. "So, what exactly is your condition? You haven't elaborated yet and I didn't want to rush in asking you."

Lola croaked out, "Y-yeah …," before clearing the clog in her throat. "Sorry about that. I honestly didn't plan on telling you for a little while longer, but after my phone call with Dr. Indigo yesterday, I think I owe it to you."

Taking a deep breath to calm her rising nerves, Lola began to explain her condition, *Alexithymia*, and what all it entailed. "I wasn't trying to shut you out. I just had an experience that I needed to process before I could even begin to explain it. I still can't tell how it made me feel but I can relay it to you if you'd like?"

Logan again remained silent but gave a quick nod as his response. Lola thought for the right words to say without sounding insane. "I might sound crazy but this is something that really happened. A few days ago when I went for a drive, I went to my dad's gravesite and read the letter I finally wrote to him. After I finished and stood to leave, I swear I saw him standing in front of me. He hugged me, Logan! It was as real as any hug I've ever experienced from you or anyone else."

After listening intently, Logan finally responded after several minutes. "What do you think about that experience? I've never had anything like that happen, but who am I to say it didn't?"

"So you don't think I'm crazy?"

"Never have, babe."

"Thank you! Truly, I thank you for believing me." Lola exclaimed as she tightly gripped Logan's hand with immense gratitude.

~

As the day drew to a close, Lola felt it was now time to continue her story. "Do you remember when we met up again at that college party **Chi Psi** frat was throwing?"

Logan chuckled at the memory, "That was one hell of a rager!"

"It definitely was! Well, I want to tell you of the events that lead up to that night and what the repercussions were."

~

June 6, 2004

Nearly one month had passed since Lola decided she was willing to give Jacob a true chance, and he had proved true to his word. Every day he showered her with love and affection, never once leaving her to feel saddened or lonely.

June 6 meant Cate and Jacob would celebrate their 26th birthdays with a very lavish dinner at Jacob's newly purchased condo. Jacob, being a man of steadfast determination, had decided that he would be telling Cate of his and Lola's relationship over dessert.

As she slipped on the black, satin cocktail dress, Lola nervously asked, "J-Jacob, are you sure it's not too soon to tell Cate? I-I mean what if she doesn't agree? I don't want to lose her friendship."

Drawing her close to his body, Jacob firmly gripped Lola's jaw as he wanted her full attention solely on him. Gazing into the clear diamonds before her, Lola felt herself slowly come undone as Jacob's husky voice reverberated through her very soul. "Now, now my little *Vixen*. Don't you worry your pretty little head about anything. Besides, Catarina knows her place and she will keep her opinion on the matter to herself."

A gasp escaped from Lola's lips as her body welcomed the memory of Jacob's familiar hands upon her. The deepest part of her soul felt guilty for moving on from Shane's death; it had been a mere seven months since his passing, but the human desire for physical affection soon outweighed the longing of her heart. *I will quiet the guilt later, but for now, I need to feel the touch of his hands on me. Shit! He really was right...*

Looking into Lola's eyes as he slid the thin strap of her dress from her shoulder, Jacob inquired, "What are you thinking about, *Vixen*?"

Turning scarlet, Lola cringed, "Ugh! It's too embarrassing!"

Gently lifting her chin, Jacob began placing delicate kisses along the sweet spot on Lola's neck. Feeling Lola's throat catch and her heartbeat quicken, Jacob chuckled against Lola's skin. "I bet I know what's got your mind turning."

Kissing a bit firmer, Jacob felt the darkness inside of him ignite once more and he knew the fiery-haired beauty before him was the fuel he needed to keep that darkness burning.

Lola gripped her long nails into Jacob's shoulders as she felt his hands trail down her bare, alabaster thighs. Leaving the spot from her neck, Jacob smirked as ran fingers across her uncovered, heated core. "Tsk. Tsk. I see my little *Vixen* has been very naughty- no panties!"

Blushing as a sudden boldness overtook her, her own darkness coming alive, Lola teased, "Well, I was hoping you'd fuck me."

Jacob smiled like a demon having captured a soul. "*Vixen*, it's not polite to tease."

Lola breathed out as seductively as possible, "Who said anything about teasing? You were right, ya know. I loved Shane for his gentle nature and sex with him was blissful, but..."

Beaming with pride, Jacob sought out the answer he already knew. "But what?"

"But ... he was so pure that I never felt that the darkness inside of me would be fully satisfied. Although I tried to deny it, I found a part of me longing for your touch."

Beginning to work his digits inside of Lola, Jacob retorted, "You should trust that I'm always right, *Vix*."

Nearing the brink of her release, Lola begged out, "Please, fuck me! I need to feel you in me."

With a guttural growl, Jacob brought Lola over to his bed where he commanded her to bend over, spread her legs, and put her arms above her head. Lifting the satin dress, so her nudity was on full display, Jacob aligned himself with the dripping center before him.

As she felt Jacob enter her, Lola shuddered in ecstasy. "Oh, god! Jacob!"

If Lola could witness the eyes of the man she was giving herself to, she would have left and never returned. Jacob's icy eyes turned obsidian as he growled out between deepened thrusts, "*Vixen*, there is no god here, but me. Do I make myself clear?"

The demanding tone in Jacob's voice both frightened and enthralled Lola as she panted out her understanding.

When Lola acknowledged his demand, Jacob's long-held promise resounded in his mind as he and Lola rode out their high together; *Good, because I can't wait to fucking tear you apart.*

~

June 12, 2004

Six days had passed since the Gallagher twins' birthday dinner, and what should have been a joyful occasion for the siblings, turned out to be anything but. Precisely as he had planned, Jacob announced that he and Lola had begun a relationship; and while she knew her place, to say Cate took the news poorly would be putting it mildly. Cate felt as if she were watching the sordid display from outside her own body; the crashing sound of a plate to the floor brought her swiftly back to reality. Cade mumbled apologies as Cate hastily ushered him out the door.

Crestfallen by her friend's reaction, Lola too found herself leaving Jacob's house. As Lola reached her car, she felt a gentle tug on her arm; turning to the source, Lola saw Jacob standing before her looking slightly bewildered. "Well, that was a complete shit show."

Nervously, Lola offered up a hug as she tried to fight back the tears of shock. "I honestly didn't think she'd take the news so poorly." Jacob kissed Lola passionately as he tried to reassure her that Cate would come around, before sending her off.

By allowing nearly a week to pass without speaking to either Lola or her brother, and smoking at least two cartons of cigarettes, Cate felt she finally had a better grasp on the situation she never thought would occur. Gathering all of the confidence she could muster, Cate finally gave Lola a call to request that she come by the café in hopes they would have a proper conversation, just the two of them.

That evening, Lola entered the building she held so dear to her heart, as the last customer of the night left. Cate finished her final tasks before bringing out two glasses of raspberry lemonade and a couple of apple tarts left from the day. Seating themselves in their favorite area, both women laughed as they began to apologize in unison. Allowing the laughter to die down, Lola was the first to speak up, "Cate, I'm so sorry. I honestly didn't think this through and I even asked Jacob if he thought it was too soon to tell you."

Sighing in disappointment, Cate relayed her concerns. "Luxie, I'm not mad at you or anything like that, so please know that now. I'm just concerned because as much as I love you like a sister, I never wanted you to have to worry about the fate that comes with being a Gallagher."

"I understand and appreciate your concern, but I do have a right to move on-," Lola started before Cate interjected.

"Luxie, I'm not saying you don't. Please just answer me this- When did you and J even get so close?"

Once more an opportunity had presented itself for Lola to finally reveal all of the past injustices Jacob had committed against her, however, Lola found herself not wanting to out the man who made her feel alive. *If I tell her now, she'll only freak out and get angry at me. I mean, he's changed and really cares about me now. Why should I ruin a good thing?*

Hearing Cate call her name once more, Lola carefully replayed the events of the previous month for Cate. "The day after Rae was born, I felt really down and I don't know why, but he was the only person I could think to call. He's been a great listening ear and very compassionate to me."

At Lola's mention of the word *compassion*, Cate couldn't help but double over in a fit of laughter. Wiping the tears from her eyes, Cate chuckled out, "Oh, sweet and precious Luxie, thanks so much for a good laugh. I honestly don't think I've laughed that hard in ages."

Noticing the look of frustration upon her friend's face, Cate quickly apologized for laughing. "Look, Luxe. I'm sorry for laughing. Just know that I love your naivety and blissful ignorance, but I want you to find a way to be wise. My father and brother are not easy men to love, nor are they compassionate without some ulterior motive. Can you at least promise me you'll be careful?"

Knowing the discussion was going nowhere fast, Lola made her promise to Cate, before driving to her lonely apartment; and while she should have moved out after Shane's death, or at the very latest, Andy's conviction, Lola simply couldn't find it in her to let that last piece of who she was dissipate. Lola vowed to herself to prove Cate wrong. *You'll see Cate, Jacob really cares for me and we'll be blissfully happy, I just know it.*

~

August 2, 2004

For a while, Jacob and Lola were as she had hoped, blissfully happy; however, shadows are not often hidden for too long. The beginning of August brought Lola's birthday, where Cate hosted a small celebration at the café, giving Lizzie and Mark a chance to officially meet Jacob for the first time; an experience Lizzie found herself wanting to forget.

While Jacob was more than welcoming and inviting, something about his icy gaze disturbed her very soul. Turning to her husband, Lizzie voiced her concerns. "Mark, there is something off about Cate's brother."

"How so, my *beautiful hurricane?*"

"I can't put my finger on it, but it's in his eyes."

Even though he hated the thought of Lola moving on from their dear friend, Mark was a reasonable man who knew she couldn't hold onto a ghost forever. "Elizabeth, look at me." Mark sternly scolded, commanding his wife's attention. "Now, while I don't particularly like the idea of Luxie moving on from Shane, she's an adult and deserves to find happiness. I mean, it's been nearly a year. Also, you can't just judge someone based on their eye color."

Trying not to let her fuse blow, Lizzie urged, "Mark, I swear to you I'm not judging just off of his eye color; it's more than that." Composing herself, Lizzie continued. "His eyes are actually haunting. It's like when you're on a frozen part of the sea and something deadly is lurking just beneath the surface."

As the guests trickled out one by one, Jacob approached Lola with his gift in hand. Lola's eyes shone vibrantly as she caught a glimpse of the small box. "And here I was thinking you forgot," Lola playfully jested.

"I could never forget you, *Vixen*," Jacob stated with a wink that made Lola's heart flutter, before placing the black box in her eagerly awaiting hands. "Now, I know we haven't been together very long, but I was thinking…"

Jacob paused as Lola gasped in surprise before she queried, "A key? What's this for?"

"Well, I know your Junior year of uni is starting soon and my place is closer to the campus than your apartment."

Lola apprehensively responded, "Umm … isn't this a bit soon?"

Jacob let out a hearty laugh that resonated throughout the café. "I'm not asking you to move in, move in. I just figured since it's a closer drive, you may want to spend the night from time to time."

Feeling utterly stupid at that point, Lola apologized, "I'm sorry for assuming. Thank you, Jacob. I mean, I've been over most of the summer anyhow, so I guess it's fitting."

~

August 9, 2004

The week proceeding her birthday, Lola found herself solely focused on the small black box with the key inside. *Everything feels like it's moving so quickly but at the same time, I feel like I'm stuck. I know Jacob isn't rushing me or even saying we have to move in together right now, but ... it would be easier to be closer to campus. Shit! I wish I had someone I could truly talk to about all of this. Am I betraying Shane and his memory?*

As her mind focused in on Shane and everything Lola held dear about him, the tears she so desperately denied herself finally broke through. Finding the familiar divots in her palms, Lola calmed herself in the only manner she knew how. The ringing of Lola's phone in the background brought her mind back to reality and she cursed herself for her weaknesses.

Watching the rust-colored water trickle down the drain as she cleansed her wounded palms, Lola resolved that now was the time to truly move on. With determination and expertly bandaged hands, she quickly packed everything of value and importance. With her own belongings loaded, Lola drove to the Carson home; the place that had been the source of so many treasured memories, now was a haunted husk of its former glory. Leaving an envelope with a letter and the apartment key, Lola drove to her intended destination.

After a somber drive through heavy traffic, Lola felt her nerves rise as she pulled up outside of what would be her new home. *Maybe I should have called Jacob and talked this through instead of being impulsive. Shit! What if he gets mad?* Pushing the negative thoughts from her mind, Lola pulled out her key and made her way inside.

~

August 20, 2004

While Lola's sudden move had been surprising to Jacob, he

couldn't help but be pleased. *Slow and steady hunting always proves victorious.* Daily, Lola asked Jacob if he was absolutely fine that she had moved in so suddenly. "I-I just don't want to overstep."

"*Vix*, look at me. I gave you the key, right?" With a nod of Lola's head as confirmation, Jacob spoke on. "Okay, then. It was yours to do with as you pleased. I was too forceful in the past and I'm really trying to change, so I wanted it to be **your** decision."

Grabbing tightly to the raven-haired man before her, Lola passionately spoke out, "Thank you, Jacob. You have no idea how much seeing you change really means to me. You make me feel so many things and for the first time I can fully be myself because it's like you understand the darkest parts of me."

Pecking Lola's lips, Jacob lifted her onto the kitchen counter. "*Vix*, what did I tell you in the past?"

"That we-we're the same?"

"That's right. Your friends will never understand that part of you. Hell, even my own twin sister who's supposed to be my other half, doesn't even understand the darkest parts of me. But you, my precarious little *vixen*, are the only one who will ever understand because we are one and the same."

It is human nature to want to be fully understood, and Lola was no different from anyone else. However, could she truly know the depths of the mind of the man ensnaring her, she would have never given him an ounce of her time; for demons only need the slightest crack in the foundation to slip through.

Giving Jacob a quick, passionate kiss, Lola hopped down from the counter as she announced that she was going to purchase her school books for the fall term and check out some clubs and events on campus. Before allowing Lola to leave, Jacob hungrily devoured Lola's neck, ensuring his mark would be left. "What the hell, Jacob? That's going to leave a mark!" Lola snapped.

Rolling his eyes, Jacob retorted, "Well, *Vixen*, I'm just wanting all of those college boys to know you're mine."

"I am a big girl who is clearly capable of letting potential suitors know she has a boyfriend. Trust me, okay?"

"It's not you I have an issue with, Lola. It's all the horny fuckers you'll be around. I know how they think after all."

Huffing in annoyance, Lola grabbed her purse as she slammed the front door. Once in her car, she quickly grabbed some concealer in hopes of covering the affectionate bruising on her neck.

~

Later that evening as Lola pulled back into Jacob's garage, she found herself feeling lighthearted; being back on campus helped her feel like normalcy was settling back in. Having seen a flyer for a back-to-school party hosted by the **Chi Psi** fraternity, Lola decided that a night just being a normal college student would do her some good. *Too bad Mark and Lizzie can't come with me. I really miss our times together, but I can't fault her for being a good momma.*

Looking through her closet, Lola wanted something perfect for summer but would also provide her with a little warmth against the cool evening breeze. After twenty minutes of searching, Lola finally decided upon a silk navy blue romper, which stopped mid-thigh and had a convertible, criss-cross top. Since the hemline of her romper was decently short, Lola chose a pair of black thigh-high stockings, which she gartered, to help provide some modesty. *No sense in looking like complete trash*, Lola laughed to herself as she put on a black and white, thick striped blazer, rolling the sleeves to her elbows; and put on a black pair of military-inspired, peep toe booties. Lola completed the ensemble by pulling her lovely curls into a high ponytail, adding a touch of red to her lips and a quick coat of mascara, Lola made her way out the door before she stopped short.

"Going somewhere, my little *vixen?*" Jacob sternly inquired as he took note of Lola's attire.

"Just to this party on campus. Wanna come with?" Lola asked.

"Not particularly, because you're not going!" Jacob firmly stated whilst crossing the room to stand before Lola.

"The fuck did you just say?" Lola asked as surprise overtook her.

"I said, you're not going!"

"See, I thought that's what your stupid ass just said. I'm a fucking adult and you don't control me, Jacob."

Lola quickly moved her arm as Jacob tried to grab it, to hold her in place. "Don't wait up, Jacob. Hopefully, by the time I'm back, you'll change your tune." Lola remarked with sadness in her voice.

Watching her leave, Jacob poured himself a glass of his favorite Scotch, **Johnnie Walker Black,** and thought to himself, *Just wait, my little vixen. We'll see how smart that pretty little mouth is when you get home.* Before slamming the glass on the granite countertop and heading out to his car.

Parking down the street from the frat house, Lola sat for a brief moment as she tried to gather her composure before partaking in the events of the night. *I seriously can't believe Jacob had the audacity to think he could tell me what to do. I'm not a fucking child! Is this what Cate meant? Honestly, I just don't know. I mean surely this has to be out of the norm for him, because he's been so sweet to me. Whatever it is, I can just deal with it later.* As she walked down the street, Lola felt her phone begin to vibrate; looking down at the screen, Lola declined the call as she wasn't in the mood to talk to Jacob.

Upon entering the frat house, Lola did her best not to feel panicked as the heavy smell of alcohol permeated the atmosphere. *Everything is fine … It's been years since I've been around mom's drunk rage. Hell, I've been around my friends when they are drunk, so why do I feel so on edge tonight?* Not wanting to have the negative emotions damper her evening, Lola grabbed a soda while doing her best to mingle.

Unfortunately for Lola, the longer she stayed, the more apprehensive she began to feel. Stepping between the sea of sweaty bodies, Lola finally made her way outside to get some fresh air. Checking her phone, she saw she had 10 missed calls from Jacob. *Shit! Shit! Shit!* Facing her fate instead of delaying the inevitable, Lola felt the bile rise in her throat as she listened to the ringing on the other end of the line.

~

March 9, 2015

Letting out a lengthy yawn, Lola turned to Logan and asked if he was fine with continuing tomorrow. "I'm mentally exhausted and what's coming is pretty heavy. Are you okay if we get some sleep and continue this tomorrow?"

Lifting Lola's hands in his own, Logan gently kissed them. "Of course, *babe*. Like I keep saying, I'm more than happy to wait, just promise you won't shut me out."

As Logan drifted off to sleep, he couldn't help but wonder just how bad what would come next truly was.

30

Habromania part 2

March 10, 2015

After her morning run and conversation with Dr. Indigo, Lola had planned to ask Logan if he would mind joining her out at the gazebo to listen to the remainder of the tale she started the night before; however, nature had other plans as a gentle snowfall began coating the earth. Turning on the gas fireplace, Lola bitterly chuckled, "Well, isn't this just irony at its finest. Logan, do you mind making some hot chocolate? I'll run down to *Cate's* and get a couple cinnamon rolls."

With treats and cocoa in hand, Logan and Lola nestled together on the couch as Lola prepared herself once more.

~

August 20, 2004

Meanwhile, on the other side of Portland, after two long years of driving four hours round trip each school day, Logan finally settled into the room he would be renting from Shaw and Avia. The young couple had wed immediately following their high school graduation and used all of their savings to purchase a quaint four-bedroom home in downtown Portland. Their hope was to have Logan, Pablo, and Pierre move in during college and use the garage as a practice space for their band, ***Beyond Oregon***.

"Logan, you about ready?" Pablo asked as he knocked on the open door.

"Hey, man. Give me ten to get changed. Is Roz gonna make it?"

Sheepishly rubbing the back of his neck, Pablo blushed at the mention of his girlfriend. "Her birthday's in two days, so I think I'm gonna see if she wants to go to Louisa and Kaleb's house and see the kids before we go to dinner or something. I may ask Shaw and Avia if they can watch the girls, so Roselyn and Louisa can have a twin night."

Trying to listen intently to his friend's spiel, Logan honed in on his wardrobe, as he called out, "Hey, Pablo, shorts or pants?"

"I say switch it up and go with shorts."

Letting Pablo's choice settle his internal debate, Logan slipped on a pair of grey and blue plaid skater shorts; which he paired with a black and grey baseball shirt; and a black pair of high-top ***Converse***. "Alright, let's get the rest of the gang and get you to your sorority girl," Logan teased.

Once everyone was gathered in the living room, Logan spoke. "Alright, here's the plan for tonight and listen up you horny fuckers in the back," Logan pointed to Shaw and Avia, as well as Pierre and his girlfriend, Kelly, while he continued. "Pablo is riding with me. Y'all can figure out who's driving because I don't want none of y'all fuckin' in my car. Let's stay at this frat party for a couple of hours before heading to ***The British Punk***; Maeve said we can get our equipment tuned after she closes. Everyone agreed?" With everyone in agreement, Logan and his friends all set off in the direction of the ***Chi Psi*** frat house.

After searching a good ten minutes for a parking space, Logan finally found an open parking space beside a cherry red ***1967 Ford***

Mustang. "Holy shit! Look at this beauty. I bet some frat boy owns her," Pablo commented in awe as he and Logan walked in the direction of their group.

Logan guffawed, "I bet his rich ass doesn't even treat her right."

Making their way inside, Pablo bid Logan adieu as he set off in search of Roselyn, while the other couples also went their separate ways, leaving Logan highly aware of his single status. On most occasions, Logan didn't mind being single; it only became awkward when completely surrounded by a sea of sexually charged bodies.

Grabbing a soda, Logan ventured outside, where he stumbled upon a sight that tore at his heart. Standing before him stood a very petite young woman, with beautiful rose-red curls, sobbing as she spoke on the phone. Trying his hardest not to eavesdrop, Logan couldn't help but overhear the broken fragments.

"I already told you I was coming here … Why are you being such an asshole? … I fucking invited you … I'm an adult, damn it! You have no right to tell me what to do … You know what, fuck you! I'll be home when I'm damn well ready"

Slamming her phone shut, the young woman belted out to no one in particular, "You stupid ass mother fucker!" The sound of an awkward cough coming from across the yard caused her to turn in the direction from which it came. Slamming her hand to her head, she spewed out her apologies. "Shit! I'm so sorry."

Walking in her direction, Logan chuckled, "Hey, no harm no foul. Aight?" Seeing the red-headed beauty before him smile, Logan extended his hand in greeting. "I'm Logan."

Thinking for a moment, the young woman hesitated before returning the favor. "I'm Luxe- actually, just call me Lola."

"Hey! Are you Cate's friend?" Logan asked inquisitively.

"Uh, yeah- Do I know you?"

"Shit, sorry!" Logan apologized before he made a proper introduction. "I'm Cade's son, Logan. We met briefly, a few years ago."

"Oh, yeah! What are the odds of running into you here of all places?" Lola chuckled at the thought before taking a seat upon the concrete slab, gesturing for Logan to do the same. Opening her purse, Lola grabbed a pack of cigarettes, offering one up to Logan. "Your loss," she chuckled as he declined, before taking a drag.

"I'm … umm … sorry about Shane. Cate told me that he died." Logan stated with utmost sincerity.

"Thanks. I really mean it. You don't know me, so you really didn't have to say anything." Lola blankly stated as she stared up into the sky.

Sitting for a few minutes, Logan finally asked, "If you don't mind me asking, what had you crying?"

Smashing her cigarette butt, Lola sighed as she shook her head, "Sorry you had to witness that fine display of lady-like behavior. Anyhow, that was my boyfriend, Jacob."

"Jacob? Is that Cate's brother?" Logan asked with a slightly disgusted tone.

Choosing to ignore Logan's tone, Lola confirmed Logan's statement before Logan asked, "Not to sound rude, but how the hell did you end up with someone like him? He's creepy as hell!"

Lighting up another cigarette, Lola bitterly laughed, "One, you don't know me, so please don't judge my choices. Two, he's been really good to me and compassionate. It can't be easy to be with someone who had their significant other die."

Holding his hands up in defense, Logan apologized, "Hey, Lola, I wasn't trying to be a dick. I just got a weird vibe off of him the couple of times I've met him. Anyhow, if I can ask one more question, why was he making you cry?" Logan tried his best to remain composed, as his justice-seeking personality often seemed to cause him more trouble than it was worth.

Taking a few slow drags, Lola let the smoke fill her lungs and calm her soul. "The short answer is, Jacob didn't want me coming tonight. He thinks some drunk, horny frat boys are going to try hitting on me or take advantage of me."

Stating the obvious, Logan queried, "If he's that worried, why didn't he just come with you?"

"Yeah … I tried. Anyhow, enough of my shitty drama. What the hell have you been up to?"

Logan and Lola found themselves so easily wrapped up in conversation; time freely slipping away from them. Standing to stretch his legs, Logan offered Lola his hand, which she happily accepted. "Oh my gosh, I fucking love this song!" Lola belted out as the melodious chords of *I Miss You* flooded the airwaves.

With a playful wink, Logan asked, "Well, my lovely Lola, may I have this dance?"

Lola smiled brightly as she blissfully accepted Logan's offer. Closing her eyes, Lola laid her head upon Logan's chest and allowed her mind to think back to the beautiful night she and Shane danced at Mark and Lizzie's reception. *I have been doing everything I can to not think of those times because it still hurts so much. I want to let go, but how can I?*

Gazing down at the small woman standing below him, Logan felt his heart flutter with affection and admiration while chastising himself for even allowing such feelings to stir. *I'm a fucking idiot! I can't just swoop in when she's clearly in a relationship. Besides, I barely even know her; even if she is the most beautiful woman I have ever laid eyes on.*

With the song drawing to a close, Lola smiled as she stepped away from Logan and thanked him for his kindness. Just as she prepared to bid Logan farewell, a masculine voice called out, "Finally! Roz and I've been looking everywhere for your pale ass."

Turning to the owner of the voice, Logan laughed, "Why don't y'all catch a ride with Pierre and Kelly. I'll meet everyone up at Maeve's soon," before facing Lola once more. "Hey, my friends and I are all going to **The British Punk**, why don't you join us?"

"As tempting as the offer is, I think I'm gonna pass. Besides, I should probably get home and deal with the squall coming my way. Why don't you give me your phone number though? Maybe we can meet on campus for lunch or something if we have class the same day."

"I'll only give you my number on the condition that I can walk you to your car," Logan teased.

"You've got yourself a deal, Warren," Lola playfully declared.

Standing before Lola's car, Logan couldn't help but laugh as he thought back to the conversation he and Pablo had earlier that evening. Confusion clearly written across Lola's face, Logan stated, "So *you're* the rich frat boy with this sweet ass ride."

Lola shrugged, "Uh … yeah, I guess? I mean Averie here was my dad's if that's any consolation. Anyhow, I'll see ya later. Thanks for the conversation and dance."

Lola smiled happily as she made her way home; however, had she known the fate awaiting her, she never would have gone out that evening.

~

August 21, 2004

Pulling into the garage, Lola saw all of the lights in the house were off; glancing at her phone, she noticed it was half-past midnight and assumed Jacob had already gone to sleep. Breathing a sigh of relief, Lola praised whoever in the universe was listening for this small victory. *I really don't feel like fighting again right now. Hopefully, we can just settle it in the morning.*

Walking into the bedroom she shared with Jacob, Lola screamed in surprise as a lamp suddenly came on. "Jacob, what the hell? You nearly scared the piss out of me." Lola wearily announced before taking notice of the unsettling sight before her. In the oversized, Victorian red velvet chair Jacob sat in nothing but his boxer briefs, sipping a glass of Scotch.

"Welcome home, my little *Vixen*. Why don't you close our door." Jacob gruffly stated. Hearing the click of the door, Jacob took one last drink of his Scotch before flinging the glass at the door frame directly behind Lola's head; shards scattering around her.

Wide-eyed fear. The only thing running through Lola's mind as her hands began to shake; she had not felt this level of fear since living with her mother. Nervously holding her hands up, Lola timidly squeaked, "J-J-Jacob! What the hell?"

Crossing his arms angrily, Jacob commanded, "You'd do best to keep that pretty little mouth of yours shut! Now, if you know what's good for you, you'll bring your ass over here."

Cautiously, Lola walked the abysmal path of perdition to stand before the icy-eyed man she thought she knew. Nervously rubbing her arm, Lola dared not move a muscle lest he command it. As a devilish smirk graced his face, Jacob spoke with devious seduction. "Why don't you strip down and tell me about your *fun* little night out?"

Swallowing the bile she found rising, Lola let out a raspy breath as she closely followed Jacob's suggested demands; not knowing what awaited her next, Lola felt it best to tell every detail, including her conversation and dance with Logan.

Drinking in the nearly nude beauty before him, Jacob bit his lower lip in an effort of stifling a groan of desire. *Don't get yourself all worked up now. We have a **very** long night ahead of us.* The cool breeze from the ceiling fan caused Lola's exposed nipples to become erect and she cursed herself for not having worn a bra earlier that evening.

"Turn," Jacob commanded, as his erection grew at the sight of Lola in nothing but a black thong with a small heart cut out on the back, and black thigh-high stockings which she had gartered. "Now, why don't you come here and have a seat?" Jacob gently spoke, "Hey, there's no need to be afraid." To all looking in at this brief glimpse in time, they would think Jacob was a gentle and compassionate lover, however, the demon raging inside of him was anything but.

Foolishly trusting in his words, Lola allowed her guard to fall as she straddled Jacob's lap, exhaling in relief. Gazing into the eyes which held her soul captive, Lola relayed the course of her evening, before tenderly placing her forehead upon his, offering up apologies for the earlier arguments. "I'm sorry we fought. Will you please forgive me?"

Allowing a dark chuckle to pass his lips, Jacob forcefully held Lola's left arm behind her back as he dug the fingers of his right hand into her ass cheek hard enough to where she knew there would be bruising. Wincing in pain, Lola tried to wriggle free, however, her attempts only caused Jacob's pressure to increase. "Oh, my little *Vixen*, I will forgive you, but first we must play a little game. One that I have always wanted to play and I think you are the perfect partner."

Tears slowly made their way down Lola's cheek as she found herself at a loss for words. Where had she gone wrong? Should she have kept silent about her growing friendship with Logan? Wasn't honesty always the best policy? After all withholding information in the past had caused her nothing but heartache. Releasing the grip he had on Lola's arm, Jacob tenderly wiped away the tears before placing a delicate kiss upon Lola's lips. "Come now, *little one*. We're going to play our game over on the bed. Just trust me, okay?"

Jacob directed Lola to place a blindfold over her eyes and lie on her stomach while spreading out her arms and legs in a starfish pattern;

which he proceeded to strap down with thick leather bindings. "Now, for the first part of our game, I'm going to turn on some music that I find very appropriate for tonight. I do hope you'll take in every single lyric, because my little *vixen*, you really should learn to think with that pretty little head of yours."

Turning on **Welcome Home** by Coheed and Cambria, Jacob set up the rest of the "game" he had planned for Lola. After hearing the song for the third time, Lola finally noticed the change in temperature and began sweating as she panted out, "Jacob w-why is it so hot in here?"

Walking back over to Lola, Jacob slid her blindfold above her eyes as he darkly spoke. "That's because things need to **heat** up a little bit for our game to truly be fun. Although, I am going to add an extra accessory to you." With those final words spoken, Jacob fastened a red and black leather ball gag to Lola's face; to which he added a rose plug to the small hole in the front.

Watching Jacob walk out of sight once more, Lola allowed the streams of tears to fall as the haunting lyrics playing in the background burrowed deep within her psyche, while failing at mentally escaping to happier times. Making his way back to Lola, Jacob held up a very familiar accessory... the ring he always wore on his right hand. The ring, a tungsten grim reaper holding a scythe that connected to an angel wing, was something he had custom-designed four years ago prior to his first encounter with Lola.

Noting the look of high alert in Lola's eyes, Jacob placed delicate kisses up and down her back and shoulders. "Like I said, *Vixen*, there's really nothing to be afraid of. We are moving on to the next part of our game and I really think you will like this part." Jacob seductively spoke before once more moving out of Lola's peripheral.

Running his long fingers up and down Lola's inner thighs, Jacob felt her shudder in delight. Moving her panties to the side, Jacob slowly began teasing Lola until he felt her nearing the point of release. Stopping, Jacob once again moved out of sight before quickly returning. With his right hand behind his back, Lola found it quite strange when Jacob used his gloved left hand to lower the blindfold over her eyes once more. Lifting her hips, Jacob aligned himself with Lola's dripping core.

It wasn't long before both partners found themselves on the brink when the words Jacob uttered between harsh thrusts would leave a haunting tear upon Lola's soul. "I'm going to break you down so fucking badly. After tonight, you will never again question who you belong to." As the words left Jacob's mouth, Lola began to writhe in pain; the likes of which she had yet to experience in all of her 20 years of life. Sadly, this would not be the last time she would feel this type of pain.

~

March 10, 2015

Looking away from Logan, Lola sobbed. "This was the first time Jacob branded my lower back with that fucking ring."

Wide-eyed, Logan asked Lola if she minded showing him her back. Horror overtook Logan's face as he bore witness to the countless branding marks all expertly placed along the sides of Lola's back so as to be hidden by most garments.

"I-I-I..." Logan stammered out, as words failed him.

Seeming to read his mind, Lola finished Logan's train of thought. "If you're wondering why you couldn't see any damage with the green velvet dress, now you know. Not even Ronan saw these scars because I refused to shower together or have sex without at least wearing a camisole. Aside from the clinic staff, Dr. Indigo included, you are the only one to see this."

Still having no words to say, Logan did the only thing he could think to do- wrap his strong arms around the woman he loved more than anything and hold her close; in hopes of providing some sort of meager safe haven.

31

Rare Moments

April 30, 2015

Over one month had passed since Lola revealed what striking up a friendship with Logan had cost her; however, in the end, it was something she would willingly do again. Logan's friendship throughout those early years had been Lola's saving grace. While she had not intended to put their conversation off for nearly this long, Logan had asked for time to truly process what he had learned.

When he finally found himself ready to hear more on April 10, time stopped for Logan and his world came crashing down. That morning as he and Lola prepared breakfast after her run and phone session with Dr. Indigo, Logan's phone rang. Glancing down he saw his mother's picture light up the screen; showing the phone to Lola, Logan stepped into the other room. Blissfully unaware of the conversation occurring in the other room, Lola began setting the table. The sound of Logan's fist meeting the wall followed by his lamenting sobs caused Lola to quickly move in Logan's direction; the plates crashing to the floor.

Trepidatiously Lola stood in front of Logan, wrapping her dainty arms around his waist as she did her best to whisper soothing words in hopes of providing some source of serenity. After several minutes, Logan kissed Lola meekly on her lips as he brokenly spoke, "M-My mom just called. M-m-my *Zia* Priscilla died this morning."

"Oh my gosh, Logan! I am so sorry. Did she say when the funeral is?"

"It's in two days … I-I don't think I can go," Logan remorsefully relayed, not ready to truly grieve the precious woman who had been very much like a second mother to him.

Taking a step back, Lola held her hands up, unable to truly believe what she was hearing. "Woah- Woah- Woah- What do you mean you don't think you can go? Logan, she was your aunt and obviously someone you loved very much."

"I've already made up my mind, besides you need me here," Logan countered.

"Logan, I will be fine but this is something you need to deal with, and don't use me as an excuse. If you don't go, you'll regret it."

Standing, as his anger overtook him, Logan walked over to the wall, punching it once more. Seeing the fear in Lola's eyes, he firmly stated, "Look, Lola. I'm not trying to scare you right now, but I'm not fucking going! I'm far too pissed off at how she died … I can't even repeat it because it's just too much. Just please drop it."

"Alright, but for what it's worth, I'm sorry. I'm going to stay with Lizzie for a few weeks. You have a lot to process right now and as much as I want to be here for you like you've been for me, I don't think that would be very healthy for either of us."

"Lola- wait! I'm sorry! I didn't mean to react that way! I'm fucking sorry." Logan cried out as he tried to grab hold of her arm in a futile attempt to make her stay.

"I know you didn't, Logan, but sorry is a valueless word that has failed me more times than I can count. Please just think about what I said. If you don't go for yourself, at the very least, go for your family."

~

Lola wasn't sure if Logan ever went to the funeral or not, it had been a sore subject and she felt it best not to rehash it again. Instead, she made plans for them to spend a couple of days at the Crater Lake National Park and the surrounding area. Loading the last bag into the trunk of Logan's car, Lola's offer to drive was met with boisterous laughter. "As much as I love you, babe, no one drives Ruby but me."

Feigning offense, Lola jested, "Geez- you act like I'm a bad driver. I'd let you drive Averie again if you wanted. But whatever …"

Kissing Lola's forehead before starting the engine, Logan honestly expressed, "Besides, since we have nearly a six-hour drive and I know you're wanting to tell me what happened … I think it's best if my mind has something to focus on in conjunction, especially after last time."

Staring out the window as the trees passed by, Lola sighed in exasperation. "I know that was hard for you to hear and probably even harder to see. The thing is, Jacob wasn't always bad-"

"How the hell can you even defend his actions?" Logan interjected.

"I'm not! I'm just stating the truth of the matter. There were times when he really did show that he cared, but I don't know … maybe I am naive and a part of me will always love him." Lola spoke as honestly as she could, hoping Logan could still truly listen without judgment. "I know it doesn't make any sense, since you have never experienced what I've gone through. I know it's really fucked up, but there's always going to be some small part of me that hopes he'll change."

"Lola-" Logan tried to interject once more.

"Please stop cutting me off. This is why I didn't want to tell you anything to begin with. If your impatient ass would just let me friggin' talk, I could say everything I wanted." Lola vented before pausing for Logan's reaction. When she was met with silence, she continued. "As I was trying to say, I *know* there is a difference between hope and knowing. The fucked up part of my mind has hope, but the fully cognitive part of my mind knows that's just not humanly possible. It would literally take an act of God for Jacob to change, but he's so far gone that he'd just deny God's very presence standing before him."

Neither said anything for several minutes, allowing Lola's truthful words to soak in. Halfway to their destination, Logan pulled over at a small fuel station for a fill-up and so they could stretch their legs. Once they were back on the road, Logan reached across for Lola's hand. "I am sorry for coming across as confrontational. I know it can't be easy for you to be emotionally naked in front of me. I really am trying my best to be understanding. If you want to continue, I'm okay to listen now."

Giving Logan's hand a gentle squeeze, Lola thanked him for his sincerity before delving into her past once more.

~

August 21, 2004

When Lola awoke late in the afternoon, her lower back felt excruciatingly tender. Reaching over to the nightstand, Lola saw a couple of missed phone calls from an unknown number. After carefully making her way to the bathroom, she planned to return the call; however, as she got ready to press the call button, Jacob entered the bathroom with remorse filling his eyes.

"H-hey, *Vixen* ... how are you feeling?"

Tears flooded Lola's eyes as the memories of their "game" came flooding back. "How could you? Why? I was honest." Lola broke down as Jacob tenderly embraced her.

Getting down on his knees to be at her level, Jacob begged, "I'm sorry, *Vix*. I got so angry and I didn't know how to channel the anger. I fucked up big time. You've gotta believe me."

Looking through her watery eyelashes, Lola knew she should leave and never return. Yet, seeing the strong man before her appear so broken gripped Lola's heart. *If he meant to hurt me, he wouldn't be apologizing, right?* Wiping the tears, Lola uttered the words that would help to permanently seal her fate. "I-I believe you, Jacob. I love you and I-I'm sorry for making you angry."

Jacob swiftly stood at Lola's heartfelt revelation and kissed her like she was the cure for his damned soul. Both parties breathlessly broke away after several minutes. Gently taking Lola by the hand, Jacob led her to the bathroom counter, where he pulled out the items needed to help heal the mark on her back.

After removing the bandage he had placed the night before, Jacob couldn't help but admire the branding of his ring as his thoughts darkened. *So fucking beautiful.*

~

December 24, 2004

After playing Jacob's twisted game, Lola did her best to stay in line with the hopes of never having to experience that level of pain again. Although, their sex life became much rougher, Lola willingly welcomed anything Jacob brought to the table as long as he promised not to brand her again. While Lola tried to comfort herself by claiming she only allowed Jacob's devious fantasies to be enacted because it meant her life was easier; nonetheless, the most corrupted parts of her reveled in his devilish pleasures.

During her school semester, Lola had been able to meet up with Logan on campus for lunch occasionally; however, she ensured that they never spoke on the phone whenever Jacob was around, as she didn't need him making a mountain out of a simple friendship. *He should know by now that I love only him, and be able to trust me enough to know that I'm faithful.*

The morning of Christmas Eve arrived, and with it, brought great anxiety to Lola, for she would finally be meeting Jacob's parents. He informed her a few days prior that dinner would be formal and that her best behavior was imperative. Entering the walk-in closet, Lola pulled out the dress she and Cate had been able to find last minute while trying to recall the information Cate had given her about their parents.

~

"Cate, are you sure they'll love me?" Lola asked while nervously searching through the limited petite section **Modern Vintage** housed. Cate suggested this boutique as her father was very old fashioned when it came to women's attire in his home, but she also wanted Lola to be able to feel comfortable since meeting Maximillian Gallagher was never an easy feat for even the bravest of men, let alone a naive young woman blinded by false aspirations of love.

Cate sighed deeply while doing her best to choose her words wisely. "Luxie, I *know* my mother will be absolutely smitten with you. Max on the other hand … I can never tell how a meeting with him will go and I'm his own flesh and blood. If you can, just stay close to either J or me, and whatever you do, don't find yourself alone with my father. He's a smooth swindler who will have you signing over your company before the first course is served."

~

Returning her focus to the task at hand, Lola applied some light make-up and pulled her curls into a lovely chignon, before slipping into the elegant long-sleeved, Gatsby inspired ivory dress. Lola was thankful the gown had a high back, as she still felt very self-conscious of the now faded branding on her lower back. Adding a pair of sparkling silver peep-toe heels, Lola set off in search of Jacob. Even though Cate repeatedly assured Lola that Jacob would be completely enamored by her appearance, Lola still couldn't help but feel apprehensive in regards to the slight plunging neckline and slit that ran mid-thigh.

Sauntering into the living room, Lola came upon Jacob, who was oblivious to her entrance as he was preoccupied with a phone conversation, which by Jacob's agitated tone, could only mean his father was on the other line. If this current conversation was anything like the others, it would be quite lengthy. Making her way to the bar, Lola prepared a glass of Scotch for Jacob, as conversations with Maximillian Gallagher always seemed to make him edgier than usual.

"Son of a bitch!" Jacob belted out while slamming his phone on the glass end table. Lola hastily scurried in his direction, with the drink in hand. "H-here y-you go, Jacob," Lola sputtered, meekly handing him the drink.

Downing it in one go, Jacob firmly placed the glass by his phone before finally taking in Lola's appearance. Desire shrouded his eyes as he snaked his hands around her waist whilst placing tender kisses along her neckline. "My, my, little *Vixen*. You certainly look delectable."

"Th-thank you, Jacob." Lola acknowledged before extolling as she looked upon Jacob's ensemble for the evening. "You look devilishly handsome in your tuxedo."

Kissing Lola passionately once more, Jacob led her to the settee in front of their Christmas tree. "I'd like to give you your gift now before we go to my parents' house," Jacob remarked, handing Lola a small black matte satin box, much similar in size to the one her house key had been presented in.

Lola gasped in delight as she opened the box. "Oh my god! Jacob … it's so beautiful!" Lola exclaimed as she was overcome by the beauty of the necklace lying inside. Jacob had given her a small copper fox-headed pendant necklace on a platinum chain; with obsidian diamond eyes and white diamonds filling in the cheek areas. Kissing Jacob once more, Lola asked for him to help her put it on.

Chuckling as he faced her once more, Jacob lifted Lola's chin while gazing into her forest-green eyes. "A vixen for *my* vixen, and only ever the best."

"I-if you're okay with it, I'd like to give you your gift as well." Lola nervously stated.

"*Vixen*, I told you that you didn't need to get me anything."

"I-I know, b-but I wanted to. You've been so good to me lately and I wanted to show you how much I love you."

"Well, you've been such a good girl, *Vix*. So of course, I'm going to be good to you."

Lola asked Jacob to close his eyes before coming back with a large white box, topped with an oversized red bow. Clapping her hands joyously, Lola encouraged Jacob to open it. The sight in the box caused Jacob to truly smile for the first time in several years. Placed at the top was a canvased print of Jacob and Cate as young teens on holiday in Sweden. When Lola asked Cate what one of her favorite childhood memories was, she recounted their last vacation before her father decided to sell her off to her ex-husband.

Looking up at the beauty before him, Jacob felt a small amount of warmth inside his dead and dark heart. *That was the trip before that bastard excuse for our father changed everything.* Holding onto Lola's hand, Jacob spoke with earnest sincerity, "Th-thank you. I thought this picture was gone. I should have known Catarina held onto it."

Beaming with pride, Lola said, "You're welcome! There's more under the black tissue paper."

Sifting through the piles of tissue paper, nestled at the bottom of the large box, Jacob found a large bottle of **Johnnie Walker Blue** along with a six-piece, monogrammed crystal decanter and glass set. Lola nervously asked if he liked the big part of his gift, to which he responded, "I love it all, as much as I *desire* you."

~

Standing outside the entrance of the Gallagher estate, Lola immediately found herself feeling very small and isolated. While her childhood home had been on the larger scale, it always had a warm and inviting atmosphere. The home before her though, was much like Jacob, exuding opulence on the surface but underneath dwelt many a haunting tale.

Turning to face Lola, Jacob lifted her chin with a firm, attention grabbing hold on her jaw. "You are to stay on your best behavior at all times this evening. If you step out of line for even a second, I have a new 'game' that I've been waiting to play with you. Am I clear?"

The mention of a "game" with Jacob made Lola's heart beat erratically as she gripped her perfectly manicured nails into her palms. "Y-y-yes, sir. I-I-I promise. I don't want to play the game."

Lola exhaled in relief as she glanced down at her palms and found that the skin had not been broken; hearing Jacob call her name, she gave him her full attention. "Now, put on a pretty face and remember what I said." Choking down all reservations, Lola did as she was told and plastered on her bravest face.

Before Jacob could even knock on the door, he was lovingly greeted by the most elegant woman Lola had ever seen. The woman embracing Jacob appeared to be in her mid 40s with perfectly layered blonde hair and the warmest deep brown eyes, which reminded Lola of the few joyful memories with her mother. Facing Lola, the woman lovingly embraced her as well. "You must be Luxe! It is so good to finally meet you. I'm Evelynn. While my sweet Jacob here has yet to fill me in on you, Catarina has been more than forthcoming in singing your praises."

"Evelynn!" A commanding voice bellowed, causing Jacob to tighten his grip on Lola's hand. "Let them come inside."

"Son, please forgive me for holding you both at the door." Evelynn meekly spoke before quickly retreating into the house.

When Jacob went to close the front door, Cate's excited shrill resonated from the walk. "Luxie!"

Turning at the sound of her name, Lola couldn't help but giggle at the sight of her beloved friend. Much to her father's chagrin, Cate ran as unladylike as possible before plowing into Lola, knocking her to the floor. Rolling his eyes in detest, Maximillian bitterly spat, "Dear Lord, Catarina. I see you are still dressing and behaving like a common street whore."

Jacob's eyes flashed with anger at their father's blatant insult of Cate. Cate, however, used to her father's ways, chose to ignore his comments and instead focused her efforts on helping Lola regain her footing. "Oh my god, girl! You look amazing in this dress. You'll never guess who came with me tonight?" Cate asked right before Max revolted in disgust.

"Catarina! What the hell have I told you about bringing trash inside this damn house."

Flipping both middle fingers at her father, Cate passionately kissed Cade in front of him, causing Max to storm off in search of his wife. All parties present couldn't help but chuckle at the childish display from the man in his 60s. A slight cough near the front door caught their attention, as Logan called out, "Is it safe to enter the war zone?"

Although Lola had made a promise to Jacob to be on her very best behavior, she worried that Logan's presence would cause unwanted jealousy, thus making her life far more difficult when they returned home. She felt relieved but also for some reason slightly jealous when Logan announced, "I hope you guys don't mind, but I brought along someone very special to me. I'd like for everyone to meet my beautiful girlfriend, Naja; or as I like to call her, Nae."

Scrunching her face in confusion, Lola wondered why she felt slightly jealous of the lovely girl standing in the black dress. *She's so pretty, of course, that's the kind of girl Logan would go for. Her caramel complexion and warm silver eyes are flawless. She has a nose bridge piercing and small cherry tattoos underneath either side of her collarbone. And don't even get me started on her beautiful burgundy curls. I would never be so daring as to wear my hair in such a carefree manner. Wait, why the hell am I jealous? He's my friend and I should be happy for him.*

~

The remainder of the evening went as well as could be expected, with Max's sour demeanor and Cate's constant pushing of his buttons. Logan and Naja excused themselves before dessert as Logan wanted to introduce her to his mother, step-father, and sisters, who all lived two hours away in Vienna. Cate and Cade left soon after as well since they would also be traveling to Vienna to stay with Cade's family. With only Jacob and Lola remaining, Max called Jacob into his office while Lola followed Evelynn to help her clean up.

"Thank you very much for inviting me into your home," Lola warmly expressed.

Giving Lola a loving hug, Evelynn sweetly mused, "Oh, my dear, I am the one who should be thanking you." Seeing the puzzled look on Lola's face, Evelynn chuckled, "I know my Jacob is very much his father's son, and that he is not an easy man to love. They are both … I guess you would say … hard-hearted. But, it has been my prayer that God will put just a little bit of me in Jacob to hopefully undo even a small amount of his father's darkness."

Lola remained silent as she didn't know what she would be allowed to say without causing her future self turmoil. Evelynn's heart faltered when she saw the look in Lola's eyes that had been housed in her own for years; the look of silent compliance and just how much loving a Gallagher man weighed upon one's soul.

The car ride back to Jacob and Lola's house was, for the first time, filled with comfortable silence. Walking through the door, Jacob lovingly hugged Lola. "Thank you so much for tonight, *Vixen*. My mom absolutely adores you. Even though I don't give two shits about what my father thinks, he deemed you perfection, which is a praise I have never heard him utter before."

Lola smiled and breathed a sigh of relief, thankful that she didn't manage to mess things up. "I-I'm really glad, Jacob. I enjoyed getting to spend time with your mother. Her hugs were so warm and caring. I feel like Cate is a lot like your mom."

Jacob laughed in agreeance, "The only difference is that Catarina is far more ballsy than my mother ever dared to be."

Leading Jacob by the hand to their bedroom, Lola told him she had one last Christmas gift for him, to which he lustfully growled. "Close your eyes," Lola called before exiting the walk-in closet wearing a sheer black, lacy bra and satin blush-colored panties with matching black, lacy trim.

When he finally opened his eyes, Jacob's breath hitched. Hearing Lola whisper into his ear that he could do whatever he wanted to her for the night, aside from the excruciating pain he had inflicted before, made him nearly come undone right then and there. "Fucking hell, *Vixen*. You look so pure and I can't wait to taint you."

Later that evening, as Lola exhaustedly lay beneath Jacob's thrusting body, she found her mind elsewhere; stuck on the fact that she had felt jealousy when it had no business taking root in the first place. An erotically painful sting to her side brought Lola back to reality. Looking down, she saw Jacob had bit her side in the same manner he had in the past. An act that had previously left her feeling disturbed, now had Lola feeling aroused; and while she hated to admit it, the darkest part of her not only loved but seemed to thrive from the painful ways Jacob made her feel alive.

~

April 30, 2015

Lola paused as they reached the end of the gravel road and the Bed & Breakfast they would stay in came fully into view. After checking in, Lola told Logan she would be taking a nap before they went out for dinner. Feeling Logan's body press against hers, Lola couldn't help but once again feel the shame not only associated with her vivaciously depraved memories … but the shame associated with the faintest part of her missing the rare moments when Jacob truly did care.

32

Mother's Day

May 10, 2015

Logan and Lola's time at the national park had helped them to feel rejuvenated. Lola had yet to tell Logan anything else in regards to her past with Jacob, but for Logan, that was quite alright. He still had a hard time wrapping his head around the fact that even a tiny part of Lola managed to remain empathetic towards her abuser.

When the pair returned to Logan's apartment, Mother's Day was around the corner; and while Logan desperately wanted his mother to see Lola for who she truly was and not be judged based upon the past, he knew that until he had learned just about everything, the idea was moot.

"Good morning, *my heart*," Logan warmly greeted Lola with a loving kiss.

Lola stretched, wrapping her arms around Logan's neck to pull his body on top of hers. The combination of nearly having sex on Valentine's Day *and* Logan not looking upon her with disgust after seeing the marks on her back, made Lola desire him even more. A smile spread across her lips as she devoured Logan's lips and felt his throbbing erection through his jeans. Breathlessly she broke away,

"You know … I can help remedy that growing problem you have."

Logan groaned in embarrassment, as he tried to fill his mind with any thoughts other than the love of his life in nothing but her dainty undergarments. "What are your plans for today? I know that Mother's Day is a sensitive subject for you, but I am going to spend the day with my mom and grandmothers. I will be driving down with dad and Cate, and we probably won't be back until a little later in the evening."

Lola pondered for a brief moment, before responding. "Well, Mark and Lizzie are celebrating Rae's birthday in conjunction with Mother's Day, so I'll be able to visit with Luke and Patricia, and I'm sure they have news of my mother. I'm gonna have to finish that letter I started to her, and face her at some point."

"Are you sure you're going to be okay?" Logan empathetically asked.

"I'm sure, Logan," Lola stated before mocking Dr. Indigo's infamous favorite words in a high-pitched voice. "It's all a part of the process."

~

Once Logan departed, Lola put on a navy blue camisole underneath a sheer sky blue top, and tucked both into a pair of white skinny jeans with matching belt, then slipped on a pair of navy blue **Sperry's**. Choosing to forgo any makeup, Lola quickly braided her hair, allowing it to fall gracefully over her right shoulder. Satisfied with the reflection staring back at her, Lola headed down to the gazebo in hopes of completing the letter to her mother.

After two hours of writing, Lola felt decently satisfied with the words she penned. Taking notice of the time, she quickly folded the letter and placed it into her back pocket, while heading back inside to grab her belongings.

During her drive to Lizzie's house, Lola gave Dr. Indigo a phone call for moral support, as this would be the first time she had any sort of contact with her mother since high school. Dr. Indigo's warm words of encouragement did Lola's heart wonders. "I won't keep you long, as I know you're with your family, but I just want to thank you for everything, Dr. Indigo. I'll let you know how everything goes tomorrow."

Parking behind Lizzie's vehicle, Lola sent Logan a quick text before making her way inside. Once in, Lola set off in search of her precious niece. "Happy birthday a couple days early, baby Rae!"

Twirling in a periwinkle-colored, ballet-inspired dress, Raelee beamed with delight. "Thank you, *Auntie Bear*. Can you believe that I'm 11 now?"

"No, sweetie. I sure can't. Time has gone by so fast and you are maturing into such a brilliant young woman."

"I'm gonna tell momma you're here," Raelee twittered as she pranced out of the living room.

A hearty laugh from behind her filled Lola's ears. "I swear that child never walks anywhere," Mark mused as he embraced Lola in a brotherly hug.

"Don't get your panties in a twist Marky-Mark. In the end, it's all part of her charm." Lola playfully jested before asking what the day entailed.

Mark informed her that the party for Raelee would be just family, as she still didn't have any friends to invite. Concern plagued Lola's heart, "I hate this so much for Rae. She's the purest soul, so I just don't understand this pre-teen jealousy. I don't know what I would have done without all of you guys when I was growing up."

With a heavy sigh, Mark relayed his concerns as well. "We're trying out a new church, that's supposed to have a bigger youth group, so hopefully Rae can make some good friends there. You should come with us sometime."

"Umm … give me the info and I'll see if I can make it. I do have a friend in Portland that has two girls pretty close in age to Rae. I'll talk to Lizzie to see if she wants me to set up a day trip to the mall so she and Rae can meet Louisa and her two daughters, Ariella and Noella."

The chiming of the doorbell caught Mark's attention, and Lola used this opportunity to check in with Lizzie. "Happy Mother's Day, *Momma Bear*." Lola expressed as she hugged her truest friend.

"Thank you, sister. Mom and dad should be here soon, so do you mind helping me carry everything into the dining room?"

When the table was set, Mark, who was followed by Luke and Patricia, entered the dining room. Lola looked upon the loving, elderly couple with deep admiration and prayed to one day find a love as deep as theirs. When all were seated, Luke prayed a blessing over the meal and asked God to bless all of the mothers as well as their precious Raelee.

"Sweet Luxie, would you please humor an old woman and join me for a walk out in the garden?" Patricia asked once everyone had finished eating. Lola obliged, as she couldn't even recall the last time she had truly spent time with either Luke or Patricia.

Walking arm in arm, the pair made their way through the small hedges, letting the warmth of the sun surround them. After several minutes, they sat upon the quiet bench perched beneath a large maple tree. Grasping Lola's hand in her frail, wrinkled one, Patricia earnestly spoke. "How have you really been, my dear? Elizabeth and Mark haven't told us much over the last couple of years and your mother doesn't seem to know anything about your life at all. I feel like Luke and I may have failed you in some way."

Lola closed her eyes as the gentle breeze brushed across her cheeks. "Patricia, you and Luke were never anything but kind to me. Please promise me you won't ever think otherwise. Okay?"

Patricia gently squeezed Lola's hand in acknowledgment as Lola continued speaking. "As for your question, honestly … I think that I'm doing okay. No, I know that I'm doing okay. I am sorry that Mark and Lizzie have kept you guys in the dark, but I asked them to. I have a lot of stuff that I've had to deal with."

"I'm so glad to hear it, sweetheart. Luke and I have prayed for you every day of your life. No matter what you are going through, please don't forget that you are a beautiful light to this world. Your father made no mistake in choosing your name." Patricia paused as she pulled a small handkerchief from the pocket of her pink floral skirt, dabbing the corners of her eyes. "I see so much of both your mother and father in you …"

Unsure as to why she asked, but Lola felt the urge to hear about her mother. "H-how's mom? We aren't on speaking terms … she made some choices that really hurt me, but … well, she's still my mother and I am thankful she chose to give me life."

"Your mother is doing well. After you left home and graduated high school, she came clean to Luke and me about her drinking and the abuse she caused you. Why did you never tell us? I am honestly surprised Elizabeth never said a word because we all know what that girl is like when it comes to injustice."

Lola laughed, "Yeah, she sure is a spitfire," before taking a somber tone. "The reason Lizzie never said anything is because I swore her to secrecy. And the reason that I never told you guys is because after she came back, I didn't want you guys to lose her again. I thought that as long as you all had her as your daughter, that I would be okay to suffer alone."

"Oh, my precious girl. We would have helped you and got your mother the help she truly needed. We never approached you about it because we felt guilty for not noticing the little signs."

Teary-eyed, both women embraced each other as they asked for one another's forgiveness. As they dried their eyes, Lola again asked how her mother was doing, to which Patricia honestly answered that Anne-Marie was doing very well. "She went to **Alcoholics Anonymous** and has been sober for almost 13 years now. She and Everett never divorced, and eventually ended up reconciling."

"I-I'm glad she's doing well. Do you know where she's living?" Lola earnestly inquired.

"She and Everett still own the house you once lived in. They traveled often, as Oregon used to hold so many painful memories for your mother, but have recently moved back."

Lola hugged the elderly woman beside her while placing a gentle kiss upon her cheek, before asking if she was ready to go back inside. *It's time to finally come face to face with my mother.*

~

Driving down the once familiar street, Lola felt her chest begin to tighten as she pulled into the driveway; trying to stave off her anxiety, Lola went through the calming techniques she and Dr. Indigo had established during those early sessions, before reading through her letter one last time. *If I know that this has to be done, why then does it feel so hard? Come on, Lola! As Logan would say, 'You're a grown ass woman,' so get out of this car and do what you came to do.*

Smoothing out her outfit, Lola walked up to the front door, where she stood for several minutes internally debating on if she should really follow through with a face-to-face meeting. Throwing caution to the wind, Lola rang the doorbell and waited. When no response came, Lola decided to try one last time, before dropping off the letter and hightailing it out of there. With the second chime earning no response, Lola turned to leave, but as luck would have it, the front door opened, with a feminine voice calling out, "Sorry it took me so long, I was in the garden."

With a heavy sigh, Lola turned to face her mother, fully taking in the woman whose affection she had so badly craved for years on end. Anne-Marie hadn't changed much over the years, save a few crows' feet around her eyes and her honey blonde hair now cut in a bob, with the faintest hints of silver peeking through. Seeing her daughter stand before her left Anne-Marie completely floored.

Finally ready to fully take charge of her life, Lola was the first to break the silence, as she retrieved the letter from her back pocket. "Hi, mom. Please just listen before you say anything. Everything I need for you to hear is in this letter. Anyhow, I hope you have a happy Mother's Day." Handing the letter to Anne-Marie, Lola hurried back to her car before her composure completely broke.

Forced to watch her child leave once more, Anne-Marie closed her front door as she slid to the floor. With shaking hands she opened the letter, taking the words fully to heart. Anne-Marie knew that while her daughter had offered forgiveness, there was no hope for reconciliation. *She truly is her father's daughter; how could I have nearly destroyed the only remaining piece of Jackson?*

Hearing the sound of his wife crying, Everett made his way over to her as he asked her what was wrong. Unable to speak, Anne-Marie handed him the letter which in turn grieved his heart, for he too had failed Lola by abandoning her during Anne-Marie's drunken days.

~

Seeing as how she was already out, Lola made a quick stop by the florist before visiting the cemetery. Since it was Mother's Day, Lola felt it only fitting to pay a visit to the woman who had truly been her mother, her grandmother. Standing before the plot shared by her grandparents, Lola wiped down their headstones, then placed the lavender roses in front.

Speaking out loud, Lola mused, "Grandpa and Grandma, I hope that I have made you both proud. I know that I haven't always done things right and life sure as hell has been hard without you guys. Grandma, thank you for being the best damn mother any girl could have ever had. I love you both and miss you always. Happy Mother's Day in heaven, Grandma."

Teary-eyed but relieved, Lola drove back home, where she couldn't wait to fill Logan in on the events of the day. While awaiting Logan's return, Lola decided to make due on her promise to Mark by phoning her friend Louisa. Louisa said that her girls would be more than happy to have a shopping day and they always enjoyed meeting new friends. Lola smiled as she sent a quick text to Mark and Lizzie, everything was set in motion for the following weekend.

Lost in her phone, Lola failed to notice Logan had returned until she gasped as his strong arms wrapped around her waist. Inhaling her intoxicating scent, Logan groaned, "My god, I have missed you today. I hope you had a nice time with Lizzie and her family."

Blushing as she giggled, Lola told Logan that she did and couldn't wait to tell him everything, before hearing about his day. "Why don't I make us a light dinner and then we can talk?" To which Logan readily agreed. Once everything was complete, they seated themselves on the couch and dove into hearty conversation, as any normal couple would.

33

Time with you is trouble for me

June 5, 2015

With prom and graduation season happening, Logan's photography business was booming and it wasn't until nearly a month later that Logan and Lola finally found a free moment to sit down for a proper conversation. Lola had now been back for nine months and while there had been painful moments, she had to admit that she was beginning to feel repaired. Dr. Indigo noticed the changes in Lola as well and suggested they move from daily phone sessions to only talking every Monday, Wednesday, and Friday.

Walking hand in hand down the forested path behind the café, Lola asked Logan if he was ready to hear the next part of her story. "This next part actually involves you, although, like any past interactions with you, I was left with a lot of heartache."

Logan looked away shamefully, "I had no idea a simple friendship would do so much damage."

Squeezing Logan's hand, Lola gently stated, "There was no way anyone could really have known, but I'd go through all of that hell again if it meant that I had your friendship waiting for me on the other side."

~

February 14, 2005

Although Valentine's Day was one of the busiest days for Cate, she closed her café early to prepare for a small birthday party for Logan and Naja to celebrate their 21st birthdays. Logan often enjoyed saying he was dating an older woman, even though in reality, Naja was only two days older.

Preparing the decorations with Cate, Lola asked, "Who all's coming?"

"I think it's just a small affair. Aside from you, Jacob, Cade, and myself, Logan said Naja's parents would be coming. As a Christmas gift, Logan helped reunite Naja with her parents."

Curiosity overtook Lola as she asked what happened between the young woman and her family. Cate relayed, "If memory serves me correctly, Logan said Naja dropped out of school and ran away from Seattle to Portland when she was 16 because her dad was awful to her mother, a bit of an alcoholic and unfaithful, and her mother just bore the brunt of it all."

"Oh, man. That had to be rough. So how did Logan and Naja meet?"

"Well, Naja was homeless for around a year when my mom's best friend, Maeve, found her. Maeve owns **The British Punk** in Portland and gave her a place to stay, a job, and helped her obtain her GED. Naja and Logan met through Maeve, I think after some frat party." With the last of the decorations in place, Cate asked Lola to follow her into the kitchen to put the final touches on the cake before everyone arrived. Once the cake was finished, Lola told Cate she needed to get Logan's birthday gift from her car.

Lola learned from her conversations at school with Logan, that they had similar tastes in music. "I'm glad we have a similar vibe because a lot of the shit Jacob listens to scares the hell out of me,"

Lola had confided in Logan.

"I still don't see why you're with a guy like that. You're funny as hell and easy to talk to," Logan admitted.

Lola had replied, that underneath his gruff vibe, Jacob treated her pretty decently. "I could do far worse."

Smiling as she hauled the large box inside, she couldn't wait to see Logan's reaction. *I really hope he likes this because some of the things were pretty hard to track down.* Setting the gift on the table, Lola headed off to find Cate once more but was stopped by a pair of strong arms entwining her. "Jacob!" Lola called out before he assaulted her lips with hungry kisses. "We're in public," she chastised.

"*Vixen,* do you really think I give a fuck what anyone thinks?" Jacob queried while rolling his eyes.

"You might not, but I do. All of the public displays make me a little uncomfortable. I mean, it's bad enough that you leave a string of hickeys on my neck. Do you even know how many times random bitches in my classes have called me a 'slut' or 'trash' because of this shit?" Lola heatedly confessed.

"Again, do you think I give a fuck?" Jacob asked before tightly grabbing Lola's arms to retain her attention. "You.are.mine! I own your mind, body, and soul, and I will do whatever the fuck I want. Do I make myself clear?" Jacob hissed through clenched teeth.

With teary eyes, Lola nodded her head as she weakly admitted that she was his. A voice calling out from behind them became Lola's saving grace. "Hey, Lola. Is everything okay?"

Giving Jacob a quick passionate kiss, Lola called out, "H-hey, Logan. Everything is fine! I was just telling Jacob about some of the girls at school."

Returning her attention to the demanding man before her, Lola looked up with pleading eyes, to which Jacob relented. "*Vixen,* would you please let Catarina know I'm here?"

Lola acknowledged his request as she made her way to the bathroom in hopes of cleaning up her flushed and teary face. Returning to the kitchen, Lola informed Cate that everyone was starting to arrive.

~

Although an intimate affair, Logan and Naja's party was turning out to be quite successful. Lola met Naja's parents and learned that when their daughter left, it was the wake-up call James needed to get his life turned around; which is why they moved from Seattle to Portland the same year Naja ran away. Naomi said they ended up opening ***Étoile Bleue*** in hopes of a new start and someday having their daughter return to them. Seeing such loving parents always stung Lola's heart, and while it was foolish thinking on her part, she often held the faintest hope that one day her mother would truly get help; however, life had yet to be kind to Lola, so she knew it was easier to give up this small desire instead of being disappointed once again.

As the party wound down, Logan and Naja began opening their gifts. While Lola didn't know Naja very well, she still wanted to give her something she hoped would be of use; even though she still felt twinges of jealousy that had no business taking root. After Naja opened the small envelope with confusion etched upon her brow, Lola meekly spoke up. "My grandparents were the owners of **Swan Hotels** and **Swan Industries**, and I constantly have penthouse rooms reserved in my name, as a part of my inheritance. I know it isn't much, but I hope a week's stay at any time this year is okay. All of the details are in the letter I included."

Naja smiled widely, silver eyes lighting up the room, as she thanked Lola for her kindness and generosity. She did find it a little odd that the two of them had only met briefly one time, yet Lola still chose to give her such an elaborate gift. *Don't overthink it too much. You know rich white people are crazy.*

By the time Logan made it to Lola's gift, she was on edge with anticipation at the thought of him possibly not liking everything she had given him. Upon opening the box, Logan's eyes widened in surprise. "Lola …" he gasped in elation. The large box contained several vintage and current rock band t-shirts, all of which had been autographed; as well as a first edition copy of Ansel Adams's first photography book; and two original prints.

Seeing the contents of the box, resentment festered inside Jacob's black heart. *What the fuck is this shit? Apparently, Lola and I need to play a new game, as she seems to have forgotten her place.* Retaining his composure, as the stealthy hunter he was, Jacob wished Logan and Naja each a happy birthday and bid everyone else adieu; before making his way to Lola and kissing her passionately. "I'll see you when you get home," he whispered in her ear, consternation trailing down her spine.

When Naja stepped away to speak with her parents, Logan made his way to Lola, embracing her in a warm, friendly hug. "Thank you so much for the amazing gifts! You know you didn't have to go all out."

"What can I say, Warren, I like to treat my friends well." Lola preened.

"Still occasionally calling me by my last name, I see."

"It's all part of my charm," Lola exclaimed with a playful wink.

While the red-headed pair joked around, Naja felt immense disdain growing in her heart for Lola. *Who the hell does this bitch think she is? Giving **my** man such expensive ass things and her hoe ass gotta man! And Logan's gonna get an earful when we leave … smiling like a damn fool over her gift, when he only treated mine like some stranger gave it to him. Just because I ain't some rich bitch, doesn't mean I didn't work my ass off for those fucking concert tickets.*

Unbeknownst to Lola that her gift would cause such animosity between her and Naja, Lola added fuel to the fire by hugging Logan as she prepared to leave. Turning towards Naja and her parents, Lola made polite conversation before finally succumbing to the inevitable fate of returning home. "Mr. and Mrs. Grey, it was such a pleasure to meet you all. Naja, it was really nice seeing you again. Maybe in the future, Jacob and I can treat you and Logan to dinner at our house. Enjoy the rest of your birthday celebration."

~

Nausea and dread settled in the pit of Lola's stomach as she slowly walked down the hallway to her bedroom. Surely nothing good was to come from Jacob's promise of seeing her at home. *Things have been going so well, how did I manage to mess everything up?* Lola thought to herself as she opened the door with shaking hands.

Again, Lola found Jacob seated in the very familiar Victorian, red velvet chair. Although this time, he wouldn't throw a Scotch glass above her head; no, this time he was far angrier. Before Lola even had a chance to close the door, Jacob stood and closed the gap between them; slamming Lola's head against the door. "What the fuck was that about? Is your stupid ass trying to make me look like a got damn fool?"

With ringing ears, Lola tried to respond, however, her stuttering was only met with another slam of her head against the door. Jacob pulled Lola's body to his and gently stroked the side of her head. "Don't cry, *Vixen*." He shushed her while wiping away the tears. "The pain you are feeling is only a fraction of the pain you made me feel this evening."

"I-I-I ... d-d-didn't ..." Lola spluttered.

"Hush now, *Vix*. I don't want to hear your fucking lies!" Jacob scolded before informing Lola of his plans for their evening. "Now, we are going to play a new 'game'. One that I think will be even more 'fun' than our last one."

Lola knew that the words 'fun' and 'game' coming from Jacob's mouth had nothing but malice in the intent. "I-I d-don't want to play any games!" Lola demanded.

With a hard slap to Lola's face, Jacob screamed, "Did I fucking ask you what you wanted?"

With watery eyes, Lola shook her head and apologized for her rudeness. Kissing Lola's head once more, Jacob began to explain the rules of their 'game'. "We're going to play a riveting rendition of 'Hide and Seek' that I like to call, 'Hunt the rabbit'. I'm going to give you 30 minutes to hide from me, if I don't find you, you are free from any consequences of your actions. However, if I find you, and oh, my little *Vixen*, I hope I do, you win my prize."

At the sound of Jacob maniacally laughing out, "Run, rabbit, run. Save yourself if you can!" Lola bolted down the hall. Trying each doorknob, Lola was met with failure as Jacob had preemptively locked every room aside from their own. *Shit! Shit! Shit! Where the hell am I supposed to hide. The garage! I came in through there, so surely I can hide inside of something out there.*

"Only 15 minutes left, *Vixen*!" Jacob taunted.

Finally finding an open space to hide in the garage, Lola slid inside the tool cabinet, doing her best to quiet her sobs and beating heart. *This is some straight up horror movie shit! How the hell did this become my life?*

Knowing Lola's only choice was to hide in the garage, Jacob took his time hunting his prey; like a snow leopard ready to pounce upon a fox. The slamming sound of every car door and trunk, made Lola nearly vomit as the tension grew. "Where, oh where, could you be my little *Vixen*? I must say that I am enjoying this new game. Only five minutes remain and I wonder who the winner will be."

Deep down, Lola knew Jacob was merely teasing her as a means of torment; clearly, he would be the victor, as the odds were stacked against her from the beginning. Sadly though, Lola's next course of action would be her undoing that evening. Having no longer heard Jacob's voice or footsteps, Lola slid open the door of her hiding place before silently stepping out. Crouching down, Lola began to crawl across the floor. Thinking she was surely in the clear, Lola exhaled in relief.

A clapping sound resonated through the darkness, as Jacob entered the dimly lit area behind Lola's car. "I must say, well done, *Vixen*. You still had 30 seconds remaining. While the hunt was fun, I am elated for the prize portion of our evening."

Lola screamed in horror, only to once more feel the sting from the back of Jacob's hand upon her face. Kissing Lola hungrily, Jacob gently wiped away her tears. "Hush, hush, *Vixen*. There's really no need to cry right now. A little later, probably, but not right now. Why don't you let me carry you back to our room?"

Lola knew that silent compliance was her only option at this moment, as she allowed herself to rest against Jacob's body. Picking her up, Jacob curtly commented upon Lola's weight, sending another painful jab to her splintering heart. "You may want to start watching what you eat. You feel a bit heavy today."

Back in their bedroom, Lola cringed as she saw the red chair had been moved beside the fireplace, which now housed a roaring fire. Seeing the glint of terror in Lola's eyes, Jacob felt himself harden. Tenderly, he undressed Lola while administering gentle kisses upon each newly barren space of her body; before finally coming to her alabaster inner thighs.

Even though she knew she should have run, Lola cursed herself for getting ensnared by the devilishly intoxicating man before her. *Surely I deserve this. After all, aren't I just as fucked up as he is?* A moan escaped from her lips as Jacob greedily lapped at her leaking core.

Just as she was about to release her high, Jacob pulled away, while laughing darkly. "I won't let you cum just yet, *Vixen*, because you still haven't earned it."

"Wh-what do you m-mean?" Lola shakily breathed.

Jacob laughed once more, slapping Lola across the face while explaining the next portion of their evening. "You really hurt me tonight, *Vixen*. Do you know how much it hurt and disrespected me to see you give Logan such ostentatious gifts?"

Unable to answer, Lola quietly shook her head; earning yet another slap to her face as Jacob continued his rant. "In order for you to make up for this blatant act of flippancy, I am forced to remind you just who you belong to. So, for every gift that was in that damn box, you *will* earn one new mark showing that I fucking own your ungrateful ass. Also, every time you cry, I will add another. I promise you, sweetheart, by the time I'm done with you, your ass will be so fucked up that I will be etched into every fiber of your being … just like you are in mine. Now, let's begin!"

~

June 5, 2015

By the time they had finished their walk, the sun was beginning to set and Lola asked Logan if he would like to sit in the gazebo with her. "I don't know what it is about this place, but to me, it feels so serene."

Silently the pair watched as the sun disappeared, making way for the stars' arrival; neither entirely certain what to say next. Finally, Lola said, "That was one of the most hellish nights I had ever experienced. I actually ended up in the hospital because of it."

"What do you mean?" Logan asked with concern lacing his voice.

"Do you remember when I missed school for two weeks after your birthday because I had the flu?"

"Yeah …"

"Well, in reality, I was hospitalized for a couple of days due to a fractured eye socket. Turns out, the side of your head meeting a solid wooden door a few times does some major damage."

"Fucking son of a bitch! I want to filet his fucking ass alive!" Logan seethed.

Exhaling in an effort to retain composure, Lola placed a tender hand upon Logan's. "Logan, please look at me…"

"How many times?" Logan asked as he cut her off.

Confused, Lola asked, "How many times, what?"

"How many fucking times did he hurt you because of me?" Logan pounded his chest as he demanded to know the painful truth.

"Not that it changes what happened, but if you really must know, after your 21st birthday and for quite some time after. Anytime I had a project with you, hung out with you, or someone even mentioned your name, Jacob gave me a 'reminder' that I was his. Now, not all of them were as bad as that night. And like I said earlier today, I'd go through it all again just to have your friendship in the end."

Logan embraced Lola as guilt overtook him. *How the hell could she have endured all of that for two years without anyone even noticing?* With his tears falling down his face, Logan asked, "What made you finally leave him?"

Lola sighed at the irony of the truth. "Ya know, I'd like to say I finally wised up and realized my stupid ass deserved better, but that's wishful thinking. In the end, it was his father, Maximillian. About a year and a half later, after Jacob and Cate's 28th birthday celebration, Max called demanding Jacob go back to their Vancouver office. I refused to go because I would be graduating and starting my internship within my own company soon. As much of a cold-blooded son of a bitch that Max is, he truly was my savior from nearly two years of pure hell."

Logan laughed uncomfortably. "I don't think Cate's dad would ever consider himself anyone's savior."

Lola agreed with his sentiment before asking Logan if they could stay a little while longer to watch the stars. Logan readily agreed, mostly for himself though. He needed time to pray and calm down. *God, the justice seeker inside of me is raging. I have never wanted to murder someone like I do Jacob. Please calm the beast within me and just help me to be the listening ear Lola needs. I'm scared to death that if this doesn't get under control I'll react so negatively that I'd end up being no better off than Jacob, and I sure as hell can't do that to her.*

34

Unintentional Deceptions

August 2, 2015

Two months had passed since the revelation of Jacob's depravity and maltreatment of Lola. After the heaviness of reliving part of her trauma, upon recommendation from Dr. Indigo, Lola asked Logan for a bit of time before moving forward. When Lola questioned why Dr. Indigo made this recommendation, Dr. Indigo remarked, "If you choose to power through, you will end up unraveling all of the progress you have made up to this point." Although he was ready to hear the rest, Logan patiently granted Lola's query. *Besides, if I'm honest with myself, I still need to be able to process this shit.*

Lola's birthday always brought about a multitude of emotions within her. Trying her best to quell the rising tide of her anxiety, Lola told Logan she was finally ready to pick up where they had left off. "Only if you're sure," Logan lovingly reassured Lola.

"I'm sure. Besides, I think it's finally time that I apologize for my actions from the night of the gala in 2006." Lola remorsefully recanted.

Logan's heart faltered slightly, as he began to reflect upon the memory of the first time Lola had unintentionally hurt him.

~

December 31, 2006

The months following the breakup with Jacob were some of the loneliest in Lola's life; even more so than after Shane's death. In Lola's mind, when Jacob left, he robbed her of everything precious: her friendship with Lizzie had become more of an acquaintanceship, as Lizzie had everything Lola's heart desired. Deeply confiding in Cate was no longer an option, for the house of lies Lola had built, felt ready to crash around her at any moment.

To combat the darkened thoughts ever present at the forefront of her mind, Lola fully submersed herself in learning the ins and outs of her company, under the tutelage of her grandfather's best friend, Gregory Miller. Gregory and Jack had agreed after Jackson's death, that should Jack step down, Gregory would run **Swan Industries** and any subsidiaries (Lorriene's clinic included), until Lola was of age and had graduated from college.

Gregory's heart swelled with pride as he watched Lola grow in her capabilities more and more each passing day. "Luxe," Gregory began before Lola interjected. "Uncle Greg, how many times do I have to tell you to call me Lola now."

Chuckling, Gregory mused, "Well, if memory serves me correctly, you always hated your first name and pouted for a week after I called you 'Lola.'"

Rolling her eyes as she laughed, Lola recalled, "Well, I was 10 at the time, so you can't really blame me." Firmly setting her tone, Lola crossed her arms, as she remarked, "Anyhow, it's time to put childishness aside and focus on making my own name in the business world."

"I think you could still do that, while going by the name you prefer," Gregory reasoned.

"Uncle Greg, I don't want anything just handed to me because of who my grandparents were. I want to earn every damn thing in my life, and that starts with going by my given name." Lola sternly stated, before walking to her desk. "Now, let's have a seat and discuss the New Year's Eve gala. This is the first task that I am fully undertaking on my own, and I need it to be a success."

~

The day of the gala had arrived far quicker than Lola had anticipated, and while Gregory had repeatedly reassured Lola this year would be a success, she couldn't help but listen to the dark thoughts once more. Tears streamed down Lola's face as she found comfort in the familiar feeling of nails embedded into her palms. *You're pathetic and a disgrace. If your grandparents were still alive, they would be so ashamed of you. You're going to ruin this company. Just look at you! You are absolutely nothing without Jacob. You were stupid to think you stood a chance to do this on your own.*

The sound of her cell phone ringing in the background brought Lola back to reality. After regaining her composure, Lola cheerily answered.

"H-hey, Lola …" Logan nervously spoke on the other end.

"Hey, Warren. What's up?"

Rolling his eyes, Logan chuckled, "Again with the last name?"

"Like I told you before, it's part of my charm and you can't help but love me for it." Lola playfully retorted.

The line fell silent for a few moments as Logan became lost in thought. If Lola only knew the feelings that had begun growing in Logan's heart, she would have never uttered her playful words. Finally finding the courage to speak, Logan continued, "So … umm … tonight's the night of your gala, right?"

"Yeah, and I'm nervous as hell," Lola stated honestly.

"Why are you nervous? I know I haven't known you nearly as long as Cate has, but it seems like every damn thing you put your mind to, you succeed."

Logan had no way of knowing his encouraging words helped quell the storm raging in Lola's mind. "Thanks for the vote of confidence, but we'll see if your words hold true at the end of the night. Anyhow, are you coming?"

"I am. I'll be there wearin' a tux with **Chuck's**."

"I wouldn't have expected anything less," Lola laughed heartily, before inquiring, "Is Naja coming?"

"Yeah, but she's going to be working with her parents, since they are catering your event tonight." Logan took a few deep breaths before he continued with the true reasoning behind his call. "Hey, Lola, would it be okay if I talked to you later on tonight? I have something important I need to tell you and I'd like to do it in person."

Worry filled Lola's voice, as she queried. "Logan, is everything okay?"

"Yeah, it's nothing major. So don't stress yourself, m'kay?" Logan nervously reassured her.

"If you say so, then I'll take your word for it. Anyhow, I need to get off of here and finish getting everything ready for the evening. See you later, Warren."

~

With final confirmation from Gregory that Naomi and James Grey's staff had everything up and running, Lola exited the hotel ballroom, in the direction of the ladies' room in hopes of giving her hair and makeup one last check. Pleased with her reflection, Lola exhaled deeply as she returned to greet her guests. *I need this to go well. I have to prove to them that I am more than capable of pulling this off.*

After an hour of greeting guests and superficial conversations, although she rarely drank, Lola found herself seeking the solitude of the bar. "What'll it be, love?" The bartender kindly queried, in her slight British accent.

"Well, I'm not much of a drinker," Lola admitted, before asking, "What do you recommend that's light and fruity?"

"Hmm … I'd say a *Cosmopolitan*; it's a classy drink, that won't leave ya feelin' hungover in the morning. Whatcha think?"

"Sounds good to me," Lola expressed with gratitude, finally taking a moment to observe the woman behind the bar.

Taking a sip from the beautiful, pink drink placed before her, Lola raved, "Oh my gosh! This is literally the best drink I have ever had. Thank you so much … umm- please forgive my ignorance in not knowing your name." Lola remarked as she flushed in embarrassment for having forgotten basic courtesy.

"The name's Maeve, love. And don't look embarrassed. I could've very well introduced myself, but most people comin' to the bar aren't too keen on knowin' their server's name." The bartender jested.

"Thank you for the drink, Maeve. If you didn't know, my name's Lola. Do you work for the Greys?"

"Pleasures all mine, Lola. And I don't work for Naomi and James, but their daughter, Naja works for me."

Lola bristled at the mention of Naja's name; while Lola, herself, had no qualms with Naja, she felt as if Naja had a disdain for her. "Oh, that's nice. I have had the pleasure of meeting Naja a handful of times."

"Have ya now? Well, then, ya must know Logan. The two of them have been damn near inseparable the past few years. Folks say ya can't fall in love at a bar, but I'd beg to differ." Maeve boasted.

Hearing Maeve speak so fondly of Naja and Logan as a couple felt bothersome to Lola, although she couldn't understand why. *He's my friend, I should be happy that he's happy.* "I am actually friends with Logan. I met Naja because of him," Lola acknowledged.

"I knew my ears were burning!" Logan exclaimed as he walked

behind the bar, lovingly embracing Maeve.

"I don't think these rich folks'll be too fond of ya comin' back here, behind the bar." Maeve teased as she shooed Logan to the front.

"Well, it helps when you're good friends with the host and owner of this establishment," Logan preened, before giving Lola a wink.

"You know, Warren, I didn't think you were the kind of person to name drop. Seeing this side of you may make me rethink our friendship." Lola quipped.

Doubling over in laughter, Maeve teasingly told Logan that Lola could end up replacing him as her favorite person.

"Maevey, why ya gotta cut me so deep?" Logan whined.

"Maybe if ya'd ever order somethin' besides water or soda, I'll consider it." Maeve retorted.

"Now, you know I can't do that. It's the straight-edge life for me." Logan remarked, as he accepted the glass of water from Maeve.

"What's straight-edge life?" Lola asked.

Turning to answer Lola's question, Logan couldn't help but blush at the sight of the beauty standing before him; Lola looked alluring. The gown she wore was truly one of a kind: a gorgeous, full length a-line dress, with a high collared, plunging neckline; the bodice was embellished with an intricate, gold metallic floral embroidery, and had sheer elbow-length sleeves; which was attached to a luxurious, matte satin black skirt. Lola's curls were elegantly pulled back into a French Braided, low ponytail that laid delicately over her left shoulder. But the thing that captivated Logan the most, were Lola's eyes, which were adorned in a rich, smokey, purple eyeshadow; causing them to glisten in the light, like freshly cut emeralds.

Noticing the heat rising in Logan's cheeks, Maeve abruptly cleared her throat, recalling Logan from his inappropriately enamoured, stupor. "Logan, I believe yer *friend* asked ya a question." Maeve curtly remarked, whilst stressing Lola's position in Logan's life.

Chuckling nervously, Logan asked Lola to repeat her question, to which he explained, "Straight-edge life just means that I abstain from drugs, cigarettes, alcohol, and even casual sex. I'll drink an occasional beer, but that's maybe once a year. I like to keep a clear and sober mind. Plus, casual sex just causes nothing but pain and heartache in the end, so why use someone for my own personal gain."

Lola sipped her drink as she intently listened to Logan's explanation of his life choice. "You know, I think that's an admirable quality. It truly is a shame that more people aren't nearly as considerate." Lola lamented, before spotting Gregory heading in her direction. Inhaling deeply to calm her nerves, Lola thanked Logan and Maeve for the drink and conversation.

Logan carefully caught Lola's hand before she slipped out of sight. "Hey, Lola, can I still talk to you later in private? It's kinda important."

Lola's breath hitched at the tenderness of Logan's touch; for it had been far too long since a man had reached out to her with delicacy instead of malice. "Y-yeah. I think that would be nice," Lola shyly admitted.

"Lola Luxe Swan! Do you have any idea how long I have been looking for you," Gregory scolded.

"Apologies, Uncle Greg. I just needed a bit of time away from the crowd."

"I understand that, my dear, but now is time for your speech. You've worked hard for this moment, and now it's time for you to prove to them what I already see, and that's that you're meant to lead **Swan Industries** and head up this gala." Gregory lovingly reassured the bright, young woman standing before him.

Giving Logan's hand a final squeeze, Lola called out as she turned to follow her uncle, "Find me before you leave, Warren."

Lost in thought as he watched the woman who had slowly and unintentionally enthralled his heart, Logan bristled as an angry voice spat in his ear, "What the fuck was that about, Logan?"

Turning to face the owner of the voice, Logan rolled his eyes in frustration. "Don't start shit, Nae. You're the one who wanted to take a break, not me."

"Does that mean you need to flirt with that stuck up bitch?!" Naja countered as Logan interjected, before turning back in the direction of the bar. "Like I said, Nae, don't start shit. I'm not doin' this here."

"You know what Maeve, I think tonight actually is a special occasion, so why don't you go ahead and pass me a beer!" Logan demanded haughtily.

"I love ya like ya'd be my own son, Logan, but I'm gonna have to deny yer request." Maeve firmly stated as she crossed her arms.

"Fuck this shit," Logan muttered under his breath as he stepped outside to cool his temper.

~

Once Lola's speech had ended with a round of riveting applause, she let Gregory know that she was stepping away for just a few moments. "Apologies once again for earlier, Uncle Greg. I'm just not used to having to be at the forefront of everyone's attention." Embracing Gregory, Lola swiftly made her way to the lobby.

Pacing back and forth, Lola tried to calm her nerves by recalling the events of the night and trying to prepare herself for what Logan could possibly want to speak with her privately about. *Oh, God, I hope everything is okay with him and Naja. I hope my friendship with Logan hasn't disturbed their relationship. If it did, I guess I really am just a slut, like mom said. Ugh! As stupid as this sounds to any logical person, and I know I shouldn't, I miss Jacob.*

Lola grasped onto the fox necklace he had given her a few years prior, as she recalled the few genuine moments they had together. *I* *know we're both fucked up in the head, but damn, it really seemed like he was the only person to truly understand **all** of me. It's been six fucking months since we broke up, I don't know why I can't get past this, even though I should be over him. And while I don't think he ever loved me, but...*

Before Lola's mind could go further down the darkened path of disastrous thoughts, a masculine voice called out from behind.

"Miss Swan, may I speak with you a moment?"

Promptly drying the few stray tears that had managed to escape, Lola turned to meet the owner of the voice and was pleasantly surprised to be greeted by a face she hadn't seen since Andy's trial; Ronan Harper. Lola took in his appearance and saw that not much had changed in three years, except for the well-kept beard he now sported. Ronan still stood at approximately 5'10, with a medium, sunkissed golden complexion. He also had warm black wavy hair, which was smartly parted to the right, and the brightest emerald green eyes Lola had ever seen; which caused her heart to skip a beat.

"Miss Swan, are you alright?" Ronan asked as he chuckled at Lola's very obvious staring.

Mentally chastising herself for her lack of professionalism, Lola spluttered, "S-sorry, Mr. Harper is it? Please forgive my rudeness in staring. I was trying to recall your name, as it has been what, three years since our last meeting."

Ronan let out a deep, boisterous laugh at Lola's obvious attempt to save face. "Yes, Miss Swan, I do think it has been about that long. And please, call me Ronan; Mr. Harper is my father."

"Apologies, Ronan. Are you enjoying the gala? And please, call me Lola."

"I am enjoying it. I was most impressed with your speech. It's not often that someone so young is so eloquently driven to undertake such a magnanimous event." Ronan stated admirably.

"I'm glad my speech came across that way, because if I can be honest, the entire time I was up there, I was seconds away from puking. My nerves were so high."

Shaking off the last of her uneasiness, Lola dared to ask the question now burning at the forefront of her mind. "How has everything been since you lost Andy's case," before quickly adding, "I'm so sorry if that was rude or impetuous. You don't have to answer if you don't want to."

Pondering for a moment, Ronan reasoned there was no harm in admitting the truth. "You know, when someone would normally ask that question, I would paint on a smile and say what people want to hear- 'Oh, everything's fine. Works going great!' But, I feel like I can be honest with you."

Lola nodded her head reassuringly as she subconsciously grabbed Ronan's hand in hers.

Exhaling, Ronan finally admitted everything that had been buried within his chest over the last three years since the crushing defeat at Andy's trial. "Truthfully, nothing has been the same ever since. Andy's case was the first one I have ever lost. I shouldn't have, and I still don't understand how.

"I lost my opportunity at the partnership, but in all honesty, I didn't really want it. I take smaller cases, but I still spend most of my time pouring over the evidence because it just doesn't make since. I made Andy a promise that I would prove his innocence and it will be the last thing that I ever do."

Before Lola knew what she was doing, she pulled Ronan closer to her and captured his lips with hers, kissing him passionately. After several intense moments, Lola shied away, her face now the same shade as her hair; a mixture of passion and embarrassment at her boldness. "I-I'm so sorry about that, Ronan."

Chuckling, Ronan lifted Lola's chin as he stated, "No need to be sorry, Lola. It was surprising, to say the least, but not an unwelcome one." Lola breathed a sigh of relief at Ronan's reassurance, as he stated, "My original intent in coming over here, was to ask you to dinner one night. If you're interested, I'd love to get to know you better over dinner one night?"

Laughing heartily, Lola readily accepted Ronan's invitation before asking if she could kiss him once more, a request he happily granted. While Lola's heart was soaring with the budding of a new relationship, another's was breaking.

After calming down in the cold night air, Logan returned in hopes of finding Lola and finally admitting the truth inside of his heart. Having searched quietly for several minutes, Logan eventually found Lola standing in the lobby, and as he prepared to walk in her direction, he was cut off by a sharply dressed man in a white tuxedo. While Logan's gut told him to turn and walk away, curiosity overrode his instincts; thus causing his heart to shatter at the passionate display of affection before him.

Turning back to the ballroom, Logan wiped away the couple of tears that had escaped down his face; he knew what he must do. Logan's next course of action went against everything he stood for, but at that moment in time, he wanted to make the bitter aching dissipate. Finding Naja packing up a table for her parents, he swiftly turned her around and kissed her, as if her lips provided life support to his shattered heart.

Placing his forehead upon Naja's as their kiss ended, Logan breathlessly spoke words laced with fallacy, "Nae, I've been miserable without you."

~

August 2, 2015
Gazing upon Logan's face, Lola painfully admitted, "You know, I never meant to kiss Ronan that night, or even hurt you like I did.

I've never been an overly bold person, but hearing how passionate Ronan was about trying to get Andy another trial, made my heart soar."

Kissing Lola's left cheek as he tenderly touched her right one, Logan confessed, "I never meant to use Naja, and that's something I'll always regret. Even though she has forgiven me, and even said she felt like she just used me in the end too, it still weighs heavy on my soul."

Wrapping his long arms around Lola, Logan inhaled her calming scent, before she reminded him that they should probably finish getting ready for her party at Lizzie's. "You know how she is," Lola warmly laughed.

35

Beauty from the ashes

August 16, 2015

Lola awoke the morning of August 16 feeling rather apprehensive, as the date was nearing the one-year anniversary of when she finally braved her fears, thus making that fateful phone call to Logan. Seeing Lola so lost in thought, Logan seized the opportunity to envelop her in a loving embrace, while placing a tender kiss on her bare shoulder. "What's going through that beautiful mind of yours, *my heart?*"

"Oh, j-just thinking … it's silly, really." Lola tried to shy away; while her walls were beginning to slowly come down, from time to time she still found herself trying to lock the door.

"Regardless of whether or not it's silly, I'd still love to hear about it. Everything that's on your mind matters to me." Logan lovingly encouraged.

Sighing wearily, Lola knew she'd have to be honest with her thoughts and feelings; after all, wasn't that her entire reasoning for coming back to face her two biggest fears: her past and herself.

"If you really want to know, I was just reflecting upon how it's nearly a year since I called you and set all of 'this' in motion," Lola motioned between the two of them before continuing, "I sometimes feel like I'm ... I don't know ... I guess, stuck in this sort of paradox."

While Lola thought of how to vocalize her next thoughts, Logan squeezed her hand tenderly as he reassured her to the best of his ability. "I can't believe it's already nearing a year. We've grown so much, but more importantly than that, you've grown."

"You think so?" Lola queried.

"I don't think so, I know so," Logan exclaimed before continuing, "I can't even imagine going through half of the shit you've gone through, let alone to have to relive it by telling someone else."

Tearing up, Lola recited Dr. Indigo's words which long since become her mantra, "Healing takes time. Back in March, I told Dr. Indigo that I was frustrated with how long everything has taken, and she again reminded me of those words."

"She's right you know?"

"Even though I hate admitting it, I know she is." Lola truthfully stated.

"I think we should celebrate!" Logan jumped out of the bed with zeal as he made his proclamation.

"We literally just celebrated my birthday, don't you think this would be overkill?"

"Nonsense! I'm gonna call Maeve and tell her I'm booking **The British Punk** for August 29, and we'll invite your friends from your company, Mark, Lizzie, Dad, and Cate, and anyone else you want." Logan announced with great excitement, as his brain went into overdrive.

Lola couldn't help but feel elated by Logan's boyish enthusiasm. "Alright, alright- you've convinced me. I do have one request though." Seeing Logan's inquisitive look, Lola continued. "My request is, that I have to finish telling you about the beginning of mine and Ronan's relationship. There should at least be some happiness shared before

I relive that downfall."

Turning on the radio, Logan walked over to Lola and extended his hand to help her up from the bed. *"My heart*, I am more than willing to move at your pace. Will you dance with me?"

Lola giggled as she nodded her head, listening to DJ Samantha's soothing voice flood the room. "Good morning, Oregon Lovers. DJ Samantha here to start your morning off with a little love. 'Collide' by **Howie Day** is up next following a word from our sponsors."

As the song ended, Logan told Lola that he would like to take her to Vienna for the day. "I don't think I'm ready to meet your mom just yet," Lola stated wearily.

Laughing, Logan remarked, "Well, it's a good thing we aren't going to meet her then. If you're up for it, I'd like for you to meet my friend and tattoo artist, Luka. And if you feel comfortable with him seeing your back, I was thinking you could look into getting a beautiful full back tattoo, to cover your marks."

Giving Logan's words some thought, Lola stated, "I'd honestly never given much thought to a tattoo, but since my skin is already damaged … I guess it couldn't hurt. Do I have to tell him what happened?"

"If you aren't comfortable with telling him what happened, you don't have to. *My heart*, it's completely up to you who you tell your story to. I'll never force you to do something you aren't comfortable with. Besides, Luka would never judge you."

"O-Okay! Let's do this before I chicken out," Lola half-heartedly jested. "I guess I can use the drive there to finish telling you about the beginning of my relationship with Ronan."

~

March 15, 2007

Since the night of the gala, Lola found herself deeply enamored by Ronan. And though they had a decade between them, Lola felt at ease talking with him. It was nice having someone around who knew nothing of her relationship with Jacob nor about her past. Lola could divulge what she wanted, when she wanted.

Glancing quickly at her reflection, Lola checked her makeup before pulling her hair into a quick ponytail; she never tried to stare for too long, as that was when the voices were the loudest. Appeased with the young woman glancing back at her, Lola moved to her closet to find something suitable for a casual date. The first few had been formal, at Ronan's insistence, so Lola requested something more laid back.

Settling on a ripped pair of black skinny jeans, a grey oversized, vintage **Nirvana** sweatshirt, and a pair of black combat boots with roses painted on them, Lola collected her purse then walked down to her car before driving in the direction of the diner Ronan had agreed to meet at.

~

Following their meal, neither Lola nor Ronan could bring themselves to call an end to their evening. Grabbing Ronan's hand, Lola suggested they enjoy a moonlit stroll around the marina. "You know, I do believe this is the first time I have ever seen you in a pair of jeans," Lola playfully pointed out.

"I don't think I've even worn a pair since college," Ronan shrugged, "I must say that's it's kind of nice since I'm usually stuck with suits or tuxes."

Two hours quickly passed with the couple walking aimlessly around the marina. Lola smiled to herself as she realized this was the first time since, Shane's passing, that she felt free and at ease.

Having arrived back at their respective vehicles, Lola embraced Ronan as she revealed the contents of her heart. "Ronan, for the first time in a long time, I'm truly happy. My mind used to overflow with so many distorted thoughts, that it was suffocating. But …"

Pausing, Lola gazed up into Ronan's bright eyes, before continuing. "… but with you, everything seems so quiet and calm. You bring me this peace, and while I know we haven't known each other long or even been together that long, I love you."

Staring wide-eyed at the young woman before him, Ronan couldn't believe the words he was hearing. During their time together, he had grown deeply fond of and attached to Lola. Not wanting to taint the magic of their moment, Ronan ludicrously tried to deceive himself when he uttered, "I love you too, Lola."

~

August 16, 2015

As Logan pulled into the parking lot of **Prohibition Ink**, Lola concurred, "Hearing Ronan's words caused my heart to euphorically erupt. I'd like to say had I known our ending, I never would have opened my heart to our beginning, but I guess that's why they say hindsight is 20/20."

Grabbing Lola's hand in his, Logan wistfully remarked, "I think that's where we can find beauty in life's mysteries. Surely some good came from your relationship with Ronan?"

Pondering momentarily, Lola flatly stated before changing the subject, "While I'm sure some did, it sure as hell didn't help with my trust issues. Anyhow, I guess we'd better head inside."

Once inside the shop, Logan led Lola to the back office where Luka had told Logan they could find him, when they spoke that morning. "Hey, brother," Logan warmly greeted the tall, blonde man seated behind the wooden desk.

Looking up from his sketchbook, Luka let out a lengthy whistle, before flirtatiously jesting, "Well, fuck me! I swear, your sweet ginger ass gets finer every time I see you."

Rolling his eyes, Logan shook his head as he turned to Lola, "*My heart*, please ignore Luka's incessant flirting. He's actually harmless,

I swear."

Crossing the room in a couple of lengthy strides, Luka walked up to Lola as he extended his hand. "It's finally nice to meet the lucky lady who has taken this fine specimen off the market. I swear, all the hot ones are straight." Turning to Logan, Luka smirked, "Although should you find yourself just a little bi-curious, you've got my number."

Growing flushed with embarrassment, Logan bellowed, "Luka, I swear to God, I will find another damn tattoo artist!"

Seeing the crimson hue now rested upon Logan's face, Lola couldn't help but laugh; the banter between the two men helped her feel slightly less apprehensive about showing Luka the damage Jacob had caused to her back and sides.

Rolling his eyes dramatically, Luka looked at Lola and said, "Always so dramatic, that one. Now, why don't you come sit by my desk and tell me a few of your favorite things so we can get comfortable with each other, before you show me my canvas, aka your back."

Lola told Luka of her love for red poppies; she also let him know that she was fond of bluebirds and liked the idea of seeing an empty birdcage. "Watching them soar so carefree, is the most beautiful form of freedom I think there is."

Having made his notes and a few minor sketches, Luka ordered lunch for the trio, wanting to create a more comfortable environment for Lola. Once their meal ended, Logan used the time Lola was in the restroom to remind Luka that while what he was about to see would be heartbreaking, to please keep his reactions internalized in Lola's presence. "This is a big step for Lola, brother. I know she didn't tell you what happened, and I can't really go into all of the details because it's not my place to say, but I don't think her best friend has even seen all of the marks that fucker put on her."

Having removed her bra in the restroom, Lola returned to her seat in the office, telling Luka she was ready for him to see what he could create from the ashes of her past. Logan held onto Lola's hands, as Luka lifted Lola's shirt, exposing the years of malevolent branding Jacob had inflicted upon her.

To say Luka was shocked would be an understatement. *Logan said it was bad, but what the actual hell? What kind of sadistic bastard repeatedly brands someone?* Luka quickly lowered Lola's shirt before clearing his throat, "Thank you for letting me see your back, Lola. That was very brave of you."

Taking a few breaths to calm his nerves, Luka stated, "Lola, if you give me about two weeks, I should be able to come up with a beautiful concept for you." Thanking Luka for his time, Logan and Lola began their journey back home.

36

Exposure

August 17, 2015

The day following the meeting with Luka, Lola had a session with Dr. Indigo. Unlike with her previous sessions as of late, Lola decided that today's should be done in person; far too much had happened in a single day, to justify a mere phone conversation.

Putting her car in park, Lola gripped the steering wheel while exhaling deeply; in hopes of calming the invasive thoughts, ever present at the forefront of her troubled mind.

~

Seated inside the soothingly, familiar office, Lola nervously picked at the weathered hole on the thigh of her white skinny jeans, as she pondered Dr. Indigo's query. "Many people have found body art, specifically in the form of tattoos, to be very helpful and healing after a traumatic experience. What do you think your main hesitation is, in regards to getting a tattoo?"

After several minutes, Lola finally spoke. "I guess my main hesitation would be knowing that once it's done, I could show my back. I have spent so many years always making sure any wounded areas were strategically covered."

"Are there any other hesitations?" Dr. Indigo asked while making notations.

"I think the second big one, would be that I have the freedom to choose." Lola decisively stated, before adding, "Freedom to choose what I want to wear and freedom to choose what people see. That freedom, I feel like is what scares me the most."

When Lola sat silently for several minutes, Dr. Indigo asked, "What are your thoughts on the party Logan has asked to have?"

Covering her face with her hands, Lola groaned, "I'm honestly **not** looking forward to having this, but I don't want to disappoint Logan nor do I want to hurt his feelings."

With pen to paper, Dr. Indigo inquired, "What do you think is the specific issue with Logan's request? Is it the party in general? The location? Or, even a person?"

Giving deep thought to this next series of questions, Lola finally reasoned, "It's not the party in general, but more of the location and a person … well, people."

"Have you had a bad experience at **The British Punk** that could be triggering? Also, who brings you these apprehensive feelings?" Dr. Indigo challenged.

Lola searched within the depths of her mind and was unable to recall having ever visited **The British Punk**. Finally having an answer, she stated, "I can't remember ever going there, but I feel like the root issue would be seeing Maeve and possibly seeing Naja. I feel guilty at the thought of seeing Naja because even though Logan has said before that their relationship was over before he confessed his love to me, I still feel like it's my fault they ended."

Once she had concluded her notes, Dr. Indigo looked up at Lola as she instructed, "From what I have gathered, it would seem that fear is the primary underlying factor here. I would like for you to take the time today and tomorrow and really think about ways of combating that fear. Since our next session is Wednesday, I want to discuss what you have come up with."

"Thanks, Dr. Indigo." Lola waved, before returning to her car.

~

The short amount of time between Lola's sessions with Dr. Indigo ensured, much to her chagrin, that Lola could not procrastinate with the task at hand. Knowing she wouldn't be good company, and as she was already in Portland, Lola decided it was best to stay in her own apartment, returning to Parkway the following evening. Having stopped by the store to pick up a few necessities for the next 24-hours, Lola briefly told Logan her plans for the evening.

Lately, entering the place that by all legal intents and purposes, was her home, felt foreign; almost as if she were entering a stranger's house or even a hotel room. Lola was slowly coming to the realization, and while she loved having something truly of her own, this was no longer her home. Settling back on the bed, Lola pulled out her well-worn copy of **The Raven's Song** and dove back into the comfortingly, familiar world of Raven and Willow.

Hours quickly passed by, and as Lola was midway through the book, a portion which she had easily read nearing a thousand times, pulled at her heart. Not wanting to lose the feeling of the moment, Lola swiftly sought out a highlighter so she would be reminded to share the passage with Logan.

Closing the book, Lola drifted off into a fantastically, peculiar dream; one where she found herself walking through the scene of the Mordovian village bazaar. *The annual bazaar was one of the few times fae and elven creatures mingled amongst mortals. Trailing behind the characters she fondly recognized as Willow, Kieran, and Briton, Lola knew she was headed in the direction of the fortune teller's tent.*

Hearing the twang of a lute playing in the distance, Lola's feet tried to carry her in the opposite direction; however, she was determined to stay the course. Seconds transitioned to hours, as Lola patiently waited her turn to speak to the one both mortal and fae creatures alike referred to as, **Lady of the Mists.** *With the last embers of sunlight kissing the horizon, a voice from within beckoned, "Please come inside, Lola."*

Stepping through the outer curtain, Lola was blanketed in a thick cloud, which transformed her pajamas into an ensemble far more fitting for this world her mind had concocted. Stepping out of the cloud, Lola found herself now before a mirror, and saw she wore a white, floor-length, lace dress; a mint green blazer cinched and belted at the waist; and a nude colored pair of suede ankle boots. Pulling her hair in a high bun, Lola then turned left to enter the next curtain.

Entering the second curtain, Lola gasped as she was momentarily blinded. The same voice from the entrance laughed out, "Don't be afraid, dear Lola. After all, it is you who sought out I. The fog will lift from your eyes and reveal to you a place that brings you peace." Once the voice was silenced, Lola entered a third curtain.

Allowing her eyes to quickly adjust to the sunlight, Lola now found herself in the beautiful grove at the base of Proxy Falls, seated at a small, circular table with a black, lace tablecloth. Placed on top of the table, was a large stone unlike any Lola had ever seen. The stone, though mostly pink, had an azure center, and was mounted upon a silver plate with four rings; one in each of the cardinal directions.

Reaching her hand out to touch the esoteric stone, Lola quickly pulled her hand back when she heard from beyond a veil, "Enchanted by my moonstone, I see. You know, dear Lola, as much as you'd like to deny it, you've always been a curious thing."

Finally finding her voice for the first time since the dream had begun, Lola cautiously asked, "How do you know my name or even anything about me?"

"Surely you know they call me **Lady of the Mists** *for a reason," the mysterious stranger laughed as her voice surrounded Lola.*

Sighing in frustration, Lola growled, "Ugh! This is stupid and getting me nowhere. I'm going to wake up and be back in my bed."

*Laughing once more, **Lady of the Mists** taunted, "Surely you are mistaken, Lola. If it really was so stupid, you wouldn't even be here."*

*Crossing her arms in defiance, Lola retorted, "Fine, **Lady of the Mists**, if you know so much, please humor me. Tell me exactly why I'm here."*

*With hands reaching through the veil, **Lady of the Mists** placed her hands upon what she had called the moonstone, instructing Lola to do the same. Doing as requested, Lola flinched as she watched the stone's center change from azure to a murky, shadowed gray. "What on earth does that mean?" Lola queried while removing her hands.*

*"Darling, that is your fear. Would you like the answer that you seek?" With a nod of Lola's head, **Lady of the Mists** instructed, "Place your hands on the stone once more." The stone's center now revealed a foggy bathroom mirror, with a single, eight-letter word written upon it.*

Confusion etched upon Lola's face as she removed her hands. A simple action that caused the mysterious fortune teller to laugh out, "All answers are found in mystery. The true meaning of your word will come to you soon. Farewell, dear Lola."

"Wait," Lola called, "Please allow me to see your face before you leave."

*"Where is the fun in that, my dear?" **Lady of the Mists** countered, before adding, "If you think hard enough, and maybe even look closely, you will find that you had the answers all this time."*

~

August 19, 2015

Lola found herself quite perplexed and fully consumed by the dream she had after her last session with Dr. Indigo. Even after returning to the apartment, Lola barely acknowledged Logan's presence.

"Lola, *my heart*, is everything okay?" Logan nervously asked.

Shaking the fog from her brain, Lola answered honestly. "I had the strangest dream."

"Do you want to talk about it? You know I'm always here to listen."

"As much as I appreciate the sentiment, I think I just need to talk to Dr. Indigo about it." Lola stated while wrapping her arms around Logan's waist, before making her phone call.

~

After rushing through the usual check-in questions, Lola belted out, "I had the strangest dream that I have literally been dying to tell you about." Smiling to herself on the other end of the line, Dr. Indigo asked Lola to proceed with the details of the dream.

Once Lola recanted every last detail, Dr. Indigo asked, "Do you recall the word you saw? Also, did you see anything else at the end of your dream that may have stood out to you?"

"As for your first question," Lola replied, "the word that appeared was *Exposure*. But honestly, I have no idea what that even means."

Dr. Indigo chuckled at the answer Lola had come up with to her assigned task. "Well, to put it plainly, Lola, exposure means to face your fears. Your subconscious is telling you that attending the party will help you to overcome the guilt and fear you have."

Sighing in frustration, Lola groaned, "Somehow I figured it would come down to that. I really don't want to face Naja, but I guess there isn't any other way around it."

Allowing silence to fill the line for a few moments, Lola finally stated with confusion lacing her words, "To answer the second question, the strangest thing happened. I seriously could have sworn that the fortune teller was … well … she was me."

Pausing to make a few notations, Dr. Indigo explained, "From what you have told me, your mind created two comforting and familiar scenarios to prepare you with the answer you needed. Do you have anything else you would like to add to our session today?"

With nothing else to add, Lola thanked Dr. Indigo for her help and time before finding Logan. "Logan, do you have anything specific planned for today?"

"Not that I know of. What's up?".

"W-well, if you are up for it, I would like to read you more from **_The Raven's Song_**. There is a special part that I'd like to share with you, but it's not until midway through the book." Lola nervously replied.

"I would like that very much, but first, I'd very much like to kiss you." Logan remarked with passion in his eyes.

Having granted Logan's request, Lola led them out to the gazebo, where she began the next chapter. "_The elven prince opened his eyes to see the silver eyes that had captivated him earlier that day. He felt worn out but was glad to discover that he was still a raven. It would have been quite an unfortunate occurrence to scare away this mortal beauty by transforming back into his elven body while he was unconscious. This maiden, though young was already quite beautiful, and he couldn't turn his eyes away._"

37

A white rose amongst the foxgloves

August 20, 2015

Taking the previous evening to meditate upon Dr. Indigo's words, Lola awoke that morning with vigor. Returning from her morning run, Lola was pleased to see Logan had breakfast ready for the two of them. With her appetite thoroughly satiated, Lola cleared her throat, "Logan, I have given a great deal of thought to both the tattoo and the party."

Placing the used dishes in the sink, Logan returned to Lola's side. "I'm glad to hear that. You know I'd never want you to do something just because you think it would make *me* happy." Lovingly embracing Lola, he asked, "What'd you decide?"

Logan couldn't help but chuckle as Lola's brow creased in its usual manner whenever she was deep in thought. "You've got your thinking face on, I see!"

Rolling her eyes playfully, Lola retorted, "Well, my beautiful brain *is* one of my best features!" Before adding, "I honestly love the idea of a full back tattoo. Although it scares me to have my skin show, and that people will want to know why I have it, I think, for the most part, people will probably just comment on its beauty."

"While I think it is important for tattoos to have meaning behind them, that's not the case with most people. Even if there is a meaning, you aren't required to indulge the curiosities of others. You can always just say it's something you found beautiful." Logan smiled as he watched Lola's body relax.

"Now, for the party, is it okay if I make one small request?" Lola shyly asked.

Enveloping her in his arms, Logan told Lola she could make any number of requests she wanted since this party was meant to be in celebration of her. Releasing a few steadying breaths, Lola requested that if Naja were to be invited, she'd like the chance to speak with her beforehand. Quickly clarifying, "I-it's not that I don't want her to be a part of your life … it's just well, we aren't that close. I don't think she's ever liked me, and I'd really like to apologize for any wrong I may have done to her."

Lifting Lola's chin, Logan reassured, "*My heart*, I know I have said countless times that if anyone was to blame for the tension between the two of you, it's me. That being said though if it will make you feel better, I can give you her number."

Thanking Logan with a quick kiss, Lola bounded down the hall to finally wash away the dried sweat from her morning jog; leaving Logan feeling slightly uncomfortable below the belt.

~

Feeling refreshed from her shower, Lola slipped on one of Logan's old, ripped concert tees, and paired it with a light wash, denim skirt that fell mid-thigh. To complete the ensemble, Lola added a pair of black, over-the-knee socks; black high tops; and Logan's army green denim jacket, rolling the sleeves to her elbows. Making her appearance in the living room, Lola blushed as Logan greeted her with a whistle. "*My heart*, you look sexy as hell in my clothes. Damn!"

Tossing her head back in laughter, Lola remarked, "Keep it in your pants, Warren!"

After several minutes of flirtatious banter, as Lola grabbed her purse and keys, Logan asked where she was headed, to which she replied, "Well, Warren, **we** are going to Portland. I'd like to visit **The British Punk** at least once before this party you're planning. Besides, it's typically customary to give the venue notice."

"Well, *Miss Sass*, I'll have you know that I already called Maeve," Logan boasted.

"Well, what are we waiting for then!" Lola exclaimed before adding an enticing tidbit for Logan's benefit. "You know, since I've never been *and* I need to continue telling you about Ronan, I figured you may want to finally drive Averie again."

"For real?" Logan asked in disbelief. Seeing Lola nod her head in affirmation, Logan bolted out the door shouting, "Fuck yeah!"

~

May 25, 2007

A little over two months had quickly passed since Lola confessed her love for Ronan. As for Ronan, what had been uttered from self-deceptive seeds, swiftly blossomed into true feelings. The more time they spent together, Ronan couldn't help but be enamored by Lola's magnetic, yet at times melancholic, persona.

Taking their relationship to the next level, Ronan knew that it was finally time to introduce Lola to his family. "Lola, I know you've said you aren't close with your mom, but my family means the world to me, and I'd love it if you would come to our annual Memorial Day celebration on Monday."

Although the request left her nothing but a ball of nerves, Lola readily accepted Ronan's invitation before asking for a little more information. Wrapping Lola in a hug, Ronan excitedly explained, "Well, this event, along with pretty much anything else my parents' host is quintessentially Americana and the epitome of opulence."

"Uh … Are you sure that I'll even fit in?" Lola gulped.

"Just be your amazing self, and I know that they'll love you just as much as I do," Ronan reassured.

Had Ronan known how the tides would turn, he never would have invited Lola that fateful Memorial Day.

~

May 28, 2007

Awaking early that morning, Lola called Ronan before she set to work on baking her signature dessert, the Black Forest Cake that had been her grandmother's recipe and her father's favorite. Although Ronan had said that surely her presence would be more than enough, propriety told Lola otherwise. "Ro, you literally told me this event was the epitome of opulence. That means no one shows up empty-handed, and besides, my grandmother would turn over in her grave if I ever did anything like that."

When he ended the call with Lola, Ronan figured now was the time to call his parents, and finally let them know he would have a guest with him. Up until this point, his parents were oblivious to the fact that he had someone special in his life. Sighing deeply as the phone rang, until going to voicemail, Ronan silently prayed. *Lord, please don't let this day be a complete fiasco.*

"Truly perfect, if I do say so myself," Lola beamed to herself as she added the final touches to her cake, before taking a well-deserved shower. No longer smelling like a bakery, Lola walked to her closet in search of something that would hopefully be elegant enough to meet Ronan's parents, Luis and Jennika Harper, for the first time. Finally settling on navy blue, tea length, tulle skirt, and white, elbow-length, lace blouse. Slipping into a pair of navy blue espadrilles, Lola pulled out her grandmother's pearl jewelry set. Pulling her hair into an elegant chignon and reapplying her lipstick, Lola picked up her cake before driving to Ronan's apartment.

~

Gazing out the window, Lola couldn't believe the sight before her eyes, as they drove up the lengthy driveway before stopping in front of a lavish estate. "I thought my grandparents' property was large … it has nothing on this place."

Chuckling at Lola's expression, Ronan remarked as he handed his keys to the valet, "Sorry if this is a bit much."

"Your parents have valet parking for this event?"

Sheepishly rubbing the back of his neck, Ronan replied, "Yeah- they had to start this a few years back, to help keep traffic flowing. Sorry again."

Taking everything in, Lola finally stated, "You have nothing to be sorry for, Ro. It's just different. Even though my grandparents were wealthy, they just preferred to live life as normally as possible. My grandpa used to say, 'Those who flaunt their money lack a moral compass.'"

Letting Lola's statement resonate with him for a few minutes, Ronan asked, "Do you believe that?"

"Honestly," Lola shrugged, "I think there is some truth to it, but at the end of the day it's up to each person to choose how they live."

Walking through the grand sitting room, Ronan led Lola into the oversized kitchen where his mother stood, giving last-minute directions to the catering staff. Lola smiled as she watched Ronan envelop his mother in a loving embrace before saying, "Mom, I'd like for you to meet my girlfriend, Lola."

At the mention of the word "girlfriend," Jennika's genuine smile turned to one so stiff, that her face might crack had she gritted her teeth any harder. Raising her eyebrows in disdain, but maintaining a tone reflective of propriety, Jennika walked over to greet Lola. "*Hello, Lola*. What is that you've got there?"

Blushing a bit, Lola sweetly replied, "Hello, Mrs. Harper. It's such a pleasure to finally meet you. I made my famous Black Forrest Cake; it's an old family recipe."

Rolling her eyes, Jennika sighed before once again feigning an air of cordiality. "Oh! Well, how thoughtful of you, dear. Why don't we just leave *this* here on the counter."

Taking a quick breath, Lola did her best not to read into Jennika's attitude. *Don't think too much on it, surely she's just stressed with hosting such a big event.*

Grabbing her son by the arm, Jennika led Ronan out to the back garden, leaving Lola to silently trail behind. "Son, I really wish you had given me more notice about bringing a guest. You'll never guess who moved back?"

Glancing back at Lola, Ronan offered her an apologetic smile before speaking to his mother. "I'm sorry about the lack of notice, but I am 33 now and not 13." Shrinking back from a side glance from Jennika, Ronan asked who had moved back.

"I understand that you are now an adult, son, and if you wanted to bring such a *lovely*, young woman to meet us, it would have been better at a time when the Abbotts are not in attendance."

Trying to get Ronan's attention, Lola hastened her pace, before grabbing his hand. "Ro, who are the Abbotts?"

Giving Lola's hand a quick squeeze, Ronan whispered in Lola's ear, "The Abbotts are old family friends."

"Really, mother. Are we on this again? Elin and I..." Ronan refuted before he was cut off by a leggy blonde. Dropping Lola's hand, Ronan embraced the lady before him, before the pair broke out in a boisterous banter.

"Hey there, Atlas. It looks like you're still carrying the weight of the world on your shoulders?"

Laughing heartily, in a way Lola had yet to see, Ronan retorted, "Only about as often as you ward off those evil spirits, Sage!"

Hearing the clearing of Lola's throat, Ronan called her over to join him. Giving Lola's cheek a quick kiss, he introduced the two women. "Elin, I'd like to introduce you to my girlfriend, Lola."

A twinge of sorrow appeared in Elin's eyes before it was quickly replaced with a look of genuine curiosity. Standing a good ten inches above Lola, Elin looked down as she extended her hand. "Well, aren't you just the most precious, *little* thing. I'm Elin and it's *so* nice to meet you."

Not one to be overly fond of false admirations, Lola blushed uncomfortably. "Umm- thank you, I think?"

Engaging in insider humor with Elin, Ronan failed to notice Lola's departure. Lola, walking the perimeter, sought out some way to occupy her time, in hopes of silencing Jacob's ever-nagging voice. *You know vixen, you really only have yourself to blame for feeling so awkward here. How many fucking times did I tell you that perfect people will never understand you?* Finally making her way to the drink table, Lola thanked the server who handed her a mimosa.

"They really are perfect for one another, don't you think?"

Hearing the voice behind her, Lola turned as she uttered, "I'm sorry … who's perfect for one another?" Her eyes going wide as Jennika now stood before her.

"Why Ronan and Elin, of course, my dear. Who else would I be talking about?" Jennika replied curtly as she took a sip of her own drink.

"With all due respect, Mrs. Harper, I believe it comes down to a matter of opinion. And as they say about opinions, well, they all stink." Lola rebutted, before excusing herself as she walked back in Ronan's direction.

"Where did you wander off to," Ronan asked when he felt Lola squeeze his hand.

"Oh, just to grab a drink," Lola surmised as she rolled her eyes, "and apparently having a *wonderful* conversation with your mother."

~

Several hours passed by with Lola feeling more like an accessory than a welcomed guest. Although Ronan did his best to introduce Lola to everyone in attendance, somehow Elin managed to retain the majority of his focus. With her nerves at the peak of exploding, Lola quietly excused herself in search of a bathroom. Finding the one just off of the kitchen occupied, Lola made her way upstairs.

Entering what appeared to be Ronan's childhood bedroom, Lola smiled at the pictures on display. Coming across what happened to be a prom picture, Lola hated to admit the truth in Jennika's words. *Ronan and Elin truly do look perfect together.*

Ensuring everything was exactly as it had been when she arrived, Lola quietly closed the bedroom door behind her before making her way to the bathroom across the hall. Once inside, with fists balled, Lola closed her eyes in hopes of easing the tension building inside of her. However, as Lola opened her eyes to look at her palms, the usual release she felt was absent. Feeling knots building in her stomach, Lola turned to the toilet, where she proceeded to empty its contents.

Stepping in front of the sink to rinse her mouth and wash her hands, Lola let out a shaky laugh. And although she uttered words of pseudo-reassurance to herself, deep down, Lola knew she was anything but okay.

Slowly slinking back down the stairs, Lola happened upon a conversation not meant for her ears. Standing with their backs turned, stood three women, completely unaware of Lola's presence. Lola instantly recognized two of them as Elin and Jennika. As for the last woman, Lola assumed her to be Elin's mother, by the loving embrace placed around Elin. Beyond the three women, on the counter where Jennika had placed it, stood Lola's cake.

Wiping her eyes with a tissue, Elin cried, "Jennika, I feel like you lied to me. You said Ronan was still single and he missed me."

Jennika held her hands up as she defended, "I had no idea, my sweet Elin."

With words cutting like a knife, the older lady embracing Elin seethed. "I swear Jennika, who are you and Luis now? The Gallaghers? I mean really, how hard is it to keep your son in line."

Lola promptly placed her hands over her mouth at the mention of Cate's family. Seeing the look of anger flash in Jennika's hazel eyes, Lola knew this mystery woman had struck a nerve.

"Josephine Ophelia Abbott," Jennika snarled. "How dare you ever compare Luis or me to the likes of the Gallaghers!"

Turning to face Jennika, Josephine retorted, "Jennika, *dear*, I think it would do you well to remember that you could have very well been Mrs. Gallagher. Unlike Evelynn's father, yours had morals and good sense not to sell you off."

"Oh my god! Would you two please just stop?" Elin cried. "Now I know why Ronan didn't tell you about his girlfriend, Jennika. You're both just awful."

Jennika tried to splutter out some sort of faux apology in order to save face but found herself cut off by Elin once more. "And you, Jennika, if you stopped being a stuck-up bitch for even five seconds, you'd find that Lola is actually a sweet girl."

"That's just it!" Jennika seethed, "She's nothing but a child!"

"Are you really that asinine? She's an adult. She may be ten years younger than Ronan, but an adult nonetheless." Elin defended before adding, "Now if you'll excuse me, I think I'm going to drown my sorrows in this lovely looking cake. Ronan said Lola worked very hard on it, and I told her I would try a piece."

Quickly grabbing hold of the cake, Jennika tore a handful before taking a rather large, and uncivilized, bite. Turning her face up in disgust, Jennika tossed the cake in the waste as she spat, "Nothing but disgusting, store-bought trash! Just like the one who brought it!"

Witnessing her cake so cruelly disposed of, was the final straw for Lola, as she stormed past the trio in search of Ronan. After several minutes of searching, Lola finally found Ronan speaking with his father. "Ex-excuse my rudeness," Lola's voice broke as she apologized.

Placing a small object in the pocket of his trousers, Ronan's face fell as he noticed Lola's disheveled state. "Lola, are you okay? What's wrong?"

"I want to go! There's only so much blatant disrespect a person can take." Lola sorrowfully exclaimed, before turning to leave.

Failing at calling her back, Ronan apologized to his father before running after Lola. "L-l-l-ola!" Ronan panted as he finally caught up to her. "You know, for someone with such tiny legs, you move surprisingly fast."

Seeing his jest fell upon deaf ears, Ronan apologized, "Sorry. I know now is not the time for a joke. Just please don't leave yet. I promise that I'll make it worth your while."

A small crowd began to form in the back, as Lola grimly stated, "Fine."

Breathing a sigh of relief, Ronan lovingly led Lola back to the party. Seeing everyone in place, Ronan nodded to his father, who tapped a fork on his glass. Clearing his throat, Luis spoke. "Friends and family, we want to thank you all for attending this year's party. Now, before we all go on our way, my son, Ronan, has asked to speak."

Lola crossed her arms defiantly as Ronan proceeded to make some sort of speech that, in that moment, she really could care less about. Finally hearing her name being called, Lola looked down to see

Ronan on a single knee, with a blue velvet box held open.

Chuckling nervously, Ronan asked again, "Lola Luxe Swan, I have never met anyone as incredible as you. And even though we have been together for just a short while, I know that I will never find another like you. Will you marry me?"

Eyes growing wide in astonishment, Lola didn't know what to say. She knew she loved Ronan and the thought of marrying him someday did cross her mind. Unsure of what to say, Lola quickly scanned the crowd for the one face she knew would help form her resolve. Finally finding it, Lola gazed upon Ronan with affection. "Ronan, I would be honored to be the *next* Mrs. Harper. Yes, I will gladly marry you."

As Ronan joyfully spun Lola around, Lola never lost eye contact with Jennika; giving a smirk that let Jennika know she had finally met her match.

~

August 20, 2015

Finding the parking lot of **The British Punk** empty, save a few employee vehicles, Logan coasted into a spot directly outside the entrance. "Man, she handles like a dream!" Logan exclaimed with a starry-eyed expression as he caressed the steering wheel.

Lola beamed with pride. "Uncle Greg said that until my dad got really sick, he maintained her well. Then, after he died, Uncle Greg garaged it until it was time to give me the keys."

"Who kept up with the maintenance while you were…" Logan asked, but let his words tapper off at the heartbreaking memory from nearly three years ago.

Placing her hand on his, Lola closed her eyes before answering. "When I went away, Uncle Greg took care of this beauty once again." Taking a few steadying breaths, Lola opened her car door as she called out, "Now, why don't we go inside so I can finally see what the big deal is about this place!"

Logan laughed at Lola's antics as he moved quickly to match Lola's pace. "You know, Ronan was right. You sure do move surprisingly fast for someone with such short legs!"

"Yeah, yeah!" Lola rolled her eyes as she ushered Logan inside the building.

38

Make Amends

August 25, 2015

The days preceding the party moved rather quickly. In order to prevent herself from overthinking, as she tended to do, Lola used the time to catch up with Lizzie and Raelee; in addition to some much-needed conversation with Cate.

~

As she had done so every year, excluding the time Lola was away, Lizzie once again invited Lola to go with her to take Raelee school shopping. Although she had wanted to decline, Lola thought better of it; knowing this was precious time that she could never get back.

Pulling into Lizzie's driveway, Lola barely had the chance to open her door before a tiny but muscular body slammed into her. *"Auntie Bear*! I'm so happy to see you! Momma said that you were coming and I almost couldn't believe it! I know that you're super busy with work, now that you aren't sick anymore. Can we go get coffee after this?"

Raelee's exuberant words left a small ache in Lola's heart, and she knew she only had herself to blame. Refusing to allow bitter thoughts to sour the day, Lola stepped out of the car to easily return the young girl's embrace. "When did you get so mature, Baby Rae?"

Placing her hands on her hips, Raelee proclaimed, "Well, I am 11 now, Auntie, and that means I'm practically an adult." Lola laughed at Raelee's silly antics, before the two proceeded in lively conversation, as they waited for Lizzie.

Closing the door behind her, Lizzie couldn't help but chuckle at the sight before her. "What are you two going on about over here?" Lizzie asked as she reached the passenger side of Lola's car.

Moving her seat forward so that Raelee could easily slide into the back, Lola jested, "Rae asked if we could go get coffee after shopping. And I told her that she was definitely her father's daughter."

"Then," Raelee piped up from the back seat as Lola started the engine, "I did your coffee gagging-face, mom! It was epic!"

Laughter filled the red **Mustang**, as the small party headed off to the mall, with the wind rushing past them on this beautiful August day.

~

After several hours at the mall, including a trip to the ballet boutique for a pointe shoe appointment, Lola pulled into the parking lot of **Brewed Awakening**. "You know," Lizzie stated, "we could have just gone to **Cate's** for coffee."

Lola shook her head in amusement. "I know, but we're already in Portland, so I figured we could stop here before heading home."

As they waited in line, Lola asked, "So, Rae, what's your favorite kind of coffee?"

"I love anything sweet! Momma says I'm a hummingbird. She said it's because I'm pretty, tiny, and love super sweet things." Raelee exclaimed joyfully.

Lola chuckled, "Want in on a little secret?" Seeing Raelee nod her head in affirmation, Lola exclaimed, "You're a lot like your momma when she was your age. She always had to have something sweet, no matter what we were doing."

Finally making their way to the front, Lola decided on a Caramel Macchiato while Raelee chose the house special of the day, a Blissful Berry Kiss; a white chocolate frappe blended with strawberries and raspberries; topped with whipped cream, and coated in a white chocolate drizzle.

Taking their drinks to go, Raelee sat in the back of the car listening to the low hum of the radio, blissfully unaware of the conversation happening in the front seat.

Breaking the silence between them, Lizzie asked, "You know, I'm really happy you came with us today."

Glancing up in her rearview mirror, Lola caught sight of Raelee's joyous expression. "You know … I am too. I'm sorry that it's taken me so long to do this, sister."

Turning to truly look at her friend, Lizzie exclaimed, "Luxie, I love you and I have forgiven you a long time ago. You are my soul sister, and my life would be meaningless without you. Mark might be my romantic soulmate, but you are my platonic soulmate and the love I have for you, knows no bounds."

Wiping a stray tear from her eyes, Lola choked out. "I honestly don't know what I did to deserve you."

~

August 27, 2015

Knowing that a proper conversation was long overdue, Lola invited Cate to spend the day with her tending to the roses at Swan Manor. After texting Cate the address, Lola drove to her childhood home.

Lola stepped inside the place that held so many treasured memories, for the first time since her grandparents' deaths. Walking into the kitchen, Lola smiled as she saw a note from Gregory, that read-
Enjoy your day here. This has been and always will be your home. Uncle

Greg.

Hearing the sound of the doorbell in the background, Lola returned to the foyer, welcoming Cate inside. Nervous tension filled the air, as neither lady truly knew how to interact with the other anymore. Finally breaking the silence, Lola said, "Why don't we get some water and get started?"

"S-sure," Cate called out, trailing behind Lola.

Two hours of pruning later, Lola asked Cate if she would like to come inside for lunch. "Thanks, Luxie. May I ask a question?" Cate asked, nervously.

"Sure! You can ask me anything you'd like." Lola replied honestly.

"Who has been looking after this place all this time? It's so amazing!" Cate exclaimed in wonder.

Laughing heartily, Lola replied, "My grandfather's best friend, Gregory, was given care of the manor. He never had any kids of his own, and he always saw me as his little niece."

"Oh!" Cate remarked in surprise, before adding, "Why didn't he ever try to get custody of you from your mom?"

"Well, before she lost the twins and started drinking again, my mother was a decent parent, and the court found her more than capable of taking care of me. Once the abuse started, I just kept it locked inside. The only people who knew were Lizzie and Shane." Lola shrugged before turning to pull out some ingredients for tacos.

Cate nervously strummed her fingers on the marble countertop, as she sat at the island before asking if there was anything she could do to help.

"Nope, you're my guest and I'd like for you to relax. I know the café is booming, so please, just enjoy this time." Lola reassured.

Several agonizing minutes passed, each one slowly eating away at Cate's resolve. Feeling the vibrating of her phone, relief flooded Cate's face as she looked down to see Cade's name flash across the screen. "Hey, Luxie. Cade's calling. I'm going to step out back and answer this really quick." Lola acknowledged Cate with a nod, before finishing the final touches to the meal.

Returning from her reassuring phone call with Cade, Cate's stomach grumbled at the delicious looks spread placed upon the kitchen island. Lola laughed heartily at the sound, "I'm glad to know I'm not the only one who worked up an appetite!"

Eating in silence for several minutes, Cate finally cleared her throat. "Uhm-hm … Luxie…"

Holding her hand up for a moment, Lola wiped her mouth with a napkin, before grabbing Cate's hand as she spoke, "Cate, I just want you to know that I don't blame you."

Hearing Lola's words caused all resolve in Cate to break. "I-I-I should have known. My gut told me something was off!" Tears freely flowed from Cate's aqua blue eyes.

"Cate, please look at me," Lola requested. Once she had Cate's full attention, Lola continued. "Never once did I blame you for Jacob's actions. The only person I have ever blamed was myself. You never stopped trying to reach me, even at my lowest, and I will forever love you for that. So, please …" Lola paused to wipe away her own tears, "… please don't ever blame yourself."

Embracing one another for longer than they could count, both women eventually broke apart, as they allowed their friendship to bloom once more.

~

August 29, 2015

When the morning of August 29 arrived, Lola stared out the bedroom window, expecting to feel some sort of way, anything other than just … fine. A gentle kiss upon her shoulder brought Lola's attention back to the space before her. "What's going on in that beautiful mind of yours, *my heart*?" Logan asked as he moved a stray curl from Lola's eyes.

Scrunching her brow in contemplation, Lola finally voiced the thoughts floating in her head. "Well … when you first asked me about the party, I was filled with so much anxiety that it was rather overwhelming, but now … I feel … fine."

"Isn't that a good thing, though?"

"I mean, it's supposed to be," Lola shrugged as she added, "but, I don't remember the last time I was ever truly fine."

Logan pressed his forehead against Lola's as he held onto her hands and looked deeply into her whimsical eyes. "You're letting yourself open up and heal. I'm sure the conversation with Cate really helped. Were you able to call Naja?"

Eventually breaking away, as the loving intensity held in Logan's gaze always made her feel as if he were looking into the depths of her soul, Lola sheepishly admitted that she hadn't. "I mean, I thought about it, but then I felt like me calling her out of the blue would make things feel even more awkward. I figured if she's at **The British Punk** tonight, I can just give her the letter I wrote her."

~

Ending his phone call with Louisa, Logan breathed a sigh of relief as he checked her and Kaleb's names off of the guest list. Although only ten friends would be in attendance, these were the ten people who were the most important to Lola.

*Now that that's done, I can finally get a...*the sound of the doorbell disrupted Logan mid-thought. "Just a minute!" Lola called out from the bedroom before Logan told her to take her time getting ready.

A look of surprise filled Logan's face as he answered the door to find his step-father standing there, uncomfortably holding an oversized shopping bag from Logan's favorite clothing store, **Anarchy's Monstrosity**. "Hey, Dean. Why don't you come on in? I wasn't expecting you to come by."

Holding out the bag to Logan, Dean gladly accepted the invitation, taking a seat on the sofa. Hearing a delicate voice call out to Logan, Dean was surprised to see a lovely young woman enter the living room. A young woman who seemed to be the complete opposite of how his wife had envisioned her to be.

"Logan, will you please help me with the button on the back of this top?" Lola called out before seeing Dean seated on the couch. "Oh! I'm so sorry! I didn't realize Logan had a guest. Please forgive my manners, my name's Lola. What's your name?"

Standing to extend his hand, Dean introduced himself. "I'm Logan's step-father, Dean. It's a pleasure to meet you."

With her top buttoned, Lola excused herself back to the bedroom to continue getting ready, as Logan turned to Dean. "So, what's with the bag?"

Rubbing his neck in an awkward manner, Dean stated, "Your mom was taking the girls' back-to-school shopping and got you some stuff."

"How are Elle-belle and Rosebud?" Logan asked, making a mental note to visit his younger sisters soon, before asking, "Would you and mom be fine if I took the girls to school and picked them up on their first day?"

"I think the girls would love that so much," Dean admitted. "Their first day is September 8."

"Awesome! I hate to rush you out, but I need to get ready for a party. Tell mom I said, 'Thanks!'" Logan remarked.

Having taken the bag in his room once Dean had departed, Logan smiled as he looked inside and pulled out each item. Although his mother, Britt, was not overly fond of Logan's clothing style, she had done a good job in picking out things he would wear. At the bottom of the bag, was a note.

Setting the clothes and shoes on the bed, Logan unfolded the letter as he read it.

Baby Mine,

The distance between us has pained my heart so much lately. You're definitely my son, as you've gotten my stubbornness. I miss you, and I hope that maybe we can mend some of the hurt soon. I'm not quite ready to meet Lola, but I think I will be soon since I know it will mean so much to you. I know you love her, and I love you, Baby Mine. Now, I know how much you love your ripped jeans, but I hope you'll love the outfit I picked for you. Perhaps it could be a bit of a peace offering.

Love you forever and always,

Mom

Smiling at his mother's words, Logan folded the note neatly before taking a good look at each piece that had been given to him. A black, vintage **Van Halen** concert tee; a black, lightweight denim jacket; a black leather belt with chains as accessories; a pair of red socks; a pair of patent leather loafers; a light grey beanie; and a pair of super skinny, black jeans.

~

Now dressed and showered, Logan stepped out into the living room, where he cleared his throat. Although he was not one to normally need a second opinion, he found himself eagerly wanting to know Lola's thoughts on his appearance.

Hearing Logan walk in, Lola looked up from her book as she felt her throat catch. Heat rising in her cheeks, Lola stuttered, "Uhhhhhhh"

"I look fine as hell, don't I" Logan preened.

Regaining her composure, Lola retorted as she rolled her eyes, "Don't let your ego get too big, now Warren," before adding in, "but yes, you do look 'fine as hell!'"

"The pants are a bit short, and definitely not ripped," Logan analyzed, "but they're comfy as hell!"

"I think them being a bit short looks good though," Lola shrugged, "I like the socks! I don't see you wear red very often, so it's a nice touch."

~

As the guests arrived, Logan stepped back to the bar, allowing Lola to have her moment to shine; after all, this was in celebration of her, so who was he to stand in the limelight. Turning to grab a soda, Logan felt a tap on his shoulder. Looking down, he was surprised to see a young woman, with curly dark brown hair standing next to him.

Extending her hand, she said, "Hi, you're Logan, right?" Seeing the nod of Logan's head, the young woman continued. "I just want to say thanks for doing this all for Lola."

"You're welcome, umm … what's your name again?" Logan inquired.

"Silly me for not making a proper introduction! I'm Marina. I was Lola's assistant, but now I work for Andre Bennett."

"Ah! Well, it's nice to finally be able to put a face with the name. If you'll excuse me, I'm gonna check in with my dad." Logan exclaimed as he started to step away.

Stopping Logan for a minute, Marina remarked, "Ya know, you look awfully familiar. Have we met before? Or, have I seen you somewhere?"

Shrugging his shoulders in uncertainty, Logan stated, "Not that I know of. I must just have one of those faces. Anyhow, Marina, it was nice to meet you. Enjoy the party."

Grabbing a glass of whiskey, Marina walked over to catch up with Daisy and Jade, the gears constantly turning in her mind.

Talking with Lizzie and Mark for a bit, Lola excused herself when she saw Louisa and Kaleb enter the pub. Running over in excitement, Lola threw her arms around Louisa's neck, "Oh my god! You made it! I can't believe it."

Returning Lola's affections, Louisa exclaimed, "Lola, you look so healthy! Dr. Indigo said you were looking great, but I didn't realize just how bright your smile is. You're totally shining!"

Blushing at Louisa's compliments, Lola grabbed the other woman's hand before leading her off in search of Logan. "Louisa, there's someone I'd love for you to meet."

"Logan, I want you to meet one of the nurses from the clinic. She was a huge help to me," Lola explained as she tapped Logan's arm.

Turning around, Logan belted out, "No fucking way! Pip is that you?"

Smirking with amusement as she socked Logan's arm, Louisa retorted, "One and the same, Redwood!"

After several minutes of playful banter, Lola interjected, "Umm …am I missing something? How do you guys know each other?"

Logan laughed heartily as he explained. "Pip here is one of Avia's cousins, and we went to high school together for a little while."

"How crazy is that?!" Lola smiled at the connection.

Once she had briefly introduced Logan to Louisa's husband, Kaleb, Lola stopped by her purse then walked in the direction of the bar. Finding Naja refilling drinks, Lola asked her for a glass of water before extending an envelope in Naja's direction.

Looking at the envelope with skepticism, Naja remarked, "What's this?"

"Uh … uh … I …" Lola began as she tried to formulate just the right words. Taking a steadying breath, Lola started again. "I'd like for you to have this. I'm not always good with words, so I wanted to explain everything in this letter."

"Thanks, I guess," Naja said, pocketing the letter. "Need anything else?"

Politely declining, Lola returned to the front of the pub. The night quickly passed, and Lola tucked it away as one of her most treasured experiences.

39

What starts with a lie…

September 3, 2015

A few days after the party, Luka called Logan saying he had a design finalized and asked if he and Lola were still okay to come to the shop for their scheduled appointment on September 5. When asked, Lola said, "I guess I'm as ready as I'll ever be."

After confirming the appointment with Luka, Logan double-checked his calendar for the day before asking Lola if she had any work plans for the day. "Not really," Lola shrugged. "Dr. Indigo is still pretty set on me doing minimal in office work. I already called Jade and Daisy to go over everything for the week, so I'm free for the rest of the day."

Checking his phone one last time, Logan quickly put it away before clapping his hands excitedly. "Fantastic! We're going to drive up to Seattle and visit the art museum there."

"Okay?" Lola said, unsure of Logan's excitement. "I guess that's good. Anything wrong with the museum in Portland?"

Laughing at Lola's expression, Logan remarked, "Don't get me wrong, I like the one in Portland, but they don't have the Ansel Adams exhibit. It's in Seattle until next week before moving on to

Los Angeles."

Catching Logan's excitement, Lola exclaimed, "Well, what are we waiting for!"

Once they were dressed and out the door, Logan and Lola stopped into **Cate's** for some coffee and muffins for the road. After some lively conversation with Cate and Cade, Lola found herself seated in the passenger's seat of Logan's car. "Since we have a decent drive, I think I'll tell you about mine and Ronan's wedding and everything leading up to the divorce? What do you think?"

Shifting into gear as they headed towards the interstate, Logan playfully remarked, "I've always wanted to relive my own foolishness."

Lola stuck out her tongue at Logan's playful quip and smiled to herself, as she realized how far she had come in right at a year's time. *Even just a couple of months ago, I would have had the hardest time with a joke like that. I can't believe how much I've grown.*

Taking a sip of her coffee, Lola began-

~

December 1, 2007

While it was typically customary for couples to be engaged a minimum of 12-18 months before getting married, Ronan and Lola chose to minimize their engagement to a mere seven months, with a lavish New Year's Eve wedding. Instead of gifts, the couple asked guests to make donations to support the **Lorriene Swan Center**, as there would not be a gala held that year.

Seated in Ronan's living room, the young couple found themselves finalizing the last-minute details. At this point, they still had yet to secure a venue for the ceremony; and the only request Ronan had for their wedding, in his best efforts to appease his mother, was that it be held in his family's church, **St. Mary's Cathedral**. Hearing this, Lola felt slightly on edge. "Ro, I'm not Catholic. In fact, I'm not anything. Is it right to be having our wedding in a church?"

Caught off guard by Lola's admission, Ronan asked in bewilderment, "What do you mean by 'I'm not anything'?"

"I mean exactly as I said; I'm agnostic. I believe there's something out there, but if it's God, He sure as hell hasn't been good to me." Lola grimly stated as she crossed her arms.

Feeling his chest tighten a bit, Ronan did his best not to panic. "Crap! How am I just now hearing about this?" Pacing back and forth for several minutes, Ronan finally came to the conclusion, "Whatever we do, we cannot tell my mother you're agnostic. We'll just tell her your Episcipallian. That should smooth things over?"

Looking at Ronan as if he had grown a second head, Lola fumed. "Are you insane? Doesn't your Bible say something about lying being a sin? What the fuck, Ro?"

Exacerbated, Ronan defended, "Well, it also says 'Thou shalt not murder,' and that's exactly what's going to happen. My mother is going to murder me if she finds out you're agnostic. Trust me, you're better off being labeled as a Protestant."

"Are you sure your God isn't going to smite me the second I step inside the church?" Lola asked, genuinely concerned. *I know I've done my fair share of lying in the past, but this just feels wrong.*

Holding Lola's hands in his own, Ronan looked at her with pleading eyes. "Please, *love*. I haven't asked for a single thing. Can you *please* just give me this one request?"

Sighing heavily, Lola relented. "Fine. I trust you, Ro. I trust you."

Breathing a sigh of relief, Ronan kissed Lola passionately before asking, "How's your dress coming along?"

Lola smiled brightly. "Uncle Greg was able to find a picture of my grandmother's dress for me, so I was able to get mine designed to resemble hers; just a bit more modern. My final fitting is today."

"I'm happy to hear it, *love*! Who's going to walk you down the aisle?"

"I've already asked Uncle Greg if he will. And before you ask, I've asked Lizzie and Cate if they will be my attendants." Lola said.

"Did you ask Elin?" Ronan inquired.

"Why would I ask Elin?!" Lola exclaimed.

"Because you need to have three attendants to have your side match mine. And, it would be a great insult to the Abbott family, as they have already said they would make a large donation to the **Center**." Ronan stated firmly.

"Shit!" Lola sighed, feeling flabbergasted. "Give me her number and I'll ask her. Cate and Lizzie are trying on dresses after my fitting, so Elin may as well join us."

Kissing Lola's forehead, Ronan expressed his gratitude. "Thank you, *love*. I know you aren't close with Elin, but she wants to get to know you better. I hope you consider giving friendship with her a chance because we will be seeing the Abbotts quite often at future events."

Leaning into Ronan's chest, Lola sighed, "For you, Ro. Only for you."

~

Pulling into the parking lot of **Leslie's Bridal Boutique**, Lola looked up at the sky and sighed heavily. While she absolutely adored her dad's car, a classic **Mustang** wasn't always the vehicle of choice when it came to inclement weather. *I probably should have taken Logan up on his offer for a ride any time the forecast calls for snow. Would that have been odd to ask him for a ride to my dress fitting? Lord knows I don't need any more issues with Naja.*

A knock on her window brought Lola out of her thoughts. Seeing Cate and Lizzie's excited faces, made Lola momentarily put her worries behind her. "Hey, girls! Thanks for coming. Why don't we go inside and wait for the last person."

Looking at each other in curiosity, Lizzie finally asked the question both she and Cate were thinking. "Who else are we waiting for?"

"Elin…" Lola sighed.

"Are you fucking kidding me?" Cate fumed.

"I wish I was, Cate," Lola acknowledged as they entered the shop, recanting the conversation between her and Ronan earlier that day.

"*Baby bear*, look at me," Lizzie commanded, before stating, "What kind of man can't stand up to his own mother? You know it's not too late to back out, right?"

Before Lola had a chance to respond, the trio was interrupted by a chipper voice coming from the back of the store. "Welcome to **Leslie's Bridal Boutique**! I'll be with you all in just a moment."

Putting the last few dresses on the rack, the owner of the voice made her way to the storefront, where her customers were waiting. "Hi, there! I'm Leslie Hageman, the owner. What can I do for you ladies today?" The young, blonde woman greeted.

"Hi, Leslie. I'm Lola Swan and I'm here for my final dress fitting. I made my appointment with Yvaine last month."

Checking the schedule, Leslie found Lola's appointment. "Oh, yes! My daughter has been helping you. I see from her notes that we also need to find two bridesmaid dresses and your color scheme is plum, gold, and champagne. Is that correct?"

"If it's okay, I need to look for three dresses today. We've had the *pleasure* of a last-minute addition to my bridal party," Lola wearily replied.

"That's fine, hun. We're here to serve you and make your big day go as smoothly as possible. Why don't you look for the style you like best for your attendants while we wait for the last member to show up. I'll call my daughter and see if she is on her way to help."

"I don't mean to sound rude, but you have a child working with you?" Cate asked.

Laughing heartily, Leslie explained. "Don't worry, I get that quite often! My daughter, Yvaine, is 17. I had her right after I turned 20, so I promise you all that no child labor laws are broken here."

While Leslie headed off to the back office, Lola sent Lizzie and Cate to look at the bridesmaid options while she gave Elin a call to see where she was. "E-Elin? This is Lola. I was just calling to see if you were close to **Leslie's Bridal Boutique?**"

"Hey, Lola! I'm so sorry for running late. I'm actually about five minutes away. I had a client meeting that ran over." Elin sheepishly explained.

After ending the call, Lola set off in the direction of her friends. Once she found them, Cate asked the question that she had been dying to know since Lola told her the color scheme. "Hey, Luxie, I was wondering about your wedding colors."

"Same here, sister." Lizzie chimed in.

"We both figured you'd have red and black to go with the champagne color since those two have been your favorite colors for quite some time." Cate pointed out.

Closing her eyes in frustration with herself, Lola explained how this had been another way for Jennika to pull the strings. "When Ro and I were having dinner with his parents, Jennika asked what colors we were planning and I did tell her that I wanted red, black, and champagne. You wanna know what this bitch had the audacity to say?"

"What?!" Both Lizzie and Cate inquired simultaneously.

"She said, and I quote, 'Do you think this is a funeral? No! No son of mine will ever be associated with a tawdry, gothic theme that is only for heathens.'" Lola explained, with sadness in her eyes.

"Oh hell to the no!" Lizzie fumed. "Y'all know that I'm tryin' to live right with Jesus, but I swear ... This heifer makes me wanna cut a bitch!"

Shaking her head in amusement at her friend's antics, Lola playfully chastised, "Reign it in, *Hurricane*." Before taking a few breaths and continuing on. "Anyhow, after I explained that it was merely a suggestion, Jennika then proceeds to say that my colors would be plum, gold, and champagne; since the wedding is being held on New Year's Eve this is the appropriate color scheme."

"What did Ronan say?" Cate asked, completely astounded. *Shit! I knew Jennika was bad from my brief interactions with her when I was growing up, but what Luxie is dealing with has to be unbearable.*

Before Lola could explain that Ronan had once again bowed down to his mother, the trio was interrupted by a timid voice. "S-sorry to interrupt. I hope I didn't keep you guys waiting too long."

Turning around, Lola knew she had to do the right thing, even if she didn't want to. "Hey, Elin. It's fine. The brunette bombshell is my best friend, and practically my sister, Lizzie. And the raven-haired beauty is my other best friend, and former boss, Cate."

After brief introductions between the bridal party, Lola sighed in relief when Leslie's daughter, Yvaine, arrived to help with the fittings and findings.

"Hi, Ms. Lola," the teen girl greeted enthusiastically. "Are you excited to see the final touches that momma added?"

"Yvaine, why don't you take our bride to her fitting room, while I help her attendants?" Leslie instructed before turning to the three remaining women. "Alright ladies, let's see what you have found to show our bride."

Inside the fitting room, Lola removed her clothing before putting on a knee-length silk slip, which would help the dress fit best without causing any unwanted static cling. Once Yvaine entered the room, Lola burst into tears of joy. "It looks even better than I imagined!"

"Just wait until you try it on," Yvaine giggled at her client's pure and genuine elation.

Having closed the final button, Yvaine fluffed the base of the dress before as she stated, "Momma had to take in the waist quite a bit from our original measurements and fitting, so I hope everything fits okay."

"It's more than perfect, Yvaine. You and your mother have outdone yourselves!"

"Alright, let's add the veil, and then we can show your friends. Sound like a plan?" Yvaine directed.

Once everything was in place, Yvaine exited the room to ensure everyone was ready for Lola's big reveal. Quickly making her way back to Lola, Yvaine gently led her by the arm to the viewing area. Lola's bridal party gasped in astonishment as she came into view; she truly looked like a dream.

Taking the floor, Leslie explained the details of the dress. "What we have created for Ms. Lola is an ivory Mikado silk gown with a column silhouette, a boat neckline, and a thin strand of natural pearls accenting the natural waistline. The sleeves are an opaque, ivory chiffon with lace cuffs, which have three pearl buttons on the inside of the wrist. If you look to the top of the shoulders, you will notice lace appliques have been added, as they are extended from the back of the gown."

Directing Lola to turn around, Leslie continued, "On the back, you will see the lace continues across each shoulder, stopping directly at the natural waistline. The lace is large and translucent at Ms. Lola's request, so as not to deviate too much from the inspiration of her grandmother's dress. Flowing from the back of the neck to the chapel length train, are the same pearl buttons used at the cuffs. Now, for those attending to Ms. Lola's dressing, the buttons from the base of the neck to directly below her rear, come undone. Everything else is decorative."

Looking across the room to ensure her clients weren't bored, Leslie continued, "For the finishing touches, I have included the same lace appliques on the train, to give one final look of pristine elegance."

Stepping aside for Lola to converse with her guests, Leslie instructed Yvaine to set up fitting rooms for the three attendants.

Lola nervously looked out at the faces staring back at her, as she asked everyone's opinion. Lizzie choked out, *"Baby bear, if I could hug you right now, I would. I-I just don't want to ruin your dress with my raccoon eyes."

Drying her own eyes, Cate looked at Lola with sisterly love. "Luxie, you truly look like a vision. When you and J were dating, I had hoped for this moment with you, and when things ended … well, I was so heartbroken because I already saw you as my sister. Thank you for making me a part of your special time."

Looking at her precious friend, Lola said, "Cate, please remember that Jacob doesn't define our friendship. You were in my life first, and I sure as hell won't lose you over his stupid ass. You're my sister, just like Lizzie, and nothing'll ever change that."

Sitting quietly by herself, Elin felt awkward and out of place; knowing that Lola had only invited her as a means of silencing Jennika's ever-nagging voice in Ronan's ear. Meekly finding the courage to speak, Elin exclaimed, "Lola, you look very beautiful. I know Atlas … I mean, Ronan, will be completely awestruck when he sees you."

Thanking everyone for their kind words, Lola told Yvaine she would like to change then see the bridesmaid options.

After two hours of trying dresses to fit each woman's height and body type, Lola finally made her choice: a dress consisting of a pale gold sequin, off-the-shoulder bodice, with a banded waist in a deep plum. The bottom portion of the dress was a charmeuse slip skirt, with a flowing organza overlay; all in a deep muted plum.

~

September 3, 2015

Lola stretched out her limbs, as Logan turned off the engine. "If you're okay with it, I can tell you the rest on our journey back. I'm not sure how late it will be when we get back, but uh …"

Looking over at the woman he loved so dearly, Logan asked, "What's that?"

Turning red, Lola blushed as she gathered up the courage to continue her inquiry. "Would you like to stay at my apartment?"

"I think that would be a great idea," Logan smiled as he stepped out of the car and went to open Lola's door.

Aside from the few groups of random strangers who came up to Logan asking for autographs, though she thought it odd, Lola chose not to think too deeply about it when Logan again told her they were just fans of his photography, Lola enjoyed the afternoon at the museum, and while she couldn't identify any particular image that was her favorite, the one thing she did know, was that seeing Logan's reactions was more than enough for her. As they walked back to Logan's car, Lola slowly slipped her hand into his, as she asked him what was next on the agenda.

"Well, *my heart*, I was thinking we would make the short walk over to **Pike's Place Market** and get an early dinner at **Pike Place Bar &** **Grill**."

"I was beginning to wonder if you were ever going to feed me, Warren!" Lola playfully pouted.

Logan smiled brightly, as he felt the warmth of Lola's hand in his. Checking the parking meter one last time, Logan led Lola down the street to their next destination.

"You know," Logan mused, "I can't believe Ronan actually wanted you to lie about being a Christian when you weren't one."

"It was very frustrating, I'll admit. However, I don't ever have to lie about my beliefs again. If someone were to ask me today, what I believe, I could proudly tell them that I am a Christian." Lola admitted.

Kissing the top of Lola's head, Logan smiled brightly as he held the restaurant's door open. "I can say the same thing. You know, right up until the **incident**, I was also agnostic." Logan revealed, with his voice wavering slightly. "With everything that happened that day and came to pass after … it really made me think long and hard about what I truly believed."

40

…ends in heartache

September 3, 2015

After Logan and Lola finished their meal, they headed off to Portland, where they would stay the night, as well as the following evening, before driving into Vienna the morning of September 5, for Lola's appointment with Luka. Looking over at Lola, as they waited for the light to change, Logan said, "You know, we'll have to come back another day to fully check out the **Market**."

"I'd like that a lot. Plus, I need to check out a coffee shop and see how they compare to **Cate's**!" Lola stated matter of factly.

Pausing for a brief moment to recall where she had left off, Lola continued her tale once more.

~

December 31, 2007

The month of December had flown by rather quickly for both Ronan and Lola. Having been advised by both Luis and Gregory, Ronan and Lola agreed to a prenup, which stated, "*Should anything other than death separate Ronan Atlas Harper and Lola Luxe Swan, neither party is entitled to the other's assets. Anything gained before or after marriage, legally remains in the ownership of the earner.*"

As for Lola's apartment, she was free to do with it as she wished, and what she had wished was to keep it. Although quite quaint, and slightly rundown, this apartment was the one thing in Lola's adult life that was truly hers by her own volition.

The morning of her wedding, Lola found herself with heightened apprehension. Lola paced the floor of her living room, as she awaited the arrival of her bridal party. Jennika had called the night before, highly annoyed that Lola had gone behind her back to tell the priest she would be getting ready in her own apartment, and not the room reserved in the back of the church.

Lola breathed a sigh of relief when her friends, and Elin, entered her apartment. Warmly embracing Cate, Lola asked, "H-have you heard anything from Logan? He didn't send an R.S.V.P., and Jennika was already a bitch about it because I put my foot down to reserve a space for him. And, I have tried calling him, but he doesn't answer."

Lovingly embracing her friend once more, Cate truthfully remarked with sadness lacing her voice, "No. I'm sorry, sweetie. Cade hasn't either."

"Oh…" Lola grimly replied. "I don't know if I have upset him in some way or not, or if he's just trying to keep his distance because of Naja. But, whatever it is, I was hoping to have him here. I don't really have a big family, so…"

"Now, you listen to me, Luxie. Logan, like most men, gets his head up his own ass. This in no way is your fault. I'm sure he'll be there, he's just stubborn is all. Besides, if he makes you cry on your wedding day, I'll have Cade give him a firm talk." Cate playfully chastised.

Feeling relieved after her talk with Cate, Lola allowed herself to relax in the bliss of her special day.

~

The ceremony went on, as all ceremonies do, without interruption.

While Jennika could have caused a scene and objected, simply causing a ruckus just wasn't her style. For Jennika knew that if she were to just patiently bide her time, everything would work out just how she wanted it to in the end.

After her dance with Ronan, Lola shared two special dances for the "Father-Daughter" portion- one with Gregory and the other with Lizzie's father, Luke. As her dance with Luke ended, Lola felt a light tap on her shoulder. Turning around, her face lit up as Logan now stood before her.

"Oh my god, Warren! You had me worried." Lola playfully chastised.

Taking Lola by the hand, Logan apologized as they danced across the floor. "I'm sorry, Lola. I've had a lot going on lately, and honestly wasn't sure if I would get to make it."

Smiling brightly at her dear friend, Lola easily forgave him before stating, "You have no idea just how much this means to me. Aside from Cate and Lizzie, you're my only other friend. No, you're my best friend, and …"

Logan and Lola's dance was cut short at Ronan's request to dance once more with his wife. Hearing the word 'friend' caused Logan's heart to falter once more. Before departing, Logan embraced Lola in a warm hug, as he whispered into her ear, "You look beautiful today, and I hope Ronan never takes you for granted."

Stepping away from the blissful couple, Logan briefly spoke with his dad and Cate before exiting the reception hall to make a phone call.

~

March 30, 2008

Winter slowly faded away, as spring arrived with its beauty and new life. This spring season should have signified a time of growth and development in Ronan and Lola's marriage, the exact opposite began to take root. Work and the everyday pressures of life quietly built a wall between the newlywed couple.

Lola arrived in Parkway that relatively warm, spring day, as she planned to have brunch with Logan before spending the day with Cate. However, unbeknownst to Lola, her past would resurface that fateful March morning.

Seated in a corner booth, Logan and Lola sat chatting merrily over a warm cup of coffee. Logan had felt guilty since the wedding; and although it hurt his heart, friendship with Lola was better than not having anything with her at all. Logan paused abruptly when Cate appeared apprehensively around the corner. "H-hey, guys. How's it goin' over here?"

Looking up in Cate's direction, Lola answered, "Hey, Cate! Everything's going great so far. The coffee is superb as always!"

"Umm ... thanks-," Cate nervously replied as she shifted her weight back and forth.

"Are you okay, Cate?" Logan asked concern etched upon his brow.

Exhaling to shake away her nerves, as she never was one to be fond of delivering bad news, Cate slowly spoke. "Wel-l ... you see ... umm ... I guess..."

Before Cate could utter a completely coherent statement, an all too familiar scent flooded Lola's nostrils, overtaking all of her senses. A gruff, yet sultry voice called over Cate's shoulder, "Did you miss me, *Vix*?"

Quickly regaining her senses, Lola immediately saw red- To say she was caught off guard would be understating Lola's feelings. Years of anger barely dwelling below the surface finally bubbled over in a fit of rage. "What the hell are you doing here, you arrogant son of a bitch?"

Rubbing the slight scruff along his jawline, Jacob playfully bit his lower lip before running his tongue across his top teeth; a tactic he knew very well would cause Lola to become weak in the knees, before speaking in his intrinsically, intoxicating voice. "Tsk tsk. My, my *Vixen*. Why all this rage? Is it a crime for a loving brother to move back to spend time with his sister?"

Mustering up what little self-control she had, Lola vowed to herself that she would not fall prey to the sadistic man before her … how sadly she was mistaken, for she had no way to know what the future would hold.

No longer able to remain seated, Lola stood as she growled through clenched teeth, "Don't show your fucking smug face to me, **ever** again!"

Slapping Jacob as hard as she could, Lola grabbed her belongings before running out the door. *Don't let him see you cry, Lola. Not this time!*

Trying to walk after Lola, Jacob was immediately stopped by a lean, yet muscular body; one that stood a good four inches above him. Looking down at the man he had long since despised, Logan seethed. "I'm pretty sure Lola told you to stay the fuck away from her. If you follow her, I have no qualms with beating the shit out of you in the parking lot! Am I clear, you demented mother fucker?"

Knowing he had already caused enough of a scene, Jacob held his hands up in defense as he slowly backed away. Finally appeased with Jacob's distance, Logan grabbed his jacket before following Lola into the parking lot.

Coming upon Lola seated against the driver's side door, on the pavement, Logan's heart completely shattered. Squatting down to be at her level, Logan rubbed Lola's back as he did his best to soothe her from her panic attack. When Lola's breathing had finally regulated, she embraced Logan like her life depended on it. "I-I'm sorry for my outburst," she apologized profusely.

Having fully sat down as his legs started to cramp in the squatted position, Logan reassured Lola that she had nothing to apologize for, before asking the question which had long since burned in the back of his mind. "If you don't mind me asking, what all happened between you and Jacob?"

Realizing she was in fact married, and it was not proper to remain in another man's embrace, Lola quickly scooted back before grabbing a tissue from her purse. "He just wasn't who I thought he was..."

"What do you mean?" Logan queried, his mind instantly going to the darkest possible outcomes.

"Look, Logan ... I know you mean well, but please-" Lola began, trying to remain composed so as not to direct all of her anger at her innocent friend. "-please don't fucking psychoanalyze me. Just trust me when I say that he wasn't who I thought he was. Okay?"

Realizing further inquiry was a moot point, Logan stood before helping Lola to her feet. "Okay, Lola. I'll trust you. Please just promise me that you will call me if he ever bothers you again?" Logan requested, before playfully flexing his muscles.

Laughing heartily, Lola reassured Logan that she would, before entering her car to drive back to her home in Portland.

~

Walking into her bedroom, Lola wearily placed her purse on the vanity, before undressing and making her way to the oversized shower in her lavish bathroom. Lost in thought, Lola was caught off guard, when a pair of lips grazed the side of her neck. Fear overtook her, as she turned around, punching the person behind her square in the nose. "Don't fucking touch me!"

Falling back against the counter, Ronan yelled out, "What the hell, Lola?"

Hearing Ronan's voice brought Lola back to reality. "Shit! Oh my god, Ro! I'm so fucking sorry. You scared the hell out of me."

Grabbing the hand towel from the hook, Ronan held it to his nose to stop the bleeding. "Look, I'm sorry, okay. But who else would be in our house?"

Not wanting to relive the events from earlier in the day, Lola deflected, "I've told you about coming up on me from behind."

Annoyed and sexually frustrated, Ronan spat, "Well, excuse the hell out of me for trying to initiate foreplay with my wife. You know these rings say that I am just as entitled to your body, as you are to mine!"

"Ro, I'm not in the fucking mood. Please just let me get a shower," Lola wearily pleaded.

"That's just it. You're never in the 'fucking mood'!" Ronan emphasized with air quotes before continuing, "God, Lola! We'll be married for three friggin' months tomorrow, and have literally had sex twice! I'm a man with needs and I don't know what the hell is wrong with you, but you're being a selfish bitch!"

Not in the mood to explain the inner workings of her mind, Lola slapped Ronan across the face before screaming at him to get out of the bathroom. To which he responded by slamming the door as he yelled, "I'm beginning to think my mother was right about you!"

Sitting on the floor of the shower, Lola allowed the scalding hot water to carry her tears down the drain. *Now I've really gone and done it! Why the hell do I keep letting Jacob have this much control over my life?*

After the water turned to ice, Lola exited the shower before entering her walk-in closet to put on a pair of silk shorts with a matching short-sleeved top. Making a pit stop in the kitchen, Lola walked down the hall to Ronan's office, knocking lightly on the door before entering.

Looking up from the case file on his desk, Ronan patted his lap for Lola to come sit, where he apologized profusely. "I'm sorry, *love*.

I shouldn't have spoken to you like that or even spitefully said that my mother was right when she isn't."

Placing the ice pack on Ronan's nose, which was still rather swollen, Lola said, "No, Ro, I'm the one who has to apologize. I haven't been fulfilling my duties as a wife and I shouldn't have punched you like that."

Tossing the ice pack to the floor, Ronan lovingly held Lola's hands as he admitted, "It looks like we both have a lot to learn about this thing called marriage."

Chuckling as she straddled her husband's lap, Lola seductively told Ronan that she would love to make it up to him in any way possible, as she shifted her hips back and forth, eagerly bringing his member to life.

~

April 27, 2008

Nearly a month had passed since Lola's argument with Ronan, and while she had done her best to fulfill her wifely duties to make herself sexually available every night, she couldn't help but be bored by the same monotonous position every night.

Laying beneath her husband's predictably, rhythmic thrusts, Lola felt ashamed as she found herself reflecting on her last sexual encounter with Jacob; in hopes of at least feeling some kind of orgasm. Pulling her camisole that had ridden up, back over her stomach, Lola's guilt rose inside her as she looked over to see Ronan smiling in his post-sex high.

Reaching out to draw his wife closer to him, Ronan asked the question burning in his brain. "Hey, *love*. May I ask something?" Hearing Lola's hum of a response, he continued. "Do you think the next time we have sex, you could take your camisole off?"

"NO!" Lola belted out, feelings of guilt transitioning to panic. *What would Ro think if he saw all of the marks? He already looked at me like I was insane when I asked about some light bondage.*

Seeing the look of confusion on Ronan's face, Lola apologized for her brashness. "Sorry, Ro. I shouldn't have yelled like that. I had an … umm…" Lola did her best to come up with a believable lie; one which would hopefully deter any further questions. "Well, I had an … accident … yeah, an accident a few years ago. I'm just not comfortable showing the scars."

"Lola, I'm your husband. You shouldn't be afraid to show me your body." Ronan countered.

"Drop it, Ro! Please-" Lola pleaded before walking into the bathroom.

Sitting on the cold, hard tile of the shower as the blistering, hot water pelted upon her back, Lola allowed the weight of her guilt to fall down her cheeks and seep out of her palms once more. *God! Jacob really has fucked me up in so many ways.*

~

July 31, 2008

Spring transitioned into summer, with the months quickly passing by Ronan and Lola, with only the physical part of their relationship thriving. Ronan wanted to feel closer to his wife emotionally but was left feeling pitiful and helpless, as Lola continued to build the icy wall around her heart.

Shutting Ronan out had never been Lola's original intent, but his incessant pushing and prodding were more than her mind could handle at that point in her life. For while Jacob had respected her wishes that fateful March morning at **Cate's**, his voice was louder than ever, echoing through the vast chambers of her mind.

Two days before Lola's 24th birthday, Ronan and Lola found themselves seated quietly at their dinner table. Ronan had some news he was dying to share with his wife and hoped it would go over well. Ronan grabbed Lola's hand, clearing his throat before he began. "*Love*, I have some pretty exciting news!"

A genuine smile formed upon Lola's lips, the first in weeks, as Lola picked up on Ronan's elation. "What's that, Ro?"

Kissing her hand lovingly, Ronan stated, "Well, before I tell you, I want to know what you have planned for your birthday Saturday night."

Thinking for a brief moment, Lola informed Ronan of the only plans she would have that morning. "Lizzie and I are celebrating our birthdays together, I'm not sure where, but most likely we'll be at her house. Cate, Cade, and Logan are coming and you can come too if you aren't working."

Hearing Logan's name mentioned Ronan asked, a little bitterly, "What's the deal with Logan?"

"He's just a friend, Ro! I promise you have nothing to worry about." Lola lovingly reassured her husband.

"If you say so, well ... I trust you, *love*," Ronan stated before moving on to his big news. "I won't be able to come to Lizzie's, because I got a promotion!"

"Oh my god, Ro! That's amazing!" Lola squealed in delight.

Smiling enthusiastically, Ronan continued, "Well, I was hired on as the lead attorney for a company that's based both here and somewhere in Canada."

"Ronan Atlas Harper, I am so fucking proud of you!" Lola beamed, before asking, "So, what does this have to do with my birthday?"

"Well, I was hoping to celebrate your birthday in combination with having the CEO over for dinner. What do you think?"

"Honestly, I think it's a great idea. You know I typically don't do much for my birthday anyhow, so why not celebrate your success of getting out from under your dad." Lola sincerely stated before asking Ronan to follow her to their bedroom, so they could have their own private celebration.

~

August 2, 2008

Lola's birthday started off merrily, as she treasured the precious moments with those she held so dear to her heart. Cate had proposed they have a picnic breakfast by the pond at the local park, where she and Cade would bring all of the food and coffee. Lizzie had given Lola a certificate for a spa day; and in turn, Lola's gift to Lizzie was a weekend getaway for her and Mark to Las Vegas. Raelee drew Lola a precious picture, which showed the two of them playing faeries together.

Walking up to Lola, Logan nervously held out the small box as he hoped Lola would like his gift. Taking the box in her hands, Lola smiled brightly as she opened it. "Concert tickets! Thanks, Warren."

"Y-you're welcome. It's for my friend's band, they have a show playing tonight at **The British Punk** in Portland, and I thought maybe..." Logan spluttered.

Logan internally chastised himself. *Why the hell am I stuttering like some damn, love-sick fool? Oh, wait, you idiot! It's because you are one.*

Inspecting the tickets more thoroughly, Lola noticed the name of the band, **Beyond Oregon**, which caused a bittersweet memory to flood her mind. Looking directly at Mark, Lola boasted, "Hey, Marky Mark! Guess who just got tickets to see **Beyond Oregon**?"

"Son of a..." Mark tapered off, realizing his very bright-eyed and repetitive six-year-old was listening in on his words. "Uh ... I mean, that's great, Luxie!"

Turning her attention back to Logan, Lola thanked him for the gift. "Ronan got a new job, so we are having his boss over for dinner tonight, but I'll try my best to make it. Thank you again."

Time quickly slipped away from Lola as she enjoyed the rest of her morning. Hearing the chime of her phone, Lola saw a text from Ronan which stated, *"Happy birthday, love! I know I told you and showed you this morning ;), but I wanted to say it again. When you get home, grab a shower, and then your presents will be waiting on the bed. Also, don't worry about dinner for tonight. I've got it covered."*

Smiling at her husband's sweet words, Lola thanked her friends for everything, before driving back to her home in Portland.

~

Feeling quite refreshed after her shower, Lola smiled as she walked into the bedroom and found a beautiful bouquet of dark red roses with baby's breath and four beautifully wrapped gifts in a variety of sizes. Starting with the smallest, Lola smiled in awe as she lifted the box lid and found a bottle of **Chanel No. 19**; this had been her grandmother's favorite perfume and was very hard to come by.

In the other three packages, Ronan had given Lola a beautiful, leather **Tahari** clutch in pale pink; a black pair of **Christian Louboutin** peep toe, slingback stilettos, with black satin ribbons to tie around her ankles; and a beautiful beige rose, satin, mid-length swing dress with lantern sleeves.

After applying her makeup, Lola styled her hair elegantly with a braided crown, which transitioned into a low ponytail, before adding a few sprigs of the baby's breath for a lovely finishing touch. Cinching the dress's ribbon snuggly around her waist, Lola quickly exited the bedroom just as the doorbell chimed.

Opening the door in expectation of meeting Ronan's new employer, Lola was quite stunned to see Elin standing on the other side, smiling giddily as she held a narrow pink bag in her hands. "Happy birthday, bestie!" Elin squealed as she bent down to hug Lola.

"Uh..." Lola spluttered. "H-hey, Elin... What brings you here?"

Stepping inside the foyer, Elin chirped, "Atlas, sorry- old habits die hard ... I mean, Ronan and I met for coffee yesterday morning and he told me it was your birthday today!"

"Okay..." Lola knew that Ronan and Elin often met for coffee, and while this would have bothered most wives, she felt it would be rather hypocritical to make a fuss when she herself met with Logan quite often.

"Anyhow, Ronan didn't want you to be bored with his boss here, so he thought you might enjoy the company." Elin recanted before making her way to the kitchen as she called, "Come on, you silly goose. This rosé isn't going to drink itself."

Lola remained perplexed by the door as she thought to herself, *Elin is weird as hell. Hopefully, this isn't a complete shit show. Fuck, speaking of show- I forgot to tell Ro about the tickets Logan gave me for tonight. Whoever is listening, please let tonight go smoothly.*

As she prepared to close the door, Lola was caught off guard by an all too familiar scent. Uneasiness washed over Lola like a brutal wave crashing upon the seashore, as she slowly brought her eyes up to meet the icy pair she knew was somehow standing before her.

"My, my. Isn't this an interesting turn of events?" Jacob crooned seductively while taking in all of Lola's elegant figure.

Balling her fists in a failed attempt to silence the squall of rage building inside of her, Lola belted out, "What the actual fuck?! Why the hell are you here, Jacob?"

Hearing commotion by the front door, Ronan swiftly left his office and headed for the front door. "Is everything okay, *love*?" Seeing their guest at the door, Ronan cleared his throat before welcoming Jacob inside. "Thank you for joining us, Mr. Gallagher."

Stepping across the threshold, Jacob thanked Ronan for his gracious invitation before winking at Lola as he stated, "By the way, happy birthday, *Vix*. I know I've missed a few."

Lola did her best to contain her embarrassment as she escorted Jacob to the dining room. Clearly confused, and rightfully so, Ronan asked, "Am I missing something here?"

Sitting in the chair offered to him, Jacob announced with his signature wink, "*Vixen* and I used to date."

Oblivious to the ongoings happening in the dining room, Elin sauntered in from the kitchen with two glasses of rosé in hand. Making note of the somber expressions upon the three faces staring back at her, Elin asked, "Uh- bestie, is everything okay?"

Plucking the extra glass from Elin's hand, Lola bitterly spat out, "My god, Elin. Read the damn room," before quickly downing the contents of her own glass, followed by Elin's.

Trying to save face in front of his new employer, Ronan clapped his hands as he asked for everyone to be seated. Two excruciatingly long and awkward hours later, Lola politely excused herself from the table, as her nerves were nearly worn completely through. Once Lola was out of sight, Ronan finally asked Jacob the question in the forefront of his mind for the majority of the evening.

"Mr. Gallagher-" Ronan began before being reminded by Jacob to address him by his first name. "Jacob, while I am grateful for the opportunity to work as the head of your company's legal team, I must know, is there anything going on between you and Lola? Are you still in love with my wife?"

Chuckling, Jacob stated honestly, "Currently, there isn't anything going on between *Vix* and me. And as for love … well, let's just say it never really was about love."

Ronan exhaled in relief. "Please forgive me for sounding accusatory, Jacob. I love my wife dearly and just wanted to make sure there wouldn't be any issues."

Having stated his piece, Ronan and Jacob made their way to Ronan's office for a glass or two of Scotch, accompanied by Ronan's personal stash of **Griffin's Robusto** cigars. Elin, on the other hand, set off in search of Lola. After several minutes of searching, Elin found Lola seated on the floor of the veranda, holding her phone and looking teary-eyed. Sitting down beside the younger woman,

Elin asked with genuine concern if everything was alright.

Wiping the tears from her eyes, Lola truthfully stated that things were anything but fine. "I just got off the phone with my best friend, Logan … and let's just say, he's mad at me…"

"But it's your birthday, why would he be mad at you?" Elin inquired.

Sighing heavily and feeling she had nothing else to lose at this point, Lola summarized her conversation with Logan to Elin. "I disappointed Logan because I told him that I wouldn't be able to make it to his friend's concert. Also, he already doesn't like Jacob, so his being here in my house really pissed Logan off." Unsure of what else to say, Elin gave Lola a warm hug.

After a few moments of idle conversation, Elin decided it was time to head back home. Lola wished her safe travels before snatching up the bottle of rosé, taking several large and unladylike swigs. Halfway to her car, Elin realized she had forgotten her phone. As she re-entered the kitchen, Elin came upon a disheartening scene not meant for her eyes.

As soon as Elin had left the house, Lola found herself flush against the kitchen sink with Jacob standing directly behind her. Doing her best to remain composed, Lola bitterly spat out, "What the hell are you doing Jacob? My **husband** is down the hall."

"Don't you see, *Vixen*, that's what makes this all the more exciting?" Jacob darkly laughed as he brushed the tip of his nose along the side of Lola's neck; an action that caused Lola to shudder in both delight and disgust.

Trying to regain full control of the situation, Lola used what little strength she had to face the icy-eyed devil head-on. "You hurt me in more ways than I could even dream to count, Jacob. Why the hell would I want to mess things up with a man who truly loves me?"

"Because, *Vixen*, if you truly loved him, you wouldn't be so sexually frustrated right now. You wouldn't think of all the ways I can instantly make your body cum, while having vanilla sex." Jacob remarked as he lifted Lola's chin, ensuring her eyes could not leave his for even a second, before uttering, "Besides, how can you truly love Ronan, when you already know that I own your mind, body, and soul."

Seeing the object of his obsession wide-eyed in bewilderment, Jacob pulled Lola's lower lip between his teeth, causing it to bust. As the blood slowly pooled upon Lola's lip, Jacob smashed his lips onto hers; devouring them as a snow leopard does its prey. Having pulled away from his victim, Jacob stepped out of the kitchen and offered Elin his signature wink.

"Now, now, *Goldie*. I think you and I both know it's best you forget everything you just saw. Besides, do you really think Ronan would believe you? How about I make you a deal?"

Sliding down to the kitchen floor, Lola felt her heart shatter with the costly weight of Jacob's words and actions.

~

December 31, 2008

Summer and autumn hastily transitioned to a long and arduously, bitter winter. A winter that brought with it a flurry of heartache and costly mistakes. Following Lola's birthday, distance began to dwell deeper within the hearts of both Ronan and Lola. Try as he might, Ronan couldn't seem to shake the feelings of dissonance that had taken root at Jacob's wording when asked if anything were going on between him and Lola. The word, "*Currently*," grew rampant like kudzu, as it all but choked out the love Ronan had for his wife.

Instead of opening up to her husband after the incident with Jacob in their kitchen, Lola retreated further into herself, leaving only an icy husk of who she once was. And although he made no other contact with Lola after her birthday, Jacob's voice reverberated louder than ever within the withering walls of Lola's decrepit mind. Diving deeper into her work, Lola spent far too many nights apart from her husband, leaving room for sin to walk on in and tear them asunder.

While the date of their first wedding anniversary would have been the perfect time for Ronan and Lola to reconnect, Lola instead, chose to focus all of her efforts and attention on the annual charity gala.

Lola walked into what was meant to be her home, for the first time in two months, and made her way down the hall to her bedroom. With all of the minute details of the gala still at the forefront of her mind, Lola was ill-prepared for the sight before her, as she opened the door- Elin and Ronan were carnally entwined, defiling what was meant to be the marital bed.

"Are you fucking kidding me?" Lola cried out, as she slammed the door into the wall hard enough for the knob to punch a hole through the sheetrock, before running out of the house.

Sending Gregory a quick text stating she had fallen ill and he would need to lead the gala that evening, Lola got in her car before blindly driving in the direction of Parkway's cemetery. Sitting down in the snow, in front of Shane's headstone, Lola couldn't help but wonder how her life had gone so off course.

As the night's darkness surrounded her, Lola laughed bitterly as she trekked back to her car. Reveling in the tingling of her limbs becoming as cold and dead as she felt on the inside, Lola pulled out her phone to call the one person who constantly reminded her that they would be available no matter what ... Logan. After the tenth unanswered call, Lola sighed to herself, *He's probably busy like everyone else is on New Year's Eve.*

Scrolling through her contacts, Lola finally came across a number she should have deleted long ago ... Jacob's. Unsure of whether or not he would answer, Lola made the ill-advised call that would finally seal her fate.

41

Hope

September 3, 2015

Once Logan pulled into Lola's assigned parking space, Lola stretched her cramped limbs as she exited the passenger's side. "If you want to grab a shower, I can wash your clothes. I think there's an old pair of your shorts floating around somewhere," Lola called over her shoulder as she entered the apartment complex's lobby.

By the time they reached Lola's door on the second floor, Logan's breathing became labored as he began to feel faint and clammy all over. Although he tried to reach out for Lola, Logan's vision blurred before he crumpled to the ground. Alerted by the sound of Logan's body crashing to the tiled floor, Lola did her best not to panic as she checked Logan's breathing before rushing to a neighbor's door in search of help.

~

September 4, 2015

Two hours later, Logan awoke to the sound of Lola's tiny feet pacing back and forth in an unfamiliar room. "L-Lola … where are we?" Logan weakly asked, not recognizing the grogginess of his own voice.

"Warren!" Lola belted out, as she rushed over to his side to embrace him before momentarily stepping out of the room. Watching Lola exit the room, Logan fully took in his surroundings and was quite surprised to find himself in a hospital bed.

Lola returned in less than five minutes, followed by a doctor, and seated herself in the chair at Logan's bedside. Looking up from the clipboard containing Logan's information, the doctor took a moment to introduce himself. "Good evening, well at this point it's morning. Anyhow, good morning, Mr. Warren. I'm Dr. Hanover."

"Umm … hey, doc-" Logan asked with confusion. "Why I am here?"

"From what Ms. Swan has told us, you blacked out, outside of her apartment. Are you able to recall how you were feeling right before you passed out?" Dr. Hanover asked.

Rubbing the bruised side of his head, Logan stated, "When we pulled into the parking lot of the complex, I honestly felt fine. However, once we made it up to the second floor, my heart started beating super fast. Then, I started having trouble breathing and my chest felt like it was caving in. I got cold chills and my ears started ringing, then the next thing I know, I'm waking up in here."

Notating Logan's symptoms, Dr. Hanover did a basic physical to ensure Logan was not concussed before asking, "How has your overall health been as of late? Are you eating well? Drinking enough water? Sleeping well? Exercising?"

While Logan relayed to Dr. Hanover that until this random moment, he had been perfectly healthy, Lola nervously tapped her foot as she was almost positive of what exactly happened to Logan.

"From everything that I am seeing now, I would say you are healthy enough to return home," Dr. Hanover announced, before stating his official diagnosis. "Mr. Warren, from the symptoms you have described, I would say you had a panic attack."

Lola squeezed Logan's hand reassuringly, as Dr. Hanover advised Logan to speak with his general practitioner regarding anti-anxiety medication if he were to experience similar symptoms in the future.

Once they were seated in Logan's car, Lola started the engine before looking at Logan remorsefully. "What the hell happened, Warren?"

Giving Lola's hand a gentle kiss before holding it in his, Logan sheepishly stated, "Well … when we arrived at your apartment complex, I wanted to tell you that I had no idea I made you cry on your birthday back then, and I felt guilty. Then, I figured you would ask why I never answered your call that night and I planned to tell you because, at that point in time, it was the most traumatic experience of my life."

Typically feeling dehydrated after her own panic attacks, Lola offered Logan a water bottle, which he gratefully accepted, before continuing his train of thought. "And after I thought about that, I then realized that I hadn't been to your apartment since … since we had that big fight… right before…"

Logan's voice trailed off, as Lola's mind finally put the pieces of the puzzle together. "That was your first time at my apartment since right before the *incident*, huh?"

Pinching the bridge of his nose, Logan fought through his internal frustrations, as he admitted that Lola was right. "Shit! I am so fucking sorry, Logan." Lola confessed. "I honestly didn't even think about there being a possibility of my place bothering you like that. I always have a room on reserve at my hotel. We can go-"

"Lola, look at me." Logan cut Lola off. "I honestly didn't even think about it until it happened. I'll be okay if we go there."

"A-are you s-sure?" Lola asked apprehensively.

"I promise you, I'll be fine." Logan lovingly reassured. "I won't be caught up in my own head this time, and besides, I really just want to go to sleep." Taking a deep breath, Lola relented, driving back in the direction of her apartment.

Stretching out on Lola's bed, Logan patted the empty space beside him, signaling Lola to join him. "*My heart*, you worry far too much. How about when we wake up in a few hours since we have a day to kill before your appointment with Luka, I tell you what happened that night in 2008?"

Lola nodded in agreement, as she ran her fingers through Logan's hair; lulling him into a peaceful slumber while leaving her alone with her anxious thoughts.

~

Lola awoke around noon to the sound of the shower being turned off. Hearing the growling of her stomach, Lola realized there was no food in the apartment, as this wasn't meant to be a long stay. "Good morning, well afternoon at this point," Logan chuckled as he entered the bedroom.

"When did you wake up? Are you feeling okay? Do you need anything?" Lola spluttered out quickly.

Wrapping Lola in a warm embrace, Logan patiently reassured Lola that he was perfectly fine. "Besides, that was just a fluke!"

"If you're absolutely, positively sure that you are fine, I'll go get a shower and then we go grab something to eat. Sound like a plan?" Lola said.

Once Lola was ready for the day, she and Logan piled back into the car. "Where to, *my heart*?"

Thinking for a moment, Lola recommended they go to **Bea's Pancake House**. "I know it's not super healthy, but I am starving." The sound of her stomach resonated loudly throughout the car, causing both passengers to laugh hysterically.

~

It didn't take long for Logan and Lola to have their order taken, once they were seated. As they waited, Lola said, "I know I apologized like a million times for missing that concert, but I still feel kinda bad. I just hate letting people down."

Reaching over to hold Lola's hand, Logan reminded her that it was just a concert. "Back then, I just wanted any excuse to hang out with you. And if I'm being completely honest, well..."

Eyeing Logan curiously, Lola queried, "Well, what?"

"Well, I think it was a blessing because, unlike Elin, I wasn't the *other* person who destroyed a marriage. Speaking of Elin, what were her and Ronan's reactions to you walking in on them?" Logan admitted.

"At the end of the day, I don't blame Elin for what happened," Lola stated truthfully.

"Really?" Logan asked in astonishment.

"I mean, it did sting for someone who claimed to be my best friend- mind you, I never said she was, she just had that idea in her head- to be in bed with my husband … well … that part hurt like hell. But as for the affair and the destruction of our marriage, only Ronan and I are to blame.

"And I guess, the part that made me miss Ronan, up until recently, was more of the 'idea' of him, and how hard he did try to love me, even though I wouldn't let him in."

Taking a drink of her water, Lola said, "I mean, if I am being truthful, not even Jacob is at fault for that." Lola surprised herself with the last statement, as she made a mental note to inform Dr. Indigo over their next session. "Anyhow, back to your original question, Elin and Ronan were super shocked. At the divorce proceedings, Ronan said he never meant for us to end like that, but he couldn't deny a big part of him still loved Elin after all of their years apart."

Lola trailed off as the server brought out their order. Enjoying a few bites of her strawberry cheesecake pancakes, Lola finally asked, "So … what happened in 2008?"

Clearing his throat, Logan said, "Well, for starters, Naja and I broke up for good after Thanksgiving. We spent more than half of 2008 hot and cold, and honestly, I just didn't like who I was becoming. So, my mom suggested that we go spend Christmas in Los Angeles with our extended family-"

"That's the Moretti family, right?" Lola interjected.

"Right!" Logan smiled, pleased Lola remembered. "Anyhow, we all went- me, my mom, Dean, Eloise, and Rosalie. We were having the best time, until New Year's Eve when we were scheduled to fly back to Oregon, late that evening."

"What happened?" Lola asked, unable to contain her anticipation any longer.

Taking a deep breath, Logan tried to shake away the rising nausea as the memories came flooding back into his mind. "My *Zio* and *Zia* gave me the two most wonderful extra siblings, Drake and Launa. Drake was 14, and Launa was 12 on New Year's Eve. Launa was upset that Drake had been given a street bike, and had been eyeing it since Christmas. I never thought that she'd take it out without permission," he swallowed.

"Launa had excused herself, saying she wasn't feeling well pretty early in the evening. Around seven, all of us were sitting around laughing about something my *Zio* had said when sirens screamed up the driveway and there was a loud knock at the door. *Zio* answered the door, and *my heart*, I have never gotten the sound he made out of my head.

"Launa had taken the bike out for a spin and was hit by a drunk driver. We all rushed to the emergency room where we were told that even though she had been wearing all of her protective gear, one of the handles had pierced clean through her abdomen. She had to have several blood transfusions, and her uterus was beyond repair, so they had to remove it. We thought we were gonna lose her. It was a fucking nightmare."

Logan shook himself from the memory and smiled sadly at the woman sitting across from him. "We were in such a hurry to get to her, that I left my phone at the house."

Hearing Logan's summation of what had occurred back then, shook Lola to her core. "Oh … oh my god…" was the only thing Lola could utter in response to the horrific events that unfolded for the poor young girl.

~

September 5, 2015

Logan and Lola awoke early the morning of September 5, as they had decided to go to bed early the night before; the lingering muscle fatigue from Logan's panic attack and Lola finding herself in a weird headspace after hearing about Launa's tragedy took a small toll on both parties.

Making a minor detour in Parkway for some breakfast at **Cate's**, with neither Logan nor Lola having much to say that morning, the couple sat back as they enjoyed the trip to Vienna, the radio playing softly in the background.

Standing outside of **Prohibition Ink**, Lola reached for Logan's hand and squeezed it to give herself some reassurance that this would be okay. "Everything is going to be okay, *my heart*. You'll see." Logan encouraged as he held open the door.

"Good morning, you sexy red duo!" Luka boisterously greeted as Logan and Lola walked into the back office. "Why don't you guys have a seat, while I pull up the concept? Then, you can tell me what you think."

While there was no doubt in Logan's mind that Luka would come up with something spectacular, even he was not prepared for the sheer beauty of what his friend had been able to draw out.

"So," Luka began as he pointed to the outer edge of the design, "what I was thinking, is that I would start with quite a few red poppies going along both sides of your back, making their way to the lower area. I'll give these a watercolor-painted look, having the stems and leaves in black. Since most of the damage seems to have been in these areas, the blooms should provide enough coverage."

"I really like that, it feels very elegant," Lola exclaimed in complete admiration.

"I'm glad you think so." Luka smiled warmly, before moving onto what would be the center portion of the tattoo. Luka pointed to the small bluebird perched atop the golden cage, which was slightly askew with its door wide open. "This is meant to represent your freedom. And as for these," Luka said as he pointed to the pink peonies, "I know you only mentioned red poppies, but I hope you don't mind me taking some creative liberties."

"Not at all," Lola answered honestly. "Peonies would be a close second as a flower I like, so I think it goes really well. What made you include them?"

"Well … back in high school I was seeing this guy that was really into flowers. And since I really liked him, I thought it'd be cool to learn the meanings behind them." Luka reminisced fondly.

"Wait a minute, did you date Andy Bennett?" Lola asked as her mind began putting pieces together.

"Yeah- umm … but how do you know him?" Luka queried.

"Oh my god! I can't believe I didn't put two and two together until now." Lola laughed heartily. "Andy would always go on about how he and his girlfriend, Zaylee, were in an open relationship with this guy named Luke."

"Crazy bastard never would add the 'a' on the end of my name; just equating it to part of his charm and charisma." Luka chuckled before adding, "So … are you the Luxie that was with his best friend, Shane?"

"Guilty as charged," Lola sassed.

"Small fucking world!" Luka chortled, before answering Lola's question. "Anyhow, I added the pink peonies because peonies are meant to symbolize prosperity. And I wanted the whole tattoo to help you remember that you are no longer caged, but free, and will have prosperity in your new life."

Logan's heart nearly burst as he sat back, watching the genuine interaction between one of his closest friends, and the woman he loved more than anything.

"I absolutely love this Luka! It truly is a masterpiece." Lola beamed.

"Alrighty then! Now, all together, this is going to be about 40 hours of work, so I'd like to start today off with just the outlining process. Then, I'd like for you to come back for a five-hour session, every day until I finish next Saturday. How's that? You guys are even welcome to crash at my house so that you can keep the drive time to a minimum."

~

September 12, 2015

By the end of one week's time, Luka had completed what he considered to be his magnum opus. Watching Lola in awe, as she admired the beauty standing in the place of torment, Luka teared up as he turned to Logan and said, "I know I joke a lot and give you a hard time, but I can't ever thank you enough for allowing me the chance to create something beautiful for Lola. Lola's expression right now is exactly why dad started this shop, and why I continue … It's all about giving someone hope to feel whole again."

42

Dissolution

November 1, 2015

Due to its size, it took approximately seven weeks for Lola's tattoo to do most of the external healing. During that time, Lola was ever so grateful Logan knew what to do and was there to help during the healing, peeling, and itching process. Looking at the latest picture of it on Logan's phone, Lola stated, "It is beautiful and I am so thankful to have this, however, I don't see how people can keep going through with it. Especially the itching."

Lola shuddered at the thought of not having been able to scratch the dried, flaky skin. "It was also really hard because I couldn't go running either."

"Well, *my heart*, most people tend to start out smaller than a full back piece," Logan playfully snickered.

"Yeah, yeah…" Lola exclaimed with a roll of her eyes as she teasingly shooed Logan away.

Settling onto the couch, Logan gestured for Lola to sit beside him. Once she was there, he moved the stray curls that had fallen down into her face. Lola blushed at the sensation of Logan's skin caressing hers, as she nestled the side of her face into his large palm. "Thank

431

you," Lola genuinely expressed after several minutes.

"For what?" Logan asked.

"Thank you for just being you. You never rush me, and are far more patient than I ever deserve." Lola stated with the utmost transparency.

Lifting Lola's chin, so that her eyes met his, Logan said in a husky voice, "*My heart*, I am really having the hardest time not kissing you right now."

"What's stopping you then, Warren?" Lola flirtatiously jested before crashing her lips upon Logan's.

Logan, never separating from their kiss, gently laid Lola back against the couch, running his fingers through her luxurious ringlets. Lola's breath quickly became labored when Logan began to trail kisses from her lips to her neck and shoulders, and his hands slowly trailed up and down her thighs and waist.

Logan broke away from their kisses long enough to remove his t-shirt, giving Lola's nails full access to his lean, yet muscular back. Logan and Lola's lusty moment would have turned into one of pure lover's bliss, had the voices in Lola's mind not gone into overdrive, the second Logan began to slide his hand into the waistband of Lola's leggings.

Panic instantly hit Lola like a freight train; yet, she did her best to remain in control of her emotions, lest she cause Logan any heartache. Tapping Logan on the arm, Lola meekly muttered, "L-let's stop … I'm sorry."

Seeing the sorrow in Lola's eyes crushed Logan's heart, as he mentally chastised himself. *Shit! I moved too fast again.* Helping Lola sit up, as he tried to adjust the discomfort in his nether regions, Logan disconcertedly remarked, "Lola, *my heart*, you've got nothing to be sorry for. If anything, I'm the one who should be sorry. I should've asked before jumping the gun."

Lola wearily rested her head against Logan's chest, allowing his heartbeat to calm her heightened senses. Kissing the top of Lola's head, Logan reaffirmed, "I will always ask for your consent. I love you more than anything, and I'm willing to wait until the ends of the earth for our first time together." Before squirming uncomfortably, "Now, if you'll excuse me, I think I'm gonna go practice for the polar bear club with an icy shower."

Lola's face reddened in embarrassment, as she uttered, "Oh my god! I can't believe I did that to you again."

"Not the first time and definitely won't be the last." Logan tossed a wink over his shoulder at Lola as he made his way to the shower.

"To make up for it," Lola yelled out, "I'll pick up where I left off a few weeks ago!"

~

After some self-care and a long, frigid shower, Logan wrapped his chilled body around Lola's, seeking out her warmth. "I'm sorry again," Lola apologized.

"Don't be sorry, Lola! I'd way rather have you be honest with me than you do something you aren't comfortable with." Logan assured while rubbing Lola's back.

Pushing the last waves of guilt to the back of her mind, Lola cleared her throat before continuing her story once again.

~

January 31, 2009

One month had passed since Lola's world took yet another unexpected spiral downward. While calling Jacob had been her rock bottom decision, seeing him again was definitely not what she had expected. With the last memories of Jacob being cruel and abusive in the forefront of her mind, Lola was caught off guard when the only thing he did that night was lend her a shoulder to cry on.

After waking up on New Year's Day, Lola left Jacob a note, thanking him for just being there for her. Even though the part of her soul that craved the consistency and understanding Jacob provided, the fully cognitive part waved red flags, as it warned Lola to protect herself at all costs. All of the calls Lola made to Logan were sent directly to voicemail. She finally stopped calling when Logan sent a brief text that stated, *"Can't talk. I'm busy. Family stuff in L.A. Be back in Oregon for my bday. Call you then."*

Though Lola could have leaned on either Cate or Lizzie for moral support after the dissipation of her marriage, she chose to retreat further within; weathering the fallout with only the voices in her head to keep her company.

No longer wanting to be alone, Lola sent a text to Jacob, inviting him for dinner at **Étoile Bleue**. Seated at a table positioned between two oversized windows, Lola and Jacob made idle small talk as they awaited the arrival of their food. Still unsure of how to react around Jacob, Lola defensively inquired, "So … *Mr. Icy Eyes*- tell me how you did it?"

"*Mr. Icy Eyes*, huh?" Jacob flirtatiously quipped.

Lola indignantly rolled her eyes as she demanded, "Yes, now answer the damn question!"

"Retract the claws, *Vixen*. There's no need for this hostility." Jacob sternly stated, before adding, "What do you mean by 'How did I do it?' How the hell did I do what?"

Trying her hardest to remain composed, Lola sighed, "How the hell did you know Ronan was my husband, you smug asshole!"

"Honestly, I had no clue. If you recall my words from your birthday, *Vixen*, I clearly stated that this was an interesting turn of events. You seem awfully full of yourself to think my thought process is solely consumed with you." Jacob seethed as he prepared to take his leave.

"Look, Jacob-" Lola called out, grabbing Jacob's arm. "I'm sorry, okay! I didn't mean to offend you. I'm just in this really weird headspace right now."

"I get it, *Vix*, but you'd do well to watch your words and mind your tone." Jacob directed, taking his seat once more.

As their food arrived, Lola asked one final question. "Where the hell do we stand, Jacob?"

Gears quickly turning within the hunter's mind, Jacob emphasized, "Where do **you** want us to stand, *Vix*?"

Silence echoed around the small table, as Lola thought long and hard about Jacob's rebuttal. Finally exiting the restaurant, Lola was able to carefully craft a response. "What I want, Jacob is a friendship to form. I don't want a relationship, because I'm still trying to process the divorce, but..."

Nervously rubbing her arm, as bile began to rise from the pit of her stomach, Lola all but handed her oppressor the key to her psychological enclosure, as she uttered her next statement. "... b-but I don't mind if we have sex. The truth is, and as fucked up as this sounds, I often find myself longing for your touch and how you made me feel- just minus the excruciating pain from your '*games*'."

Jacob smirked in satisfaction, "Well, *Vixen*, if that's what you **really** want, then who am I to deny you."

"More than anything, I am beginning to see just how right you really have been all along. You are the only one who actually gets me."

~

February 14, 2009

True to his word, Logan returned to Oregon on the date of his 25th birthday; giving Lola a call as soon as he pulled into the driveway of his dad's house. Exiting his driver's side, Logan held his phone to his ear, making his way inside. "Yeah- well, I just walked into Dad's house. Why don't you come over to the house and join us for a little birthday dinner? Alright, see you tonight, Lola. Lo … uh, bye."

Hanging up, Logan sighed heavily, before seeking out his dad and Cate. Warmly embracing the couple, Logan filled them in on everything that had occurred in Los Angeles. Wiping the tears from her eyes, Cate choked out, "Th-that poor girl! Is she healing okay?"

Before Logan could answer, Cade somberly asked, "How's Antonio **really** holding up? Your mom said he kept putting on a brave face."

Logan sighed once more as he fought back the bitter tears that threatened to break free. "Launa is healing okay, physical therapy is really helping. And as for *Zio*, he's keeping a brave face like mom said, but he was crumbling. We both got some use out of his shooting range." Wanting to change the subject to anything other than what had heavily weighed on his mind over the last month, Logan asked what all had gone on for Cate and Cade.

Cate stated that it had been business as usual before asking, "H-have you talked to Luxie any since you've been gone?"

Seeing Cate's sorrowful expression, Logan grew concerned. "Honestly, not until right before I walked in to talk with you guys. I saw she called- I don't even know how many times, but I just wasn't in the right headspace to talk to her."

"Shit!" Cate groaned. Seeing the perplexed look on Logan's face, Cate filled him in on the dismal demise of Lola's marriage; the news hitting Logan like a ton of bricks.

"Are you serious? She didn't even say anything when I talked to her just a little bit ago. Have you guys talked to her lately?" Logan fumed.

"I haven't heard anything from her since she called me a few days after walking in on Ronan and Elin. I'm honestly worried about her. I called Lizzie, and she said the same thing." Cate confessed.

Having let the heavy news settle into the background, like an early morning fog, Cade spoke several minutes later. "Son, we don't want your birthday to be so focused on everyone else's sadness, so if you're ready, Cate and I would like to give you your gift."

With Logan's nod of approval, Cate took a small, white box from her purse before handing it to Logan as she spoke. "I know you love staying here at our house when you come up to visit, and we love having you, but…"

"Is this what I think it is?" Logan gleefully interjected, taking the small item from the box.

Cade laughed at his son's excitement. "Yes, it's the key to Cate's- well, now your- apartment above the café; if you want it, that is."

Logan thanked Cate and Cade profusely for their generous gift before the trio settled into lively conversation as they worked together to prepare the evening's meal. Two hours later, Logan rushed to the front door with the sounding of the bell. Opening the door, he smiled brightly at the rosy-haired beauty standing before him.

"I know I look good, Warren, but are you gonna let me in or sit there and stare?" Lola playfully teased, as she extended a medium-sized, blue gift bag.

Accepting the bag with bashful laughter, Logan let Lola in, before leading her into the dining room. The delicious aromas permeated the house, causing Lola's stomach to growl with a vengeance. "Everything smells amazing, Cate!" Lola exclaimed as she pulled out her chair.

In each seat, was a beautifully dressed plate consisting of a tenderloin steak, grilled to perfection, seasoned winter greens, roasted potatoes, and a loaf of homemade white bread. Once everyone had eaten their fill, Logan told Lola he'd like to unpack his suitcase before opening his gift. "You're welcome to join me if you'd like." Nodding in agreement, Lola politely excused herself from the table as she followed Logan down the hall.

When Logan had put all of his belongings away, he sat on the bed, patting the open space beside him. After Lola was seated, Logan opened the gift; awestruck by yet another amazing gift from Lola. "I wasn't sure what to get you, or if you're even still into photography," Lola began to explain, "but I thought you might like a custom leather, camera bag."

Before he could speak, Logan was cut off by the buzzing of Lola's phone, followed by a giddy laugh as a blush crept upon her face. Never one to shy away from his curious nature, Logan boldly asked who she was messaging.

Not wanting to cause tension or ruin Logan's birthday, Lola quickly slipped back into the erroneous haven of her lies. "Oh, umm, just a friend that I met through a business meeting with another company. He just sent me a funny inside joke."

Deep within his gut, Logan knew something was off in Lola's sentiment. However, he chose to forego his instincts to savor the small window of time he had with the woman he was falling in love with.

"So...," Lola began, sitting cross-legged on Logan's bed, as she contemplated whether or not she should even ask her questions.

"So, what?"

"So, what happened in Los Angeles? You just straight up ghosted me!"

Not wanting to delve into this subject for a second time that evening, Logan bitterly spat, "Don't- I don't want to fucking talk about it!"

"I-I'm sorry, Logan!" Lola cried out, a bit wide-eyed and weepy.

"No, I'm the one who should be sorry," Logan confessed. "I was a complete ass just now." Seeing Lola give a weak smile, Logan continued, "It's still pretty fresh, and hurts like hell. I'll tell you anything else you wanna know. M'kay?"

Trying her best to fight back the tears, as she had never once heard Logan raise his voice, Lola excused herself to the restroom. Feeling overwhelmed by both the weight of her emotions and her meal, Lola knew one of those things had to go.

After rinsing the bile's residue from her mouth, Lola sighed as she gazed upon her reflection. *Surely everyone has things they wish to keep to themselves. God- how many times have I snapped at people when they hit a sore subject?*

Walking back into the room, Lola was thankful Logan didn't seem to notice the length of her absence. "Do you think I can ask another question?" Lola meekly inquired as she sat back upon the bed.

"Like I said, you can ask me anything else."

"Okay, so what happened with you and Naja? I was surprised that she wasn't here tonight."

Yawning as he glanced at the time, Logan replied, "I'll give you the abridged version for now. I didn't like the person I was becoming. I chose to let her go because we spent more time fighting than getting along. We both deserve happiness, and that meant me letting her go."

"That makes sense," Lola stated as she stood to leave.

"Don't go just yet, I figured we could end the night with a movie," Logan suggested as he clicked on the t.v.

"Oh, fine!" Lola jested. "Only 'cause it's your birthday!"

Laying her head against the pillow, Lola succumbed to the weight of her exhaustion, not making it past the opening credits.

~

August 2, 2009

August arrived in the blink of an eye, and with it, the decomposition of a lifelong companionship. Although coming to an agreement with Jacob back in January had gone far smoother than Lola could have expected, and he made sure to respect the boundaries *she* put in place, Lola couldn't help but slowly become consumed by him once again. This consumption would have occurred at a much faster pace had Jacob not traveled frequently for work, and had Logan not continually made his presence known.

Lola awoke the morning of her 25th birthday feeling elated. She had decided a month prior to host her own birthday dinner in the ballroom of her hotel. After a brief phone call with the kitchen's chef, finalizing the last-minute details of the dinner menu, Lola began working on her own birthday cake. *Hopefully, today is going to be a great day. Well, at this point, anything has to be better than last year's fiasco.*

Later that afternoon, as Lola glanced at the clock, she realized time had quickly slipped away. After the quickest shower of her life, Lola put on a midi length, sage green, silk, slip dress with spaghetti straps; and a pair of nude-colored, dressy sandals. Glancing at her reflection, Lola touched up her curls with some defining cream, before adding a tiny bit of makeup.

Lola beamed brightly as she walked into the venue; though her party was small, it still brought joy to her heart to see almost all of the people she cared for the most, present. Gazing around the room, Lola became lost in thought. *Looks like Jacob isn't going to make it. I know he said that he may have to work, but oh, well.*

Pushing the discouraging ideas to the back of her mind, Lola smiled as she saw Cate and Lizzie engaging in what looked like a rather serious, yet jovial, conversation. Had Lola known the true contents of their conversation, her smile would have faltered. Having connected during Lola's wedding planning, Cate and Lizzie began meeting weekly to hang out as friends. However, after the divorce, they also began discussing their growing concern for Lola's well-being. Both women felt helpless, as they slowly watched their friend's waistline diminish, day by day.

Setting off in the direction of her friends, Lola was cut off by Logan, as he held out an obnoxiously large gift bag in his right hand while rubbing the back of his neck nervously with the left. "Happy birthday, Lola!"

Graciously accepting the gift, Lola set it on the floor before embracing Logan and offering her thanks. "Thank you for the gift, Logan. I'm really glad you could make it."

Moving back a couple of steps, Logan cleared his throat in hopes of covering the blush which now resided upon his cheeks. "Ahem- N-no need to thank me, Lola. I'm happy to be here with you. So, where would you like me to set this monstrosity?" Logan asked as he reached for the gift once more before Lola quickly grabbed it.

"Let me set this with the others. I want you to just enjoy your time here. Why don't you go over and talk with Mark or your dad?" Lola directed before taking a peek inside the bag, as she walked to the gift table; eyes going wide with delight. Tucked safely inside was a beautiful merlot-colored tote, made from the softest leather Lola had ever felt.

After a quick embrace from Gregory, along with Lizzie's parents, Luke and Patricia, everyone sat down to enjoy their meal.

~

As the night wore on, Lola found herself checking her phone far more than what would be deemed socially acceptable, while absent-mindedly pushing her food around on her plate; before finally slipping out quietly to the restroom. The generous amount of wine she had consumed throughout the evening was now painfully pushing against her bladder.

After relieving herself and washing her hands, Lola was startled by a voice as she exited the bathroom. "Happy birthday, *Vixen.*"

"Shit!" Lola called out as Jacob chuckled. "You scared the hell out of me, Jacob."

Wrapping his arms around Lola's waist as he pressed her body against the wall, Jacob took in Lola's scent as playfully noted, "Someone's rather drunk!"

Sloppily bringing her finger to Jacob's lips, Lola shushed him, "Only a little, but don't tell anyone." Before kissing him passionately.

"Damn, *Vix*, if you kiss me like that again, I'm gonna fuck you right here." Jacob breathlessly spoke once the kiss ended.

"That's what the after-party is for, *Mr. Icy Eyes!*" Lola tantalized while leading Jacob into the ballroom.

When Jacob's dark aura crossed the threshold of the ballroom, all conversation ceased. Shock resonated inside the minds of several guests, while others were simply confused by the presence of such a powerful man. A glass shattering in the background followed by a guttural scream caught everyone's attention.

"Shit, shit, shit!" Mark repeated, instantly recognizing the scream, before running in vain towards his wife.

A mixture of anger and heartache filled Logan's countenance as he watched Lizzie move at an almost inhumanly quick pace before slapping Jacob across his smug face. Not wanting to see anymore, Logan sent Lola a text stating *"I hope you know what you're doing-"*, before slipping out unnoticed.

Finally reaching his wife, it took all of Mark's strength to pull Lizzie away, but not before she drew blood from Jacob's neck with her fingernails. Wiping the blood from his neck, Jacob looked at Mark with darkened eyes, as he spat out, "A wise man keeps his *beast* locked away!"

"Lola Luxe Swan. Lobby. **Now!**" Lizzie seethed after shaking herself free from Mark.

"What the hell is going on, Luxie?" Lizzie asked once they were out of the ballroom.

"Oh, hell no! If anyone gets to ask that question, it's me, *Elizabeth*!" Lola spat.

"What the fuck is wrong with you, Luxie? Why would you bring that evil bastard here? Why would you hurt Logan like that?"

"What does Logan have to do with anything?" Lola asked, clearly confused.

"Everyone in that fucking room can see how much he loves you, but you're too stupid to see it!" Lizzie raged on.

"Fuck you, Lizzie! Logan is my friend, just like Jacob. I'm a fucking adult who doesn't need permission from the likes of *you*, as to who the hell I invite to my own damn party!" Lola retorted before adding words to cut Lizzie deep within her core. "I'm so fucking sorry that my life is shit compared to your ideal one, *Elizabeth*! We can't always have the perfect dream, so take whatever this is between us, and shove it so far up your stuck-up ass! I don't need you in my life, *bitch*!"

43

Blue Moon, Guinness, and Blarney

November 1, 2015

After reliving the memories of the dissolution of her lifelong friendship with Lizzie, Lola asked for a few days before moving forward. "I appreciate the mental break, Logan. Besides, where we pick back up will be a pretty big move forward in time. So … I guess, I should probably prepare myself for that." Giving Logan a tender peck on the lips, Lola readied herself for bed.

Reciprocating Lola's affection, Logan quickly glanced at the time on his phone. "Since it's only a little after ten, and I'm not tired yet, I think I'll go for a drive. Are you okay with that?"

Seeing Lola nod in affirmation, before resting her weary head upon the pillow, Logan grabbed his keys and a jacket, making his way to his car.

Driving aimlessly through the night, Logan found himself parked outside of **The British Punk**. Feeling thankful it was a Sunday night, and the bar wasn't overly packed, Logan sent a quick text before making his way inside. Greeting Maeve and Naja with a warm embrace, Logan took a seat while strumming his fingers absentmindedly on the bar.

"Ya keep that up, yer gonna wear a hole through my bar top," Maeve teased before asking, "What ya gettin' tonight? And none of this 'straight-edge' nonsense. Yer face clearly says ya need a beer."

"That transparent tonight, huh?" Logan chuckled with a shake of his head, moving his bangs from his eyes. Receiving a wink from Maeve, Logan asked her to pass him a bottle of **Blue Moon**. "How much is it?"

"For you, darlin', it's on the house," Maeve acknowledged, giving Logan a motherly peck on his cheek. Never having children of her own, Logan and his friends held a special place inside of Maeve's heart.

Walking over to Naja, who was serving a dapper gentleman, Maeve pulled her to the side. "Does Logan seem a bit off to ya tonight?"

"Not really any different than any other time Lola has been in his life," Naja crossed her arms with a huff.

"I feel it in my gut, Nae. Somethin's different. Almost like somethin' changed in him after the party."

"I don't know, Maeve. I still care for Logan a lot, same as you, but I can't be dealin' with him when he's stuck so far up that soulless, ginger bitch's ass. Now if you'll excuse me, Maeve, Derek's needin' a refill."

The clock behind the bar slowly ticked away as Logan watched the condensation pool at the base of his bottle. Hearing a familiar voice greeting Maeve, Logan looked up to see Mark had finally made an appearance. "Hey, Maeve! Hit me with a pitcher of **Guinness** and a bottle of whatever Logan has," before walking over to greet Logan with brotherly affection.

"Why don't we grab a table," Logan suggested.

Gathering his order from Maeve, Mark led the way to a back table. "So- what's up, man? Not that I'm not happy to hang out, but usually Lola'd be with you and you'd ask me to bring *The Hurricane* along."

Logan laughed at Mark's nickname for his wife. "Lizzie being that crazy, huh?"

"Ugh- you don't even know the half of it man," Mark groaned before smiling to himself. "But that's why I love her. She keeps me on my toes."

"Y'all definitely balance each other out," Logan mused, as he fell silent. Taking a sip from his lukewarm beer, Logan finally answered Mark's initial question with a hefty sigh. "Since you've known Lola the longest, aside from Lizzie, I feel like I can talk to you about what's goin' on in my head lately."

"Sure, man. Shoot!" Mark encouraged.

"The only person I have been able to talk to so far is my *Zio*, but he doesn't know Lola. I could talk to my dad and Cate, but I think dad's just trying to be there for Cate. Everything that came out about Jacob really took its toll on her. And the rest of my friends and family, aside from Luka … well … let's just say they all think I'm bat shit crazy for even having anything to do with Lola." Logan paused, trying to get his thoughts in order.

"I can understand how they think that because the whole situation is fucked up. But it's just because they care about you and hate seeing you hurt. They don't know Luxie, so in their minds, it's pretty easy to paint her as this soulless siren." Mark paused seeing the look of confusion on Logan's face. "Your friend at the bar, Naja, was going off to another customer about Luxie."

Logan chuckled as he shook his head, "Let's just say that's mild compared to the things my mom has said."

"That bad, huh?" Mark asked. Seeing Logan's grimacing nod, he continued, "Look, even though Lizzie knows more than I do, which I'm sure probably isn't even half of what Luxie has confided in you, she's one of the most selfless people I know. It pisses me off when other people are so fucking closed-minded and just judge her from their damn high horses!" Mark protested, aggressively slamming his hand on the table before chugging his beer.

"That's exactly how I feel," Logan admitted, as he took another swig. "Back in September, I ended up having a fucking panic attack. And I can't talk about it, because everyone will, again, blame Lola."

"Shit! What happened?"

Logan relayed the events leading up to his panic attack to Mark, who listened intently while pouring himself another glass from the pitcher. Once Logan had filled Mark in on what happened, he downed the rest of his room-temperature bottle and grabbed the one Mark had waiting for him.

"I know you probably don't want to hear this," Mark suggested, "but have you considered talking to a therapist? Luxie's tellin' you some heavy shit, and it's gotta be hard as hell holding it in on your own."

"Honestly, no," Logan confessed. "I've started trying to write some songs here and there because the guys have been on my ass about getting back together and debuting a new album. Music has always helped in the past when things have been too deep, but I just feel like I have to be there for her all the time."

"Did you ever tell Luxie you were the lead singer of **Beyond Oregon**?"

"No. I guess I just always liked the fact that she enjoyed my company for who I am as a person, and not for some kind of celeb clout." Logan confided.

"My dude, that's a hella big secret to keep from her all these years." Mark admonished.

"I know … I fucking know … ugh- on a level of one to I need to change my identity, how pissed do you think she'll be?" Logan warily inquired.

"If it were Lizzie, she would rain down hellfire and brimstone, but Luxie- I honestly think she'd be hurt more than anything," Mark admitted as he sadly patted his friend on the back.

Settling into a more relaxed conversation, Mark flagged Naja down for two more pitchers of beer, along with a glass for Logan. Minutes quickly slipped into hours, with Mark and Logan laughing boisterously at their table. "Alright, lads," Maeve chastised, "it's time ya be gettin' on. I'd like to close up shop."

With a failed attempt at batting his large eyes, Logan doubled over in laughter before proceeding to sweet talk Maeve in his drunken stupor. "Oh, Maevey. You's luuusss me!"

"Hells bells!" Maeve cursed under her breath. "Mark, yer takin' his drunken ass home wit' ya."

"Nah, Maeve," Mark giggled excitedly. "Daddy's about to get laid! And if I brink him home, Lizzie's gonna fret and I ain't gettin' none."

Hearing her husband's obnoxiously, drunken giggle, Lizzie sighed. "Thanks for calling me, Maeve," before leaning into Maeve's ear and whispering, "He only thinks he's gettin' laid. He's a damn fool if he thinks I want to be fucking his sloppy, drunk self. Trust me, you only make that mistake twice."

Cringing at the image now flashing like a neon sign in her mind, Maeve paused for a minute before replying, "No need to thank me, hun. I guess I'll be puttin' Logan up in Naja's apartment upstairs." Turning to the man still seated at the bar, Maeve requested for him to help get Mark to Lizzie's car. "Once yer done, help Nae and I get this lush to her apartment."

"Nae, Nae, Nae! Guess what?" Logan yelled out as he ran up to Naja, where he announced that it was a slumber party.

Shaking her head as she placed Logan's arm over her shoulders, Naja chuffed. "Now I know why your ass never drinks. You're about as easy to maneuver as a fucking tree, given you're roughly the same size."

Walking up the stairs, Logan babbled on nonsensically, before saying, "I gots a secret. I luuusss Lola so much, it fucccking hursss. You know, gingerrrsss has souls, right?"

Naja sighed in relief as Derek arrived just in time to help her lie Logan back across the sofa. Feeling Logan pull on her hand, she responded to his statements, "I know, bud. I know."

Sitting back up, Logan patted the couch for Naja to sit down beside him. "I has another secrets, Nae. You there," he said to Derek, "you sits too. M'kay?"

"I'm sorry D," Naja apologized. "For as long as I have known Logan, I swear I have never seen him drunk. Maeve said she felt something was off tonight, and well, I guess she was right."

Looking down into the silver eyes that complimented Naja's golden complexion, Derek kissed the young woman he was deeply falling for, though ten years his junior, gently upon the forehead. Smiling weakly at Derek's tender compassion, Naja allowed herself to sit beside her ex and ask, "What's your secret Logan?"

Rubbing his eyes as he fought to stay awake, the mass quantity of alcohol now trying to lull him into its comforting slumber, Logan slurred. "Nae, I's sorries for being a shit boyfriend." When Naja began to interject, Logan placed his finger upon her lips to silence her. "Shh! Listen, m'kay?"

Seeing Naja's nodded agreement, Logan continued. "I was shit 'cause I useded you. I loveded Lola since college, but I became a man I didn't wants to be." Stopping to organize the drunken thoughts that otherwise would have stayed buried within the caverns of his heart, Logan finally started once more. "Ya know, I haven't had sex with anyone since you, Nae."

"What the hell, Logan?" Naja groaned out in deep embarrassment.

Silencing her once again with a finger to her lips, Logan repri-manded. "You no talky, only listen. Now, it's not that I haven't wanted to … with Lola … but Jacob has fucked her up sssooo bad. Not jussss all over her body, butttt in here." Logan stated as he tapped Naja's temple. Finally allowing sleep to overtake him, Logan drowsily murmured, "I just hope she knows how much I luuusss hers."

Hearing Logan's words deeply pained Naja; while, admittedly, she wasn't Lola's biggest fan, feelings of shame arose within her. Grabbing Logan's phone, as she fought back her tears, Naja sent Lola a quick text. *Hey- it's Naja. Logan came down to the bar. Met Mark and both got drunk. Maeve moved Logan up to my apartment- he's on my couch. My man, Derek, is gonna help me keep an eye on him. I'll have Logan call you when he's awake.*

"Hey, *Ail*," Derek called as he gently caught Naja by the hand. "Are you okay? And don't lie to me, because you do know that reading people is literally my job."

"Trust me, I know, *Mr. Therapist*," Naja retorted before taking a few calming breaths. "Let me grab a blanket to cover up Logan, and then we can head into my room to talk. Deal?"

After Derek's nod of agreement, Naja covered Logan with a blanket, before moving his hair from his eyes as she whispered, "While I still don't like her, I'm trying to hate Lola a little less for you."

Finally making her way to her bedroom, Naja slipped out of her work clothes and into a comfortable, silk sleep set. Settling in beside Derek on her bed, Naja breathed a sigh of contentment. "Wanna finally fill me in on what's going on in that beautifully braided head?"

"Not really, but I guess I have no other choice. Since *Dr. D* is makin' a house call." Naja jested with a wiggle of her eyebrows.

"You know what that does to me, *Ail*!" Derek groaned.

"Why do you think I said it, *Dr. D*?" Naja smirked before switching to a more serious tone. "As you are more than well aware, I don't like Lola. Never have really. I just felt like she always came off as this stuck-up, rich, white bitch who could just throw money around and make everything better. And it just seemed like she was always *too* friendly with Logan."

Listening intently, Derek asked, "Okay, so- what about Logan's words caused tears to well up. It was like your whole countenance changed."

Thinking for a few moments, Naja finally admitted her transgressions. "I guess I didn't realize how deranged Jacob really was."

Naja's past with Jacob was not particularly her finest hour, however, at the time being able to rub it in Lola's face made Naja feel like she was paying Lola back. "I know sleeping with an already involved guy is petty as hell, but that's who I was at that time. Angry and petty. I was angry that Logan and I broke up. I know we weren't good together, but it pissed me off that he was so in love with someone who continued to put herself and Jacob constantly in front of him."

Pausing for a drink of water, Naja continued, "That's why, when Jacob started flirting with me at the bar, I didn't hesitate to take him up on his offer. So now, I have this stupid letter Lola gave me back at the end of August, that I haven't read *and* Logan's words both weighing on me."

"How do you know the letter is stupid if you haven't read it?" Derek countered.

"Your smart ass knows what I mean, D." Naja snapped.

"It may ease your conscience and your heart if you read it." Derek stated while adding, "And by that look on your face, you know I'm right!"

With a roll of her eyes, Naja walked over to her dresser to retrieve the letter. Settling back in beside Derek, Naja read contents aloud.

Dear Naja,

While I've never been one to be good with words or even emotions for that matter, my therapist recommended that I write letters to important people in my life. I have no idea if you'll ever read this, and if you don't, no hard feelings. I just wanted to say that I am truly sorry for any heartache or harm I may have caused you in the past. It was never my intention for you and Logan to break up, and I'm sorry if for some reason that was my fault. As for finding you with Jacob, I don't blame you for that.

Hell, I know better than anyone just how magnetic he truly is. I know you probably think of me as a 'dumb bitch' for having stayed with him for so long when the very reason I divorced my husband was for infidelity. But, hey- low self-esteem and diminished self-worth makes us all do 'dumb bitch' things. I don't expect that we will ever be the best of friends, and I'm okay with that. What I would like is for us to at least be cordial for Logan's sake if nothing else.

~Always, Lola.

Unsure of what to truly make of Lola's words, Naja stored them away in her heart, as she placed the letter back on her dresser before allowing sleep to overtake her.

~

November 2, 2015

"I feel like shit!" Logan announced as he awoke the following morning. "Ugh- I'm never drinking that much again."

Taking in his surroundings, Logan first wondered how he ended up in Naja's apartment, then, concern for Lola hit him like an avalanche. *Shit! The last thing she knew was that I was just going for a drive.*

Grabbing his phone from the coffee table, Logan sighed in relief when he saw that Naja had graciously sent Lola a message. Seeing Naja in the kitchen, Logan stretched out his limbs as spoke. "Hey, Nae. Thanks for letting me crash here. I don't even know what the hell happened last night, but I appreciate it. Also, thanks for texting

Lola."

"Don't mention it, Logan. Friends gotta look out for each other. Anyhow, your lanky ass is heavy as hell!"

"It's all muscle, Nae!" Logan teased as he exited the apartment. Finally reaching his car, Logan called Lola to let her know he was on his way back and asked if she wanted any breakfast. Stopping in a drive-thru just outside of Parkway, Logan placed their order, then made his way home.

Opening the door, Logan was greeted by the smell of fresh coffee. "Mmm- smells amazing! What flavor did Cate send up?"

"Good morning," Lola greeted cheerily. "Cate sent up a maple roast; however, none for you until you drink some water. Lizzie called me after she picked up Mark and explained everything, but I'm glad Naja sent that text."

The cool water slid down Logan's parched throat, refreshing every cell inside of his body. "This is why I don't drink," Logan groaned. "Hangovers are a bitch!"

"Why don't we have breakfast and a movie?" Lola suggested. "After that, I need to call Dr. Indigo and make a few phone calls for work."

Scarfing down the breakfast sandwich, greasy hashbrowns, and two cups of coffee, Logan finally felt content as the hangover's symptoms had all but dissipated. "Best pillow ever," Logan exclaimed as he plopped his head onto Lola's thighs; he knew that **this** was everything he needed in life.

44

Lonely Days

November 16, 2015

Two weeks had passed since Logan and Lola's last conversation regarding her past, and Logan's drunken evening. During that time, Lola filled her days with regular phone sessions with Dr. Indigo, as well as teleconferences with Gregory, Marina, Jade, and Daisy. Although she was no longer directly employed by Lola, Marina enjoyed keeping in touch and helping in whatever ways she could.

After this morning's session with Dr. Indigo, Lola felt slightly disheartened, but knew by now that Dr. Indigo's words often held great value. Sighing deeply as she ended the call, Lola decided to walk over to the café for a quick chat with Cate before having to pick back up with Logan.

"I hope you have a good time with Cate, *my heart*," Logan said, catching Lola as she headed out the door.

Lola smiled as she saw Logan hoist the camera bag she had given him six years ago, onto his shoulder. "I'm glad to see my gift was such a hit."

"It's definitely my favorite to take for shoots that don't require many lens changes." Logan remarked, before adding, "That reminds me- I have that five-generation photo shoot outside of Vienna, so I probably won't be back until sometime tomorrow. Will you be okay?" To which Lola reassured him with a passionate kiss, preceding her exit.

Inside the café, Cate smiled brightly as she saw Lola come in. While things would never fully be the same between the two women, a door Jacob closed long ago, Cate's heart was filled with hope for the new path they were forging. "Hey, Luxie! What can I get you this morning?"

"Hey, Cate..." Lola sighed heavily once more. "If you have a few minutes, I'd love to have scones and a chat like we used to."

"Well, my dear, you're in luck. I just so happened to pull out the recipe for those orange-cranberry scones you loved so much back in high school." Cate beamed as she added, "Why don't you go take these plates to our favorite spot, while I get the coffee and a tray of fresh scones that are about to come from the oven."

Taking the plates, Lola walked to the small table that was now directly in front of an oversized bookshelf. "This shelf is new!" Lola exclaimed when Cate arrived, hands full.

"What do you think? I thought a little reading nook would be perfect here. I mean I already had the oversized armchairs and this vintage side table."

"I think it's absolutely perfect, Cate," Lola said before taking a sip of her warm coffee.

Enjoying their baked goods for a few minutes, Cate finally asked, "What did you want to talk about?"

"I had a session with Dr. Indigo, and while I know she's right, I just want to vent a little," Lola admitted. With Cate's encouraging nod, Lola recanted her earlier conversation. "I'm not sure if you're aware or not, but the annual gala for **Swan Industries** is next month. The last one I attended was right before ... well, I don't think I need to go into details on that."

Wiping a stray tear from her cheek, Cate asked Lola to continue on. "I know that Uncle Greg, Jade, and Daisy have all done a tremendous job in managing everything, but I was really hoping to move forward and finally attend my first gala in four years."

"By your tone, I take it Dr. Indigo didn't agree with this."

"No-" Lola replied flatly. "She said that I have made such amazing progress with the pace we're moving at now, that she'd hate for me to have another relapse."

"What do you mean by 'another relapse'?" Cate inquired with confusion etched upon her brow.

Mentally face-palming herself, Lola went on to explain that her original stay at the clinic had only been for six months; fighting Dr. Indigo with everything she had. Upon her release from the clinic, Lola immediately tried returning to work. However, as soon as she entered the floor of her office, panic set in. "My heart started to feel like it was going to burst through my chest. I felt like everyone was staring … whispering … judging all of my hidden secrets. According to Uncle Greg, I hit my head on the corner of a desk as I crashed to the ground."

"Oh my gosh!" Cate worriedly interjected.

"After that, Uncle Greg was pretty firm. Actually, I think that was the strictest I've ever seen him in my life. He told me that if I didn't adhere to the proper guidelines from Dr. Indigo, then everything would be taken from me." Lola explained.

"Damn, girl! That's some crazy shit." Cate exclaimed, before trying to encourage her friend, "I can see why Dr. Indigo wants you to wait though."

"Even though I hate to admit it, I honestly can too," Lola exclaimed before finishing up her treats. Glancing at her watch, she realized two hours had easily slipped on by. "Thanks for listening, Cate. I'd better get back to the apartment. It's been two weeks, and I should probably ready my mind to pick back up with telling Logan how things transpired the way they did."

Hugging her friend warmly, before she left, Cate prayed a silent prayer asking God to give Lola the strength she needed to carry on.

~

November 17, 2015

It was mid-afternoon by the time Logan had returned home. Entering the door, he smiled as he saw Lola curled up on the sofa, once again devouring her favorite book. Draping his lanky arms around her shoulders, Logan announced, "There are other books, you know?"

Dog earring her spot, Lola closed the book, then glanced up at Logan. "I know there are other books, but this one just holds such a soft spot for me. Plus, I'm just biding my time until *E.R. Blackwell* releases something new."

After playfully ruffling Lola's hair, Logan jumped over the back of the couch before Lola had a chance to swat at him. "You asshole! How many times do I have to tell you that you can't just mess with my curls." Lola laughed as she feigned anger.

"I can't help it, *my heart,* I just love them." Logan expressed as he batted his deep azure eyes at her.

Rolling her own eyes back at him, Lola smoothed out her disheveled hair as she asked how Logan's trip had been. "It was really nice. The family I did the shoot for was celebrating the great-great-grandfather's 100th birthday, and since his health is declining, they wanted to commemorate the event with a shoot of the five family generations."

"Wow! That's so amazing." Lola exclaimed in awe.

Following an early dinner filled with light-hearted conversation, Lola asked Logan if they could go on an evening stroll. "I think I have delayed the past long enough," she remarked as she held up a few items. "Besides, the night's supposed to be clear, so I was thinking we could find an open clearing on the trail, roast some marshmallows for s'mores, and set up a quilt to do a little star gazing."

Logan readily agreed to Lola's plan; of course, he would willingly do almost anything that meant more time with her. Loading up the oversized canvas tote with their supplies, Logan placed the bag on his shoulder, before grabbing Lola's hand and walking out the door.

~

December 31, 2009

After the fiasco better known as her 25th birthday, Lola began to fall into a dismal state of despair; her only companions, aside from the deleterious voices in her head, were Logan and Jacob. Both of whom vied for her attention in such drastically different means, but only one would shine a light bright enough to channel her demise. For he truly was a demon in disguise, with nefarious intent laced behind such enchanting, icy eyes.

Though the seasons around her had changed, inside of Lola's mind, there was only a cold, lonely winter. Standing upon the stage to give her annual speech, a stagnant misery filled Lola's countenance. *Do they even really care about the* **Center***? Hell, do I even really care? Do I care about anything at all? Would anyone even truly miss me if I was gone?*

Stepping off the stage, Lola plastered on her best smile as countless guests began to barrage her with queries and trivial pleasantries until she was finally able to successfully deflect the guests in Gregory's direction.

Walking out to the garden area, Lola inhaled the crisp, frosty air as she allowed its bite to settle on her barren shoulders and arms. Pulling a pack of cigarettes from her clutch purse, a voice scoffed in the background. "You know those things will kill you, right?"

Not needing to turn around to face the owner, Lola chattered out, "Apparently so will a million other things, but hey- we're all gonna die at some point, right, Warren?"

Placing his jacket on Lola's shoulders before removing the cigarette from her lips, Logan scolded, "While that may be true, Lola, I don't think you should speed the process along with this weird combo of frostbite and lung cancer."

Far too mentally exhausted to come back with her usual quip, Lola's only response was a weathered sigh as she stared blankly into the starry abyss.

"Hey, Lola-" Logan began, finally finding the courage to speak again. Hearing her hum in response, he continued, "Are you okay? I mean like really-really okay? You seem so different after your birthday."

"I'm just … tired, I guess. Don't worry so much, especially about someone like me, Logan." Lola remarked while patting Logan on the arm, and returning his jacket.

"Before you go, can I ask you something?"

"What's up, Warren?"

"I know it's still a couple of months away from my birthday, and I was thinking of going to see the **Winterhawks** play a game. Not sure if you're a hockey fan, but I thought it would be a fun thing to do this year." Logan spoke as he nervously awaited Lola's response. *What the hell was I just thinking? I'm not even a hockey fan- shit! I guess I had better ask Dean for his passes that night. I just hope mom doesn't kill me.*

Allowing herself to genuinely smile for the first time since her birthday, Lola accepted Logan's offer. "I'll be honest, I'm not really into sports, but I think it could be fun." Giving Logan a friendly peck on his cheek, Lola thanked Logan for his gracious invitation before excusing herself. "As I said, I'm tired, so I'm gonna head out.

We'll talk soon though. Yeah?"

~

February 14, 2010

Logan nervously paced back and forth outside the arena, as he waited for Lola to walk up. Feeling the night air slice through him, Logan rubbed his gloved hands together, to keep the blood flow moving. A tap on the glass behind him caught Logan's attention.

"Hey, mate. We're gonna have to shut the gates. Are you sure the rest of your party's on the way?"

"She will be, sir, she promised," Logan answered the impatient Will Call attendant.

"Must be a nice piece of ass for you to wait in the damn cold," the attendant mocked.

Before Logan could lay into the crude man, Lola reached Logan, as she wheezed. "S-sorry t-t-to … Oh god! I am out of shape!" Catching her breath, Lola offered a proper apology.

Smiling brightly as he puffed out his chest, Logan handed the attendant his tickets; then took Lola by the hand, leading her inside the arena. "My step-dad always buys center ice tickets, he says they're the best to see the game overall," Logan said as they settled in.

"Sorry again for cutting it so close," Lola admitted. "Normally I wouldn't have to work on a Sunday, but I have a meeting this coming week to discuss the financial projections for the next quarter. I know it's not an excuse, but I really did lose track of time."

"No need to apologize, I'm just glad you made it."

"I'm glad I made it too, Warren. How's your birthday so far?" Lola inquired.

"Well, I'll be honest that it can suck sharing your birthday with the biggest couples' holiday, particularly when you're single. But, my friends and I celebrated last night with a gig at ***The British Punk***."

Curiosity peaked in Lola's mind, as she jested, "A gig? Are you in some kind of band?"

Although there was no real reason for him to lie, that is precisely what Logan did. "My friends are, but me … Nah! I typically am not one to like being in the spotlight. I just help set up events and run their website." Breathing a sigh of relief as Lola seemed to buy into his lie, Logan continued, "This morning I took dad and Cate over to Vienna for a big family celebration with my grandparents, mom, step-dad, and sisters."

After the game, Logan escorted Lola back to her car. "Thanks for celebrating my birthday with me, Lola. I'll be honest, I had no clue what was happening out there on the ice."

"I'm glad I wasn't the only one," Lola laughed out while giving Logan a congenial hug before entering her car. "As much as I'd love to stay and chat, work comes early in the morning."

Sadness flooded Logan's heart as he watched Lola leave. *You stupid idiot! Why didn't you ask her out when you had the chance?*

~

April 25, 2010

Lola awoke the morning of Andy's 26th birthday feeling hollow, and wondered how seven years had passed since she last celebrated with him, and almost nearly just as long from the time of his conviction. Though she initially had every intention of keeping in touch with Andy, Lola realized this, too, was yet another one of her failures. Not having Lizzie in her life was far more difficult than she could have imagined; Lizzie's presence was like a bandage over the wounds of Lola's past, and without her, the hidden turmoil now oozed and festered within Lola, like an infected sore.

Had she known how dismally the day would have ended, Lola would have never visited Andy. In the end, though, Andy saw through Lola's feeble attempts as simply a way to placate her own feelings of guilt.

After verifying that she was in fact on Andy's approved visitor list, and reviewing the dress code, Lola drove to **Oregon State Penitentiary**, located a little over an hour away in Salem, Oregon. While the drive to the prison would have been the perfect time for Lola to contact Lizzie and make things right, Lola's hubris dictated otherwise.

Leaving all of her personal effects with the front guard, Lola strummed her long, red fingernails upon the chipped Formica table, in sync with the ticking of the wall clock, as she patiently waited at the designated visitor's table. The minutes crawled into hours, taking Lola's fleeting hope with them. Turning to leave, Lola was startled by the clearing of a throat behind her. "What the hell are you doing here, Luxie?"

Facing the owner of the voice, tears welled in Lola's eyes as the man who now stood before her was a stark contrast from the boy she knew seven years prior. As Andy took his place at the table across from Lola, she couldn't help but observe all of the changes Andy had gone through. Replacing the waifish, lanky build Andy donned a majority of his life, now sat a broad man, whose rugged aura sliced straight through Lola's spirit. "Happy birthday, Andy," Lola stated weakly.

"Cut the shit, Luxie, and tell me why the hell you are here," Andy spat.

"Is it wrong for a friend to come and wish another friend a happy birthday?"

Laughing wildly for a few moments, before taking on an eerily calm demeanor, Andy gazed across the table with jaded green eyes shooting daggers straight into Lola; his next words dripped acid onto Lola's feeble heart. "Friend? Friend? You stupid, selfish bitch! Do you **really** think you can call yourself my friend? Huh?"

Lola tried to defend herself before Andy cut her off. "If your self-centered ass really cared, you wouldn't be here six-and-a-half years too fucking late! You wanna know who true friends are, bitch?"

Biting her lower lip to keep the tears from falling, Lola let the metallic taste flood her mouth, as Andy continued his deafening rant. "Mark and Lizzie are true friends, unlike you they have visited, written, or called regularly. And, you wanna know something Lizzie finally told me this morning? The real reason why your senseless ass chose to let me rot in this hell?"

Unsure of what Lizzie could have told Andy, Lola foolishly nodded her head, allowing several large tears to splatter upon the table. Leaning in as far as his shackles would allow, Andy uttered the cruelest words he could conjure. "Lizzie told me that you decided to whore yourself out to the one fucking person that you knew Shane detested the most. How can you even claim to have loved him when you allowed yourself to end up with someone like Jacob?

"Ya know, it's honestly probably a good thing Shane is dead at this point because if he knew what you'd done, it would kill him. Fuck! You may as well have been the one to kill him, Luxie! You're a stupid bitch who thinks of only herself and what's going to benefit her the best."

Dumbfounded, Lola sobbed out, "How can you be so cruel, Andy? Look, I'm sorry that I haven't visited. I'll admit that's fucked up on my part, okay? But that doesn't **ever** give you the right to pin Shane's death on me. You don't even know half the shit I've gone through. So, fuck you!"

Laughing once again, as the guard came to retrieve him, Andy mocked, "Oh, boo fucking hoo! Poor Luxie had her little feelings hurt. I'll tell ya right now, being nice only makes you someone's bitch, Luxie."

Watching Andy walk toward the inmate exit, Lola composed

herself before she called out, "For what it's worth Andy, even though you're a dick, I still hope that one day the truth will come out. I know you're innocent. Whether you choose to believe me or not is on you."

Collecting her personal effects, Lola returned to her car before finally letting the last of her hurt flow down her cheeks and out of her palms.

~

May 5, 2010

While Logan and Lola continued to spend time together in the friendliest of manners, nothing more than friendship blossomed between them. Though Logan desired so much more, and his heart literally felt like it would burst with every moment spent together, Lola was content with their current state. On more than one occasion, Lola told Logan that his friendship was truly the only thing that helped her to feel grounded.

"Without Lizzie, I feel lost and hopeless. Cate hasn't pushed me away, but I know she isn't fond of me interacting with Jacob again, so I guess in a way, I've distanced myself from her."

"What exactly is going on between you and Jacob?" Logan finally asked the question that had bore many a hole in the back of his brain. "I don't trust his shady ass as far as I could throw him!"

"Oh, come on, Warren! He isn't **that** bad." Lola quipped, before taking a few moments to carefully craft her next response. "Well … as for Jacob and I … it's complicated at best. I guess the easiest way to label it would be, 'Friends with benefits.'"

Failing at hiding the disgust on his face, Logan cringed when he saw the look of hurt creep into Lola's weathered eyes; her next words lacerating him. "Look, Logan- I know you mean well, and you're a hell of a friend, but I don't need your fucking judgment."

Holding his hands up as he started to defend himself, Lola cut him off. "I know this isn't ideal, and Jacob's a man who's harder than a diamond, but- it is what it is. As my *friend*, you should just support me!"

Knowing the point was now moot, Logan internalized the words he so desperately wanted to speak, hoping that one day he would be able to tell Lola the truth. *Don't you see, Lola, that he is killing you? Supporting you and being your friend doesn't mean that I should stand by and watch him slowly chip away at your soul, leaving you just a husk. But, what do I really know? I'm just a lovesick fool, damned by your captivating presence.*

Feeling the vibration of an incoming text message, Lola removed her phone from her back pocket. Reading the message a couple of times to ensure she read it correctly, she thanked Logan for their time spent together. "I hate to cut our hangout time short, but that was Jacob."

"Speak of the fucking devil," Logan cursed under his breath.

Choosing to ignore Logan's vilifying comment, Lola continued, "I guess we'll get the answer to your earlier question about where Jacob and I stand because he wants me to come over to his house and discuss just that."

Even though Logan wasn't a praying man, nor one who truly knew if God existed, he prayed for Lola. *Whoever is listening out there, please help Lola to see how dangerous this tightrope she's walking on, is. Both ends are burning far too quickly, and it's my fear that she's gonna burn in the midst of it all.*

~

Apprehension settled within the pit of Lola's stomach as she sat in the driveway of Jacob's house. The weighty truth of Andy's words repeatedly stung Lola's heart; she knew Shane detested Jacob more than anything, but Shane wasn't here, so at this point, did it truly matter what he would have thought?

Crossing the threshold of Jacob's door, Lola knew there was no turning back. Pushing back the terrifying memories of the past, Lola crept forward until she found Jacob seated at the dining room table with his laptop, a glass of Scotch, and a cigar smoldering in the ashtray. Lola lightly cleared her throat to garner Jacob's attention.

Lola shuddered excitedly as Jacob looked up from his work, only to seductively run the tip of his tongue across his teeth, as he crooned, "Welcome home, *Vixen*."

45

Ineffable Ferly

November 18, 2015

"If you're good with it, I'd like to continue this tomorrow," Lola yawned and stretched out her cramped limbs, before glancing at her watch. "Well- make that later today, seeing as how it's now three in the morning."

Nodding his head in agreeance, Logan put out the fire before helping Lola pack up their supplies, and heading home.

~

After a few hours of relatively restful sleep, Lola awoke and readied herself for the day. Quickly tossing her hair into a messy bun, before pulling on a pair of black leggings, and a lilac-colored, oversized cable knit sweater; Lola sat down at the kitchen table making a list of final preparations for the friends' Thanksgiving feast she was planning the Saturday after Thanksgiving. Scribbling away, Lola chuckled as she was caught off guard by a warm embrace from behind, and the feeling of two days' scruff nuzzling against the exposed portion of her neck.

"Good morning, *my heart*. Whatcha workin' on?" Logan asked inquisitively.

Tapping Logan's arm affectionately, Lola placed her pen on the table before turning to face Logan. "Oh, just the last-minute details for next Saturday."

"Need any help?" Logan offered as he poured himself a cup of coffee.

"Sure!" Lola exclaimed enthusiastically before adding, "I was thinking of staying at the manor so that I can get everything set up. I know you'll be going to Vienna with your dad and Cate next Thursday, but if you're up for it, I'd love for you to see where I grew up."

"I'd love that more than anything. Let me get a shower, and then we can go to the store, before going to the manor." Pausing before heading back in the direction of his bedroom, Logan remarked, "Ya know, I've always been kinda curious about where you grew up. I'm excited to finally see your foundation."

~

Having asked him to drive separately, Logan looked on in wide-eyed amazement, as Lola filled the trunks of both vehicles, as well as the back seats, with several bulging grocery sacks. Grimacing once more at the unusually long receipt, Logan again inquired, "Are you *sure* you need all of this?"

Although she was slightly annoyed, Lola did her best to keep her tone and temperament in check. "Yes, Logan, for the fiftieth time, I promise you, all of this is needed. No one stays at the manor, and I haven't been since summertime with Cate. I'm hosting Lizzie, Mark, Raelee, Luke, Patricia, and Uncle Greg on Thanksgiving Day, so … yeah."

"If you want, I can call mom and tell her that I'm not gonna be home this year," Logan obliviously offered.

Lola's eyes grew wide with apprehension as she firmly belted out, "NO!" Laughing at Logan's surprised face, Lola explained herself.

"Look, you can help me from now through Wednesday, but you are **not** under any circumstances allowed to miss Thanksgiving with your family. Your mother already despises me, and I really don't need more shit heaped upon me with her blaming me for you not being home."

"I doubt…" Logan began before Lola cut him off.

"Ah, ah, ah, Warren!" Lola chastised as she playfully tapped Logan's lips with her index finger. "We both know I'm right. Now, hush your pretty face, and let's get a move on."

It took all the self-control Logan could muster, to stop himself from pressing Lola firmly against his car and kiss her like there was no tomorrow. Feeling Logan's desire press against her leg, Lola chuckled as she patted Logan's chest, reminding him that they should get a move on.

~

When everything was put away properly, Lola gave Logan a quick tour of the manor, before stopping outside of the room that had belonged to her father. "As a little girl," Lola began reminiscently as she guided Logan inside the room, "this was my favorite place to be. Since my grandparents had always left it the same, when my dad moved out with my mother, it just seemed like…"

Seeing the tears well up in Lola's eyes, Logan wrapped his arms around her and brought her into his warm embrace. Uttering muffled words, Lola weakly laughed as she took a step back and sat upon the bed. "I know it's silly-"

"It's not silly," Logan interjected. "I think it's perfectly logical to have spent your time here. It's really no different than looking at an old family photo album, and trying to get a feel for a relative who's long since passed."

Turning her face up thoughtfully as she tried to blink away the last stray tears, Lola cleared her throat, as she offered, "Anyhow, if you want, you can stay in here, or you can stay in my old room with me."

"As badass as this room looks with the combination of **Foreigner** and **Styx** vinyls, classic **Mustang** decor, and **Mariners** memorabilia, I think it might be rather lonely without you." Logan acknowledged before kissing Lola's forehead. "Now, *my heart*, when are you going to feed me? I'm a growing boy, after all!"

Rolling her eyes, Lola grabbed Logan's hand, as she condescendingly jested, "We can't have that, now can we?"

"You know, I hear the sarcasm in your voice, but I'm going to take it as a sign of your love and affection," Logan quipped.

"Whatever helps you sleep at night, big boy!"

Heading to the den after a light dinner, Lola asked Logan to have a seat on the couch, so that she could finally continue where she left off. Lola fidgeted nervously with her fingers, for several minutes, before finally speaking. "The parts that are coming up … please, **please**," Lola begged, "don't judge me too harshly for the things I said back then. I am still coming to terms with everything, but it doesn't change what was done."

"I'm here every step of the way, and will never judge you. If I didn't back then, I sure as hell won't now."

Logan's reassurance gave Lola the confidence she needed to start once more.

~

May 5, 2010

Jacob's utterance of "Welcome home, *Vixen*," caused Lola to exhale raggedly as she summoned the last ounce of her courage. Sauntering over to Jacob's side, Lola circled her delicate fingertips around the Scotch glass's rim, before whispering seductively into Jacob's ear, "Who said *this* was my home, *Mr. Icy Eyes*? We both know the *real* reason I'm here."

Growling lustfully, Jacob pushed his paperwork to the back of the table before firmly placing Lola in what had been his workspace. The pair wasted no time in shedding their clothing before Jacob skillfully attuned to Lola's body, as a maestro would an orchestra.

Even though Lola had originally arrived at Jacob's house seeking answers, she instead, received hours of orgasmic pleasure, thus leaving her back at square one. Feeling refreshed after a warm shower, the question of where she and Jacob stood now presented itself once more at the forefront of Lola's mind. Crawling in bed beside him, Lola nervously asked, "Sooo … Jacob, where do we stand?"

Knowing the best way to keep Lola where he wanted her, Jacob placed the file he had been reviewing on the nightstand, before feigning interest in what Lola had to say. "What do you mean, *Vix?*"

"Well, are we like a couple now, or are we still mutually beneficial to one another? I just don't know!" Lola blurted out.

As always, Jacob chose his words carefully. "Like I asked when we met for dinner in January of 2009, where do **you** want us to stand, *Vix?* If you want a relationship, I'll give you a relationship. Just know, that like before, the success of **our** relationship is all dependent upon how **you** behave."

Feeling Jacob's words cut deep within her, Lola hung her head, as she spoke the words that would seal her fate, "O-okay, Jacob. I think we should try 'us' again. Heaven only knows how hard I tried to move on from you, but you are ingrained into every fiber of me. I know we had a few rough times, but it was my own stupidity that led us there. The good really did outweigh the bad. People will think I'm stupid, but I don't fucking care. I love you, so damn much that it hurts."

Smirking like the vile devil he was, Jacob passionately kissed Lola, before smugly whispering into her ear, "I know you do, *Vixen.*"

Before thinking to himself, After all, *I own you mind, body, and my absolute favorite part, soul.*

~

August 2, 2010

Lola's officially renewed relationship with Jacob was utterly blissful … until it wasn't. Awakening the morning of her 26th birthday, Lola told herself that it would be just like any other day, before sighing in dismay as she dressed. *What is the point of even celebrating the worst day in history, when I'm not even on speaking terms with the last of my family?*

Making her way into the kitchen, Lola smiled when she saw Jacob preparing two mugs of coffee. "Thank you," Lola murmured in satisfaction while embracing Jacob from behind.

"Anything for you, *Vix.*" Jacob chuckled before swiftly pulling Lola before him, capturing her lips with his own. "Happy birthday," he vocalized, much to Lola's chagrin.

"Jacob, what did I say?"

"That this is just a regular day," Jacob recited Lola's words from the day before, with a mischievous gleam in his eye.

"Exactly," Lola called over her shoulder as she turned to add a spoonful of honey and a dash of cinnamon to her coffee. "My birthday is nothing of importance, and therefore, not worth wasting time in celebrating."

Walking to the dining room, Jacob retorted, "Just trust me, *Vix.* Besides, you wouldn't want to break Catarina's heart, now would you?"

"What's that supposed to mean?" Lola clamored as she hastily followed Jacob, doing her best not to spill the contents of her mug.

Having seated himself in his usual place at the dining room table, Jacob waited until Lola sat beside him before he proceeded to tell her that Cate had insisted on hosting a birthday dinner for Lola. When

Lola last saw Cate at Maximillian and Evelynn's home to celebrate the twins' birthday, Cate refused to believe Lola when she said she would be treating her birthday as just another day on the calendar.

"Oh, Cate!" Lola chuckled as she shook her head. "Even though I wish she'd just let me be, I sure do love her to pieces for her persistence."

"It's one of the best Gallagher traits," Jacob winked, before handing Lola a small, black matte gift bag.

Peering into the bag, Lola smiled brightly as she pulled out a small, black velvet box. "Oh my god, Jacob…" Lola gasped, unable to process the exquisite grandeur of the black diamond, rose stud earrings. "They're so, so beautiful!"

Jacob handed Lola the certificate of authenticity, which she read silently to herself. *Holy shit! Each earring has a 5.0mm, round cut, AAA clarity black diamond; which weighs in at 1.20 carats. Certified 14k black gold.* Lola's eyes nearly bulged from their sockets, as she honed in on the price. Closing the box, Lola said, "Jacob- this is too much. I can't believe you spent nearly two grand on a pair of earrings."

"As I said, anything for you, *Vix.*" Jacob impishly rejoindered.

~

"Something feels different," Lola started as she looked out the passenger's side window of Jacob's car.

"How so?" Jacob mused as he prepared to park in the driveway of his childhood home.

"I'm not really sure," Lola said, as she turned to face the man beside her. "It just seems like my birthday always brings trouble."

Lifting Lola's chin in a firm, but gentle manner, Jacob kissed her passionately yet possessively; an action which onlookers would deem as romantic. However, things never were what they seemed with Jacob Sterling Gallagher. "You think far too much, *Vixen*. After all, someone as appealing as you, shouldn't waste their time and energy on such frivolous things as empty thoughts."

"I guess you're right," Lola stated, doing her best to suppress the sting of Jacob's backhanded compliment before she allowed him to help her out of the car.

With a heavy sigh, Lola reached out for Jacob's hand, in the hopes that it would provide some means of comfort since she still was unable to shake the off-putting feeling which had settled in her gut. Crossing the threshold, Lola barely had a chance to announce her presence, when she was ambushed by Cate's warm embrace.

"Catarina Adeline, I swear to God, your childish antics would drive any normal man over the edge. Although-," Maximillian chastised before cutting his eyes in Cade's direction, "I guess it's not a failure on *my* part as a father, but the simple fact that you have chosen to make your bed with someone of such a *lower* stature."

Refusing to let her father's poor attitude sour her friend's special day, Cate called out "Love you too, Pops!" before wrenching Lola's hand from Jacob's, and leading Lola down the hall.

"For fuck's sake, Max, can you for once in your life not be a complete asshole to your kids?" Jacob fumed before quickly following his sister and girlfriend.

Upon entering the kitchen, Jacob leaned against the doorframe and smiled as he saw Lola interacting with his mother; very few things, aside from his mother and sister, brought warmth into his blackened heart. However, Jacob's demeanor would quickly transform as Logan made his way into the kitchen from the back patio.

Jacob moved faster than a hummingbird in search of nectar, as Logan leaned down to give Lola, what most would consider a friendly hug. Jacob extended his right hand in Logan's direction, while simultaneously holding steadfast to Lola's with his left, as he grimaced, "What a **pleasant surprise** this is, Logan! Catarina failed to mention that **you** would be joining us."

"Hey, Jacob." Logan greeted in confusion at the anger radiating from the man standing four inches below him. "Cate asked if I wanted to tag along with her for Lola's birthday, and I figured why not. I was gonna text Lola later anyhow and see if she wanted to go to a concert this weekend."

Doing his best not to completely lose his cool, Jacob scoffed, "Well, Logan, I doubt it'd be proper for **my** girlfriend to attend a concert with another man."

All eyes suddenly turned as Cate fell to the floor in a fit of laughter. "Oh my god, J, you kill me! Since when have you ever given a damn about propriety?"

"Shut the fuck up, Catarina?" Jacob retorted.

"No seriously, weren't you the one who skipped out on his own wedding ceremony, leaving *Bunni*, I mean Beckii, at the altar, while you decided to have an orgy in dad's old office?" Cate remarked, after wiping the tears from her eyes.

Firmly gripping Lola's hand, Jacob all but dragged Lola out of the kitchen before yelling back, "Fuck you, Catarina! Fuck you!"

"No thanks, J! I'm not into incest, besides Cade did me real good right before we got here!" Cate sassed.

Hanging her head in shame, poor Evelynn uttered out, "Dear, sweet, Jesus!" before patting both Logan and Cade on the arms as she said, "I see, once again, that it was foolish of me to hope for a peaceful family event two times in a row." Embracing her mother affectionately, Cate offered her sincerest apologies for making a scene.

Finally able to remove her arm from Jacob's grasp, Lola rubbed the tender area as she questioned Cate's words. "You were almost married?! We've known each other for how long, and I'm just now learning this?"

"It was a long time ago, *Vix-*" Jacob started before Lola cut him off with a barrage of questions. "Look, Lola-" Jacob spat out Lola's first name as he closed his eyes, in hopes of regaining his composure. "I don't care what my sister's bitch ass decided to bring up tonight, *Bunni* is not up for discussion! Am I clear?"

"But…"

Pressing Lola against the nearest wall, Jacob firmly gripped her jaw as he demanded, "Am.I.fucking.clear?"

Closing her eyes in submission, Lola nodded her head in acknowledgment. Smirking to himself, Jacob delicately lifted Lola's chin and gave her a tender kiss on the lips, before offering up words of praise. "That's a good girl."

Hearing the clearing of a throat behind him, Jacob turned as his father stated, "Evelynn has sent me to find you two. Dinner's ready on the back patio. Lola, my dear, why don't you head that way while I have a quick word with my son."

"Y-y-yes, sir!" Lola stammered before swiftly making her way to join the others.

When Lola was completely out of view, Jacob scowled, "What the hell do you want, Max"

"Now, now, son. I was merely going to invite you to have a glass of Bourbon with me in my office after dinner. It would seem that your darling, *Bunni,* as you affectionately refer to Rebecca as has sent a bottle to your mother and me just this morning" Maximillian said as he patted Jacob on the shoulder.

Slinking from his father's grasp, Jacob rolled his eyes in annoyance. "Why the hell should I be concerned with *Bunni,* or her sending you a bottle of Bourbon?"

"I guess you'll just have to join me to find out," Maximillian chuckled darkly.

~

After an oddly strained, yet humorous meal, Maximillian cleared his throat as he stood, "If you all would excuse us, Jacob and I have several things we need to discuss in my office." Prior to heeding his father's command, Jacob leaned over to kiss Lola's cheek as he whispered a chastising reminder for her to be on her best behavior.

With her husband and son now out of earshot, Evelynn turned to Lola, and quietly asked, "Lola my dear, would you please join me on a short walk through the front garden. You have been a part of my son's life for quite some time now, and I feel as though we haven't really had the chance to have a meaningful conversation."

Walking peacefully for several minutes, Evelynn finally found the courage to speak the words that had long since been buried deep within her heart. "Lola, my dear, I have something of great importance to say to you. Please know that I think you are the loveliest of young women, and you remind me a bit of my younger self."

"Uh, thanks, Evelynn…"

"Ever since Jacob first brought you here several years ago, something just hasn't settled well with me," Evelynn began as she noticed Lola's countenance falter slightly. "Please do not be dismayed. My words come from a place of love, and most importantly as Jacob's mother."

Exhaling in relief, Lola nodded her consent for Evelynn to proceed.

"I tried my hardest to raise both of my children to the best of my ability, but sadly, my husband has a way of ruining people. Max may be one heck of a businessman, but personal relationships are his folly. Every person, place, and thing is solely viewed for monetary value and gain.

"Now had you met my son before he turned 18, I honestly feel from the depths of my soul that he wouldn't be the dark, hardened man he is now. However, that is neither here nor there." Evelynn paused her spiel as she prayed for the courage to press on. "I see the way that sweet, redheaded man, Logan, looks at you in complete adoration-"

Lola laughed at the thought of Logan viewing her in any way other than friendship. "I can promise you, Evelynn, that Logan and I are simply friends. Nothing more, nothing less. Besides, I really love Jacob, and even though I've made mistakes and messed things up with him in the past, I'm grateful he's given me another chance."

Tapping Lola's hand in an almost pitying manner, Evelynn stated her final piece. "Lola, even though your heart is blinded right now, I hope my words will bury themselves deep within your heart and resurface when you need them the most. My son, as much as I love him with my whole heart, is a man who is damned. He will never be worthy of your love and affection. I pray you find someone who will treat you like the precious gem you are. For no Gallagher man truly loved anyone but himself."

Before she could deny Evelynn's truth, the buzzing of Lola's phone quickly captured her attention. Seeing an unknown number flash across the screen, Lola declined the call, thus losing her defensive thoughts. "Thanks for the talk, Evelynn. If it's okay with you, I'd like to head back now for a piece of birthday cake."

"About time, you slowpokes! I thought I was going to have to send out a search party," Cate teased as Evelynn and Lola took the original seats.

"Where's your father and brother?" Evelynn asked Cate, once Lola blew out the candles.

"Still inside, I assume. You know how dad gets when it comes to anything to do with the Blackmores. His ass is still pissed at J. I mean I am too for how he did Beckii, but dad is just a greedy bastard!"

Cate ranted as she slammed the knife into the cake.

"Easy there killer! Just put down the knife!" Cade said as he slowly slipped the knife from Cate's hand. "Why don't you let me finish slicing up this masterpiece? I don't think Luxie wants a pile of crumbs on her plate."

Lola sighed in delight as she reveled in the first bite. "Oh my god, Cate! This is amazing!"

"Thank you, my sweet Luxie! I know black forest cakes are typically your favorite, but I wanted to try this new variation on it. It's called a white forest cake."

"I think-" Lola was cut off by the continued buzzing from her phone. "If you all would excuse me, I'm going to take this call out front. I worry it may be someone from work."

~

Concurrently in Maximillian's home office, Jacob found his minimal amount of patience wearing thin. "Max, I'm through playing your fucking games! Either you tell me what the fuck is going on or I'm leaving."

Maximillian chuckled at the sight of his son's annoyance. "Still acting like a spoiled child, I see. Do you think I have made it this far in business by acting like a bitch? No. Now sit your ass back down and listen like the grown man you pretend to be!" Jacob begrudgingly complied with his father's demands as he poured himself another glass of Bourbon.

"Now," Maximillian began, "I'm sure you remember how you failed to secure the Blackmore account not once, but twice."

"I have no further interest in *Bunni*, she was a good lay, but nothing more."

"Whatever the case may be, *son*," Maximillian spat, "I was rather surprised when your mother and I received this bottle of Bourbon along with an invitation to Rebecca's wedding."

"Okay … she's getting married. What the hell does that have to do with me or the past?" Jacob argued.

"Oh, my boy- it has everything to do with you. For it would seem that our dear Rebecca is marrying Elijah Silver." Seeing the uninterested look in Jacob's eyes, Maximillian continued. "My god, you are an idiot, aren't you? Elijah Silver is the owner of **Silver Lining Exclusives**. His company is our biggest competitor."

"Max, I really don't give a fuck. I head the company now, so I really don't see how this concerns you. If *Bunni* wants to marry him, then it is what it is. Besides, I now have someone far more interesting," Jacob stated with a devious gleam in his eye.

"Oh, son- you still have a lot to learn," Maximillian retorted.

"What the fuck is that supposed to mean?"

"Nothing, except for the fact that you might want to keep a tighter hold on your little **obsession** out there. After all, the Swan name is rather good for business." Maximillian exclaimed with a satisfied smirk.

Turning to look out the window that overlooked the front garden in its entirety, Jacob was filled with pure, unadulterated rage.

~

November 18, 2015

"I'm pretty sure I didn't drink enough water today, my head is killing me," Lola remarked as she rubbed her temples. "Let me get a quick drink."

Returning to the den with a glass of water in hand, Lola took several drinks before she spoke once more. "Remember how I said a little while back that time with you meant trouble for me?"

Logan nodded his head in remembrance. "Well," Lola said, "I'm not sure if you remember hugging me when I was upset about my mother calling me that night. But … but, after that hug, I began to feel a new level of Jacob's anger."

"What do you mean?" Logan asked as he scrunched his brow in confusion.

"I know this sounds really stupid and completely backwards, but he started sleeping around with other people. First, it was Naja and then too many others to count. That honestly hurt me far deeper than any physical pain he caused me."

Seeing the gears turn in Logan's head as he tried to process how infidelity could possibly hurt worse than physical abuse, Lola said with tears in her eyes, "Back then, I felt like when he hurt me, he was showing how much he cared. When he ignored me and messed around with other women, it was just devastating, and I would do anything to get some kind of attention. Bad attention felt better than nothing at all. It's just really hard to explain, let alone comprehend unless you've been there."

Unable to speak, because what could anyone really say about a revelation such as Lola's, Logan did the only thing that came naturally to him, and that was to embrace Lola and pray she could somehow feel even a fraction of the magnitude of his love for her.

<h1 align="center">46</h1>

<h1 align="center">Blue Hyacinth Holidays</h1>

November 26, 2015

Lola felt a deep sense of accomplishment as she looked at the feast spread across the manor's dining room table and side buffet; a sight that would have made her grandparents proud. Taking one last deep breath, Lola sent Logan a quick text before retrieving one last item, a small letter, from her childhood bedroom, which she safely tucked away in a kitchen drawer. While Lola couldn't quite yet picture herself living at Swan Manor permanently, the last week had been the calm she needed to brave the upcoming storm of memories.

~

With all in attendance, Gregory took a moment to bless the food, before everyone dug in. After a delightful main course, idle chatter filled the room, causing Lola to quietly take in the lovely sight before her; no matter how hard the past tried to hauntingly slice through her moments of joy. Looking across the table, Lola saw the tell-tale signs of a curious question nestled deep within Raelee's brain; something she had inherited from her mother.

"Baby Rae," Lola lovingly called, "what's on your mind?"

Fidgeting nervously, Raelee glanced at her mother before returning her gaze to Lola. "Well, *Auntie Bear*, I have a question, but…"

"But what, sweet girl?"

"Well, momma said I am sometimes too nosy for my own good, so I shouldn't ask anything personal."

Sighing heavily, Lizzie prepared to defend herself, before Lola patiently interjected. "Rae, your momma loves you very much and just knows that some things that go on in life are too much for a girl your age to understand."

Rolling her eyes as she tossed her napkin hastily upon the table, Raelee bristled. "I'm not a little kid anymore. I'm 11 for crying out loud!"

Shaking her head humorously, Lola asked Raelee to help her in the kitchen. Annoyed by what she perceived as her aunt poking fun at her irritation, Raelee huffed out a haughty, "Fine!" before following Lola's request.

Pulling out the dessert plates, Lola called over her shoulder, "You know, Rae, while you are the spitting image of your mom- minus the eyes- those are your dad through and through, you definitely have your dad's laid back personality. Well," Lola paused as she turned to lovingly face her precious niece, "that is until that little *tropical storm* in the dining room just now."

Trying her best to hide her smile, Raelee pouted, "Ugh! I know- Daddy always calls momma a *hurricane* because of her temper."

"It's not always a bad thing, you know- having a mother who loves you fiercely."

"Yeah, yeah." Raelee retorted as she playfully shooed Lola away. "Anyhow, sorry about that, Auntie. I know that momma has her reasons, but I still have a lot of questions. I just love you so much and we missed out on a lot of time together."

Walking over to the young girl who stood around four inches

taller than her, Lola embraced her affectionately. "I love you so much too, Rae. I was sick for a long time in my heart and in my mind, and it made it really hard for me to be around anyone. Some days I still feel sick, but I am getting better."

"Is that why you love Mr. Logan? 'Cause he makes you feel better." Raelee proclaimed as she broke away.

Blushing deeply, Lola felt the air leave her lungs before she sputtered out her reply. "W-well, I don't know if I love Logan just yet, but I do care about him. He does make me happy, but-" Lola paused as she lovingly grabbed her niece's shoulders, before continuing. "-don't ever find your self-worth or identity solely in a man. Remember, *baby*, you are amazing just the way God made you."

"I know, Auntie. Daddy and momma tell me that all the time."

"And that's because they love you so much, Rae. Please don't ever forget that, okay?"

Raelee nodded in affirmation before circling back to the query which had led to her initial outburst. "Auntie, can I ask you my question now?"

After a few thoughtful moments, Lola carefully replied, "How about this- You can go ahead and ask your question, but your mom has to be present. As long as it's something she thinks you're ready to hear, I will gladly answer. However, if she thinks you're still too young, we'll wait a few years."

Noticing the corners of Raelee's mouth fall into a pout, Lola teased, "Alright, *Elizabeth junior*- yes, I know your mom's signature pout, and just so you know, it only works on your dad. Anyhow, that's my best offer. As much as I love you, I love your parents even more and have worked hard to regain their trust. So, if they say 'no', I have to respect it."

Realizing she would get nowhere by being stubborn, Raelee hung her head in defeat, "Okay, Auntie. I know you're right," before exiting to retrieve Lizzie. Upon her quick return with her mother in tow, Raelee sincerely apologized for her outburst before asking her mother if she could please ask her question.

Lola relayed her conditions to Lizzie, in hopes of being able to help ease her mother's heart. "Sister, you know that I'm not going to go over your head, but at the same time, I do think Rae has a right to know some things."

Looking at her only child with love and admiration, Lizzie sighed wistfully. "Raelee, I know you're growing up, and that's hard for me. You're literally the best parts of your dad and me, and I can't help but want to shelter you from everything that is bad in this life, but you're right, you aren't a little girl anymore. So, as long as it's not an inappropriate question, I don't see the harm in you asking."

Quickly wiping the shocked expression from her face, Raelee finally asked, "Auntie, I don't remember much about the man with the scary white eyes, what was his name again?"

"Jacob..." Lola hesitantly replied.

"Oh, yeah! Mr. Jacob- anyhow, I don't remember much about him, but I know you were with him for a super long time. Even though you are with Mr. Logan now, I was wondering if you ever missed Mr. Jacob? Did you love him a lot? Did-"

"Raelee Sommer Keane!" Lizzie chastised, before granting Lola permission to respond because, in truth, she too wanted to know Lola's thoughts.

"Umm ... well ... uh, why do you ask?" Lola started, caught slightly off guard by the depth of her niece's questions.

"The reason I ask is because when I was at the dance studio and had some downtime, I was reading a book when I overheard my teacher talking to one of the moms about how she was worried because her sister is in a toxic relationship," Raelee explained.

Receiving a chastising look from her mother, Raelee defended, "What?! It's not like I was being nosy *this* time."

"Raelee Sommer Keane! What do you mean by *this* time?" Lizzie admonished.

"What?! It's not like it's *my* fault that adults are so noisy." Raelee sassed before continuing, "I may or may not have been listening in on one of momma and daddy's conversations - that I heard momma say that she was glad you weren't with someone so toxic anymore."

"Do you know exactly what that means, Rae?" Lola asked.

"Oh, yeah! I looked it up on the internet when I was waiting for momma and daddy to pick me up from ballet. The only couples I really know are my parents and grandparents, but they've been together for, like, ever."

"Son of a bitch! Jesus, please place Your hand upon this child before I **yeet** her from this earth!" Lizzie cursed under her breath. "Raelee, I can see now that your father and I are going to have to rethink your phone privileges."

Not knowing what to do in this very awkward situation, Lola asked if she should entertain Raelee's query, which Lizzie allowed. "At this point, it's fine. I mean who knows what else she's looked at on the damn internet. May as well hear an honest answer from someone we know and trust."

Choosing her words as carefully as she could, Lola answered honestly, "Well, Rae, there are times in our lives when we fool ourselves into thinking that something is good for us, no matter how much it hurts or makes us feel alone. Kinda like what you've probably started to read in some of your stories, and apparent research. And, after a while, your mind tricks you into only remembering the few good moments and holding onto those like you've found gold. When in reality, it was nothing but pyrite.

"So, to answer your question in the best way that I can for your age, I would say that while definitely not so much now, there were many times when I did miss the *idea* of a life and relationship with Jacob. And while I know your curious mind longs to know more, I think that's really all that I can say."

~

After bidding one final farewell to the Keanes, Lola turned to Gregory, as she asked him to join her in the living room for a cup of tea before he, too, left for the evening.

With everything prepared and neatly organized on the silver serving tray, Lola grabbed the letter she had stashed earlier in the evening and expertly made her way to accompany the elderly gentleman seated near the fireplace.

"I wish you'd let me help you with that tray, Luxe."

"Nonsense, Uncle Greg! You're my guest; besides, it brings me joy to do something nice for you … especially after all you have done for me." Lola exclaimed with deep sincerity.

"Sweet child, I often wish I could have done more for you after Jack and Lorriene passed, but-" Gregory paused as his voice broke slightly.

Noticing the corners of her beloved uncle's eyes slightly moisten, Lola tenderly patted his arm. "Oh, Uncle Greg! Everything that you did for me, was more than enough." Pausing for a brief moment, Lola grabbed a tissue, along with the letter, before handing them to Gregory.

"What's this?" Gregory asked, looking at the envelope with immense curiosity.

"It's a letter, silly!" Lola playfully teased, before proceeding to tell Gregory about the path Dr. Indigo had her on to help with her healing. "Even though Dr. Indigo had told me that I didn't have to hand them out, and they could be just for me, it feels more … what's the word … real, I guess, when I give them out."

"I can understand that, I would say it seems like handing them out gives you some closure." Gregory acknowledged, before asking, " How many more do you have to write until this part of your treatment is complete?"

"Just two," Lola stated firmly. "I guess you could say two and an ongoing oral reiteration with Logan. You know, I thought about just writing him a brief letter, but after some encouragement from Dr. Indigo-" Lola paused as she dabbed the tears from her own eyes. "I realized that there isn't enough paper in the world to retell my tragic tale."

"Well, my dear," Gregory said as he stifled a yawn, "would you be willing to humor an old man before he calls it a night?" Seeing Lola turn her head curiously, Gregory held up the letter. Laughing sheepishly at the true meaning behind her uncle's query, Lola smiled whilst nodding in agreement.

With the letter back in her possession once more, Lola cleared her throat, took a sip of her warm tea, and began reading the bittersweet words she had penned.

Dearest Uncle Greg,

If I haven't told you already, I have been tasked by Dr. Indigo with writing letters to the people in my life to help with my healing after everything that went down nearly three years ago. I have tried to write this letter countless times- in fact, the amount of paper I wasted would make an environmentalist cry bitter tears.

I think, up to this point, yours has been the hardest for me to write, because where do I even begin. Do I start with an expression of gratitude for being there to guide me and mentor me through my adulthood and career path? Do I start with thanking you for being the closest damn thing to a father figure in my fucked up life? Or ... and the hardest one of all ... Do I start with an apology for the cruel grief I so selfishly pierced your heart with?

I'm honestly not sure where to start, because I know that I can't take back the hurt or even begin to repay your loving kindness, but please know that I truly am both remorseful and appreciative.

Always,

Lola Luxe

When the letter drew to a close, Gregory warmly embraced Lola, as several fat tears slowly fell down his weathered face. "My precious girl, you don't have to apologize, but since you feel you must, please know that you are already forgiven. As for repayment, you can't repay love that is freely given. The only thing you can do is pass it on."

~

December 6, 2015

Having spent such a pleasant time in her childhood home over Thanksgiving, Lola decided to stay through the end of the year; and while she had originally planned to invite Logan to stay with her, after consulting Dr. Indigo on the matter, Lola felt it best she spend this time alone … lest they both become far more codependent than what was deemed the "healthy norm".

Looking down at the sheet of paper set before her, as she penned the last few lines, Lola exhaled in relief as she realized she had finally completed her second to last letter. Placing the neatly folded letter in her purse, Lola called the florist to check the status of her order. "Hi, this is Lola Swan. I'm just calling to check on my order for a bouquet mixed with blue hyacinths and white lilies." Which the clerk kindly confirmed would be ready at seven o'clock that evening.

After ending her call with the florist, Lola sent Logan a text asking if he would like to accompany her this evening, before making her last call of the morning, to ensure everything was still a go. "You're absolutely *positive* that it's okay for us to stop by, right Mar?" Lola asked nervously.

Laughing sweetly on the other end, Marina once again reassured Lola that she and Logan were fine. "Lola, I know you're worried since it's the first night of Hanukkah, but I promise my family won't mind at all. I mean if they went out of their way to ensure Andy would feel welcome, even though he's an Atheist, I know you guys will be fine."

"How's everything with you and Andy going, by the way? Do you think wedding bells will be happening any time soon," Lola asked with genuine curiosity.

Marina sighed into the receiver, recalling the bittersweet conversation that occurred just two days prior. "At first, my family had a bit of a hard time with the fact that the first guy I'm actually serious about isn't a 'Good Jewish boy,' but an Atheist; but once they were able to meet Andy, they loved how respectful he was, which made me really happy.

"As for wedding bells … I don't want to go into too much because it's still a bit tender."

"You only have to tell me whatever you're comfortable with, okay?" Lola kindly reassured Marina.

Exhaling the remaining remnants of her frustration, Marina swiftly explained. "Well, after Andy and I attended the wedding of one of my cousins, I started looking at wedding dresses online, just to have an idea of what I might like in the future, ya know?

"While we had yet to initially discuss marriage, I figured we would one day end up there because Andy continually tells me that he is eternally devoted to me and that I saved him from his miserable and agonizingly bitter existence; so I just naturally assumed, ya know?

"Anyhow, Andy told me that he never lied to me and was sorry for giving me the wrong impression, but he would never marry me. He gave me an ultimatum-" Marina paused to finally catch her breath.

"Oh, Lord! What was the ultimatum?" Lola wearily asked.

"Andy's ultimatum was that if I could set aside the idea of marriage, which he called the death of a real relationship, he would be far more devoted to me than any man has ever been to a woman. He said why should a piece of paper that is easily torn signify the foundation of our relationship.

"He then went on to say that everything he has is already mine, but if I can't let go of the idea of a wedding and a marriage, then it is best we go our separate ways now," Marina concluded with yet another heavy sigh.

While her knowledge of Andy as an adult was very limited, Lola did know firsthand why Andy felt the way he did. "Mar, I know it's rough, but I think Andy's view stems from how his parents treated him growing up. And even though they got divorced in the end because of infidelity on both ends, they still abandoned him with the Carsons."

Marina concluded the call by letting Lola know that even though a wedding and marriage had been important to her, her love for Andy outweighed all of that, and if a wedding meant a life without him, it wasn't a life worth living.

~

At twenty till seven, Lola's heart joyfully skipped a beat when she heard Logan's all too familiar knock. Grabbing her belongings, Lola rushed out the door, straight into the arms of the man who had slowly helped to revive her dead and lonely heart, greeting him with a passionate kiss.

"It seems someone has missed little 'ole me," Logan teased after breaking the kiss.

"In your dreams, Warren!" Lola sassed as she grabbed Logan by the arm, leading him in the direction of his vehicle.

Logan halted his movements as he wrapped an arm around Lola's waist thus bringing her closer to him, as he whispered huskily into her ear, "Of course, *my heart*, especially the dirtiest ones," before kissing the exposed side of her neck.

"*Logan Asher Warren!*" Lola screeched as embarrassment shone brightly upon her fair face.

Before Lola could say anything else, Logan belted out with laughter as he quickly ran past her, calling out his affections.

~

With the beautiful floral arrangement in hand, Lola nervously bit her lower lip as she looked out the passenger's side of the window; anticipation and what-ifs continually building within her. Quickly picking up on the sudden shift in Lola's mood, Logan asked if she was absolutely certain that Marina was okay with him tagging along.

"Of course she is silly. What makes you think she wouldn't?"

"Well, I just get the feeling that she doesn't like me." Logan stated before glancing over to see a skeptical expression etched across Lola's face, thus causing him to elaborate, "I'm being serious! I have seen the death glares she gives me."

Laughing heartily as she wiped a couple of stray tears away before pondering the weight of Logan's inquiry. "Well, now that I think of it, Marina has said on more than one occasion that she feels like you're hiding something from me."

"Uh … weird. No clue why she would think that" Logan nervously chuckled.

Clearing his throat as he turned down the crowded street his GPS had directed him to, Logan couldn't seem to shake the dreadful feeling which had taken up residence within the pit of his stomach. While he knew that Marina was rightfully justified in her thinking, Logan still couldn't bring himself to tell Lola the truth about who he really was. *It's not like she's going to hate that I'm actually in a band … I just know shit is going to hit the fan when she finds out that I have lied to her numerous times, even though she's asked me repeatedly.*

"Move that sweet, ginger ass of yours, Warren. It's cold as hell out here!" Lola's bellow abruptly shook Logan from his guilt-ridden thoughts.

~

Greeting her guests, Marina quickly introduced Logan and Lola to her very large, extended family. Seeing the look of astonishment in Lola's eyes, Marina chuckled as she explained how Andy had kindly offered to host the first night of Hanukkah celebrations in their home. "Every year, we draw eight names to see who will host the family each night. My *Shavta*- sorry, my grandma- used to host every single night, but as our family grew and she aged, it just became too much."

Marina led Logan and Lola down a small hallway, to the office where Andy was seated. Though he was quietly looking over a document, Lola could tell by the way the corner of his mouth twitched, that Andy was doing his calming exercises. "I see Andy still recites his favorite flowers," Lola whispered to Marina.

With a knowing wink, Marina walked over to Andy, giving him a loving kiss, before sternly telling Logan that they would be having a serious conversation. Wide-eyed, Logan looked to Lola for help, only to be met with a fit of laughter.

"If this crazy lady kills me, *my heart*, tell my mom I love her." Logan pitifully mused.

Rolling her eyes at his childish antics, Lola playfully shooed Logan away before nervously moving to stand before the man who had truly become nothing but a stranger to her. "Uh … th-these are for you, Andy." Lola sputtered out while handing the lovely blue and white floral arrangements across the desk.

With a heavy sigh, Andy placed the document he had been looking over to the side, before accepting the flowers that were being held in front of his face. "By the looks of this bouquet, Luxe, it seems as if you have come here sincerely asking my forgiveness."

"That-that's if you'll hear me out," Lola admitted, nervously fidgeting with the hem of her sleeve as she stood.

"Well, have a seat why don't you? I really don't have all night for you to waste my time by just standing there like an imbecile." Andy hastily admonished.

Though the words cut through her patched-up soul like a knife, Lola knew this conversation wouldn't be easy by any means. Removing the letter from her purse, Lola slid it across the desk in front of Andy, before sitting in the cold, leather chair.

Several minutes passed by at an agonizingly, lackadaisical pace; neither party honestly knew where to begin. Finally clearing his throat, Andy picked up the letter, only to place it in a drawer. Turning his attention back to Lola, Andy bristled, "Well, Mar said you wanted to talk, so I'd suggest you start, or you can get the hell out of my house, Luxe."

Lola sent up a quick prayer that whether by miracle or fortune, Andy's heart would be open to hearing the weighty depths of her words.

"First, I really want to thank you for taking the time to meet with me. I know you didn't have to." Noticing the approving nod coming from across the desk, Lola continued.

"I don't remember everything I wrote, but I'll do my best to explain myself. I'm not the best with conveying my emotions and thoughts out loud, so I'm sorry if I stumble along the way." Lola confessed.

"Alright- moving on," Andy replied flatly.

"When I came to visit you in prison on your birthday five years ago, the words you spoke really did have an impact on me. I loved you so much, like a brother, yet I literally left you there to rot away. Shane really would have been disappointed in me … and well …" Lola paused as her voice broke.

Wiping the stray tears away, Lola continued down the road she had started. "I know that no amount of sorry will ever take away from the betrayal you must have felt. I truly am sorry. I also want to thank you for calling me out on my shit. Because in the end, though it was unintentional, I betrayed Shane every time I allowed Jacob to continually drag me down to the pits of hell.

"I know that I could make a million other excuses, and they would all be shit ... and while I know that we can never have the same level of friendship-"

"You're damn right, we'll never have the same fucking level of friendship, Luxe," Andy authoritatively declared, before offering an olive branch, "but I am not an unreasonable man. As my gratitude for sending Mar my way, I will forgive you..."

"Thank you so much, Andy!" Lola joyfully interjected, then swiftly changed her demeanor as she took notice of the look upon Andy's face. "I sense a 'but' coming."

"You'd be correct, Luxe." Andy acknowledged. "My forgiveness comes with a price." Smirking as he saw Lola's wide-eyed expression, Andy continued. "It's honestly not that big of a price. All I'm asking is that you and me, we're nothing. The only thing you'll ever know me as from this day forward is Marina's partner and the CEO of *Carson Tech*."

Lola was rendered speechless and dumbfounded. While she knew it wouldn't be nearly as easy to patch things up with Andy as it had been with everyone else, she truly had not expected such an abrasive response. Doing her best to control her aching heart, Lola simply asked, "Why?"

"The answer's quite simple, Luxe," Andy mocked. "The boy you think you knew died the same night his best friend did. And the pathetic remnant that was left was so easy for you to forget, as he rotted away in a prison cell. So, yeah ... if you could just forget you ever knew me, that'd be great.

"I'll be cordial enough to you in Marina's presence and at company events, but other than that, we're nothing. If that's all you've got for today, I'd like for you to **kindly** get the hell out of my house." Andy ruthlessly concluded.

Thanking Andy for his time once more, Lola stepped off into the restroom she had noticed prior to entering the office. Splashing some water on her face, Lola did her best to avoid the reflection gawking back at her; knowing one glance is all that it would take to break the fragile wall she had slowly built to keep the damning thoughts at bay. Finally pulling herself back together, Lola set off in search of Logan.

After several minutes of searching, Lola happened upon what appeared to be the tail end of a very heated conversation between Logan and Marina. "All I'm saying, **lover boy**," Marina spat, "is that I'm giving you two months to tell her the truth. If you don't, well then … I'm going to have to, and I don't think she'll appreciate your lies."

Before Logan could muster up an answer to defend himself, there came the intrusion of a throat being cleared.

"Uh, hey guys," Lola called out. "Did I miss anything?"

Marina hastily rushed over and embraced Lola. "How did it go? I'm sure Andy was a hard-ass as always, and even though he might not show it, I know that it really did mean a lot to him that you came. Okay?"

"Well, Mar, let's just say, some memories are just better off left in the past." Lola morosely stated. "At any rate, I'm really thankful you allowed us to interrupt your family's festivities. I'll talk to you soon, yeah?"

47

Enigmatically Facinorous

December 6, 2015

The drive back to Swan Manor was somber at best. No longer wishing to give thought to Marina's valid demand, Logan instead chose to focus on the original intent of the evening. "By your melancholy state, I take it the conversation didn't go well with Andy. Did it, *my heart?*"

Lola sorrowfully recanted the contents of her conversation with Andy. "As much as it hurts, I know that this isn't some sort of fairytale. Not everything is resolved with a tidy little bow."

"It's not," Logan stated as he pulled into the driveway, before continuing, "but you've got two choices in this instant. You can either grieve properly and then move forward or let it consume you, only to reset all of your progress."

"It sounds like you've been talking to Dr. Indigo." Lola chuckled.

"Well … after the panic attack, I did reach out to her, but she said it would be a conflict of interest to see me since you are her patient. I did take the time recently, though, to reach out to one of her colleagues. Especially after yet another conversation with my mom." Logan acknowledged.

Grabbing the hand of the man who treasured her heart, Lola asked Logan if he would stay the night with her. "I must admit, I really have missed your closeness. You help me feel safe."

Putting her belongings away, Lola called over her shoulder, "I'm going to get a shower before heading to bed … feel free to join me if you'd like."

Shock resonated upon Logan's face as the magnitude of Lola's words hit him like a ton of bricks. "Uh- what'd you just say?"

"You heard me, Warren!" Lola retorted with a playful wink before running up the stairs.

Completely dumbfounded, Logan walked over to the fridge to pour himself a glass of water. *Umm … I swear I heard her right, but shit! Why the hell am I having so many fucking reservations? Fuck it! Now is not the time to be a little bitch about this.* Finally overcoming his apprehensive thoughts, Logan downed the water in a single gulp before allowing his surging hormones to guide him up the stairs to where Lola awaited him.

~

Standing beneath the hot water, Logan felt his breath hitch in his throat; while he had seen a decent share of Lola's body, he couldn't help but become even more enraptured by the beauty standing in front of him. Though she had been one to put on a brave front whilst on the stairs, now that Logan stood before her, bearing just as much vulnerability as she did, Lola couldn't help but feel slightly timid. And while this was far from the first time either person were to look upon the natural glory of another, somehow, this time felt far more meaningful.

Surrounded by the serenity of the falling water, Logan quickly closed the gap between the two of them, as he tenderly pressed Lola's back against the cool tile wall. Though he longed to kiss her, Logan instead chose to study Lola as she reflexively reached out with shaking hands to trace the tattoos adorning Logan's body, until they finally found their way to the one Logan treasured the most, upon his heart.

When the tension was almost too much for him to bear, Logan gently lifted Lola's chin, to only once more become lost deep within her forested gaze. Overcome with emotions she couldn't even begin to name, Lola closed her eyes as a single tear slowly faded into the cascading waters.

"Logan … I think I love you. Like, I really love you." Lola choked out.

Before Lola could even continue her heartfelt revelation, Logan had completely captured her lips; kissing her like his life was dependent upon it. "Say it again, please." Logan pleaded, his voice raspy from the kiss they had just shared. "Say it again, so that I know this isn't just a dream."

"I love you, Logan." Lola happily cried out, as Logan peppered her face with delicate kisses before slowly trailing them down the length of her body. Just as he was about to reach her most sensitive spot, Logan gazed up at Lola to ensure he had her full consent.

"If anything gets to be too much, I will let you know- I promise. But for now, please don't stop." Lola lovingly pleaded. Hearing all he needed, Logan lovingly attuned to Lola's body; his nimble fingers upon her like the finest of instruments. Having reached her high, Lola hungrily pulled Logan's face to hers; the desire to reciprocate his love overtook her.

"Y-you don't have to, *my heart.*" Logan rasped.

"I know I don't, and that's all the more reason why I want to. So please, let me shower you with love as well."

"Well then, who am I to deny the keeper of my heart!" Logan mischievously chuckled. As Lola positioned herself on her knees, only to tease him slowly, Logan earnestly wrapped his hands in

Lola's sodden curls. And while the shower's water had long since run frigid, the newly blossomed love radiated more than enough heat to cause either party to take notice.

After the blissful shower, Lola now rested her head upon Logan's chest, doing her best to stifle a yawn, she asked, "Do you mind if we wait just a little bit longer to fully have sex? I don't want to rush this."

"Lola, *my heart*, I will always wait for however long you want." Logan lovingly reminded Lola before placing a gentle kiss upon her head.

"This is why I love you, Logan." Lola called out before finally succumbing to sleep's blissful song.

~

December 12, 2015

Lola awoke to the gentle sound of rain hitting the window, and stretched out her limbs, only to find Logan's side of the bed had gone cold. Doing her best not to overthink his absence, Lola expelled one final yawn, before warmly dressing for her morning run.

Upon entering the kitchen, Lola smiled brightly as she saw Logan seated at the bar with brows furrowed in concentration; completely unaware of her entrance. Seeing an open opportunity, Lola stealthily slunk up behind Logan, before wrapping her arms around his waist.

"You're too damn tall!" Lola huffed into Logan's back.

Logan's laughter reverberated through Lola's body, causing her heart to skip a beat. Turning to face the woman behind him, Logan playfully patted her head, before seductively teasing her about her short stature.

Thoroughly red-faced, Lola did her best to change the subject by inquiring about what Logan had been working on. "Well, since Christmas is coming, and you plan to stay here through the end of the year, I was thinking of making a little road trip down to Salem to the Christmas Tree farm my family and I always go to, and we can get you a tree," Logan answered.

"Oh, umm … okay. I think that could be a lot of fun. Can we go after my run?"

"Sure. I'll go ahead and let mom know that we're joining them!" Logan excitedly proclaimed.

"Are you sure it's okay that I intrude on your family's outing? I mean, I know your mom isn't my biggest fan. What do I say if she starts grilling me about what we are to each other?"

Taking Lola's hands in his, Logan pressed his forehead to hers, in hopes that this kindly affection would help to temper her overthinking mind. "Hey, hey! I am bringing you, so of course, it's fine. And if mom asks you what we are, just answer what feels the most natural to you at that moment. Okay?"

Relief flooded Lola's soul, as she kissed Logan goodbye. Upon Lola's exit, Logan gave his mom a quick call to let her know Lola would be joining him. While he could have chosen his typical "Fuck it!" attitude towards anyone with a negative opinion regarding Lola, Logan knew their newly sprouted love was still quite fragile; which meant giving his mom enough notice, so as not to create an uncomfortable scene.

~

Two hours later, along a serenely, scenic route Lola found herself gazing out the window at the snow-covered evergreens. "You wanna know what I just realized?"

Hearing a curious hum from Logan, Lola elaborated. "I just realized that it's been nearly a month since I last told you anything."

"Ya know, I guess it has. What, with Thanksgiving and then your meeting with Andy." Logan recalled. "If you feel up to it, we've got an hour left on our drive, so you can pick up where you left off."

"If it's alright with you, I'd like to talk about the reconciliation of my friendship with Lizzie. It's still during the time where my relationship with Jacob began to fade. I'll tell you a little bit about that day, but keep as much of the heavy stuff as I can to a minimum because I'd like to try to be in a cheerful mood when I finally meet your family."

"Whatever you want, *my heart*," Logan affirmed as he picked up Lola's hand and placed a kiss on it.

~

October 6, 2010

Lola awoke that Wednesday morning, feeling hollow. Looking over at Jacob's sleeping form, she couldn't help but feel disgusted by what had occurred the night before. *If he's going to fuck around with other women, I really wish he'd wash the stench of betrayal off of himself before taking his turn with me.* While Lola's thoughts were wishful, she knew the real reason Jacob acted in such an egregious manner was to punish her for remaining steadfast in her friendship with Logan.

Lola quietly exhaled, as she slowly shifted her weight, in hopes of sneaking out of the bed without waking the wretched man beside her. Sadly, much like the rest of her life, fortune was anywhere but on her side. "And just where do you think you're going, *Vix?*" Jacob gruffly whispered in her ear after firmly pulling her unveiled body flush against his own.

If past experiences with Jacob taught her anything, it was that it was best to just give in to his inquiries, lest she find herself on the receiving end of a beating, that somehow she would end up believing she was deserving of. Plastering on an adoring facade, Lola simply uttered, "Good morning, Jacob. I was just going to use the bathroom."

Having relieved herself, Lola found herself caged once more in the arms of the man she couldn't help but love. "Have you given any more thought to what I've asked? You know I don't enjoy having to be harsh with you, *Vix*." Jacob asked between kisses down Lola's neck, right shoulder, and forearm.

Every instinct of self-preservation screamed at Lola to just give into Jacob's singular request; yet for some reason, the small flicker of hope- the hope of a better life- would not let her relent. "Jacob, I wish you would just please trust me. Logan is nothing but a friend. Why can't you see that it's you who I love?" Lola begged before screaming out in pain as Jacob savagely bit Lola's forearm, causing it to bleed quite heavily.

"What the hell is wrong with you, Jacob?!"

The only answer Lola received was a firm backhand to her face, and an eerily firm chastising as heavy sobs poured out of her. "*Vix*, you'd do well to remember who the fuck you're talking to. Now clean yourself up, because you look ugly as hell when you cry. No Gallagher man wants to be seen with a woman who can't even look halfway decent."

Once Jacob left for the day, Lola showered before carefully examining her wounds; praying and hoping with what little self-resolve she could find at the moment. *God, or anyone who will listen, if you're real, please save me from this love.*

The ringing of her phone in the background shook Lola from her own mind. Seeing an unknown number, Lola would normally decline but something urged her to answer. After answering, the caller on the other end asked, "Is this Ms. Lola Luxe Swan?" Acknowledging who she was, Lola learned the caller was the nurse from Raelee's school.

"Mrs. Keane has listed you as Raelee's emergency contact in case we are unable to get ahold of her or Mr. Keane." The nurse proceeded to inform Lola that Raelee had a very high fever and began vomiting after recess, and should be taken to the doctor before being allowed to return to school.

~

"*Auntie Bear*, I missed you. Why are you wearing sunglasses inside? Momma always says it's not good for our eyes." Raelee weakly asked while she and Lola were seated in the exam room, awaiting the doctor's arrival.

"I missed you too, Baby Rae. And yes, normally your momma's one-hundred percent right, but Auntie has a really bad headache, and the light makes it hurt worse." Lola acknowledged as truthfully as possible while trying to protect the precious innocence of the six-year-old girl seated beside her.

Twenty minutes later, Lizzie frantically rushed into the exam. "Oh my gosh, *baby*! Are you okay?" Turning to Lola, Lizzie awkwardly offered her thanks, to which Lola responded, "It's fine, sist … I mean, Lizzie. Well, since you're here, I'm gonna head out."

No longer wishing to keep the distance between them, Lizzie hastily threw her arms around Lola in hopes of stopping her. "Please don't go, sister." Doing her best not to cry, as the salty tears would sting her wounded eye hidden behind her glasses, Lola smiled brightly, taking her place by Raelee once more as the doctor entered the room.

An hour later, Lola found herself seated in Lizzie's living room; a place that simultaneously felt both familiar and foreign. Having set Raelee up in her room with everything she might need in case she fell ill once again, Lizzie asked Lola if she'd like a cup of coffee.

"No thanks, Lizzie. Honestly, I should probably head out I don't want to get the stomach bug too, and I really should do something about this killer headache."

"Okay, Luxie. Just please promise that if I call you when Rae is better, that you'll consider answering." Lizzie begged.

After promising that she would answer, Lola hugged Lizzie once more as she rushed out the door; doing her best to evade the onslaught of questions resting at the forefront of Lizzie's mind.

~

December 12, 2015

"What happened after Raelee got the stomach bug? How were you and Lizzie able to patch things up?" Logan asked as he removed his key from the ignition.

"Honestly, we weren't close again like we are now until after the **incident**. I know without a shadow of a doubt that she wanted to know everything, but I purposely kept her at arm's length." Lola admitted.

Stepping out of the car, Logan raced over to Lola's door to hold it open for her. "Thank you, *my love*," Lola said happily before giving him a kiss. "Alright, Warren, let's go find your mom and a tree. Please promise you won't leave me alone with her just yet!"

"I hadn't planned on it, but why do you ask?"

"Umm … well … you've told me a little bit about your uncle Antonio, your mom dislikes me, and there will be sharp objects about! You do the math, Logan." Lola nervously admitted.

Doing his best to ease Lola's nervousness, Logan squeezed her hand and offered semi-reassuring words that even he had a hard time believing. "I don't think it will be *that* bad."

Making their way to the back half of the lot, Logan and Lola finally met up with Logan's family. Noticing his wife's grim expression, Dean chose to risk the argument with Britt and gave Lola a warm, fatherly embrace. "Thanks for joining us today, Lola. I'd like to introduce you to the rest of the crew here."

"The mini-Britt," Dean introduced the blonde pre-teen who was the spitting image of his wife, "is our Eloise Rose. She's 13, and her birthday is two days after Logan's."

"Elle-belle is the best birthday present I ever got." Logan mused while affectionately ruffling his sister's hair.

"And this tiny *cherry bomb*, as we lovingly call her," Dean teased, bringing forth a younger, strawberry blonde girl, who looked quite similar to Logan, just with a more muted color palette, "is our Rosalie Cerise. She's 10 and definitely gives us a run for our money."

Rosalie gave Logan a firm fist bump before accepting a hug. "Love you too, Rosebud," Logan called happily before making his way over to his mother. "You know, mom, *hardass* is a better-suited look for *Zio*." Logan teased while leaning down to hug her.

"Love you too, *Baby Mine*." Britt warmly returned her son's affections before briskly introducing herself to Lola.

Gathering up her courage, Lola took the time to officially introduce herself. "It's wonderful to finally meet everyone, and see you again, Dean." Turning to Eloise and Rosalie, Lola said, "You know girls, this is my very first time picking my own Christmas tree. In fact, this just might be the first time having a real one; so would you two be willing to help me find the very best tree?"

The two young girls looked at each other in bewilderment, unable to believe someone their brother's age never had a real Christmas tree, before shouting, "Yes!", in joyful unison and dragging Lola off in search of the perfect tree. As the three searched, Lola told the girls stories from her happy memories of Christmas with her grandparents. Logan laughed heartily at the look of pure joy on Lola's face, before turning to his mom and step-dad and suggesting they should start their own search.

Forty-five minutes later, with two trees in tow- an 8' Grand Fir for Lola, and a 6' Douglas Fir for the Anderson family- the small party sipped on hot chocolate, making small talk before heading off to their respective homes. "You know, girls," Lola said to Eloise and Rosalie, "my niece, Raelee, is 11 and I think you'd really enjoy playing with her. If it's okay with your mom and dad, how would you all like to come to the house I grew up in on December 23?"

Though she preferred to keep her distance from the seductress who she believed to be her son's downfall, Britt agreed to Lola's offer after seeing the pleading look in her son's eyes. *After all, I never could deny him anything, no matter how much I fear he will get hurt.*

"Lola, you're so pretty! I love your hair. Do you love Logie? Like momma loves daddy?" Rosalie chatted on.

"Yeah, do you? Momma seems skeptical." Eloise added.

"Well, Eloise, your momma has every right to be skeptical. I would be the same way if I was in her place. And to answer your question, Rosalie. Yes, I love Logan very much. He's the best boyfriend I've ever had, and I know I would be so blessed to spend the rest of my life with him." Lola truthfully stated without even an ounce of hesitation as she smiled brightly at Logan's sisters.

Standing outside his car, with the tree firmly strapped to the roof, Logan couldn't help but blush brightly at the recollection of Lola's words. Turning to face her directly, he smiled as he exclaimed, "So … I'm your boyfriend now, huh?"

Patting Logan on the chest, Lola nonchalantly smirked, "Seems that way, Warren. Seems that way," before having her lips lovingly captured by Logan's.

As soon as they were headed back in the direction of Swan Manor, Lola decided to pick back up where she left off that morning. "Before you start," Logan interjected, "If this is the time that I am thinking of in late 2010 to early 2011, that's when my mom started disliking you. She felt that you were just using me to fill the void in your heart."

"I mean, well, she's not wrong. And for that, I will forever be sorry."

With his eyes still on the road, Logan instinctively brought Lola's hand to his lips, as he placed a tender kiss on it, before encouraging

Lola to continue with her tale. *I know she used me, but I'd go through every fucking hurt and heartache again just to be near her. I know it's fucked up as hell, God, but I can't change it.*

~

October 6, 2010

Once her time with Lizzie was over, Lola changed into a white, satin camisole and shorts pajama set, and stood in her bathroom tending to the bite wound on her forearm; wincing in a mixture of pain and relief as she poured the antiseptic wash. "How's it looking?" Jacob's unnaturally gentle voice echoed off the marble walls.

Taking Lola's arm in his hands, Jacob kissed the wound he inflicted that morning. "It's okay, but I think it might scar," Lola admitted.

"I'm sorry, *Vix-*"

"What?" Lola remarked while bringing her suspicious gaze to look Jacob square in the eye. Lola instantly felt guilty as she came to find Jacob's eyes genuinely softened and his brow etched with deep concern.

Jacob went on to explain that while in the moment he felt justified in his anger, as the day wore on, his concern grew for Lola and he needed to leave early to check in on her. Pulling Lola's head to his chest, Jacob went on to say, "You know that I'm a possessive man, *Vix*, and while I do trust you, I also can't help but notice the lovesick looks that bastard gives you. I've done a lot to keep you, and I'd like to think you'd respect me enough to do this one small thing that I request."

Lola smiled brightly as she fooled herself into believing the words spoken were love-filled, instead of repugnantly saccharine. "I know that I was wrong, Jacob, and I'm sorry. I love you so much and I hate it when we fight, and that I keep messing up. Is it okay though if I'm at least polite to Logan in social settings? I won't be overly cordial, but I can't be rude either."

Sighing in satisfaction that Lola was back where she should be, Jacob chose to entertain her request. "Now you know, this favor comes at a cost, don't you?"

Panic flooded Lola as she realized she had unwittingly walked into yet another carefully laid trap. Becoming aroused at the look of pure fear that had taken up residence in Lola's eyes, Jacob kissed her fiercely; biting her lower lip hard enough to pool blood, which he proceeded to smear across her jaw.

Silent tears slowly fell down Lola's face as Jacob turned her to face her reflection while he harshly kissed her neck and shoulders, leaving a trail of blood behind; forever staining the satin white pajamas. Making his way back to her ear as his hand worked its way into her shorts, Jacob reveled in the wet heat that began to flood Lola's core. "You see, *Vix*, you're just as fucked up as I am. The sight of me fiercely marking you as my property has you so turned on. Do you think Logan, or any other man, could **ever** make you feel like this?"

Feeling the rush of her first orgasm on the verge of boiling over, Lola gripped onto the bathroom counter and cried out through labored breathing that she would only ever be Jacob's. Hearing the words he needed, Jacob victoriously smirked, "Just as it should always be, my little *Vixen*. Now let's play a little game."

48

Ouroboros

December 15, 2015

Three days after meeting Logan's family, Lola found herself seated across from Dr. Indigo, telling her everything that had occurred from facing Andy to realizing the full weight of her feelings for Logan, to finally meeting his family.

Having made several notes as Lola recounted the events of the last nine days, Dr. Indigo finally took her turn to speak. "I'm glad to hear things went better than you expected with Logan's family, specifically his mother, as I know that filled you with a great deal of apprehension. How are you feeling after hearing what some would view as harsh criticism from Andy?"

Lola thought for several moments before finally saying, "Well, at first I was super devastated because I did love him so much, just like he was a brother. But then as I grieved the loss of the past, I realized that in this case, I'm really not so different from Anne-Marie as I thought I was."

Upon Dr. Indigo's prompting for further explanation, Lola elaborated. "I basically told Anne-Marie the same thing Andy told me, and that made me realize that my actions in the past really were hurtful. And while I don't live there anymore, every action still has consequences."

"With the revelation of your feelings for Logan, how did it feel to finally admit them out loud?" Dr. Indigo asked after scribbling down more notes.

"I guess … I feel … free. Yeah- I feel free. Like I'm one step closer to finally being able to step out of the cage I allowed Jacob to trap me in. And it feels really good to start letting myself out.

"I think having some time away from Logan, in a natural way, helped me to realize just how real these feelings I have for him are." Lola acknowledged.

"One last question before we end our session today that I'd like for you to reflect on and answer in our next session in January. Now that you are drawing closer to the *incident*, do you plan on facing Jacob one last time for final closure?" Noticing Lola's panicked expression, Dr. Indigo elaborated upon her query.

"Please know, that this is in no way mandatory for treatment. Many survivors find peace and comfort when being able to stand before their abusers. However, many others can never face them again. Neither choice is wrong, as each survivor has to make the choice that is best for them at their stage of recovery."

Doing her best to remain completely composed, Lola bid Dr. Indigo farewell before driving back to Swan Manor.

~

December 18, 2015

Three days after her session with Dr. Indigo, Lola awoke with determination; feeling it was finally time to tell Logan about the incident. "Good morning, *my love*." Lola warmly greeted Logan with a kiss.

"You know, I don't think I'll ever get tired of hearing you say these words, *my heart*." Logan admitted, for fear this truly would be a dream and his joy would once again slip through his fingers.

"If you're ready to listen, I'd like for us to sit in the sunroom so that I can finally start telling you about the pivotal moments that lead up to the *incident*." With an understanding nod, Logan followed Lola into the well-lit sunroom.

Seated comfortably on the plush sofa, Lola macabrely jested, "You know, it's kinda funny that this room has witnessed both the word of my beginning and now what was nearly the-" Logan cut Lola off with a kiss; selfishly hoping to give himself the strength to relive the darkest and cruelest days of his life.

~

February 14, 2011

Four months had passed since Lola made the shackled promise in the bathroom that fateful day; even going so far as to completely change her number. Though all but dissolving her friendship with Logan killed her inside, Lola felt that for the well-being of her sanity, which was barely hanging on by a thread, this was the lesser of two evils. And while the last four months with Jacob had been some of the best within their relationship, Lola couldn't help but await the moment the ground split beneath her feet, and she was utterly consumed by her own demise.

Having settled herself in at her work desk, Lola quickly became thoroughly engrossed in the file staring back at her on the computer screen. The chiming of the office phone, combined with the gnawing ache of her stomach, caught Lola's attention. *How is it already near noon?* Lola asked herself before answering the phone.

On the other end of the line, Lola's assistant, Jade, informed Lola that a Ms. Catarina was dropping by for lunch. "It would be like Cate to just show up," Lola warmly teased.

"She's got a fit looking fella with her. You know, I wouldn't mind climbing him like a tree right now." Jade remarked in her thick,

British accent, before adding, "He looks rather famous, I feel like I've seen him somewhere before."

"Umm … as far as I'm aware, Cate doesn't know anyone famous, but why don't you send them on up." Lola mused before asking Jade to hold her calls for the remainder of the day; then sent a quick text to Jacob, letting him know she would be with Cate the rest of the day. Stowing her phone away in her purse, Lola put her desk back in order for Cate's arrival.

"Hi, Luxie!" Cate warmly greeted her friend, whose back was turned to her.

Moving around to return Cate's greeting, Lola felt her skin pale as shock left her mouth arid. "Uh … hey Cate … and … Logan. What brings the **two** of you here?" Lola nervously asked, while doing her best to keep the onset of a panic attack at bay. *Shit! Shit! Shit! This is so bad. If Jacob finds out that Logan was here- Fuck! I'm as good as dead. God, why do you hate me?*

Lola reached for her phone to tell Jacob about Logan also being with Cate but was stopped short when Cate grabbed her hand. "Alright, Ms. CEO. I see you're too busy for your best friends now."

"I-It's not like that, Cate. I … I just have to send an important message to send really quick." Lola all but pleaded.

"Nonsense, Luxie. Besides, I highly doubt it's a life or death type thing, and-" Cate admonished before being cut off by the chime of an incoming text from Jacob flashed across Lola's screen. "I think my brother will be fine letting you be. I know that you two are in love, but my god woman, don't forget about your friends."

Oh, Cate...if you only knew how dire this situation really is- Is what Lola wanted to scream out loud, however, she simply resigned to agreeing with Cate's words while plastering on her best, fake smile. "Anyhow, why don't you guys sit on the sofa while I have Jade get our lunch order; then, you can fill me in on this **surprising** visit."

Logan who up to this point had remained silent finally spoke. "Well, today is my birthday-"

"Shit!" Lola interjected before offering her apologies for forgetting Logan's birthday. "With taking on more responsibilities here, I've had a lot of things slip my mind."

Doing his best to hide his downtrodden expression, Logan continued. "It's okay, Lola. Anyhow, uh- like I was saying, today's my birthday and Cate asked me what I wanted to do. This led me to asking if she'd heard from you because I hadn't been able to reach you since the beginning of October. Hell- I didn't even see you at the holiday events."

Logan briefly paused to catch his breath. "Anyhow, I guess I just wanted to know if there was something I'd done to upset you. Our friendship is something special to me, and if I've upset you in any way, I'd like to make amends."

Fighting back the tears that threatened to break the protective wall of her defenses, Lola cleared her throat, before offering a meager apology- one that she hoped would smooth things over with Logan but still maintain the distance that would keep Jacob content.

"I'm really sorry, Logan. I didn't mean to make you feel that way. In October, Jacob took me to Vancouver to show me some of the sights and I ended up losing my phone. Anyhow, by the time we came back stateside, I got a new phone and phone number. I just collected the few phone numbers Jacob had … then everything else going on with work … yeah. I know it's a shit excuse, but I do hope you'll forgive me."

Even though he felt there was far more to Lola's story than what she led on, Logan chose to forgive Lola. Before Logan could say another word, Jade entered the office with the lunch order Lola had requested. "Hey, Luxie, I think I'm gonna have to take mine to go." Cate suddenly remarked.

"Well, I guess I'll be heading out then, too, Lola." Logan dolefully remarked, but quickly changed his demeanor when Cate reassured him that it would be fine if he stayed.

"What do you think, Luxie? Why don't you and Logan take this time to catch up?" Cate sternly requested.

Feeling the stress build within her, Lola dug her nails into her palms, allowing the all too familiar warmth to stain her nail beds. "Ugh, yeah … I think that sh-should be fine." Lola meekly replied.

As soon as Cate was out of earshot, Logan set his fork on the table and cleared his throat before speaking words that caused Lola to pale, and nearly crumble her weakly crafted walls. "Lola, I don't know what is going on in your life, but you're my best friend, and I can tell when you're blatantly lying. So, I'm begging you, please tell me what's really going on? Are you being abused?"

Not yet able to fully call her situation what it was, Lola screamed out her frustrations at Logan. "What the hell would you even know, Logan? Huh? Sometimes I step out of line, but I know Jacob loves me enough to help me see when I'm wrong. If you're gonna make judgmental assumptions, you can just get the fuck out of my office!"

Logan quickly apologized for overstepping with his care and concerns, while enveloping Lola in the warmest hug he could. "I'm sorry for assuming, Lola, I really am. If you say you're fine, then I'll believe you for now. However, please take my number again. You call me or text me anytime you need me. I swear I'll be there, okay?"

Though it took her a couple of minutes to reciprocate Logan's friendly action, Lola eventually did. *How the hell could Logan even know? Shit! He can't begin to understand even half of it- but still … his warm embrace somehow feels safe.*

~

December 18, 2015
Logan couldn't help but laugh as Lola's stomach mercilessly

growled. "Geez, Lola, do you have a bear trapped in there?"

"Yes, and a hangry, rabid one at that! So let's pause for lunch, okay?"

When the table was set with turkey club sandwiches and tomato bisque soup, Logan finally asked Lola what really happened to her phone in 2011, to which she truthfully responded. "The part about being in Vancouver was true. However, I didn't actually lose it … Jacob broke it because you were calling me. I'm just thankful my punishment wasn't too bad because of that phone call."

"Well, that explains why you looked so skittish when I showed up with Cate, and when she left me there."

"Yeah- anyhow, why don't we go over the menu for the Christmas party before I start back?" Lola offered, hoping a little extra break would push her through to the next parts to come.

Three hours later, with the menu completely finalized and dish requests sent out to the guests, Lola asked Logan if he would bring a couple of blankets and the space heater out to the sunroom. "Since we started out here, might as well finish out here. Besides, they're calling for rain later this evening, and the sound of the rain against the roof and windows of this room is very soothing."

Lola gave Logan a kiss for courage and began once more.

~

June 4, 2011

When Lola awoke that Saturday morning, she couldn't help but be weighed down; with what, she could not exactly say. Reaching over, only to find Jacob's spot had long since grown cold, Lola sighed, though she wasn't surprised to once again wake up alone. Several weeks prior, beginning in April, Maximillian demanded that Jacob meet with him daily; for what, Lola could not say. Only knowing that the more time Jacob spent with his father, the more on edge he became.

As Lola carefully made her way to the shower, it dawned on her that it had been eight months since Jacob last hit her in anger for something she had done, he still made sure Lola felt the full force of his control and personal frustrations; because sex never was something for her love and pleasure. The proof of his masochism stared angrily back at Lola as she tried to wash herself with the utmost care.

Stepping out of the shower, Lola saw a message on her phone from Jacob demanding she dress appropriately for dinner at his parents' house for his and Cate's birthday dinner. Having sifted through her closet for something, most likely a simple summer dress, that would not only provide full coverage to her back, stomach, and arms; but also was lightweight enough so as not to irritate the painful abrasions.

Having three options laid across her bed, Lola found herself wondering if Logan would make an appearance, and if he did, which color would he find the most attractive. While nearly four months had passed since Lola last saw or spoke with Logan, and though she had his number once more, she dared not to contact him, for fear of disrupting the delicate balance she currently had with Jacob. Nonetheless, that carefully crafted balance would suddenly shift in a direction no one truly expected.

Finally, she settled upon a beautiful, sheer blue-grey polyester, mini wrap dress with long, bubble-style sleeves, and had the faintest rose detailing in white. Lola then pulled out an elegant pair of nude leather high heels, with handmade ivory lace. Next, adding her watch, and the black, rose earrings and fox necklace Jacob had gifted her in the past, before completing the look by securing her curls into a romantic side ponytail and adding her usual makeup look.

Satisfied that her appearance would bring her the least amount of trouble, Lola made her way into the kitchen for a glass of water. "Fuck, *Vix*. You look sexy as hell." Jacob called out as he entered the kitchen, before pressing Lola's stomach against the marble countertop and running his hands along her exposed thighs.

Lola couldn't help but blush while biting her lip at Jacob's compliment. "Th-thank you, Jacob." Lola meekly stuttered before trying to turn to face the man she blindly loved, only to be stopped by Jacob's firm hold.

"Just where do you think you're going, my little *Vixen?*" Jacob huskily breathed, while toying with the hem of Lola's lacy thong.

"W-won't we be late?" Lola spoke with a mixture of discomfort due to her previous abrasions being pressed into the counter and the arousal building from the tender caresses near her sensitive area.

"*Vix*, you should know well enough by now that I'm frustrated as hell after meeting with my father- and fuck! Seeing you in this color is doing my head in. Either you let me fuck you right now, like the good girl you are, or..."

Lola gulped nervously at the word "or," knowing well enough by now that an unfinished thought from Jacob was the devil's playground. The next words she would utter made Lola die a little more inside, but knew it was best to play the part of a willing victim, lest another garment become permanently stained like a war-torn rose. "Please ... please fuck me, Jacob. After all, my body and soul are yours and yours alone, to do with as you wish."

When Jacob finished his voracious ravishment of her body, he gracefully positioned Lola so that their eyes met. And while the running lines of mascara stirred no feelings within him, Jacob knew that to properly keep Lola, feigning care and consideration was the route he must travel. Wrapping his arms around Lola, Jacob held her close as he became lost in his own thoughts-

For in another place and time, he could see himself possibly falling madly in love with the rose-colored beauty clinging to him. However, for a man like Jacob Sterling Gallagher power, domination, and possession far outweighed any other emotional sentiment. *Why have something as useless as love, when watching a person completely break is far more satisfying.*

~

Having sorted out her appearance once more, Lola found herself seated in the passenger's seat of Jacob's car, as Jacob made the drive to his family's home. While Lola had planned to exit the vehicle as hastily as possible because at that moment in time, the further she was from Jacob, the better; she was stopped short by Jacob's grasp the instant he parked the car.

"When we get inside, you are allowed to say a quick hello to my mother and Catarina before we meet with my father." Jacob asserted.

Though she wanted to protest the meeting with Maximillian, self-preservation got the best of her. With a heavy-hearted sigh, Lola simply uttered, "Fine, Jacob."

"That's a good girl, *Vix.*" Jacob commended as he pulled her in for a tender kiss. With his hand still resting on the back of Lola's neck, Jacob squeezed just tight enough to show the severity of his warning as he spoke his next demand. "And remember, *Vix*, you'd do well to remember the promise you made in October. In no way possible are you to be alone with Logan. If he approaches you, turn the other way. Am I clear?"

"Crystal..." Lola flatly replied, bowing her head in submission, before exiting the car.

Enveloping Lola in a hug once more, Jacob whispered more to himself than anyone else, "Good, because I'm not afraid to reinforce the measures I've had to take just to be able to keep you."

While curiosity at the meaning of Jacob's statement tried to settle into Lola's primary focus, it soon was replaced with the uneasy thoughts of meeting face-to-face with Maximillian.

Since Cate had yet to arrive, Lola exchanged brief pleasantries with Evelynn, who seemed to appear more somber than usual as she gave Lola a pitying embrace. Evelynn briefly hugged her son as well, before praying silently as she watched them walk down the hall to Maximillian's office. *I'm so sorry, you sweet, precious woman. Lord, please know that I tried my hardest to save her, even though my hands are completely bound, and my voice is practically useless.*

Now seated in the office that, on the outside bore no difference to the one her grandfather had occupied in their home, Lola somehow felt strangled by the power emanating from the man seated directly across from her. The powerful aura was so intense that had Lola eaten anything that day, surely the contents from her stomach would have revealed themselves.

As for Jacob, while he said nothing, irritation radiated through him- causing him to firmly grip the leather arms of the chair where he was seated. The less his father meddled in his personal affairs, the better. After all, wasn't he now the one who was supposed to be in charge of the financial empire?

When several uneasy minutes had passed, Maximillian finally cleared his throat; speaking in a gentle tone that somehow seemed far more off-putting than his normal one. "Lola, my dear, it is lovely to see you."

"Th-tha-thank you, Maximillian, sir." Lola stuttered, her body shaking like the sole remaining leaf on a blustery autumn day.

"You're not nervous are you, dear?" Maximillian queried in a nearly condescending tone.

"J-just a little, sir." Lola, who wished Jacob would offer his hand to her for a source of strength and comfort, hated herself for the weakness her voice displayed.

"Well, my dear, there's no need for you to be nervous. After all, unlike my two children, you have yet to be a disappointment to me. Now, why don't you tell me about your relationship and feelings with my son."

The weight of Maximillian's question severely caught Lola by surprise, leaving her unable to really begin to understand how to answer. Having remained silent for far longer than she should have, Jacob firmly squeezed Lola's hand, earning him a satisfying squeak of surprise. Though the action was painful, Lola took it as a loving nudge, thus restoring her voice. "I love Jacob very much. So much so in fact, that he's interwoven into every fiber of my soul."

Offering Jacob a wink of approval, Maximillian continued with his odd array of questioning. "Well, as a *loving* father, those words are exactly what I want to hear. In fact, it reminds me of my early days with Evelynn. Since we've established precisely how much you love my son, are you willing to do anything for him?"

"Uh … I mean, I guess so, just as long as it's legal. W-why do you ask?"

"Wonderful!" Maximillian exclaimed with an echoing clap of his hands, prior to addressing his son. "Now to you, Jacob, or better yet- the greatest disappointment of my life- since I have officially paved the way for you, would you like to rectify the mistakes you made with *Bunni?* And by all means, do fill your little '*Vixen*' in on our conversations the last several weeks."

While he wanted nothing more than to reach across the desk and watch the life leave the eyes of his father as he strangled him, Jacob exhaled in deep frustration, as he impertinently proceeded to tell Lola his brief history with Rebecca, more affectionately referred to as *Bunni.* "Since I chose not to get married, the smug asshole sitting across from us has apparently maintained control of everything that is rightfully mine."

"Isn't it just the most wonderful turn of events, my dear?" Maximillian chuckled darkly as he addressed Lola.

"Oh, okay. Uh, what does this have to do with me?" Lola cautiously asked.

"I was hoping you'd ask that, Lola!" Maximillian exclaimed while reaching into the side drawer of his desk. Pulling out a small, black velvet box; sliding it to Lola as he proceeded. "Since we have established that you love my son enough to do anything, barring it is within the realm of legality, why don't you go ahead and slip this on your pretty little finger."

"Just put the fucking ring on, *Vix!*" Jacob brashly spat out as a result of Lola's hesitation; before jamming the ring on Lola's slender finger. Years of pent-up anger and frustration finally boiled over within Lola as she fiercely slapped Jacob across the face, busting his lip in the process.

A burst of dark and demented laughter erupted from Jacob, as his icy, white eyes shifted, allowing his inner demons to surface. "Kinky, my little *Vixen.*" Jacob ferociously growled out before standing to slam Lola's body against the office's solid, oak door. "I'm gonna give you two fucking choices," Jacob seethed. "One, you can act like a stupid bitch one more got damn time, and I fuck you into submission, right here and now. Or, you can get your act together and realize you're never going anywhere."

Lola was instantly filled with regret the moment her hand collided with Jacob's face; and while she wanted to beg for forgiveness, she knew it was futile, as Jacob never was the forgiving type. Feeling yet another piece of her slowly disintegrate when Jacob laid out his ultimatum, Lola defeatedly took the second option; uttering the harrowing words, which once again cemented her dismal fate. "I will marry you, Jacob. Besides, my body and soul are yours and yours alone, to do with as you wish."

Jacob oppressively entangled his mouth with Lola's the second she fully accepted the carefully crafted destiny he had laid out before her. Breaking the kiss, Jacob gently wiped Lola's tears for the second time that day. "Hush now, *Vix*. You know I don't enjoy having to be harsh with you, don't you? I'm honestly just as stuck as you." Jacob whispered into her ear, as he set to release her, but not before crudely stating, "Now clean yourself up, because you look ugly as hell when you cry. You'd do well to remember that no Gallagher man wants to be seen with a woman who can't even look halfway decent."

Lola sluggishly stepped into the bathroom just to the right of Maximillian's office. The mirror's reflection of a hollow shell did little to comfort Lola as she reapplied her makeup for the third time that day. Drying her hands, Lola finally took the time to fully inspect the tiny shackle disguised as jewelry. The black gold band was of standard thickness, approximately 2mm in width, housed a total of ten, 0.5-carat garnet stones; five on each side of the band, with a stunning 3.0-carat garnet stone faceted perfectly in the middle. Even though the color, clarity, and design were all on par with the items Jacob had gifted her in the past, Lola couldn't help but hate it. *How can something so lovely tighten the noose dangling from my neck?*

Stepping back out into the hall, Lola squeaked in surprise as she ran face-first into Jacob, whose expression was now one that made her heart melt all over again. With a softened smile and eyes that appeared to hint at his fondness for Lola, Jacob brought her to his chest and tenderly kissed her head. "I don't like scaring you so harshly. You know that don't you, *Vix*?"

"I know you don't, Jacob. It was my own fault for not being obedient and answering quickly. I'm sorry." Lola continually bewitched herself by believing love blossomed in the wasteland of Jacob's heart. Satisfied with the complacency of his obsession, Jacob led Lola into the main room of the house. "Now, let's go announce our engagement to the family before Max decides to take another shit on my day."

~

December 18, 2015

Lola stifled a yawn as she glanced down at her watch, hardly believing that it was already drawing close to midnight; she apologized for not making it very far before asking if they could reconvene after the Christmas party, to which Logan readily agreed.

"If you're okay with it, *my heart*, I'd like to go back to my apartment for a couple of days. I have some jobs that I need to finish up." Lola acknowledged that she was fine with that, before kissing Logan good night as she saw him to the door.

While Logan's request held a decent measure of truth, his real reasoning for wanting to leave was so that he wouldn't break down in front of Lola. His one goal through this whole painful ordeal was to remain strong for the woman he loved, but how could he do that, when feelings of guilt, devastation, and anger that had festered just below his supportive surface, finally overflowed into bitter sobs.

49

She dances with marigolds at her feet...

December 23, 2015

The day of the Christmas party quickly arrived, and with it, great excitement in Swan Manor. With a good majority of the house decorated, Lola moved her things into the room which had been her grandparents, before adding a few extra touches to her childhood bedroom, in hopes that Raelee, Eloise, and Rosalie would have a fun place to hang out when the adults became too boring for them. Pleased with the layout of the room, Lola proceeded to the master bathroom to finish getting herself ready but was cut off by the chiming of the doorbell.

When she answered the door, Lola was happy to see both Britt and Lizzie standing there, while Raelee pointed the familiar surroundings out to Eloise and Rosalie. After ushering everyone inside, Lola asked where Logan, Dean, and Mark were. Lizzie said Mark had an emergency at work but would be there as soon as everything was handled. As for Logan and Dean, Britt explained that they had stopped to pick up Cate and Cade before arriving.

"Wonderful!" Lola joyfully exclaimed as she directed Britt and Lizzie to the rooms set aside for their stay. "Once you ladies have your bags set down, I'd like to show everyone where the girls will be staying."

Standing outside the bedroom door, Lola asked for the girls to close their eyes, because she had a special surprise. When they finally entered the room, all three girls squealed in delight. Across the bed, she laid three similar-looking lace, tea-length, a-line dresses with cap sleeves; each dress had a pearled satin ribbon around the waist. The only difference between the three dresses was the color; periwinkle for Raelee, royal blue for Eloise, and aubergine for Rosalie.

With her guests settled, Lola headed to her bathroom to ready herself. Instead of her usual, more muted eyeshadow look, Lola chose to apply a smokey mauve base with a glittery gold top layer, then applied her signature deep red, matte lipstick; she then proceeded to pull her hair half up, while leaving a few stray curls to frame her face. As soon as she started to step into her dress, there came a knock at her door; expecting Lizzie to be standing on the other side, Lola blindly called for the owner of the knock to enter. Instead of Lizzie standing on the other side of the door, Lola found Logan's mother.

Doing her best to hide her discomfort, Lola invited Britt inside. "Is everything okay with your room?" Lola asked, in hopes of making the situation not feel so awkward. "I'm about to put my dress on, and if you don't mind, would you be able to help me with the zipper?"

Britt went on to say that everything was just fine with the room, before extending her gratitude for Lola's generosity in gifting her daughters the beautiful dresses. "I know that I have never been silent with my son, in regards to my disdain for you, but" Britt began to explain as she finished zipping the neck of Lola's dress, "it's only because I love him so very much."

Patting Lola's back to signal she was finished helping with the dress, Britt went on to provide further explanation, with a look of wonder and admiration shining through her bright, blue eyes. "I absolutely adore my daughters, and I do thank God for them every single day. However, Logan is far more precious to me. When he was born, I had only just turned 16 twelve days prior. And in a way, I guess you could say that we grew up together. Now, while I am still not your biggest fan, I see how much my son truly loves you, so … I guess … I'm willing to give you a chance." Without changing her pleasant expression, Britt added, "Just know that, if you break his heart again, it will be the **very last** heart you ever break. Okay?"

After stating her piece, Britt gently patted Lola on the arm, before making her exit. Lola couldn't help but be left wide-eyed and speechless at what she knew was the sincere promise of a mother's heart. Slipping into a pair of glittery, champagne stilettos, Lola quickly took one last look at her reflection, hoping Logan would find her appearance agreeable, before making her way to the foyer to greet her guests.

Having greeted the final guest, Lola set off in search of Logan who had managed to slip in the back entrance as he helped Cate carry in a few packages; and was delighted to find him joyfully dancing with his sisters and Raelee. A blush crept across her face as she took in Logan's physique, as seeing him in a suit was quite the rare, but very welcome, annual occurrence. For the evening, Logan chose a slim-fitting three-piece suit in royal blue that made his eyes shine like the brightest star on a clear night, which he paired with an ebony-colored shirt and tie, and black leather dress shoes.

Looking up from dancing with her brother, little Rosalie squealed with delight as she saw Lola, before all but demanding he stop dancing, and take sight of his beloved. "Logie! Logie! Look at how pretty Lola is."

"Wow!" Was the only word Logan could even think to utter, as he was instantly captivated once more by Lola's appearance. The full-length, onyx-colored, long-sleeved velvet dress with a turtleneck contrasted flawlessly with her fair skin and rose-red hair. After thanking Raelee and his sisters for the wonderful dances, Logan hastily moved in Lola's direction.

Having met each other in the middle, Lola wrapped her arms around Logan, before asking his thoughts on her outfit. Upon closer inspection, Logan noticed the uniqueness of Lola's dress; and while he had seen her in many formal dresses throughout the years, this one would have to be his favorite, as it had refined elegance with a slight punk flair. "You look so stunning, *my heart.* I think my favorite part is how the sleeves go down to your hands and even have thumb holes; kinda like punk gloves."

"I really thought you'd like that," Lola happily exclaimed, before turning around, "but my favorite part is the fully open back. I can finally show off Luka's handy work!"

Doing his best to keep his lewd thoughts at bay, Logan took Lola in his arms and fervidly captured her lips. "I love you so, so fucking much, *my heart.*" Logan breathlessly spoke after breaking their kiss. Lola returned Logan's affections, as they joined the rest of the party.

~

January 7, 2016

Logan awoke before sunrise the morning of January 7 feeling deeply burdened, in fact, he didn't think he could possibly hate a singular day more. While this date had been of little thought or consequence last year, this year was quite the opposite. All of the feelings he had somehow managed to suppress seemed to overwhelm him at an alarming pace.

Though he may not have known the **why** or **how** of what led to the events that took place on this date four years ago, Logan knew the devastating **what** of those events. And although he knew what he was getting into when Lola asked to start explaining everything, it had never dawned on Logan … until this very moment … how painful reliving some memories could truly be.

Logan sighed heavily as he looked over at the now empty bed, realizing he was once again alone in his apartment; while he wished for nothing more than to wake up surrounded by Lola's cascading curls, Logan knew he had to respect her wishes of staying by herself at Swan Manor. Finally willing himself out of bed, Logan made his way to the shower, in hopes of allowing the hot water to wash away his pensive thoughts.

Once out of the shower, Logan saw a good morning text from Lola, followed by another asking him to come to Swan Manor so that she could start back up from where she had last left off. Quickly throwing on a charcoal grey, cable knit sweater; a pair of dark wash, ripped skinny jeans; and a pair of black combat boots, Logan replied to Lola's message as he headed out the door.

~

Lola yelped in surprise as strong arms embraced her from behind. "Easy there, *my heart.*" Logan soothed, before nuzzling into the crook of her neck. "Mmm- I have missed you so damn much."

"I'm glad you missed me, and I missed you too, but I barely got your text ten minutes ago, Warren!" Lola admonished while trying to hide the blush that had managed to take up residence upon her porcelain face.

"I may or may not have sped the whole way here," Logan shrugged nonchalantly.

"Don't do that ever again, okay, Warren?" Lola began as she took note of Logan's nodding head. "Please promise me, because seeing me isn't worth risking your life or someone else's."

"Okay, okay! I promise, alright?" Logan surrendered before Lola affectionately wrapped her arms around him.

"I know why you did though…" Lola started while rubbing her forehead against Logan's chest. "…and I don't blame you. After all, it's exactly four years to the date that the **incident** occurred." Lola held Logan tightly, doing her best to comfort the man who held almost all of her heart. After several passing minutes, Lola broke away from Logan's embrace to finish preparing their breakfast.

When the kitchen was once again in order, Lola clapped her hands together before pushing Logan towards the garage. "Alright, Warren, we're going on a little field trip- and just let me finish before you ask- I will still be starting from where I stopped, but the main part of this will happen in Dr. Indigo's office."

Logan responded he understood by giving Lola's hand a gentle squeeze. As soon as she had pulled out of the garage, and onto the road, Lola began.

~

June 4, 2011

After the twins' birthday dinner, Jacob proceeded to announce his engagement to Lola- something that took Cate, Cade, and Logan completely by surprise; while leaving Evelynn in a lugubrious state, and Maximillian thoroughly satisfied.

Two hours preceding the announcement, Lola found herself aimlessly gazing out at the setting sun. "Hey- is everything okay? You don't seem like someone who's happy to be engaged." A deep voice called out, taking the seat beside her.

Never turning her gaze from the view before her, lest she was to completely crumble, Lola answered with what she hoped would be the most satisfying answer, while doling out the least amount of trouble for herself. "It is what it is, Logan … It is what it is." Logan placed his hand on Lola's in hopes of providing comfort and did his best to hide his dismay when Lola quickly snatched hers away.

"Well, I'd better see if Jacob is ready to go." Lola timidly called while standing with haste. Though she had wanted to escape as quickly as possible, Lola's hopes were once again dashed when Logan embraced her, in a manner that was no different from the countless hugs of the past.

Once again, neither fate nor fortune was on Lola's side; for the moment Logan hugged Lola, was the exact moment Jacob stepped out onto the back patio. And though any rational person who chanced to look upon the situation would have been able to easily read Lola's visible discomfort- Jacob Gallagher, on the other hand, was far from rational in that heated moment.

"Are you fucking kidding me?!" Jacob fumed as he snatched Lola from Logan's arms, pushing her behind him. "Listen here, you stupid son of a bitch, if you touch what is mine again, I'll fucking kill you! Can you get that through your stupid ass head?" Jacob seethed as he bowed up to Logan.

"Come at me then, you abusive mother fucker! Or is your narcissistic ass only afraid to fight a man? Let me guess, you only get off hitting defenseless women?" Logan challenged before sending a swift right hook to Jacob's jaw.

"Stop it, right now!" Lola screamed before swiftly positioning herself between the two men who towered over her greatly. The sound of Lola's scream brought forth the rushing footsteps of Cate and Cade. Upon seeing her brother and stepson about to kill one another, Cate yelled, "What the hell is going on?"

"Jacob, please stop, okay? Let's just go home." Lola begged, while weakly trying to redirect Jacob toward the door.

"Just remember what I said, Logan. It's a fucking promise." Jacob seethed, as he spat out the blood that had pooled in his mouth, before yanking Lola by the arm and whispering in her ear, that he would make sure to deal with her when they got home.

~

January 7, 2016

Lola paused as she pulled into her usual parking space; taking note of the nervous manner in which Logan's right leg bounced, she reached over to squeeze his left hand, in what she hoped would help bring him some form of comfort. "Ya know," she started, "it's kinda funny that I am now doing the things you used to do, to help me calm down."

Returning Lola's affection, Logan exhaled in the most plaintive of manners. On most days, Logan would have been able to quickly mask his emotions, however, the longer this day went on, the more it felt like he was drowning in the resurfaced memories of the past.

Making their way inside the office building, Lola checked in for her session, then told Logan once again, "I know I've said it several times by now, but time with you back then, **really** was trouble for me. Just please remember, that I'd go through it all again just to have your friendship at the end. Your friendship was the last lifeline I had."

Fifteen minutes later, Logan and Lola were seated, side-by-side, across from Dr. Indigo. "Thank you for joining us today, Logan." Dr. Indigo warmly greeted, before proceeding to tell Logan that she would be taking several notes throughout the session. "Logan, please know that if at any point things get too heavy, you are allowed to stop the session by stepping out of the room- no explanation will be necessary. If you choose to leave, I'll just proceed with Lola's normal session. Is that okay?"

Once Logan nodded his head in understanding, Dr. Indigo directed her next two questions to Lola. "Lola, would you mind telling me where you left off with Logan, and are you at a point where you are finally ready to call what happened by its name?"

"I left off at the fight that went down between Jacob and Logan," Lola started before jesting, "well- I guess you couldn't call it much of a fight, since Logan knocked the shit out of Jacob's jaw." Lola then allowed her expression to turn serious, "I'm still not quite ready to call it by name, but I think once I get there, I will be."

"Alright, Lola, let's get started then." Dr. Indigo directed while making a couple of small notes.

~

July 16, 2011

The month and a half following her engagement to Jacob showed Lola an even more depraved side of him that she wished would have never surfaced- for a single boundary, his cruelty knew not.

At first, Lola tried to justify Jacob's actions, because once again it was her fault Logan decided to hug her. Then, she tried to deceive herself by claiming Jacob was simply teaching her "valuable life lessons," such as: How the structural integrity of a glass coffee table is rather misleading when it can hold the weight of a variety of thick books and other solid centerpieces; yet it can't even begin to fathom the density of an adult woman who barely weighed 90 pounds, as she came crashing in. Or, how if she were going to pull a knife on someone out of anger, she should be fully willing to commit to the act, lest she once again was to wind up with a fractured wrist.

While the beatings may have hurt her body, Jacob found a new way to chip away at Lola's soul even quicker. Instead of trying to hide his infidelities, Jacob brought them front and center, by tying Lola to the armchair in their bedroom, making her watch as he ravaged countless women. The recurring dizzy spells were a reminder that looking away from the vile lascivious acts occurring in front of her, was **not** an option.

And as if this cruelty wasn't enough, the thing that ate away at Lola's heart the most, was Jacob's newest game- one that instantly became his favorite. Every time Jacob finished spending his time with various pieces of trash, he always made sure he had his way with her, before holding her hostage in his arms as they slept.

~

August 2, 2011

Now that Maximillian had revealed the truth to Jacob regarding his position within the company, Jacob once again began to jump through hoops, with futile hopes of getting his father off of his back. Thus, leading Lola to awaken by herself on the morning of her 27th birthday.

Just as she started to dream of treating this particular day without consequence, her phone began chiming with a barrage of texts. *Is it really too much to ask that people forget this worthless day?* Lola sighed heavily before rolling over to pick up her phone. Glancing at the screen, she noticed a total of 31 missed text messages. Two of the messages came from Cate: one wished her a happy birthday, before asking her what kind of cake she would like to have. While the other one asked for her to please text Logan, as he desperately wanted to wish her a happy birthday.

One message came from Gregory, who also wished her a happy birthday, before inquiring if she was feeling better. One message was from Jacob, who did wish her a happy birthday, before reminding her, as if she were a child, to be on her best behavior.

The remaining 27 text messages came from Lizzie, one character at a time, but when viewed horizontally, they read, *"Happy 27th Birthday Lola Luxe!!,"* which greatly amused Lola. Lola took the time to respond to each person's message, even Jacob's backhanded one, before finally texting Logan to ask if he would like to spend the day with her.

Not even a full minute had passed when Logan's reply came across Lola's screen; they agreed to meet at **Cate's** in about three hours so that Cate would have time to finish the cake she planned every year. While this action would most likely have ruinous ramifications for her, and with Jacob's threatening promise to Logan the furthest thing from her mind, Lola decided that she would take whatever Jacob threw at her, literally and figuratively.

After checking the weather, Lola threw on a pair of mid-wash, skinny jeans with rolled cuffs; a dark grey, v-neck t-shirt; a pair of black leather Mary Jane style Dr. Martens; and a lightweight, vintage army jacket. She was quite thankful for the relatively cool, summer day because even though her bruises had begun to heal, they were still visible enough to garner unwanted attention. Finding her appearance passable, Lola quickly left for **Cate's**.

Pulling into her usual parking space at **Cate's**, Lola felt her stomach begin to tense up. Unsure if the unsettled feeling was due to lack of nourishment, or just general anxiety, Lola took a few deep breaths as she willed herself out of the car. Once inside the café, all sense of unsettledness began to melt away. Though the decorations were the same ones Cate used any time she held a party there, Lola couldn't help but smile at the momentary feeling of peace they brought her, which she used to help carry her through the room before it faded away once more.

Using this temporary feeling of peace to her advantage, Lola quickly sought out Logan, who gave her his hug laced with compassion and some other emotion she couldn't quite figure out. And although a small part of Lola's damaged heart wanted nothing more than to reciprocate Logan's hug, the much larger, misgiving part simply wouldn't have it.

When Lola had greeted everyone else, Cate brought out the cake which left Lola awestruck. "Ya know, I only asked for something simple this year." Lola teased after everyone finished singing. Though the cake was simple in color, the intricately piped flowers, each topped with raspberries, were nothing short of impressive.

"What?! You don't think this is simple?" Cate exclaimed as she feigned offense while cutting the first slice. "It does have all of the elements you asked for: a dark chocolate cake, white frosting, and some raspberries. You should know by now, Luxie, that when creative liberties are left to me, I will take the full force."

"I should've known what I was getting into," Lola laughed merrily, before thanking her friend for putting in the time and effort.

When very little of the cake remained, Logan walked over to Lola to ask what she would like to do for the remainder of her birthday. After careful consideration, Lola finally decided that she would like to sit at the marina and just watch the sunset. "I know it's probably the most boring thing to do on a birthday, but I think I'm just about peopled out."

"Lola, it's your birthday, so whatever you want to do, we'll do it. Okay?"

"Thanks, Warren. I'm gonna start driving there now, so I'll see you in a bit, yeah?" Lola remarked before turning to say goodbye to the last few remaining guests and making her leave.

As he was about to head out the door to his vehicle, Logan was stopped by Cate. "Hey, Logan. While you're out there with Lola, do you think you can see if she's really okay? She won't talk to me about anything to do with her engagement to my brother. And when I tried to reach out to her after you and Jacob had that altercation, she was even more distant.

"I've been even more concerned because you said something about abuse, and … I guess it just scares me. I love both Luxie and my brother, and I don't want to believe he would actually do something like that, or even be capable of such an unspeakable act. Ya know?" Cate frantically admitted.

"All I can do is try, Cate. But hell, Lola shuts me out far more than anyone else." Logan stated as he stepped out the front door.

With the sun sinking slowly into the harbor, Logan took notice of how Lola continuously fidgeted with her engagement ring. "Is it uncomfortable," he finally asked.

Pondering this query for several moments, Lola finally answered, "It's just heavy ... everything feels so heavy," before slipping her untethered hand into Logan's, while they silently sat to watch the last of the sunset.

~

January 7, 2016

The constant buzzing of Logan's phone caused Lola to pause. "Sorry about that," Logan apologized as he looked at the screen. "Do you mind if I step out to take this? Pablo never calls this much, so I wanna make sure it's not an emergency."

"That's quite alright, Logan. Besides, this will give me some time to ask Lola a few questions regarding our standard session today." Dr. Indigo cordially replied.

Stepping out into the parking lot, Logan returned Pablo's call. "Hey, brother. What's up? Everything okay?" Logan carefully asked.

Excitement flooded the other side of the phone line as Pablo asked Logan what he would be doing in February. "Well, to be honest, I really don't know yet." Logan truthfully replied.

"Well, why don't you get that sweet ginger ass over here to L.A. at the beginning of next month and plan on staying through your birthday?"

"I'll have to think about it. Besides, I'm not sure what Lola will have planned."

Pablo bristled at the mention of Lola's name. "Logan, my brother, please don't tell me you're still hung up on that bitch."

"Pablo, call my girl a bitch one more fucking time and I swear it'll be the last time I fucking talk to you. Got it?" Logan seethed, before taking a few breaths to calm his nerves. "Now, what's the big deal about me coming then?"

"Sorry, man. I won't call your girl a 'bitch' again. Alright? Uh- anyhow, there's this music festival, **Elysium Underground**, happening at **Grand Park**, and since Shaw said you were workin' on some new material, Pierre and I thought I'd be great to get out there and play again."

"I don't know man…"

"Look, Logan, we understand you went through some scary shit. Hell, the three of us even agreed to go on hiatus, because without you, **Beyond Oregon** doesn't exist. But don't you think you owe it to us to perform at least once. Shit, you can even bring your girl if it helps." Pablo pleaded.

Mulling it over in his mind, Logan finally relented to his friend's request. "Fine. I'll come, but I'm not going to bring Lola. It'll be good for us to have a little time apart, plus … she still may or may not know that I'm in a band."

"What the hell, Logan?"

"I know, I know. I'll tell her. Besides, any time I tried in the past it just never worked out, but I will one day, just not today. Anyhow, before I get off of here, tell Pierre and Shaw that I'll have a new song ready so that we can practice and perform at the festival."

Logan returned his phone to his pocket with a heavy sigh, before making his way back into the office.

50

...and white carnations in her hand

January 7, 2016

As soon as Logan left the room, Dr. Indigo began with the standard questions regarding Lola's eating and sleeping habits, to which Lola replied that everything was fine. "Wonderful to hear, Lola. Now, would you mind telling me if you have noticed any significant behavioral changes in yourself?"

Lola then told Dr. Indigo how she found herself doing the small acts of comfort for Logan, that he had done for her over the last year and a half. "It's kinda weird, but in a really good way, that I don't even second guess reaching out to hold his hand first, or give him a hug or a kiss. It's like it's just instinctual at this point."

Notating Lola's progress, Dr. Indigo asked, "In our last session you told me about how you and Logan crossed a new threshold with your relationship, both with an official label and reaching a new level of physical intimacy. Since that session, have you and Logan had any other discussions regarding physical intimacy, or are you still feeling apprehensive?"

"Other than the usual hugs, kissing, and holding hands, we haven't had any kind of intense physical intimacy like we did in the shower.

As much as I have the desire to fully have sex with Logan, parts of my brain still become blindsided by fear. I am wanting to wait until after I fully discuss the incident in its entirety with Logan before we move any further in the direction of physical intimacy."

"One last question before Logan returns," Dr. Indigo began after marking down Lola's progress and thoughts, "have you been able to reach a decision in regards to the question I ended our last session on? Do you think you will soon be ready to face Jacob, or is that something you can't answer just yet?" Taking note of the uncomfortable look on Lola's face, Dr. Indigo added, "Please remember, that whatever decision you choose to make, has no negative ramifications upon your healing."

Thinking for several minutes, Lola finally admitted that at this particular moment, she was unable to say one way or the other. "I would like to say, 'Yes! I am more than ready to face that smug asshole and show him just how wrong he was.' But then I think, 'What if I'm in over my head? What if I reset every ounce of progress I have made?' So, as much as I'd like to decide right here and now, I just can't."

Logan returned shortly after Lola finished her statement. When Logan had taken his seat, Lola asked if everything was okay. "Everything's great, *my heart*!" Logan exclaimed, before explaining the details of the conversation. "I'd love for you to meet my friends soon, but for this trip, I think it'd be good to see them on my own, especially since it's been nearly a year since I last saw them."

Though she was a little disheartened at the thought of still not meeting Logan's friends, Lola understood Logan's reasoning; her only requests were that Logan call her periodically and bring her home a t-shirt from whichever band he felt was the sickest.

Clearing her throat, Dr. Indigo asked, "Alright, Lola, are you ready to continue?"

~

December 31, 2011

Lola spent the next few months after her birthday desperately clinging to Logan's friendship, but always just out of sight of Jacob's watchful eye; almost as if Logan were her dirty little secret, even though nothing remotely dirty ever occurred. And while most people would say Lola was just using Logan for her own selfish needs, a fact in which she couldn't deny even if she tried, Lola simply couldn't bring herself to let him go.

The apartment she had first rented after Shane's passing and had held onto all this time, quickly became the one safe haven from Jacob's abuse and aggression, thus making it the perfect place for Logan to spend time with her. When she first began spending time with Logan, she always made sure to coordinate it around Jacob's schedule. But, as the days went by, Lola ever so slowly began letting her guard down. Instead of returning home as she should, Lola could often be found in Logan's safe embrace. However, as with all secret things, Lola's time with Logan would soon be discovered by Jacob.

The night of the annual gala benefiting the **Lorriene Swan Center** started no differently than it had every year prior ... for no one expected that this night would end with both Lola and Jacob revealing their dark secrets to one another.

Standing behind the black curtain, Lola nervously fidgeted with the long satin belt of her navy blue floor-length, evening gown; though she couldn't put her finger on it, something about this night had Lola more on edge than usual. At the sound of Gregory announcing her presence on stage, Lola stuffed down her nerves before walking out to give the same tired and worn-out speech she could now recite in her sleep.

Once her speech was finished, Lola gave Gregory a quick hug, leaving him to handle the hob-knobbing, while she first, went to flag down a server for a cocktail then, she set off in search of Jacob. The more time Lola spent with Logan, the more she began to realize that something wasn't right in her relationship with Jacob. And while Lola felt nothing more than friendship for Logan, he was helping to show her that love shouldn't hurt … at least not in the way loving Jacob hurt her more and more every day.

Unable to locate Jacob, Lola walked out into the garden area allowing the snow to crunch beneath her stilettos, making her way to a secluded area for a smoke. When she was sure no one was in sight, Lola took a pack of cigarettes from her clutch purse when a voice scoffed in the background. "Didn't I tell you two years ago that you know those things will kill you, right?"

Not needing to turn around to face the owner, Lola chattered out, "And didn't I tell you back then, that apparently so will a million other things, but hey- we're all gonna die at some point, right, Warren?"

Removing his suit jacket just as he had two years prior, Logan placed it around Lola's shoulders as he boldly placed a kiss on her cheek. "If memory serves me right, my retort went something along the lines of, 'While that may be true, Lola, I don't think you should speed the process along with this weird combo of frostbite and lung cancer.'"

Shirking away from Logan's affection, Lola sighed before chastising him. "Thanks for the coat, Warren. But please, don't do those sweet little gestures. We're just friends and we're in public. I don't need more shit from Jacob because he thinks there's more to this than there is."

"But, Lola…"

"No buts, Logan. For fuck's sake! Can you even begin to understand my life or how hard it is? Probably not, so please don't make it even harder for me."

"Wow! You're really fucking selfish, you know that? Or stupid. I can't figure out which it is though. If your life is as hard as you claim, why don't you do something to make it better- like leave the abusive asshole you're with, Lola?"

"Do you think it's that easy, Logan? Jacob is the only fucking thing in my life that has been constant for the past eleven years. Even though we've been off and on, it's just not that easy to separate from someone who's so intertwined into your soul!" Lola fumed as she extinguished her cigarette before throwing Logan's coat at him. "I don't expect you to understand, but shit ... as my friend, just support me."

Letting his coat hit the ground, Logan grabbed Lola's arm to stop her from leaving, an action that caused Lola's chest to tighten in fear. "What the hell do you think I've been trying to do, Lola? I try to be your fucking friend even though it kills me inside!"

"What the hell ... is that ... supposed to mean, Warren?" Lola finally managed to say through panicked breaths, as she took a couple of steps back in hopes of creating distance between them.

No longer able to put his feelings into words, Logan hastily closed the gap between them, before kissing Lola as if his life depended upon it.

Giving into Logan's passion only for a moment, Lola quickly came to her senses as she pushed Logan away. "What the fuck? Why would you kiss me like that, Logan?"

"Because, if it's not obvious by now, I love you, Lola. I love you so much that it fucking hurts." Logan admitted as he grabbed Lola by her shoulders, in hopes of fully getting her attention.

"No!" That was all Lola could say before rushing out of Logan's arms, with tears in her eyes, and back into the safety of the building. Blurry-eyed, Lola allowed her feet to carry her until she bumped into Jacob's sturdy figure.

Though he had witnessed Logan and Lola's garden interaction, Jacob decided that for now, it was best to remain quiet; after all, despite her best efforts, Lola's shattered soul continuously craved Jacob's validation, which always resulted in her eventually revealing even her best hidden secrets. Feeling the warmth of Jacob's familiar embrace, anaxiphilia-laced delusions once more clouded Lola's better judgment.

"Don't cry, *Vix*. You shouldn't waste your tears on something so trivial. Besides, I'm sure you'll feel better once we get home. Okay?" Jacob said while kissing the top of Lola's head. Any passersby remained blissfully unaware of the noxious intent behind Jacob's euphonically, considerate words.

~

By the time they had arrived home, though Lola's tears had long since dissipated, the guilt ran rampantly through the inner workings of her mind; which only increased with Jacob's unusually gentle touch and words. The voice in Lola's mind wickedly taunted her worst fears. *You truly are a stupid bitch! How many times did Jacob try to warn you that Logan was after more? And here you sat, selfishly using that poor fool to fill the void. My god, Lola. You're even crueler than Jacob- you two really are fucking perfect for each other.*

"*Vix*- Hey, earth to Lola!" Jacob called out.

"Uh- sorry, Jacob." Lola quickly apologized, shaking free from the voice inside her head. "What were you saying?"

"I was suggesting that we take a shower and then have a little **chat** about what was bothering you earlier. M'kay?"

Lola's heart instantly dropped and her stomach knotted at Jacob's phrasing of the word "chat," but did her best to keep her expression as neutral as possible while agreeing to Jacob's request. On the inside though, Lola began to panic. *Surely he didn't see Logan kiss me. He couldn't have, right? No, there's no way. Because if he did, he would have made a huge scene. Stop overthinking right now. It's fine ... It's fine ... everything is going to be fine.*

Standing naked in the shower, with the front of her body pressed against the glass shower wall, while the man who owned every fiber of her aggressively kissed the side of her neck, with his erection firmly poking her in the back as his fingers expertly maneuvered their way through her core, Lola's body shook fiercely from a mixture of arousal and her overactive thoughts.

Just as her knees were about to buckle, Jacob slowly entered her dripping center, as he growled out, "Fuck, *Vix*! Tell me you love me!"

"I... love ... you ... Jacob! So damn ... much!" Lola breathlessly spoke between Jacob's fierce but tender thrusts.

Grabbing her luxurious curls in his right hand, Jacob put his left hand to work against Lola's clit- an action that was met with Lola's pleading of Jacob to fuck her harder. "Tsk! Tsk!" Jacob chuckled while letting go of Lola's hair. "Someone is getting impatient. First, tell me just **how** much you love me," he commanded while squeezing Lola's throat just hard enough to cause her to cum once again.

"I love you so much that I can't live without you, Jacob. You are in every single atom of my being." Lola admitted as she fought to catch her breath because once those words left her mouth, the pressure Jacob placed on her throat increased slightly while increasing the speed at which he plummeted into her body.

Tears began to fall down Lola's face, as Jacob's pace, along with his firm grip on her throat, switched from pleasurable to aggressive. When she tried tapping his arm to signal she was having difficulty breathing, Jacob loosened his grip only long enough to bring Lola's arms behind her back so that he could restrain them with his right hand, and once again squeeze her throat with his left.

"If you love me that fucking much, you stupid whore, then why the fuck did you kiss that pathetic asshole," he demanded while reaching his climax. The last thing Lola would remember that night was the feeling of the side of her head hitting the glass shower door so hard she thought it would break, and the familiar scent of iron that seemed to mock her for once again blindly falling into Jacob's wicked "game time."

~

January 1, 2012

When she finally came to her senses, Lola had no idea how long she had been knocked out for, all she knew was that the sun brilliantly shone through the bedroom window. Blinking her eyes to remove the final foggy remnants, panic set in as Lola fully took in her surroundings; she was once again seated nakedly in Jacob's wretched armchair, with her arms held down by rope, while the fireplace roared ruthlessly beside her.

"Glad to see my little whore is finally awake." Jacob cruelly mocked, as he gulped down his Scotch before shattering the glass behind Lola's head, causing her to flinch. Satisfied with Lola's reaction, Jacob laughed dementedly as walked around to stand directly in front of her.

Fear coursed through Lola's veins as she frantically tried to escape the demon before her. "Well, well, well. It looks like I've got myself a beautiful fox." Jacob remarked with a wink while running the tip of his tongue across his teeth.

"Please, let me go, Jacob! Whatever I did, I'm sorry! I'm fucking sorry, okay? Can't we just talk things out like a normal couple for once?" Lola begged as bitter tears fell upon her bare breasts.

"PlEaSe LeT mE gO!" Jacob mocked, before backhanding Lola. "Bitch, I will never let you go! How have you still not gotten it through that thick-ass skull of yours? I own every fucking part of you!"

"How can you be so cruel? Do you even love me the way I love you?"

"Oh, *Vix*- your naivety never ceases to amaze me. How could I possibly love you? Love is useless and makes you weak. What I 'love,' for lack of a better word, is the **power** I have over you. Although the things **you've** forced my hand to do to obtain this power were rather ... messy. And, unfortunately for your little bitch, it looks like I'm going to have to get messy again."

Uncertain if she was understanding Jacob's words correctly, Lola closed her teary eyes as she asked the single question that would spring forth a well of heartache and demise deeper than she ever thought possible. "Jacob, what do you mean by 'messy?'"

Back handing Lola once more, Jacob proceeded to smear the blood from Lola's lip across her right cheek before kissing her possessively. "Now, *Vix*, before I explain my part, don't you think it stands to reason that you owe me some explanations? And, while you're speaking, just know that if you lie, like the stupid whore you are, well then it's going to be a long fucking day." Jacob deviously stated while turning around to grab something behind him.

As Jacob faced Lola once again, he placed his ring, which Lola knew all too well, along with a medium-sized kitchen knife on the end table beside her. Kneeling onto the floor, to kiss Lola's inner thighs, Jacob went on to explain that Lola would be given the chance to explain exactly why Logan had kissed her, and if she told the truth, she could pick her punishment; either being branded once more with his ring or being branded with the knife. "I'm not an unreasonable man, my little *Vixen*. However, if you lie ... well, let's just say if you aren't broken yet, you will be. Understood?"

Doing her best not to be completely overcome with fear, as Jacob seemed to be holding onto something she should know, Lola bravely stuttered, "Wh-whe-when will you tell me what you mean by 'messy?'" Trailing kisses from Lola's thighs up to her lips, Jacob told Lola it was all dependent upon how honest she was.

Over the next several minutes, Lola took a long, hard look at the two options placed beside her; and while she hated herself for having to throw Logan under the bus, picking her own punishment was the lesser of two evils. She prayed to whoever would listen that Logan would forgive her, then went on to tell Jacob about all of the time she and Logan spent together at her apartment; never omitting even the tiniest of details.

The entire time Lola recanted the events of her innocent tryst with Logan, Jacob remained eerily silent- hoping to catch Lola in a lie- after all, where was the *fun* in her honesty. Finding no deceit in her words, Jacob sighed heavily while half-heartedly clapping. "Well, *Vix*, I've gotta hand it to you. I'm impressed you managed to tell the truth." Taking a moment to clear his throat, Jacob continued in his condescending tone, "And, since you were such a ***good*** girl, I've decided that I'll tell you what I meant as I dole out your punishment. Now, what'll it be?"

Lola closed her eyes, the never-ending tears burning down her cheeks, as she told Jacob she would choose to be branded once again by his ring; for in her mind, it was better to face the punishment she knew. Jacob couldn't help but laugh at the predictability in Lola's choice. Placing the ring in the fireplace, Jacob carefully undid Lola's restraints, guided her to the bathroom to relieve herself, then led her to sit on the floor, facing the foot of their bed.

When Lola was properly seated on the floor, she held her arms up so that Jacob could restrain her wrists to the bolster directly ahead of her. Satisfied that her arms were properly bound, Jacob gagged Lola, so as not to disturb the neighbors with her punishment; then peppered kisses across the fleshy canvas that marvelously displayed his handiwork throughout the years. Placing one final kiss on the back of Lola's neck, Jacob collected his ring with the metal tongs and set to work.

With each searing indentation, Jacob disclosed every sordid detail of his insidious actions- from being the one who murdered Shane, while having the District Attorney in his pocket to frame Andy; to **encouraging** Elin to pursue Ronan once more; and finally, the thing he was looking forward to the most ... his plan to eliminate Logan- who just so happened to be the last piece standing in his way of completely owning Lola.

Numb- this was the only feeling left within Lola as the scales of naivety finally fell from her eyes and mind. Even though her back festered and her arms throbbed, she felt none of it; numbness at the horrors of how she willingly allowed herself to be trapped by the demon who disguised himself as someone she loved, was all that remained. And while she heard Jacob speaking in the background, and felt his violent hands once again turn deceptively gentle- she was desensitized to it all.

Several hours later, Lola regained her senses, only to find herself once again smothered by Jacob's oppressive grip. Unable to move or sleep, the only thing left for Lola to do was think. In that darkened room of horrors, disastrous thoughts seeped into her fully splintered mind, before leaving her with only one solution to her problems. *I vow that I will do whatever it takes to save Logan.*

~

January 7, 2016

Lola stopped as she reached for her bottle of water; taking a drink, she looked over at Logan, whose face was pale, and rightfully so. Just as she was about to speak, Logan asked if they could break for lunch. Dr. Indigo agreed before asking if they would be continuing later that day, or if they needed to reschedule; a decision Lola left up to Logan.

Weighing all of his options, Logan finally decided that it was best to power through. "I know it's been a long time coming, but Lola, if you're okay with it, I'd like to just keep going. I don't think I'll be okay just leaving off at that point."

"Dr. Indigo, I agree with Logan. And in all honesty, retelling this part isn't as hard as I thought it would be."

"It would seem as if that matter is settled then. Now, before we break for lunch, Lola, would you mind briefly explaining what makes this part not as difficult to retell as you thought it would be?"

Grabbing Logan's hand in hers, Lola confidently exclaimed, "It's because Logan hasn't left my side throughout this whole retelling. His love and patience are what give me the strength to keep moving forward."

51

An amatively sévir occurence

January 7, 2016

While they were meant to break for lunch, neither Logan nor Lola had much of an appetite; their nerves were at an all-time high. So much so, that the drive back to Dr. Indigo's office was filled with an uncomfortable level of silence; the likes of which Logan and Lola hadn't experienced since Lola first came back to Parkway.

"Hey," both Logan and Lola exclaimed simultaneously when Lola put the car in park; nervous laughter cutting through the tension. "Why don't you go first?" Lola said as she looked into Logan's worry-filled eyes.

"If you're sure," Logan stated, earning a nod from Lola. "I just wanted to say that I'm sorry for being awkward and silent today. It's just that..."

"I get it, Logan, I really do. It's just that it's hard, and the hardest part is still yet to come." Lola affirmed, tenderly patting Logan's hand. "If you're ready, Warren, we'll head back inside. Okay?"

Squeezing the hand of the woman he treasured more than anything in this life, Logan exited his side, before opening Lola's door. "Let's get going, I guess."

When Logan and Lola had taken their seats, Dr. Indigo asked Logan if he had any questions before Lola started back up. Seeing as he had none, Dr. Indigo directed Lola to begin once more.

~

January 7, 2012

For Lola, the days following Jacob's harrowing revelation were filled with bittersweet misery. Though she had made up her mind to do whatever it took to save Logan, she still had to save face in front of Jacob, by remaining aloof. At first, he refused to listen to anything she had to say, deeming her completely untrustworthy; but little by little her persistence won him over. Finally able to state her piece, Lola enacted the first part of her plan to save Logan.

Under the guise of getting rid of her apartment to permanently remain at Jacob's side, Lola now found herself seated at the small kitchen counter. With pen and paper in hand, Lola scribbled out what she hoped would rectify her every sin, while sparring Logan in the process. If she thought too hard, for even a moment, her resolve would crumble, leaving her once again second-guessing her every action.

Satisfied with the words penned upon the page, Lola carefully folded her letter before sealing it in an envelope with a tender kiss. Placing the letter in her purse, Lola sent a text to Logan asking him to come by her apartment, then moved to her bedroom to get dressed and pack her suitcase. After putting on a royal blue, cable knit sweater with an oversized v-neck collar, that slouched down over her left shoulder; a pair of white skinny jeans; and a pair of black suede booties, Lola placed what little clothing remained in her suitcase. As soon as she rolled the suitcase into the living room, the doorbell rang.

Closing her eyes to stop the tears which threatened to fall, Lola exhaled briefly, then opened the door to find Logan standing there looking rather disheveled. "Can I come in?"

"Uh- sure, but just for a minute." Lola nervously replied as she grabbed her purse and suitcase.

Anxiously shoving his hands in his pockets, Logan tapped his foot in hopes of settling the uneasiness festering in the pit of his stomach. "So … what did you want to talk about, Lola?" Logan finally asked.

Removing her keys, along with the letter, from her purse, Lola ushered Logan out the door as she turned to lock it. Turning back to face her most precious friend, Lola felt the stabbing pang of guilt well up within her heart, as she began to second guess her decision. *I know this is selfish, but what else can I do to save him?*

"Here, take this." Lola directed as she held out the letter to Logan. "But please promise me that you won't read it for a few days."

"What's going on, Lola?" Logan asked, as he finally took notice of the suitcase positioned behind Lola.

Sighing deeply, Lola went on to explain that her leaving was the only option she had left. And when Logan asked how long she would be gone, her heart shattered as she simply responded, "A while, Logan. That's really all I can say."

"My god, Lola. You really are selfish! I love you so fucking much, can't you see that? Whatever it is with Jacob, I can protect you. Just don't leave, please!" Logan fell to his knees as he begged.

Looking down at him with pity and remorse in her deep green eyes, Lola sobbed. "Logan, right now, this is the most selfless thing I will ever do. I know you can't understand, and that's okay. I promise. Just please wait a few days and read the letter; I think it'll make everything a little easier."

Pausing for a moment to wipe the tears from her eyes, Lola bent down and kissed Logan deeply. "Thank you for your friendship, and thank you for loving me. I'm just sorry I couldn't do the same for you." Breaking away from the disheartened, kneeling man, Lola hastily grabbed her belongings, lest she completely cave.

~

Though he couldn't say exactly how long he sat outside of Lola's front door, Logan knew one thing was certain, and that was Lola would not be returning to her apartment any time soon. And though he was one to typically honor her requests, something in his gut told him the severity of this situation was unlike any other he had experienced before. Taking his time to open the letter, Logan sobbed as he carefully read Lola's heartfelt words.

Barely finishing the letter, Logan shoved it into his back pocket, before quickly running out to his car with the hopes that he wouldn't be too late. Logan sped the entire way to Jacob's house, making an urgent phone call in case his worst fears were to come true.

Meanwhile, Lola, who was oblivious to Logan's frantic nature, found herself unable to move from her driver's seat and into the house. The memory of Logan's shattered countenance nearly crumbled her resolve; causing the inner voices to resonate even louder than normal. *Don't chicken out now, Lola! You know this is the only way to truly have freedom. But is it? Isn't there another way? No-you've come too far to back out now! You're right, I really have come too far. I just hope they'll all forgive me.*

With her mind made up once more, Lola let the tears fall as she walked into the house that had never been a home, to reclaim her freedom the only way her tortured mind knew how. "Jacob, I'm back..." She called, locking the front door behind her.

The drive from Lola's apartment was a complete blur for Logan, and while his thoughts were erratic, he did his best not to drive too recklessly, lest he cause more trouble or delays for himself. Finally pulling into the driveway of Jacob's house, Logan bolted from his car without even turning off the engine, for time was far too precious. Using all of his might, Logan slammed his body into the locked front door several times, before it finally gave way.

"Lola! Are you here?" Logan called frantically throughout the house until he heard what could only be described as delirious laughter coming from the back of the house. Sirens wailed in the background as he made his way down the hall, the sight Logan stumbled upon would have completely destroyed him then and there, had it not been for the adrenaline surging through his veins. Seated against the velvet red chair, was Jacob holding his left arm, with blood dripping from what appeared to be a knife wound. Not too far from him lay Lola's nearly lifeless body.

"Shit! Shit! Shit!" Logan cried out as he ran to her body while trying not to lose the contents of his stomach at the sight of crimson that not only stained her clothes but continually flowed from her arm. Ripping his white shirt without a second thought, Logan wrapped Lola's left wrist with feeble hopes that this small action would save the woman he foolishly loved. Feeling weak and not exactly sure what to do next, Logan closed his eyes while he cried out and prayed to the God his mother believed in and begged that if He were real, Lola would not die in such a cruel manner.

~

March 7, 2012

Two months had passed since that fateful day inside of Jacob's house, and in those two months Logan exhausted every effort he could to see Lola, however, due to hospital regulations, no one other than immediate family was allowed to visit. Even his high school friend (and Avia's cousin), Louisa Johnson, who happened to be a nurse was of little help.

"What the hell, Pip? Why can't you let me fucking see her?" Logan bellowed as he punched the vending machine next to him.

"Redwood, you know I love you like a brother, but my hands are tied," Louisa admitted before stretching up to pull Logan's ear as she firmly admonished him. "And, if you don't straighten your ass up, the doctors have agreed to get a restraining order."

"Ow! What the hell, Pip? Why you gotta pinch my ear like I'm a fucking child? For someone so short, you sure are mean as hell!" Logan pouted as he rubbed his ear.

"Well, if you'd stop acting like a damn child, I wouldn't treat you like one. Now, sit your giant ass down, so I can talk to you like an adult!" Louisa demanded.

Logan sat down haughtily before offering Louisa his sincerest apologies. "Look, Pip, I know I've been a complete ass, but … I'm fucking scared. No one will tell me a damn thing. You're literally my last hope."

Louisa sighed wearily as she sat down beside her longtime friend. "Look, Logan, I get it. I really do. You remember how worried Roz was when I went through my relapse, right?" When Logan nodded, Louisa continued. "Alright, well, that's how you're feeling right now. I know it's stressful, but you freaking out like this, literally changes nothing."

Taking a deep breath, Louisa leaned in closer to Logan's ear, so as not to be overheard by the administration and run the risk of losing her job. "Now, what I'm about to tell you is the most that I can say without violating HIPAA, but can still run me the risk of getting fired. You gotta swear on your car that you'll keep that pretty mouth of yours shut."

"Alright, alright, I swear to it."

"Aside from Ms. Harper's self-inflicted wound, the doctors say her body was in one of the worst traumatic states they had ever seen." Catching sight of her nursing director, Louisa quickly stood up and switched back to her professional demeanor. "Now, Mr. Warren, as we have told you time and time again, you can't be here. Until the patient is released into a regular room, it is immediate family only.

Even then, it will be Ms. Harper's choice on whom she wishes to see."

With Louisa's final words, Logan realized his hands truly were tied; and while he didn't give up hope of one day seeing Lola again, he knew jail time wouldn't help his cause in any way.

~

Looking out the window of her hospital room, Lola felt her heart clench in sorrow as she watched Logan, once again, walk morosely to his car. Sighing to herself, Lola feebly returned to her bed, just as the door opened. "How are you feeling today, Ms. Harper?"

"The same as always, Louisa." Lola flatly replied, before stating for what she felt must be at least the hundredth time, "And how many times have I told you not to call me Ms. Harper? It's Swan, Lola Swan."

"My apologies, Lola. Anyhow, you had a visitor just now. We turned him away again since you've just barely begun your recovery, but we will be moving you to a regular room soon, at least until a room at the **Lorriene Swan Center** opens up. And you can do with this what you will, but it might do you some good to see him before you go to the clinic, since they are pretty strict about visitors for the first little while." Louisa suggested while checking all of Lola's vitals.

Though she knew who the visitor was, part of Lola hoped it had been Jacob who came to see her, just like all of the other times she was admitted into the hospital. "Who was the visitor? Did Jacob come to see me this time? I hope he knows I'm really sorry for hurting him. I was crazy in that moment and didn't want him to stop me from trying to find freedom."

~

April 7, 2012
Another month had passed, thus marking the third month since

Lola's **incident**. On this particular Saturday morning, Lola found herself seated in front of the therapist who had been assigned to her, for her first session. While the woman seated across from Lola looked harmless enough, Lola couldn't help but instantly feel animosity towards her and her compassionate demeanor. "Good morning, Ms. Harper. My name is Dr. Indigo Callena Rogers, but please just call me Dr. Indigo."

At the sound of her old name, Lola's frail body radiated hate and anger. "My god, how many fucking times do I have to tell you people that It's Swan, Lola fucking Swan."

Dr. Indigo spoke with remorse, "I do apologize, but I am going by the name that appears on all of your paperwork, and you are still legally listed as Ms. Lola Luxe Harper." Trying to salvage what she could for the remainder of their session, Dr. Indigo stated how she would run each session.

"During each session, you are free to say what you like. I will ask some leading questions that I'd like for you to take the time to think upon, then answer them in our next session. I will also be taking several notes that I'll share with my colleague, Dr. Kaleb Johnson, who will be your nutritional therapist." Handing Lola a notebook, Dr. Indigo continued, "We do ask that you keep a food journal and adhere to daily weight checks, as you are currently severely malnourished."

Snatching the notebook presented to her, Lola curtly asked if she could finally return to her room. "Before you go, Ms. Harper, I'd like to leave you with one question to think on before our meeting tomorrow."

"What?!" Lola rudely demanded.

"Since today marks three months, how do you feel knowing that your friend saved you?"

Turning towards the door, with the notebook in hand, Lola

answered truthfully, before making her exit. "Honestly, I wish he hadn't."

~

January 7, 2016

Lola gripped Logan's hand as she turned to face him, and for the very first time in four years, found the courage to finally call the incident by name. "Logan, when Dr. Indigo first asked me how I felt about you saving me, I was bitter and angry. I was so angry because it was me who was supposed to save you. When Jacob revealed everything he had done to Shane and Ronan and was planning to do to you … well … in my mind, I saw that the main problem was me."

Pausing for just a moment, so as not to be completely overcome with emotion, Lola continued, "Then, I figured that if I could remove myself … well, then you would be okay. You would be safe, and you could fall in love and find happiness. And I could finally be free. Please know that it wasn't ever my intention to hurt you as badly as I did. I do know now though, that **suicide** doesn't solve anything."

52

A letter ends where healing begins

January 28, 2016

Three weeks after her revelation of the truth behind her suicide attempt, Lola found herself seated at the desk in her grandparents' bedroom, staring blankly at the sheet of paper before her. While revealing almost everything had been cathartic, she still felt as though she was tethered by an emotional weight.

Dr. Indigo's question regarding whether or not Lola would face Jacob one final time plagued the forefront of her mind; and though she probably should have spoken with Logan about whether or not she was going to face Jacob, she chose not to, for two reasons. One reason being, that Jacob was already a sensitive subject between them and since the truth was still fresh in their minds, Lola couldn't bear to heap more pain upon Logan's tender heart. The other reason was that in the end, this was a choice that only she could make.

Lola suddenly felt her heart jump as Logan excitedly rushed into the room; his sudden movements jarred the fight or flight response in her brain, causing Lola to break down. "Hey, *my heart*! Guess wha…" Logan excitedly announced before tapering off as he saw Lola's body shaking. Cautiously walking up beside her, Logan held up his arms, as one would for a skittish animal. "Hey- Hey, Lola. It's just me, Logan. I'm sorry that I scared you."

After several calming breaths, Lola regained her composure as she accepted Logan's apology. "It's okay, Warren, I promise. While I know you wouldn't purposely try to scare or hurt me, my brain gets startled by loud noises, especially from behind when I am the most vulnerable. Dr. Indigo calls it a trigger."

"I'll do my best to alert you when I come in the room from now on, hell- I'll even send a text before I announce my presence." Logan genuinely suggested as he pulled his girlfriend in closely.

"Thank you, Warren. I truly don't know what I did to deserve your love, but now that I'm in too deep, I can't imagine **life without you**." Lola rested in the warm embrace which enveloped her for a few moments longer before asking Logan what he had originally come into the room to ask.

"Oh, yeah!" Logan exclaimed while taking a step back. "I wanna take you on a date to my favorite spot in Vienna. It'll just be for the day, and then we can come back here if you'd like."

"Uh, sure! I think that sounds fine. What do you have in mind?"

"Well, I really want you to meet my mom's parents, so I figured we would go to the businesses my grandfather started, **Alsup's Pizzaria** for an early dinner, then step next door for some arcade gaming at **Retro Redux**." Logan joyfully explained.

"Sounds like a plan. Let me pick this mess up, get some cute jeans and a sweater on, and then we can head that way."

"A fun fact about the arcade," Logan rambled as he waited for Lola to change, "my dad and step-dad actually convinced my *morfar* (grandpa) to open it when mom was still pregnant with me."

~

The drive to Vienna was peaceful, despite heavier than normal traffic. Though this wasn't her first visit to Vienna with Logan,

Lola really took the time to take in her surroundings, and couldn't help but smile at the thought of a younger version of Logan running around through the quaint little town. Thinking of a younger Logan quickly morphed into thoughts of having children with him; just the idea of it instantly made Lola blush. *Dear, Lord! What the hell is wrong with me? How can I possibly think of having children with him? We are just barely in a good place. We haven't even had sex yet.*

Logan couldn't help but laugh as he stole a quick glance at Lola, only to find her usually fair face completely matching her hair. "For shame, *my heart*! Are you having indecent thoughts about me? I am but a virtuous, young man!"

Logan's playful teasing caused Lola's blush to deepen further. "Shut up, Warren! I did no such thing. And, I know for a fact, that you are **far** from virtuous."

After parking his car and removing his key from the ignition, Logan leaned over as he gently grabbed the back of Lola's head to pull her closer to kiss her deeply, before whispering in her ear with a sultry tone, "I'll only be as naughty as you want to me to be," an act that rendered her speechless and in desperate need of new panties.

Having regained her composure, Lola opened the mirror on her sun visor to properly reapply her lip gloss. "Before we go inside, would you mind telling me a little bit about your grandparents?"

"Sure!" Logan exclaimed before requesting, "If it's okay, I'd like to keep it brief because I'd like for them to tell you their full story one day." When Lola stated that that was perfectly fine, Logan went on to say, "My grandparents, Marcus and Dianne, are naturalized U.S. citizens, who are originally from Sweden. My mom is a first-gen citizen, which makes me a second-gen citizen."

"Wow! That's really cool, Logan." Lola enthusiastically responded as she made her way out of the car. "Now, let's go meet your grandparents and get some food, 'cause I'm starving."

Walking hand in hand through the front door of the pizza shop, Logan was greatly surprised to find his grandparents nowhere in sight. Logan scrunched his brow in confusion as he spotted his mother walking away from a customer. "Hey, mom!"

Though it had been only a little over a month since she last saw her son, Britt eagerly ran to embrace him. "What a nice surprise, *baby mine* … and …Lola." Britt's elation turned flat as she willed herself to remain polite. While she had promised to give the red-headed temptress a fair chance, old habits seemed to die hard.

"Mom, where are *Morfar* and *Mormor*? I know they're practically retired, but aren't Thursdays still the days they like to come by and help out here at the shop?"

"Normally, yes, but they're in L.A. right now. Why didn't you call?"

"Well, I was kinda hoping to surprise them with a visit and introduce them to Lola. Why are they in L.A.?"

Britt sighed heavily, for though it had nearly been a year, the death of the sister of her heart was still quite painful. Brushing back the tears that dared to creep out, Britt explained, "Mamma and Pappa left shortly after Christmas, to stay the whole month of January with *Björn*, because it's just a few months shy of the one-year anniversary of Priscilla's death. You know…"

Logan quickly cut his mother off before she could scold him once more for not attending his aunt's funeral. Not wanting to spoil any more of his date with Lola, Logan requested a table before letting his mother know he would be going to L.A. for the first two weeks of February. "When I get back, we'll have to celebrate yours, Elle-belle's, and my birthdays all together."

Having yet to say a word, Lola graciously took the menu from Britt before thanking her. Turning to Logan, Lola said, "It's okay that I don't get to meet your grandparents just yet. Maybe I'm meant to meet them when we have more time for me to listen to their story like you wanted."

~

Although the date didn't start off the way in which Logan had hoped, he was quite pleased to see Lola enjoying herself. The discovery of Lola's well-hidden, competitive side left Logan feeling both intrigued and thoroughly aroused, making the drive back to Swan Manor feel as if it took even longer than normal. Lola also felt her arousal pique from once again watching Logan's playful yet considerate demeanor.

As soon as the car was turned off, Lola gave Logan a knowing look, as she bit her bottom lip seductively, bidding him to follow her. And though they had many close encounters up until this point, Logan couldn't help but get his hopes up, as tonight, the atmosphere felt carnally different.

Leading Logan by the hand into the room she had now claimed as her own, Lola gently pushed Logan on the bed, kissing him desperately, before asking him to wait right there. Retreating to the bathroom, Lola relieved herself, as the nerves building put immense pressure on her bladder. Feeling in control of her nerves once more, Lola stepped into the walk-in closet, removing the outfit from their date, only to replace it with a pale pink, chiffon pleated babydoll negligee with a matching thong; the color just barely a shade above her own complexion, helped enhance her lovely, rosy undertones.

God, I haven't felt this nervous since I lost my virginity. And it's not like he hasn't seen all of my body at this point, but still... Lola did her best to keep her thoughts from overpowering her, as she bravely walked out before the man who willingly and lovingly waited for her all this time.

When Lola left the room, Logan hastily stripped down to his boxers- hoping he hadn't misread the atmosphere- while his own thoughts unknowingly raced in a manner quite similar to Lola's. *Fuck! It's been like six or seven years since I've been with anyone, so I hope I don't disappoint Lola. God, if I've misread the intent, please forgive me.* All worry and apprehension quickly faded from Logan's mind the instant Lola stepped out of the bathroom; a sight so beautiful tears threatened to fall. While he wasn't one to find crying unmanly, Logan didn't want to ruin this moment by having Lola grow concerned by misreading his jubilation.

Meekly standing before Logan, Lola bowed her head while nervously asking him how she looked. "Mmh … *my heart* …shit! I can't even find the words to describe how fucking beautiful you are, both inside and out."

Logan's genuine words of affection gave Lola the courage she needed to once again push him onto the bed, where she kissed him hungrily while straddling him. Logan sent titillating chills up Lola's spine as he caressed her skin, before settling his hands upon her rear; guiding her hips to grind back and forth upon his erection. "Tell me if anything gets to be too much," Logan breathlessly called out after breaking their kiss, before taking Lola's right breast in his mouth, teasing her nipple with the tip of his tongue; an action which help to spurn forth the first of what would be many orgasms for her.

Flipping his position with Lola, so that he could pleasure her, Logan deftly removed her lacy thong with his teeth, before kissing, nibbling, and altogether devouring her dripping core, while his fingers worked to meticulously stroke her like the finest of instruments. Unable to take the build-up any longer, Lola hastily pulled Logan's head up to kiss him once more, before telling him that she needed to feel all of him within her. "Please, Logan, please fill me with your love."

"Are you sure?" Logan cautiously asked, to which Lola breathlessly called out a resounding yes. "Umm … okay … uh, so … I kinda wasn't expecting this to happen, so … I don't have a condom. Is that okay?"

"It's fine, Logan. We'll deal with it later, okay? Please, for everything that is good and pure in this world, just fucking love me already!" Lola hastily demanded before aggressively kissing Logan. Not needing it spelled out any further, Logan removed Lola's negligee, then carefully slipped inside of her warm, wet entrance, pouring out years of love and adoration. Though their moment didn't last long, as it had been years since either was intimate with another, that didn't matter in the slightest. It was a moment solely for them- a moment of pure, unadulterated bliss, that could never be taken away or tainted.

53

Red dahlias and yellow daffodils

January 29, 2016

Logan awoke the next morning to find himself tangled in Lola's flowing tresses. Gently freeing himself, so as not to wake her, he took in the intoxicating view of the sunlight tenderly kissing her bare shoulder. Reaching for his phone, Logan found four messages from Pierre reminding him to have a song ready for the festival. Under normal circumstances, Logan would have been annoyed with his friend's nagging, however, nothing could shake the grin from his face, as the memories of last night played on repeat.

Nothing that is, until the phone began to vibrate, showing the name of the last person he wanted to speak with. Quietly slipping out of the bed so as not to awaken Lola, Logan slipped out of the bedroom, making his way to the kitchen. "What the hell do you want, Marina?"

"Good morning to you too, lover boy!" Marina mocked before demanding to know if Logan finally told Lola his truth.

"My god, woman! It's way too early for this shit. Besides, you've given me 'til my birthday, and guess what, it's not even February yet, so chill the fuck out."

"I know what month it is, Logan! I'm not completely inept-" Marina began before being cut off by Logan.

"I'm not inept either, Marina! I get that you care about her, but you'll never care about her as much as I do. This is my business, so let me fucking handle it."

"Logan, you've had how long to tell her? And guess what, your non-confrontational ass hasn't. If you want a relationship, you can't have it built on a bed of lies. The last thing I'll say is this- Don't blame me when it all blows up in your face!" Marina groused, cutting the call before Logan could utter another word.

Feeling far too irritated to lie back down, Logan took a quick shower to rinse the post-sex stickiness from his body, before leaving Lola a note telling her that he was going out to pick up the things he needed to make his *Mormor's* Swedish pancake recipe.

Pulling back into the driveway at Swan Manor, Logan was thankful there weren't many people out at the international market, and he had been able to find everything he needed, most specifically the lingonberry jam. As he was removing the last bag from the trunk of his car, Logan felt his phone vibrate, signaling an incoming call. *Why the hell am I so popular this morning?* Logan sighed to himself before glancing at the screen. Seeing Shaw's name flash across, Logan sighed once more. "Hey, brother. Tell Pierre I got all **four** of his texts. I've got some shit in mind, but get off my ass. Y'all know I'm not into that."

"Ha ha ha," Shaw replied flatly, then proceeded to explain the reasoning behind his phone call. "I know that's the main reason I call, brother, but not today. Today, I'm calling 'cause Av wants to know if you'll be bringing your camera when you come down."

"As if I'd ever go anywhere without my baby." Logan teased while walking into the kitchen. "Let me guess, Vee is wanting one-year pictures of Celeste, and some family pictures of all y'all."

Shaw laughed heartily at Logan's knowing response. "How'd ya know?"

"It's a badass uncle skill." Logan bragged. "Any specific requests?"

"Z-man has a request if you're down to honor it," Shaw stated before elaborating. "Zelig wants a special picture with his babysitter, Aggelina. She's 14, and even though he's only six, he keeps telling us that he's going to marry her. She said she'd take a picture with him because he's the best six-year-old she has ever watched."

Logan's hearty laugh echoed through the halls as Lola made her way into the kitchen, and thanked him for the note when his call came to a close. "What's all of this?" Lola asked, her curiosity piqued.

"Well, *my heart,* since you didn't get to meet my grandparents on my mom's side, which in Swedish is *morföräldrar.* I wanted to make my *Mormor's* pancake recipe." Logan pleasantly explained, then suggested Lola go out for her morning run. "It'll all be ready by the time you get back."

~

Later that evening, as the couple lay entwined together, enjoying the calm after making love once more, Lola asked with a playful pout, "Do you really have to leave in the morning?"

"It's just a couple days earlier than planned. I haven't seen my nieces and nephews, friends, or hell, even my *Zio* and *Zia* in right at a year. Time will fly by quickly while I'm gone, you'll see." Logan lovingly reassured Lola with a passionate kiss.

"I know, I know. I'm just gonna miss your pretty face." Lola whispered as she drifted off into a peaceful slumber.

~

February 7, 2016

One month since her last session, Lola found herself seated once more in front of Dr. Indigo. After recounting the events of the past month, Lola leaned nervously against the back of her chair, wishing it would swallow her whole, for she knew she needed to make a decision on whether or not she should face Jacob once more. Clearing her arid throat with a sip of water, Lola meekly tried to ask the question heavy on her heart but failed miserably.

Looking across the desk at her patient, Dr. Indigo seemed to guess where Lola's thought process was going. "Before you solidify your decision on whether or not to face Jacob, would you like to know any information in regards to his trial? This is something we have yet to talk about. I have waited to even mention it because up until recently, you weren't in a place, mentally, to be able to handle it."

Lola nodded her head before asking, voice trembling, "M-may I see the c-court d-d-document?"

Dr. Indigo handed over the file, cautioning Lola to stop reading if at any time she began to feel overwhelmed. "One thing that I hope will bring you peace of mind, is that this is not public record. Apparently, both Maximillian Gallagher and an anonymous donor paid top dollar to keep the events quiet. I was able to request this summary directly from the judge, because I am your therapist, and stood in for you by proxy."

Lola quickly exhaled in relief as she realized all of the times she had thought people were staring at her as if they knew the darkest days of her life had only ever been in her head. "Th-thank you for doing that, Dr. Indigo. I don't think I ever said it before, but I want you to know how truly thankful I am."

With a knowing nod, Dr. Indigo handed over the weighty file, along with a large box of tissues. Lola readily accepted both, exhaling a shaky breath, as she slowly started to read. The first thing that caught Lola by surprise was the name of the prosecuting attorney. "Ronan acted on behalf of the state?"

~

This summary judgment is provided by the Honorable Judge Felix

Martin at the request of Indigo Rogers, PsyD, LMHC, on this twenty-fifth day of April 2014.

In regards to the court case, **Oregon v. Gallagher***, On the twentieth day of April 2014 an unbiased jury reached the verdict of guilty on all counts of psychological abuse/manipulation, domestic violence, 2003 frame-up of Andre Roman Bennett, along with the 2003 murder of Shane Michael Carson. In their deliberation, the jury noted that due to the compelling evidentiary testimony provided by Dr. Indigo Rogers in proxy for the plaintiff, Lola Luxe Harper, there was little doubt in the minds of the jury that the defendant, Jacob Sterling Gallagher, was unquestionably guilty.*

District Attorney Ronan Harper, counsel for the prosecution, noted that this was one of the worst cases of trauma caused by years of psychological abuse and manipulation that he had ever seen, to date, in his career.

With all testimonies heard, in conjunction with jury deliberation, the court therefore has unbiasedly sentenced the defendant, Jacob Sterling Gallagher, to life in prison, plus twenty years, without the possibility of parole.

~

Tears of relief streamed down Lola's cheeks as she re-read the verdict several times, to ensure that her mind was not playing any sort of trick on her. "So, Jacob's really and truly gone? There's no way he can ever get out to hurt me again?"

"No. Had it not been for your written permission to share our sessions with the court, there could have very well been a different ending." Dr. Indigo explained, reassuring Lola as best she could.

"Okay, I think … no! I **know** that I am finally ready to face Jacob one last time. I need to finally close this wretched chapter of my past to be able to move on with both my present and my future!" Lola mightily declared before thanking Dr. Indigo for her time once more.

Seated again in the driver's seat of her car, Lola fidgeted with her phone. Even though her communication skills had greatly improved after her sessions with Dr. Indigo, there were still times she found it quite difficult to put her feelings into words. Hoping that any sort of music would help settle her mind and give her the strength to push send on her text, Lola tuned in to her favorite radio station, and smiled as DJ Samantha's voice carried across the airwaves.

"Hello, Oregon lovers! DJ Samantha here, and I'm broadcasting LIVE from sunny L.A. I've come out to the first annual **Elysium Underground** rock music festival, because I have it on good authority that our very own **Beyond Oregon** will be performing for the first time since their abrupt hiatus in 2012. But for now, a quick word from our sponsors, followed by some classic **Social D** with "Ring of Fire.""

Letting the melodious rock tunes that spoke deeply to her soul fade into the background, Lola quickly pressed send on the text, hoping it would be received with good intent, before making two phone calls; one to the **Oregon State Penitentiary** to set up her visitation with Jacob, while the other was to Logan, for she desperately missed the sound of his voice.

~

Meanwhile, in L.A., Logan couldn't help but smile to himself as he stepped away from the mic to grab a drink of water. *Fuck, I forgot how great it feels to be performing.* His jubilation would only last a brief moment, as the weight of his deceit began to catch up with him, and as if by instinct Lola's name flashed up on the screen of his phone. After letting his friends know he was stepping out to take a call, Logan hastily made his way outside. "H-hey, *my heart.* How's everything in Oregon?"

"It's going alright. I had a session with Dr. Indigo-" Lola began before being cut off by Logan.

"Oh, yeah? How'd that go?"

"It was … okay. Umm, but that's not the reason I'm calling."

"Shit! Sorry for cutting you off. What's up?" Logan apologized for his impatient behavior.

Choosing to forego any details in regards to her session or her decision to face Jacob one last time, Lola filled Logan in on what she'd heard on the radio after her session with Dr. Indigo. "Since you're going to be at **Elysium Underground**, and since DJ Samantha seems convinced that **Beyond Oregon** will be there, and I remember you said you did some work for them in the past, do you think you could possibly get their autographs? Mark's birthday is March 2, and that man is still salty as hell that we missed seeing them perform 14 years ago.

"Uh- I guess I can try. I mean, that's even if they do autographs. Anyhow, *my heart*, I need to get going. I love you!" As soon as Lola returned her affections, Logan ended the call before wearily making his way back inside. While it shouldn't have been that hard for him to tell Lola the truth of who he really was, Logan justified his silence by reminding himself that this was a conversation better suited face-to-face.

~

Back in Oregon, though Logan's tone seemed a bit off, Lola did her best not to think too much on it. Checking her text messages, Lola was pleased to see the response she had been waiting for. *Here goes everything and nothing all at the same time.* Lola thought to herself as she headed off in the direction **Brewed Awakening** for the very impromptu meeting confirmed via text.

Stepping inside her favorite coffee spot, still second only to **Cate's**, Lola ordered her usual drink, then took a seat in the upstairs addition, as she hoped to have this meeting in a relatively undisturbed location. Pulling out her well-worn copy of **The Raven's**

Song, Lola quickly got lost in the tale she knew verbatim, but still enjoyed as though it were her first time reading it.

The vibrating of Lola's phone brought her back to reality, as she hurriedly answered the call. "Hey! Yeah, I'm here. I'm in the upstairs addition. It's okay, I've been reading, so I didn't even notice the time. Okay, sounds good. See you after you get your order."

Fifteen minutes later, the people she thought she'd never see again, who discreetly did her the biggest favor, made their way up the stairs, followed by a trio of children. "Thank you for meeting with me, Ronan and Elin," Lola warmly greeted as they took a seat at the table.

"Sorry for bringing these rascals along, but with the limited notification, we didn't have time to get a sitter." Elin sweetly apologized.

"No need to apologize at all. If anything, I'm the one who should apologize for interrupting your evening like this." Lola admitted, before inquiring about the children. She couldn't help but notice that the only thing all three children inherited from their father was his warm black hair; their rose-toned complexion, and lovely sandy, brown eyes definitely belonged to their mother.

Looking upon his children with the utmost pride, Ronan introduced them one-by-one. "Our oldest is Remington, and he's six. In the middle, we have our second son, Erik, who is four. And bringing up the rear, is our little Thalia, who is two."

"Although," Elin chipperly interjected, while pointing to her barely visible baby bump, "Thalia won't be bringing up the rear for too much longer."

"That's right, *love*," Ronan mused as he tenderly rubbed his wife's pregnant belly. "Our second daughter, Penelope, is due in just a couple of months!"

"Oh, wow! That's truly amazing, you guys." Lola stated honestly, before getting down to the reason behind this meeting. "The reason

I asked you guys to meet me here today, is because at my session with Dr. Indigo, my therapist, this morning, I learned that you, Ronan, were the prosecuting attorney, and ...”

Lola briefly paused to wipe away the stray tears, then concluded her statement. “And I just wanted to thank you from the bottom of my heart. I know you didn't have to take the case, but I am so thankful you did.”

Ronan tried to refute Lola's thanks, before sheepishly admitting the real reason behind taking the case. “You honestly don't have to thank me, Lola, but you're welcome nonetheless. After our divorce was finalized, Jacob instantly removed me from the legal team at **Gallagher Enterprises**. I thought this was really weird at the time, but didn't think too much of it. Since I was out of a job, I took other small cases before Elin encouraged me to finally run for District Attorney. Then...”

Elin picked up where her husband's voice faltered. “Then, shortly after he won the election, your case came across his desk. And as you know, the loss of Andre Bennett's case was something that still haunted Ronan, so when he saw that your case was tied to that one, and his former employer was the guilty party of it all ... well, Ronan was shocked.”

“After much discussion,” Ronan began once more, “Elin encouraged me to take the case. After all, we figured it's the least we could do to make amends for how we hurt you back then.”

“Thank you, truly!” Lola stated once more, as she prepared to leave. “And, Elin, just so you know, I never hated you or blamed you. Not even once. It was Ronan and I who were both at fault for how things went down, but in the end, everything worked out well. I wish you all nothing but the best.”

~

February 14, 2016

Never in her wildest dreams did Lola imagine that she would be spending the morning of Logan's 32nd birthday in the visitor's section of the **Oregon State Penitentiary**. This, however, was the only date available upon such short notice. Remembering the dress code from her visit with Andy, six years prior, Lola made sure to dress accordingly. Upon her arrival at the prison, Lola couldn't help but chuckle as she passed her personal effects to the very same guard as she did before.

Seated at the familiar table with chipped Formica, Lola strummed her long, black fingernails in rhythmic timing with the daunting sound of the ticking clock; each slowly, intrinsic tick seeming to mock her resolve. Though the minutes haltingly transitioned into hours, Lola refused to leave. For if she wanted to break the final chain keeping her from freedom, she knew she must face her tormentor, lest she forever be eternally bonded to Jacob.

"Inmate entering!" A guard announced, and a loud buzzer sounded as the door opened.

The second Jacob crossed the threshold, Lola's breath hitched; while she didn't know how prison would have changed his appearance, Lola was quite shocked to find that if anything, Jacob somehow appeared even more alluring. *Keep your shit together, Lola. This. This right here is what you are trying to break away from. Do **not** fall for the devil's lies! Do you hear me? Do not!*

"Have a seat, inmate, and don't get cocky! You know the rules." The guard firmly reminded Jacob, and he forcefully pushed him down into the seat across from Lola.

Having sent the guard a haughty wink in response, Jacob quickly turned to face the woman on the other side of the table, where he proceeded to pull out his old tricks. "Well, hello, my little *Vixen.*" Jacob seductively boasted, running his tongue across the top of his teeth.

"Cut the shit, Jacob!" Lola snapped, doing her best to keep the rising bile at bay.

"Oh, come on now, *Vix*. You know you love our little **games**. Don't you think it's time we end this one? After all, I know you must miss me. I mean, we're the same. You can't deny me- I'm like the oxygen that fuels your beautiful blood ... the beautiful blood that stains your flawless skin."

"Shut the fuck up, Jacob!" Lola screeched as she slammed her hand on the table, garnering immediate attention from the guards, one of whom immediately reprimanded Jacob. "Inmate, settle down and stop harassing the visitor!"

Sending a thankful wave to the guards, Lola stood up; an action which helped her regain her courage. "Jacob Sterling Gallagher, never- and I mean **never**- will you and I be the same. You have no control over my mind, body, or soul anymore. You are a sick and twisted man, and it's my own fault for having thought I could have enough love for the both of us to make you change.

"You abused me, tormented me, and tortured me. You stole my voice and my mind..." Lola wavered briefly to catch her breath, before continuing her empowering tirade. "...but no more. I am finally free, and you can never hold me hostage in any way again."

Having stated her piece, Lola hastily turned to leave, but not before Jacob could utter one last damning statement. "Just wait, my little *Vixen*. After all, I am quite the patient man."

Thanking the front guard for watching her items, Lola made her way to the main bathroom, where she rapidly wretched up the entirety of her stomach. *Freedom never tasted so painfully, bitter,* Lola thought as she washed the acidity from her mouth.

~

Seated in the driver's seat of her car once more, Lola took out her phone to check her messages before making the hour drive back to

Portland. Finding several missed calls and texts from Logan, Lola promptly called him back. "Hey, Warren! What's up?"

Taking no notice of the hoarseness of Lola's voice, Logan excitedly told Lola he was back in Oregon. "I'm heading back to my apartment in Parkway, so if you don't mind, would you meet me here?"

"Sounds like a plan, so I'll see you in a few hours. Oh! Before I forget, Happy birthday, Logan. I love you." Lola cut the call after Logan returned his affections.

About halfway to Parkway, Lola felt her stomach ache and growl, a reminder that she had lost everything she had eaten that morning. Pulling into a fuel station, she topped off her tank and went inside to buy a snack. As she was about to make her way back onto the highway, her phone rang. Stealing a quick glance at the screen, Lola quickly answered. "Hey, Marina. What's up?"

"H-hey, Lola. Umm … what are you doing right now?" Marina gulped into her end of the receiver.

Unused to hearing apprehension laced through Marina's words, Lola told Marina she would be going to visit Logan in Parkway; then asked if everything was okay.

"Yeah, everything is fine. Uh- anyhow, has Logan told you anything about himself yet?" Marina wearily asked, as she did not want to be the bearer of bad news, but felt it her duty as Lola's friend to be truthful with her, even if Logan couldn't.

"Well, I mean, he's told me bits here and there, but nothing like, major. What's going on, Marina?"

With a heavy sigh Marina asked for Lola to meet her at **Brewed Awakening** before going to see Logan. "I know that it's his birthday, and I've given him ample time to tell you the truth. Please just meet me, and I'll tell you everything. Okay?"

"Alright, alright. I guess I'll see you in about 45. Meet me in the upper addition." Lola stammered, ending the call.

~

Four hours later, Logan anxiously paced back and forth in the living room of his apartment, his thoughts a wreck. He had been trying to contact Lola for over an hour now, and every time he tried to call, he was sent directly to voicemail. *What the hell is going on? She should be here by now.*

Just as he was about to try calling her phone again, Lola stormed into Logan's apartment- the rage of a thousand furies furrowed upon her face. "What the fuck is wrong with you, Logan? Do you think I'm so stupid, or what's worse, so weak and fragile that you can't be honest with me? Didn't I even ask you if your ass was in a fucking band? But what did you do? You straight up, fucking lied to me!" Lola fumed, and rightfully so.

"Let me guess, fucking Marina." Logan exhaled.

Pushing Logan forcefully against the sofa, Lola hastily threw all of Marina's evidence onto his lap. "Don't you **dare** slander or think ill of Marina. This rage is one you brought upon yourself. Here I was thinking I'm fucking crazy, and that all of the random looks you got and people coming up to you out of the blue, was in my head. And what's worse, your ass was content to let me think I'm actually crazy!"

"Hey, Lola. Look at me, okay?" Logan cautioned, with his hands held up in defense, as he slowly approached Lola. "I'm sorry I made you feel that way, and it honestly wasn't my intent to make you question your sanity. Okay?"

Lola finally released the bitter, angry tears she had stored up, as she allowed Logan to embrace her. "Hey-" Logan started, lifting Lola's chin. "I promise, no more secrets. Alright?"

"How are you going to keep that promise?" Lola somberly probed.

Guiding Lola back to the couch, Logan avowed, "By starting at the very beginning … the time before my time … just like you did."

Then proceeded to inquire, with an outstretched hand, "Do you trust me?"

About the Author

Ellsie Anne, having grown up in several parts of the United States, now resides in the mid-south with her husband and two children. Literature has always held a special place in her heart, whether it be delving deep into the latest fantasy novel or penning a quick poem. Aside from spending time with a good book, Ellsie enjoys spending time with her family, helping out at her church, time with friends, and the never-failing cup of coffee.

To connect with Ellsie, you can find her at the following:
Instagram: @ellsiewrites
E-mail: ellsiewrites@gmail.com
Carrd.co: https://ellsieanne.carrd.co/